ALSO BY ALEXANDER BESHER

Rim

A NOVEL OF VIRTUAL REALITY

M I R

ALEXANDER BESHER

SIMON & SCHUSTER

SIMON & SCHUSTER
Rockefeller Center
1230 Avenue of the Americas
New York, NY 10020

SIMON AND SCHUSTER and colophon are registered trademarks
of Simon & Schuster Inc.

Designed by Ruth Lee

Manufactured in the United States of America

1   3   5   7   9   10   8   6   4   2

Library of Congress Cataloging-in-Publication Data
Besher, Alexander.
Mir : a novel of virtual reality / Alexander Besher.
p.   cm.
I. Title.
PS3552.E7942M5   1998
813'.54—dc21
98-3496
CIP

ISBN 0-684-83087-6

ACKNOWLEDGMENTS

I would like to express my grateful appreciation to Pamela Engebretson for all the bits including the lyrics to the song "Cat Shit Cookies" and the pathology of the Aryudashigda B9 virus; Manabu Ishikawa, for conjuring up the beast; Françoise Bollerot, for her patient editing and helpful suggestions; and Alexandra Moari for sharing all the Russian stories and scams and for her overall input.

I would also like to thank Geoff Leach, Serafina Clarke, Tim Holman, Sky Nonhoff, Joachim Burger, and all the others who assisted and encouraged me in the writing of the novel. Thanks to Bob Mecoy, my editor at Simon & Schuster, for his faith in the *Rim* series. And thank you, Dostoevsky and all the other great tortured Russian writers for blazing the way.

For Shurinka,
for opening the Russian door—and more

For Françoise,
for always being there

For Pam,
thanks for all the sentient tattoos and piercings

For Nicky,
for sharing the writer's journey

For Mama, Papa, the family everywhere

In memory of David Kidd—and for Morimoto

And for all the stray cats
of the world . . .

Mir

EXTROPIAN LIBRARY OF CONGRESS: FILE 10819//
GOBI ARCHIVES; GOBI, TREVOR, BORN APRIL 26, 2013//
SON OF GOBI, FRANK, AND FREDERICK, MELISSA//
FROM COLLECTED E-MAILS ("ALAYA LETTERS"), 2036-2048//
SUBJECT: "REMINISCENCES, MIR/ARYUDASHIGDA B9 VIRUS
         (AyDDA B9)"

Dear Nelly,

I thought you'd be interested in reading Sergei and Vladimir
Kaminsky's article describing the pathology of the
"Aryudashigda B9" virus. It just appeared in the current
edition of their *Encyclopedia of Psychosyncratic Virology*. Ah,
those Russians!

Would you believe that it's been classified as a
"Psyloviridae"—a psychological virus that is transmitted
psychoenergetically? After all these years, they have finally
given it a scientific name. I almost prefer the old classification
we gave it—"love."

Of course, there are all kinds of love—it's a pretty wide-
open field. And it's always evolving, isn't it? Just like we are.
Talk about the science fiction of the heart!

It's pretty ironic how we're being forced to regard
everything from a much less anthropocentric perspective—all
our emotions, the human drama, the whole cosmic shebang.
We are now officially an "illusion." Who would have thought
that *we* are part of a virtual world that is being generated
elsewhere by some other species? We are *their* VR . . .

Life—and love—goes on, through all the transformations,
whatever they may be, wherever they may lead us.

With lots of cosmic hugs & kisses & love always,

Trevor
Big Sur–San Francisco
December 22, 2046

Avatar Immigration
and Naturalization Service
San Francisco, April 26, 2036, 23:42 GMT

"Anything happening out there tonight, Burt?" the young
woman with red hair asked her colleague as she came into the
office. She casually dropped her bag on her desk and shook the
damp out of her hair. It was a typical San Francisco evening,
and the fog was as thick as mascara at the Avatars Black &
White Ball.

Burt was a beefy dispatcher in his early twenties. He'd
been working at AINS/SF ever since he graduated from Cal
Neuro in Pasadena. "Nah, not much," he replied, taking a bite
out of the take-out burrito he was eating. "The usual blips on
TijuanaNet . . . plus, the usual bunch of Russians scamming us
for political asylum from Kremlinsoft." He half-turned on his
chair to wave a free hand at her.

"Hi, Alex, how's it going?"

"I'm hanging in there." She glanced at the duty screen.
"Who's out there in Vector six? Lena? That's my scheduled pa-
trol. Shouldn't she be jacking back in already? She's late."

"Lena's always farting around." Burt shrugged. "You know
her, she can never pass up a bargain. She's got this collection of
bootleg digital bonsais and antique Calvin Klein underwear
ads. She has such kitschy taste."

Burt made a face as he studied the personnel-control stream on the monitor. The visual scan had frozen on an image of a row of warehouses, part of the Digibank complex where the nationalized avatar identities were continuously being processed. He rapped the screen, but it remained stuck.

"You can head back home now, Lena," he said into the mike. "The graveyard shift has arrived. Lena? You there? Report, babe."

Alex stole a glance at Burt, who was hunched over his screen. Funny how nerds always had the cracks of their asses showing above their drag-down trousers, she thought. It was almost an emblem of their faith. Not that she cared, but they seemed to be almost vain about their sloppy looks.

She frowned as she began to catch up on the reports that had come in from HQ in Washington, D.C., along with some general-info items culled by Langley.

"They're rounding up Jewish avatars again on the ReichNet and putting them in 'concentration camps' for 'reeducation in the nationalist ideals.' Doesn't all this seem horribly familiar?"

"History clones itself, I guess . . . But have you heard what their minister of propamedia, Josef Grossmeister, is now saying? That it's no worse than what we're doing with our own foreign problem—our own 'gypsies south of the border.'"

"Yeah, but at least we're not proclaiming the 'New Völkisch'—the 'master race of avatars' . . . That is really fucked."

Burt gave her a sympathetic look. Alex was Jewish. "Yeah, it sucks all right . . . *Shit,* Alex!" he exclaimed as the screen began to flash and buzz erratically. "I don't believe it! It's a Code 1! Emergency Red! What the hell is going on here?!"

"Officer Lyubovich," Burt said as he switched on the alternate visual channel. "Report on your status immediately . . . " Frantically, he began to toggle the AVC. "Lena, for chrissakes! If you're having a problem, bail out right now!"

Burt gave Alex a deadly serious look. His face was as white as the corn chips scattered on his paper plate. "If she doesn't get out soon, she's gonna get the bends. Look, her brainwaves are already bouncing all over the place. Go check her out, Alex! Now!"

Alex was already at the door to the jack chamber. She entered and quickly located Officer Lyubovich's trek capsule. Lena was a thin brunette, in her mid-twenties. Alex found her still dressed in her street clothes, a blue cashmere sweater and a pair of jeans. Her shoes were arranged neatly on the floor.

But Alex could see that she was spasming badly. Her 'trodes were coming undone, her skin was sallow and sweaty, and her soft brown hair was plastered wetly against her head. Her teeth clenched in agony.

Alex stared at the virtual-reality life-support monitor. Lena's vitals were erratic, broken lines indicating impending synapse failure. As Alex watched helplessly, Lena's nostrils flared and gushed with an almost floral-red nosebleed.

"I'm going in, Burt!" she called out to the dispatcher. Alex ran to her locker, which stood right next to Lena's, in the corner of the large, halogen-lit room. She pulled out her customized 'trode suit and stepped into it, zipping it all the way up to her neck. She grabbed her Omni visor off the hook and hurried to find an empty chute in the bank of AINS stations.

Half of them were occupied this evening—Alfonso, on his Caribbean beat; Patrice, Free French Canada; Hanako, East Asia Net; and Emily, who was monitoring Neutral Omnispace, were all on the job, but oblivious to the plight of their neighbor in capsule 8.

Alex crawled into capsule 7 and slid the overhead chute shut. "Countdown—ten—nine—eight—" The motions were all automatic; she'd made the transit a thousand times in her career, but they were all routine jacks. This was different. "Hold on, Lena!" she called through the window to her glassy-eyed neighbor in the next capsule. "I'll be there in a jiff . . . seven—six—five—four—three—two—one—zero . . ."

15

"Burt, fly me in on the exact coordinates," she communicated with the dispatch jock.

"Roger, got it, you're there," she heard the reply from a million light-years away in the next room. A second later, she bounced through the mirror matrix and was rising to her feet as she adjusted to the floor of Vector 6.

The initial step was always wobbly, but Alex was off and running. She was in a dark warehouse of Digibank 22 in Vector 6. This was where they stored the identities—source codes—of the legal avatars, those that had been approved and registered by the Immigration and Naturalization Service and were thus permitted to work, travel, or dwell in U.S. Omnispace. It represented millions of lives in nanocosm, but the place was usually as quiet as a tomb. Tonight, though, something was definitely amiss.

A hissing sound coming from the far end of the warehouse attracted Alex's attention.

"Lena?" Alex called out cautiously, shining her cache-light in the direction of the noise.

"Alex, you all right? What's going on? You found Lena? Kick it, she's curling . . ."

Curling was the first stage of the virtual bends, where the seams of the three-dimensional holoskeleton began to contract until the image-entity collapsed into its own abdominal cavity. What followed was too terrible to contemplate—mental fission that followed you back into the real world. You couldn't jack out if it. They called it "death" in the meat dimension.

"Hang tight—" Alex turned the corner of the metro archive and froze for a moment, her hand moving instinctively to the Av-guard clipped to her belt. If she had to blast them, she would. But she hesitated, afraid she might hit Lena instead.

"Alex—what is it?! I show that you're right there. What's happening, for chrissakes—" Burt's voice echoed in her distant ear.

They were crawling all over Lena's avatar like a toxic tide of venomous centipedes, disappearing into all of her cavities. One crawled out of her open mouth, another ducked under one of her eyelids.

Alex ran forward, blasting at either side, trying to avoid temporal contact with Lena's holobody. Thousands of them! They raced under the stacks, disappearing into cracks, vanishing in the blink of an eye. What were they feasting on in there? She shuddered when she saw the desiccated biofractals scattered on the floor by a stack of files. Lena must have surprised them in the act of cannibalizing the source-identities of the green-carded avs . . .

Alex knelt by her friend and turned her over. She felt for her virtual pulse.

Negative.

Lena's eyes were just as glassy in projection as they were back at base in the jack-chamber capsule.

"Shit!" Alex screamed as one of the centipedes skittered across her wrist. She brushed it off with the curved handle of her cache-light. But it left a mark anyway, like a delicate imprint of a letter on her skin. Alex now shone the light fully on Lena's face, trying to make sense of the blemish that was spiraling into a purplish cobweb design before her very eyes. Alex had seen something like it before—she blinked as she recognized it. She had seen it in a picture book, in one of the tattoo parlors on Haight Street. It was the Wheel of Life, a Tibetan design, turned inside out.

ACT ONE

"The revolutionary is a doomed *man."*

—MIKHAIL BAKUNIN

Tattoo

Cagnes-sur-Mer
The French Riviera, July 13, 2036

"Wish I'd never been tattooed," the red-haired, freckled young man said to his companion morosely.

He was wearing a brief blue swimsuit and a *Bakunin* t-shirt with a slogan in small Russian Cyrillic letters that read: A MAGAZINE FOR THE DEAD RUSSIAN ANARCHIST INSIDE ALL OF US. A contributing editor to the samizdat publication, he was on permanent leave from his homeland, where he was on the short list of violent revolutionaries wanted by the tsar's secret police.

"Well, there's nothing to be done for it, Alyosha," the young man's companion, who was named Boris, replied softly. He was dark complexioned, with a Georgian mustache that hung from his upper lip like an upside-down candelabra. "What's done is done."

They were sitting together on the beach at this small French seaside town between Nice and Cannes looking at the flat blue Mediterranean. Not a wave in sight; not a single cloud in the reflecting blue sky. The stone *gallets* on the beach were scorching his bottom, and Alyosha kept sitting up and stretching out uncomfortably. He flicked the ashes of his Gauloise at a one-legged seagull hopping on its crippled stem among the stones.

Alyosha brooded. He could relate to that sorry bird.

A French boy of about eight was stalking the bird with a slingshot. His parents beamed at him with approval from their folding beach chairs nearby. A radio played North African pop music by the hit group of the summer, the Nasty Chiracs. All around them were bodies, bodies, and bodies, including the usual summer harvest of bare-breasted women young, old, and in between, sipping bottles of water and spraying their bronzed flesh with Evian mist.

In the distance across the bay, the two Russians could see the sleek white yachts of the super-rich anchored at Antibes and gaily festooned with French flags. It was late afternoon on the eve of Bastille Day, approaching six o'clock, and the sun was still broiling, with no breeze to relieve the heat.

The fireworks were already starting on the promenade of the town. *Pop! Pop! Pop!* A string of Chinese firecrackers erupted like explosive knuckles cracking.

They heard the *whizzz* of an ill-aimed rocket fired somewhere close above their heads, and they both instinctively ducked. Boris threw himself down on the hot stones, much to the amusement of the eight-year-old's parents. The child paused in his rubber flip-flops, the seagull now flown away.

He pointed at the two men. "Look, Maman, that foreigner's digging into the beach with his big nose!"

The boy's mouth opened in surprise when he saw the red-headed man pull what looked like a gun from his knapsack. Their eyes met. The Russian's cold stare made the boy shrink as if he'd been threatened by a dangerous toy. The gun was back inside the man's knapsack, just as swiftly as it had appeared.

The French boy blinked, then blurted, "Papa, that man's got a gun!"

"That's enough slapstick out of you, Marcel!" His father, a tall, lanky accountant on holiday with his family from Paris, slapped the kid on his head. His nose and shoulders were red, the rest of him pasty white. The family had arrived that morning.

"Come on, now, you missed that bird when you had the chance! Serves you right!" The father wagged a warning finger at the kid and dragged him back to their spot on the beach. As

22

he passed Alyosha, the Frenchman gave him a wary and scornful look.

"Damn fucking Russians, they think they own the south of France now, all that mafiya money buying up the place . . . ," they could hear him bitching at his wife.

"Let's get going, Boris," Alyosha said, jumping to his feet. "It's almost time, anyway."

"Shit, I thought you were going to shoot somebody, Alyosha! You've got to keep a lid on yourself. Don't lose it now."

"Easy for you to say," Alyosha muttered as they made their way through the labyrinth of sprawling bodies. "You're not going to be at the drop. I am."

"Listen, Alyosha," his mustachioed companion snapped, pressing his swarthy face up close as soon as they had reached the stairs leading up to the street. He grabbed Alyosha by the t-shirt. "Don't fuck up now. You know what's going to happen if you fuck up, don't you? A lot of people are counting on you. Got that?"

"*Spokoyna,* calm down!" Alyosha pushed his friend away. "I'm not going to fuck up. If anyone fucks up, it's going to be you."

"*Durak,* you idiot!" his accomplice snapped at him. "That tattoo you got was not a brilliant stroke of genius. If the French police haven't already—they download all the tattoos that are posted each day—they do that, you know, every twenty-four hours, Alyosha—then the *Azef*—" he spat out the name of the dreaded Russian secret police—"is probably scanning right now to match up with the dossiers of all Russian subversives known to be abroad. Fucking fascists! Fuck them and the tsar! And fuck you, too, for putting us both at risk with your stupidity."

"How was I to know?" Alyosha pleaded, a note of panic rising in his voice as he rubbed his forearm where he had been tattooed the night before in the old town of Nice.

"Where is it?!" Boris swore as they both stared at the blank spot on his arm. "Damn, turn around!" He pulled his comrade's t-shirt up from behind. "There, it's crawling around your back."

"Honestly, how was I supposed to know?" Alyosha protested as he peered over his own shoulder at the spidery tattoo that was even now scuttling to hide under his armpit. It was a sentient tattoo, a newfangled thing imprinted with the owner's personal avatar code. Conceptually, it was like one of those sponge-animal toys that spring to full size in the bath. But it was programmed with intelligence, so that it could travel *off* the owner's body and go on-line, where it assumed the full avatar functions of its master. The owner could download files into the tattoo for release onto the Net. At least, that was how it was supposed to work. Epidermal programming was still a brand-new field. The inventor/programmer of this particular line of novelty tattoos had gone into hiding after the malpractice lawsuits began to multiply. He couldn't be found because he'd erased his trail.

"Why'd you have to go get yourself tattooed, for Christ's sake, the night before the operation?" Boris said, shaking his head, flabbergasted.

"And where were you? Shopping for souvenirs?" Alyosha replied testily. "So did you find that hand-tooled Moroccan garrote you were looking for? Big art collector! Anyway, this thing is supposed to be encrypted, that's what the guy said. It's safe. No one's going to pick up on it."

Boris scowled. "First of all, it's against the law to encrypt tattoos. They have to be registered. Second, it takes a lot more work to *encrypt* a tattoo, that's why they cost more. He didn't give a fuck about you—he just wanted your money. If it *were* encrypted, it would be dormant, not live and running all over your body. Your tattoo is active. *Active.* Do you understand, Alyosha? You always think you're so fucking smart. After this is over, you and me—we go our own separate ways. Sorry."

Alyosha glowered back at Boris. "Fine with me."

"Here, lift your arm," Boris ordered. "Let's have another look at it. What's it up to now?"

Alyosha lifted his arm dutifully. There it was, hiding in the thicket of his curly underarm hair like a cornered cockroach, its bio-feelers responding to their scrutiny with a slight shiver of its sensors.

Boris's face reddened as he exploded again. "Jesus, are you fucking stupid or what? How could you pick *that* design?!"

"No one's gonna get it," Alyosha retorted with teeth bared. "Not even Trotsky if he were alive today. It's just an acronym, that's all. It could stand for anything. The initials of girlfriends, come on, what's wrong with that? *M* for 'Marie,' *M* for 'Margot,' *M* for 'Michelle' . . . It doesn't necessarily *have* to mean anything special!" He didn't sound nearly as confident as he was trying to.

In fact, the damned tattoo was an acronym for one of the slogans of their revolutionary-terrorist group.

MMM. It stood for "Murder the Mass Media."

Both men blinked at the same time. The tattoo was now making a dash for it; it flipped on its back above Alyosha's heart, where it assumed an interesting new position that revealed yet another secret meaning of their organization.

There, it was unmistakable . . . *WWW.* Inverted, it was the sign of the Antichrist of the Matrix—the "666" of the World Wide Web.

The bell tower on the promenade of Cagnes-sur-Mer began to toll the sonorous chimes of six o'clock.

"I've got to go. I don't want to be late. Meet you at the corner of rue Le Pen at six-thirty sharp. Be there," Alyosha said authoritatively as he slipped on a windbreaker over his *Bakunin* t-shirt. He wanted to recover from his humiliation by taking charge once more.

"I will," Boris replied. "Just get the fucking thing so we can get the hell out of here."

"Don't worry, I will," Alyosha assured him and began to walk away in the direction of the town.

"And be careful," Boris called out after him, but Alyosha did not turn around. He was already lost in the milling crowd of revelers preparing to greet Bastille Day. The streets were full of them this evening, happy faces of vacationers bent on enjoying the French national holiday. If they only knew what was about to be unleashed tonight, Boris thought to himself. They might not be so happy.

Monocle

Alyosha quickly put his bickering with Boris behind him as he blended in anonymously with the bustling crowd in the marketplace. The excitement in the square had an oddly calming effect on him.

He walked briskly past the busy shops, the overflowing cafés, the outdoor restaurants, and the colorful flower stalls with their Rubenesque bouquets of red roses and Mediterranean blooms. The warm, sweet scent of fragrant lilies, orange blossoms, violets, mimosa, and jasmine wafted to his nostrils in the golden sunshine.

Aromatherapy for a terrorist? Alyosha smiled at the thought and felt happy and free again like a kid whose parents told him it was okay to go ahead and smash the neighbor's windows. Like that kid who wanted to stone that seagull on the beach. A right proper little bastard. Maybe one day he would grow up to lob bombs at some loony-tune French politician. So who was the real terrorist then? Papa, Mama, *Babushka, Dedushka*? How far back did the genealogy of terrorism go? To Adam and Eve? Look what they did in the Garden, and all the more power to them . . .

We are all terrorists at heart, he thought. But only a few of us are motivated enough to become true revolutionaries. That was the main difference. He felt centered again, confident of his task.

He smiled at the pretty girls selling fruit, melons, dates, figs, olives, mounds of pistachios, and pyramids of sweets and pastries. They were the picture of Mediterranean beauty with their olive skin, dark Italian features, long, tanned legs, and tiny gold crucifixes buried in the shapely hilltops of their breasts.

"Eh, bien, m'sieur!" One of them offered him a juicy slice of peach with a smile. *"Non, merci!"* he answered her.

See, he could resist temptation. Another notch in his favor.

Alyosha passed the stalls of gleaming fish reclining on beds of shaved ice, the sea bass, cod, red gurnett, the horny-finned *rascasse*—hogfish, to be sure, with their bristles and snouts—crabs, langoustes, and a kindergarten of little baby squids that lay huddled together helplessly.

Life is a bouillabaisse, he thought darkly. A stew of all those who manage to get caught in its net. Add olive oil, mayonnaise, crushed garlic and eat. Better still, devour . . .

My own life, he decided, is more like a borscht, truly. A difference in taste, I suppose. Heavy with cream, with cabbage and meat floating at its bottom, and unpalatable to most of these Continentals who prefer their cannibalism seasoned with more culture.

Alyosha caught a sudden whiff of spices in the air, pepper, saffron, thyme, bay leaves, sage, fennel, and orange peel. His nose prickled, and he felt a sneeze coming. Before he could react, he was hit by another, more pungent odor coming from a table stacked with French cheeses.

Pfoo! he sniffed. No wonder Picasso painted his faces with more than one nose! You practically had to be a cubist just to take a simple breath around here!

It was something he could never quite get used to, these reeking *fromages,* like old socks with a bad conscience . . .

Leave it to the French to assault you through your senses, a far better defense than the New Maginot Line, the virtual fire wall they had erected along the French-Belgian border as a defense against seepage from the ReichNet.

Alyosha hurried past the cheeses, covering his face. He entered a cobbled side street. Here the houses had pink and ochre walls, with overhanging red-tiled roofs and balconies

27

laden with wisteria and climbing plants. Lines of colorful wash hung out to dry. A stone lion's head spouted a thin stream of water into a weathered stone basin. In a recessed square, sheltered from the sun by plane trees, old men and young ones alike played *boules,* lining up the iron balls and rolling them. *Pock!*

He slowed down as he approached the Bistro du Chat Noir at the far end of the street. Steady now. Make sure the coast is clear at both ends.

He lit a Gauloise, cupping his hands around the flame, and his narrowed eyes took inventory of the situation. Waiters were carrying trays of aperitifs, setting them down on tables. He heard ripples of laughter. People were snacking on pizzettas, drinking glasses of red wine, eating plates of ravioli, dipping their bread into little dishes of puréed anchovies and black olives.

Alyosha stood there for a few minutes just to make sure. He saw a Neapolitan-looking waitress come out of the kitchen swinging her wide hips, her tight black skirt with a palm print etched in flour upon her rump.

She stepped back into the kitchen and came out again. Two palm prints this time. *Vive le chef.*

Nu davai, Alyosha thought to himself. Let's go. Time to take the plunge. He threw his cigarette into the gutter, and felt the reassuring weight of his pistol in his knapsack as he walked up to the bistro.

He took up a seat at a table next to the baldheaded Russian who was reading a copy of yesterday's *Le Figaro.* The man was dressed in a short-sleeved white shirt, gray trousers, and a pair of old-fashioned leather sandals with socks, as though that was his idea of what the proletariat wore. Too bad his monocle gave him away. Fucking aristocrat.

After a moment, the man folded the newspaper on his lap. "Looks like Olympique de Marseilles are going to take the pennant."

"I'm sorry, but I don't follow football."

"You're here on holiday?" His pale eyes peered at Alyosha carefully. The exchange of passwords began.

"Yes, I've come to see the jazz festival in Nice."

"Ah yes, jazz, do you like Chet Baker?"

"I prefer Charlie Parker."

"How about Mingus?"

"Khachaturian is more to my taste."

"Khachaturian? Isn't he classical?"

"The Khachaturian Quartet. They're opening at the Festival."

"The rest are dead, aren't they?"

"Virtual. It's a *festival de jazz virtuel.* All new compositions from beyond the grave channeled through cryosynthesizers."

The baldheaded man paused. "I have a CD that may interest you."

"Group?"

"The Monoclos. They're unknown outside of certain circles in Russia."

"I look forward to hearing it."

So far, so good. All the words were in the right order. The man relaxed an iota, but the tension followed him like the wake of badly discharged energy. "You must understand," the aristo suddenly stated, casting aside all precaution, as waves of worry thundered down on his shaved head. "I'm a patriot. I'm not doing this willingly. You people haven't given me any choice."

"*Spokoyna!* Calm down!" Alyosha ordered him sharply, glancing around to see if anyone was in earshot. The fool was going to blab out his entire life story. With all his pathetic self-justifications, uttered not for Alyosha's sake, but for his own.

It's never easy to betray your country, especially when you've got your balls in the guillotine and the blade is about to fall, Alyosha thought.

The color drained out of the man's face. "Very well then, that's my own affair. I apologize," he said, chastised. "But if you will permit me to mention a word of precaution about the handling of the—er—hazardous material . . . That's the very least I can do to minimize the potential danger involved. Many innocent people may be hurt otherwise."

Alyosha stared at him. Listen to him, the fucking hypocrite! Alyosha *was* listening, but in the back of his head something was already coming down.

Something that he could recognize, that he had been *trained* to recognize, but which he had never imagined he would ever experience in quite this manner.

On an afternoon like this one. At a café like this one. With the people who had faces like these faces, who were in a few moments going to watch dumbfounded as you took your tumble . . .

There was a young American sitting a few tables away with his girlfriend, having a lover's spat. Another couple, French, middle aged, pretending not to notice anything at all, were smoking and exchanging small talk.

The waitress with the handprints on her behind approached them now in slow motion, holding a tray with something hidden under the napkin.

That's how fast perceptions can change. The men in the Citroën cruised ever so slowly down the street, two in the back, two in the front, in the trademark sunglasses of La Picine. The French counterintelligence.

Lies! Suddenly Alyosha felt enraged. He was trapped and he knew it, but his business with this man remained unfinished. He would have to see it through to the end, and the end was coming all too soon.

"Do you have it with you?" he snarled. "I don't have all day." Maybe there was a chance he could get out of this trap and make a clean escape. Each moment counted. *Hurry up, you fool!*

The baldheaded man removed his monocle and held it in the palm of his hand. "Here," he said, offering him the eyepiece.

"What's this?" Alyosha stared at the monocle suspiciously.

30

"This is the carrying case," the man explained. "You open it like this." He pressed a hinge and the monocle snapped open like an oyster, two halves of glass enclosing a vial within. Alyosha saw something that looked like a contact lens floating inside the vial.

"It's stored in a basic chlorhexedine-saline solution. Be careful when you put the contact lens inside your eye. It's an ocular-sensitive liquid algorithm that's activated when absorbed by the optic nerve. You'll become a little disoriented at first, but you should be able to read the code without any problem."

But Alyosha was no longer listening to the man's instructions. Too late. He grabbed the monocle and rose from the table, his hand drawing his blue snub-nosed Stalin Depth Charge out of his knapsack. It was a small .22 handgun from the twentieth century, but with explosive bullets that could tear a hole through a wall of the Kremlin.

"What's the matter?!" But before the baldheaded man could finish his sentence, all hell broke loose, because there was no heaven to keep it from doing otherwise. The flash of light was so intense that all Alyosha could think was, "My tattoo . . . I should never have gotten it . . ."

But the tattoo never looked back, nor did it say goodbye. Not even *au revoir.*

The Count

Earlier . . .
Monte Carlo, Principality of Monaco

Count Viktor Trobolsky cut an imposing figure. With his shaved head and a monocle perpetually implanted in his eye socket, he was a six-foot-two *presence,* a grand piano built for the world stage. Finely tuned and with an innate understanding of what the real score was, he had an intuitive grasp of all the pianissimos as well as the fortes of public affairs.

Nominally, he was the senior aide to the Russian Minister of the Interior Sergei Voronov. Nominally. His real position was director of Special Projects, Cyber Intelligence Department. The unit was so clandestine that even Tsar Nicholas III and other high officials in the government were unaware of its existence. The SPCID had grown out of the psychological-warfare section of the old KGB. Mind control on the Net was its specialty.

The count was vacationing in Monte Carlo with his French mistress, Regine de Pompignac. That's how it all started.

On the face of it, he was there to relax, to play the roulette tables at the Casino, and to mingle with the Russian nobility that flocked to this famous resort just as they did back in the grand old days of the nineteenth century, when the Romanovs were in their heyday. These were the *new* good old days.

There was something about the color of the light here, so sparkling and clear that even the pastels sprang to life before your eyes. And of course, there was the healthy exuberance that comes from breathing in the tangy sea air that blows in from the Mediterranean. That's what the Russians craved.

That and the joie de vivre that came of knowing that they had escaped the stifling humidity of another oppressive Russian summer in St. Petersburg.

Here he was, Count Viktor Mikhailovich Trobolsky, dutifully hobnobbing with Black Sea oil moguls and Balkan software tycoons, attending one luncheon and dinner party after another in a continuous stream, while spending languorous afternoons bathing in the turquoise waters of the Larvotto, punctuated by boating, tennis, and harmless trysts of amour.

It was all as heady as one of Chekhov's more lighthearted plays.

32

Days passed in this manner, like the steam of conversation that rose around the silver-plated samovars at teatime, when the Russians would regroup on shaded terraces to eat petits fours, and custard-layered napoleons, to gossip, to reflect, and to predict the destiny of nations and of individual love affairs.

It was a perfect cover for what Count Trobolsky was planning to do: To betray all this. He wouldn't save his soul in the process, he was sure of that. But perhaps he could buy a time-share in some corner of salvation somewhere. The alternative was—well, the alternative was worse than exile to Siberia in the days before Siberia became a raw-goods and leisure province leased to New Nippon in 2029. No, the punishment for treason these days was biochemical gulagization.

Trobolsky knew what that meant because he had overseen the program himself. You—the criminal—were injected with the Gulag virus. Every moment was a living agony, complete with programmed flashbacks of torture and hopelessness that would have made Dostoevsky's *House of the Dead* seem like a paradise for members only. The beauty of this form of state control was that the gulag became a permanent state of your personal consciousness. It was no longer a *physical* place—it was a psychic penal colony.

Everywhere you went in your daily life, the gulag was there beside you like a shadow. It was inside your head. The savings over having to maintain and operate actual labor camps was incalculable. You were your own jailer, your own torturer. There was no escape. Prisoners who exhibited good behavior were permitted to apply for euthanasia, but this was a rare occurrence. You *had* to serve your time.

Everything was proceeding quite smoothly. There was a silent auction going on even as he played the roulette tables in Monte Carlo and the count's contacts were responding with encouraging bids. The Americans were dubious, but where would they be if they weren't? The Americans were always the first to smell a stinking fish, but the last to reel in a fresh live one. There was a group in Libya that had made the highest offer so far, but their money was no good. The Virtual Security Council of the New U.N. had seen to that—Libyan money self-destructed whenever it was transferred on the Net. The Serbs were chafing to win the prize, but they couldn't be trusted further than they could toss a brain-grenade.

Milosevic was in his late nineties and suffering from Kevorkian Anxiety. Mr. War Crimes himself had converted to Tibetan Buddhism, imagine that. Good luck in the next world. There are only so many angels that you can bludgeon with a catheter.

It looked like the Germans, then. The chancellor of the Fourth Reich, Rudolf Wessel, was impressed by the way the neuro-gulag program had succeeded in quelling social deviance and unrest in Russia. He was an old-world Scientologist, so he could understand the metaphysical implications of technology. And its limits, of course.

His minister of propamedia, Josef Grossmeister, affected a clubbed foot like his historical predecessor Goebbels—he'd had it *surgically* done, for God's sake—but he was swifter on the uptake. It didn't take him long to restore the Berlin Wall on the ReichNet.

If it weren't for the Germans and the Russians and the Americans who endlessly squabbled over hegemony on the Matrix, the New Cold War might have been just a blip on the radar of history. Even the Japanese had risen to the challenge with their Greater East Asia Co-Prosperity Net.

Some old archetypes obviously had yet to be worked out in the collective unconscious that was now masquerading as the global brain. ("Just Say No to the Noosphere," was the Luddites' rallying cry, a slogan that featured prominently on their Web site.)

Aryans in gray Wehrmacht uniforms goose-stepping through Omnispace had ceased to be something that only editorial cartoonists took note of. Ever since ReichNet had annexed PolskayaNet and began eyeing the rest of Europe, the goose-steppers were a frightening reality. The conquest of PolskayaNet had been a blitzkrieg of master programming. It was the same old story being played out again. To the victor go the pixels.

But the count had to be extremely cautious in carrying out his mission. He had been relying on third-party avatars to conduct the negotiations; the slightest trace put on any of his Net-reps, and they would self-destruct, leaving a wake of toxic nodefreeze that could swiftly incapacitate an entire network.

In some ways, net death was much more effective than its biological antecedent. Born-again mainframes were one thing, but the residue of psychic damage was permanently archived in the *real* collective unconscious of the world, which some Japanese Zen master had dubbed the "Wired Akashic Records."

True enough, the mental sphere that now enveloped the entire planet was an unerasable memory. The information may not always be *accessible,* but its imprint on the collective psyche was permanent. The individual might not be able to download specific details, to reflect vertically through time, but as far as the System itself was set up, total amnesia was *impossible.*

Despite this, the count felt secure in his plan. Nothing can go wrong, he reasoned to himself. There is nothing that I have not foreseen. Not even the ghost of Beria, Stalin's satanic executioner, could track me down . . .

Yaponchik

That was why Count Trobolsky suffered a severe shock to his nervous system that morning when he strode confidently into the elevator at the Hôtel Prince Albert, where he and the indefatigable Madame de Pompignac shared the top-floor Princess Grace suite. He had been feeling quite sure of himself, ebullient and strong. He had even made love twice before breakfast, though he had withheld his essence just as his tantric trainer Mantiak Tchaikovsky had instructed him.

Before the elevator door closed all the way, a ham-fisted

hand caught it and pried it open. In stepped a squat Russian gangster followed by two towering Cossack goons.

Count Trobolsky had no trouble recognizing the Russo-Japanese mafioso who headed the Siberian Ginseng syndicate. This was none other than the Yaponchik, a.k.a. "the Japanese." He was the son of a famous Japanese sushi chef in Nakhodka and a notorious Russian hit woman named Toothpick, so-called for her trademark style of execution. She prepared for her hits by creating a lethal but ingenious mix of poison drawn from the liver of the Greenland shark and a hallucinatory fish toxin extracted from the South Pacific goatfish, and then jabbed her victims with a plain wooden toothpick soaked in this deadly mixture. Many of her hits were, in fact, performed at her husband's sushi bar, the victims having been lured there with a promise of a fine Japanese dinner and sake, in order to discuss "business."

Death must have been a blessed relief, the coroner testified at her trial, as it followed a prolonged period of horrific halluci-nations, accompanied by a burning sensation about the mouth, lips, and tongue. "And," he continued, "just before the victim's breathing ceased, this excruciating fire would spread ever so slowly to the face, scalp, neck, and finally to the finger tips and toes."

After pronouncing the death sentence, the judge asked the Toothpick if she felt any remorse about committing these grisly crimes. Her response sent a powerful shiver through the gallery of spectators in the crowded courtroom; the remark was widely quoted in the press and found an immortal place in the colorful annals of Russia's "Roaring Twenties" (2023–29). "I didn't kill them," the Toothpick asserted and shrugged, with-out a trace of emotion on her pancake-flat face. "The fish didn't agree with them, that's all." She was sent to the gallows.

Yaponchik began his swift rise to the top ranks of the Siberian underworld in the city of Novo-Yokohama, a place formerly known as Vladivostok. He was an accomplished sushi chef like his father, but the missing tip of his little finger on his left hand, cut off at the last knuckle, testified to loftier career goals that he ruthlessly pursued within the brotherhood of the Russo-Japanese yakuza.

In the elevator, Yaponchik glanced up at Trobolsky with his slanted, ice-cold blue eyes as he brushed some imaginary lint off the count's Valentino poolside-smoking jacket. "Good morning, Your Excellency, it's a fine day, isn't it?"

Count Trobolsky nodded, but otherwise remained silent, his adrenaline pumping like water from a broken fire hydrant. This was not good. Not good at all.

He had been careful to stay clear of Russian mafiya who, like other nouveaux riches, flocked to the south of France in droves. They liked to jet in on their private planes from their offshore tax havens in the Caspian.

Yaponchik's overpowering cologne, Eau de Fugu, made the small space in the elevator a stifling matchbox. The two Cossack bodyguards stood looking straight ahead with their arms crossed, closing the count in even further. He couldn't take much more of this, but the elevator wasn't moving. That's when he noticed that one of the Cossacks had punched the ARRÊT button.

The count began to sweat. He was trapped.

"If there's anything that I can ever do for Your Excellency, please don't hesitate to ask," Yaponchik said with an almost sneering click of his heels. "Here's my card. Please accept it."

But the count remained frozen on his feet. Yaponchik slipped his card into the count's pocket with a broad smile that showed his small white teeth.

"Danik." The mafioso nodded at one of his two men, and the goon pulled out the stop button. The elevator began its downward descent, whining all the way.

It may have been the count's imagination running amok, but he felt as if the elevator cable would come whipping through the ceiling at any moment and yank him up into the black confines of the elevator chute like a hanged man who was getting off on the wrong floor . . .

37

Trobolsky felt a sense of trembling relief—his knees were actually wobbling—when he reached the ground level and the door opened to a marble lobby filled with a bustling mob of people. He knew it had been a close call. He mopped his brow with his handkerchief.

"Remember, Count," he heard Yaponchik's voice, an unnerving falsetto with a semiotic lisp, call out from behind. "We can do business together. Don't be afraid to call."

Thank God, Regine wasn't with me, the count thought, regaining his composure in the safety of the hotel's grand entrance and its brightly lit crystal chandeliers, smattering of Matisse and Renoir paintings in ornate gilt frames, and sixteenth-century Flemish tapestries hanging from the dark-green walls. The acute radar of Regine's sixth sense—a survival trait of the de Pompignacs, a distinguished but chronically impoverished family since the late eighteenth century—would have known immediately that there was something more to this exchange than the Yaponchik's superficial social pleasantry might have suggested.

Slipping his monogrammed handkerchief back into his breast pocket with a sigh, the count went off to lunch acting as though nothing unusual had happened. But he was still shaken.

Holorina

Arriving at Baroness Von Kreutzberg's sixty-foot yacht, *A Course in Miracles,* which was anchored in Monaco's scenic harbor of Fontvieille, Count Trobolsky was once again the witty, debonair model of St. Petersburg charm.

On the yacht's gleaming, polished-mahogany deck, barefoot but white-gloved waiters dressed in blue-striped Russo-French *matrosse* jerseys and crisply starched white shorts bore trays of champagne and caviar to guests.

"Ah, Maria Andreyevna," the count said, greeting his hostess warmly as he bowed to kiss her delicately extended hand. The Baroness Von Kreutzberg was a cherubic-faced, chestnut-haired eighty-year-old dowager with bright eyes and the cleavage of a far younger woman.

She looked not a day over forty, thanks to the services of her personal gerontologist, Dr. Yuri Sheremenko, who was also rumored to be her lover. All as part of his duties, of course.

Sheremenko, a small, pensive man wearing a gold pince-nez and a double-breasted white Panama suit, stood attentively by her side, ready to administer a Gerovital-9 injection at the slightest sign of a wrinkle on his charge's brow—which was, *spasi Bogu,* thank God, still as smooth as a baby's bare bottom.

He's forty-two, but he looks fifty-five, Count Trobolsky thought as he gave Sheremenko a cordial nod. Longevity must be bad for your health, especially if you're in the business of dishing it out to others.

The Baroness Von Kreutzberg's salon was the most famous among St. Petersburg society. An invitation to attend one of the weekly soirees at her palace on the Nevsky Prospekt was highly prized. There you could meet celebrated painters, writers, raconteurs, artists, and ballet dancers as well as an endless procession of wandering *startsy,* men of God, and "holy fools"—the *yurodivye*—who were part of the baroness's inner circle.

Many were the evenings that the ghost of Nicholas II, who had been so cruelly assassinated during the Russian Revolution of 1917, could be heard around the parlor table offering advice on how to cure Russia's ills.

Not that the ill-fated Nicholas knew any better when he was alive, the count mused.

"You are looking spiritually radiant today, my dear baroness," the count addressed his hostess brightly. "That must mean that you either have a clean conscience—or," he teased, "you must have had a successful séance last night with Monsieur Philippe, your psychic from Lyons. Or is it Papus these days?

Your dear husband, may he rest in peace, is he well?" he inquired solicitously.

"He's very well, Viktor Mikhailovich. He sends his regards. I told him you were coming today."

"Please convey my respects."

"I certainly will. You've met young Volodya?" she asked, pointing out an aloof man in his early thirties who was lounging a few feet away with a cigarette, a sloppy smile, and a *ryumka,* a tiny-stemmed shot glass of vodka, in his hand.

The baroness, with a curt nod at the count, walked off to mingle with her other guests, Dr. Sheremenko trailing a few steps behind her.

Count Trobolsky turned to the young man, whom he of course knew. Prince Yusupov was the heir to the vast Yusupov fortune, another old titled family that was closely related to the Romanov dynasty.

"Did I say something to offend her?" the count asked the prince with some concern.

Volodya's suntanned face radiated the good humor and bleary-eyed amusement at the world that he fueled with frequent shots of Stolichnaya.

"Hello, Viktor Mikhailovich," the prince said as he tossed his custom-made Turkish cigarette into the harbor. "She's just a bit touchy about her dear old husband these days."

He rolled his blue eyes upward and lit another cigarette with a platinum lighter from Kyrgyzstan.

"I hear there's marital strife brewing in the netherworld. Monsieur Philippe has been heard whispering that the old man's now threatening divorce. He disapproves of her wanton ways."

"So." The count nodded, accepting the explanation. It was all right then, so long as the baroness's displeasure was not directed at him personally.

"What about you, Volodya?" he inquired. "Still cruising the ports of the Mediterranean? I thought you were at Mallorca. And speaking of wanton ways, are you staying out of trouble?"

"Oh, don't worry about me," the young prince replied with a sly grin. "Where there's a will, there's a way."

"You mean your father's will. Be careful, my friend, there's been an epidemic of disinheritances lately. If you want to keep what you have—"

"I've been disinherited twice already."

"Just be sensible; you know what I mean. Mind your health. What's with the smoking? I thought you didn't smoke."

"Oh, this." Volodya grinned as he waved his lit cigarette in the count's face. "I light up only when I'm drinking. But I drink continuously, which is why many people mistakenly think that I smoke." He squinted across the deck. "I'll be damned."

Count Trobolsky's eyes followed in the same direction. A striking-looking woman leading a massive Russian wolfhound on a gold leash stepped off the gangplank onto the deck.

There was a pause in the conversation as Baroness Von Kreutzberg rushed to greet her new guest.

"Natasha! What a surprise! We hardly *ever* see you!" There was a mutual kissing of cheeks as the wolfhound sat obediently by his mistress's side, panting.

"A bowl of water for Raskolnikov," the woman snapped at a waiter. The servant immediately produced a gold tureen with mineral water from the Savoy. The hound slurped at it thirstily.

"Who's that?" Count Trobolsky asked, intrigued.

"You mean you don't know?" Young Yusupov's eyes widened in disbelief. "That's Natasha Nijinskaya, prima donna of the Neo-Kirov Ballet. She danced forty-two fouettés in *ROM Lake* in her last public appearance, then after the audience broke into thunderous applause, she danced forty-two more."

"Oh, that explains it." Count Trobolsky took a sip from his long-stemmed champagne glass. "She never appears in person, does she? She's a tele-ballerina—"

"The word is *holorina,* my friend," Prince Yusupov chastised him. "I can see that you're not a connoisseur of the fine arts. No, of course, she doesn't appear in *person*. She never has, in fact. She's one of those free spirits. She can't bear to be

41

confined to the stage. That's too artificial for her. She's got it programmed so that she can dance on a street, in the woods, anyplace, wherever she might be, if she's feeling up to it, and the result gets mixed in live with the dancers onstage. Anyway, KirovNet is a big enough stage these days, as big as the world."

The prince paused to have his shot glass refilled by a waiter who had been hovering behind a potted palm. He grabbed the bottle of Absolut Stoli from the waiter's hand. "No use pouring for a Russian, there's no end to it, and much as I've grown fond of you hiding behind those palms, you're starting to get on my nerves. What's your name?"

"Vadim, sir."

"Vadim, to your health then." The prince grinned. "Now get lost." The flustered waiter scurried away with a napkin over his arm; the hand that had been holding the bottle still clenched clawlike over its missing form. Something about the phantom pain of missing bottles, a common-enough waiter's malady, at least in Russia. He'd get over it.

The prince turned back to Count Trobolsky, who was still eyeing Natasha Nijinskaya with fascination. Yusupov flicked his ashes and then continued with his explanation.

"Just look at her," he said. "No one's sure what she even looks like at any given time. Her nickname is 'Kameleon.' She's so passionately secretive about her privacy. Or private about her secrecy, or whatever . . ."

He took a refined swig from the bottle. "I wonder what brings her out here today. I heard she was vacationing at St. Tropez."

"Hmm," the count murmured as he spooned up some caviar with a piece of toast and munched on it. "She's not very attractive, is she? Yet she is still somehow, ah, *electrifying.*"

He studied the woman at a distance. Her face was rather mannish, he decided, with strong cheekbones and a nose that looked like it had been hooked into place. Her lips were sensual but leering, above (here the masculine symmetry fell apart) a delicate chin. Her skin was the color of an old Japanese

42

porcelain doll in a glass case; that is to say, it looked like it had been stained white. Was it makeup? he wondered. It looked a bit unnatural. Her hair was cut simply, with thick black bangs that hung above her piercing, coal-black eyes like a coutured visor. She had a muscular build, with the barest hint of a bosom beneath the plain white t-shirt she wore with her Pravda jeans.

She wore sandals, the nails on her hands and feet unpainted though varnished. Her legs seemed too short for a ballerina, but then, young Yusupov was right, dance was not his forte, not his medium. Give him the curves and the pillowy breasts of his Regine any day, or any night . . .

That wolfhound of hers, too, the way he looked up slavishly at his mistress as though he knew on which side of the dish his filet mignon was stacked. Even now, her hand played with his ears, ruffled his back, digging deep into the fur till the dog—out of adoration, or was it consternation?—couldn't restrain himself and began to lick each finger as if it were a delicious treat.

My God, no, Count Trobolsky restrained his overactive imagination. He had heard of such things, but this was still a *Christian* world, and pets were meant to be pets, not necessarily petted in *that* way . . . Did the count detect an unholy relationship there?

"She's quite an eyeful, isn't she, Viktor Mikhailovich?" Young Yusupov, grinning, broke his reverie. "She's got presence, all right. I know what you're thinking. So she's not a raving beauty, but what is it that counts these days? The last revolution was supposed to have swept all those false distinctions away, democratized beauty and ugliness."

"So you're a philosopher now as well as a libertine?" Count Trobolsky indulged Volodya, giving him a playful jab in the side.

Prince Yusupov took a long draw on his cigarette before flicking it away into the azure water of the harbor. Little white twinkling fish darted to the surface to intercept it.

43

"Sure, why not?" His eyes were still fixed on the live image of the holorina. "These days, everyone equalizes themselves with a handicap. If you're beautiful, your plastic surgeon emphasizes your beauty with a scar. People who are really ugly don't have to do anything. They equalize themselves by doing something beautiful."

"What about the baroness?" Count Trobolsky asked, observing the dowager, who was engaged in an animated conversation with the mysterious dancer. "Is she part of the old world, or a representative of the new one as you describe it?"

"Her?" Prince Yusupov thought for a moment. "Oh, she's already got two tits in the grave. And I'm speaking literally, mind you. Dying would bring color to her cheeks at this point. What do you say we have another drink?" He finished off the rest of the vodka in the bottle before the count could reply.

The Wolfhound

Maybe it was the heat. Or maybe it was the champagne. Count Trobolsky had lost count of the glasses of Moët he had downed at the baroness's party. He stood by himself on a quiet corner of the deck, taking in the view of the harbor.

He could see the Prince's Palace, a medieval fortress built on a giant rock promontory overlooking the principality of Monaco. The Grimaldi coat of arms fluttered from a Moorish tower on the precipice. The picture-perfect Middle Ages in the twenty-first century.

It was a splendid day. But the count was despondent.

He listened to a small gypsy orchestra that had been set up beneath a folksy garlanded awning on the deck. The singer was doing a good job doling out a spirited but melancholy love song, "Ochi Chorniye," ("Dark Eyes"), a favorite tune of the tortured Russian soul.

"I'm in love with you, but I fear you, oh my beautiful Dark Eyes, we met too late for our love to start anew . . ."

Love and loss, preferably occurring at the same time. There was nothing like a good tearjerker to make a man want to kill himself. What could one say? That was the national spirit.

The count wiped a stray tear from his eye and counted the bubbles in his champagne glass.

He was still obsessing about the Yaponchik and their encounter at the hotel earlier that morning. *"If there's anything that I can ever do for Your Excellency, please don't hesitate to ask . . . ,"* the Russian gangster had said with a suffocating smoothness.

The gall of the man, as if the count would have anything to do with his kind. *What possessed him?*

Perhaps it was no accident that Yaponchik had followed him into the elevator. He could still feel the man's business card burning like an ember in his pocket whenever he fingered it, which is precisely what he had been doing for the past half hour . . .

For a moment, the count imagined that it was more than just an ordinary calling card. In his position as head of the Russian SPCID, he was familiar with accounts of underworld hits in which such cards were used to blow up unsuspecting victims. Fashioned of plastique, they were an ingenious instrument of destruction. The Japanese yakuza had perfected this Oriental ritual of murder during the Keiretsu Wars, when the megacorporations were fighting their bloody feudal battles over turf in the VR marketplace.

The polite bow, the presentation of the card with both hands; of course you had to accept it, you could hardly refuse. That would be horribly impolite. The "meishi bomb" was activated when the receiver pressed the two corners of the card in the prescribed fashion. In good time—time enough for the card giver to depart, of course—the bomb would go off. There you had it. The perfect etiquette behind a successfully staged assassination . . .

It could be a bomb—but then again, it could be salvation.
Once again, as he was naturally prone to do, the count wavered
between self-doubt and self-denial.

What if this were a God-given opportunity? He needed
time to think. But he was running out of time as fast as he was
running out of ideas.

"Viktor Mikhailovich, pssst, Viktor Mikhailovich . . ."

Count Trobolsky spun around. There was no one in sight
except the ballerina's Russian wolfhound, which had been
sniffing its way around the deck. Crotches, hands, feet, whatever its hairy heart desired.

Natasha Nijinskaya was still chatting it up with the Baroness
Von Kreutzberg and her cronies, and the hound had wandered
off to explore on his own.

"Eh, who's there?" the count asked, a bit too drunk for his
own good.

The voice called to him again. "Viktor Mikhailovich,
pssst."

Beelzebub in the Caucasus, it was the *wolfhound* speaking
to him! It had to be, unless this was some sort of an elaborate
joke that the baroness's séance table-thumpers had devised for
his benefit.

The count fumbled for his monocle. "Ah, yes," he replied
with a half-smile. "Whom do I have the honor of addressing?"

"Never mind," the hound snapped back. Was that its tongue
hanging out of the side of its face, that yard of mottled flesh? It
was disgusting, fascinating but disgusting. "Listen to me," the
wolfhound slobbered.

"Er, I'm listening," the count said, not knowing whether to
be amused or horrified. "So you're not, ah, a regular wolfhound
then? Some new breed perhaps?"

The science of genetics had advanced far beyond the phenomenon of the humpbacked mouse with the human ear growing out of its spine. Hybrids were all the rage. Racehorses that
played chess with their jockeys, monkeys that programmed
soap operas for the Web, pigs that gave communion to their fel-

low farmyard animals. Presbyterian ducks, agnostic platy-
puses, Hindu mongooses. Dogs with doctorates. It was all
rather straightforward fantasy. Pedestrian really, until you
stepped in it.

Which was what the count was in the process of doing.
Virtual dog doo had the same consistency as the real thing, but
with a different accent, another texture altogether.

"Forgive my ignorance," the count said to the wolfhound,
which was now sitting on its haunches. It was scratching itself.
Cavalierly. "Excuse me, but were you just speaking to me?"

"Indeed I was," the wolfhound growled. "If you have any
sense, you'll pay careful attention. I'm not going to repeat this
a second time."

My God, this was unbelievable! The count almost wanted
to laugh and call out to the others, "See here, a talking hound!
Isn't this priceless, or what?"

Très amusant, ce chien . . . . It would make a great story. He
now focused on the animal. "You have my complete and undivided attention."

Then the hound said one word that froze the count from
head to toe. "Mir."

Mir. It was the Russian word for "Peace," or "World." It was
also the code name of the secret neural-software program that the
count had come to the Riviera to sell to the highest bidder.

For the first time, the count struggled against both his
tipsiness *and* his sobriety. This was new information coming
from a new quarter. So what if it was a wolfhound? A dog. You
never knew where the voice of truth might emanate from. *This*
was the major breakthrough of the age. Truth was limitless,
man was limited. Your normal senses were a handicap in the
context of the big picture.

"Go on," he said soberly. "I'm listening."

"Good," the wolfhound said. "Now listen to me very, very
carefully."

47

The count listened. Indeed, he listened so carefully that he
soon discovered it was not the dog that was the messenger, but

one of the fleas on its back. And it was not a flea either. It was an electronic transmitter. From Hades.

The count felt another chill. He looked across the deck and saw that the holorina was staring at him with a bemused expression. The bitch was swaying lightly to the rhythm of a gypsy tango. And he had the eerie sensation that he was an unwitting dancer in some evil pas de deux.

Regine

"Sex is highly overrated," Count Trobolsky said later that evening to Regine de Pompignac. She was wearing a skimpy milkmaid's outfit from the French Alps.

Back in his suite at the Hotel Prince Albert, nursing a splitting headache from drinking too much champagne and facing work to do—*work!*—he was hardly in the mood to engage the saucy little vixen who was preening herself at the dresser table. She had paid twenty thousand francs for the outfit at Stormy Milkmaid, a boutique in Nice that catered to the naughty rich. They had given her a complimentary riding crop with her purchase.

"Viktor," she said, as she turned around to face him sternly, putting down her hairbrush. "You're seeing someone else, aren't you?" Her expression softened just as quickly. "I don't mind if you are, really. You Russians are animals."

"Oh, Regine! *Honestly!*" he said with exasperation. This was all he needed. Another scene with the volatile Regine.

He adored her, but she was a lance in his latex. Lately, they had been having three big fights a day and half a dozen minor arguments at night. Over what? *Orgasm.* She was positively ideological about orgasm. There was the *economy* of orgasm, the *political science* of orgasm, the *metaphysics* of orgasm, the *human rights* of orgasm, even the *astrophysics* of orgasm.

It didn't have anything to do with the *kind* of sex that they had—which for him was lyrical; she called him her "darling Pushkin" when he engaged in his bouts of Slavic foreplay, and she teased him about his caresses, which were more like lines of iambic pentameter than blank verse.

No, Regine had an apocalyptic view of sex, which drove him crazy. "It's the greenhouse effect, darling," she frequently reminded him, as she did now. "Negative orgasm—orgasm without the essential orgone cohesion that comes from the mixing of the male and the female fluids—is responsible—listen to me, Viktor, don't turn away! Negative orgasm is contributing to the growing hole in the ozone layer. Pierre Flambay has clearly explained this in his seminal work, *The Demise of Desire*. I wish you would read it. It would do you a world of good, *chéri*."

"That's that neotantric claptrap," the count snapped impatiently. "He's got his orgasm mixed up with his origami."

"Don't make fun, Viktor. We are not talking paper animals here. Regardless of what you think, there are many people who agree with his views. You're not being fair."

"Please, *please,* not tonight, *chérie,* I have a *mal de tête.* Do you have anything for it besides those Reichian flower drops of yours? Some Aspégic? Anything with *aspirin*?"

"People are coming less and less," she went on, relentlessly. "They hoard their seed like wheats in a barn. Nature is missing the joie de vivre. Sex is a dry riverbed. You have a headache, darling?"

She came up behind him and massaged his temples. "Lobes of steel," she marveled as she inserted one hand into his dressing gown and traced it down from his chest to his abdomen.

"*Please,* Regine!"

She snarled. "So you *are* seeing someone else? Regine is not enough for you. You must deviate with your Russian *condoms*!" She spat out her retort. "You never give me your seed anymore, Viktor Mikhailovich!"

It was an old, tired argument, and he had no strength for it anymore. "Yes, yes, yes! I *am* seeing someone else, if you really want to know! Someone very special! Someone who has my complete—" he paused, "—my complete and undivided attention."

"Who is it?" she held her hand to her plump breast and sank back into her chair. He had to hand it to her. When she was ruffled, she was very, very beautiful. He almost wanted to make love to her here and now. But there was this damned business he had to think through!

"Who is she, Viktor?" she pressed him. The anger had gone out of her voice, replaced by the coldness of anticipation. She could take a blow. God knows, she had taken many. Begged for them even. But that was passion, not the atrophy of submission, which was what she was exhibiting now. He felt sorry for her, but she had started it.

"You want to know who I am seeing?" he asked her, rising up to the challenge, a demonic look in his eye.

"Yes, I can take it. You are a brute, but I am strong. You cannot hurt me anymore than you have already. Who is she?"

"A dog," he said quietly.

"*Comment?* What? You are making the joke. I do not understand." There was a frown under her delicate Mediterranean seashell eyes that he loved so much.

"*Oui, un chien.* A very big dog, if you must know. *Trop grand.*" He made a big expanse with his hands in the air. "A Russian wolfhound."

"You are seeing a dog, *chéri*?"

"*Woof, woof,*" he said maliciously. There, the dice were thrown. Or the bone.

"Oh, *chéri,*" she exclaimed suddenly, with tremendous surge of empathy and forbearance.

"I put this on my credit card," she opined, stroking her milkmaid's vest. "It's not from our joint account. You are angry at your poor foolish Regine, yes? I spend too much moneys on trifles to make you want me."

"No, darling, I'm not angry," he replied wearily. The tables had already turned. Her sudden compliance made him putty in her hands. That was the way they were. An old unmarried couple. He was thirty years older than her, true. He was sixty-two and she was thirty-three.

But they had their pattern. *La guerre,* and then—*then,* passionate armistice.

"It's very beautiful on you. You are beautiful."

"Oh, *chéri,*" she laughed as she kissed his cheek. "Why don't you tell your Regine all that worries you?"

"I'm no good, Regine. I'm an old fool paralyzed by his fears. You would never understand."

"Don't ever say that to me, *mon amour.* That would be an insult to the de Pompignacs. You must confess your heart to me. You are the man of my life. My tower. My *master.*"

She knew how to turn the screw. He was putty in her hands. A hopeless gladiator in the arena of her love. She knew how to throw the net over him, how to overpower him while giving him the illusion that he was invincible.

"What did you do today, besides shopping?" he asked as he sank his head on her breast.

She stroked his brow, watching in the mirror as his shaved head reflected the soft green light of her eyes. "Nothing, *chéri.* I went to the *plage.* I read some dumb bitch magazines that I bought—"

"Dumb *beach* magazines?" he laughed incredulously.

"*Oui,* with the naked-assed Hidalgos, horny Italian men in the centerfolds, that make me want you so much. *And*—" she paused to tickle him under the arm with her long, lithe fingers. "—and the advertisements that you pretend not to enjoy because you don't want to hurt my feelings. My poor *chéri!*" She caressed his buried head.

"The ones with the big breasts and the nipples like rose petals. You like them, *oui?*"

"*Oui,*" he said, muffling a sob. He no longer wanted to breathe. He wanted to die here between her bosoms. He loved

51

her. He was confused. He was dancing on the edge of the guillotine of remorse at what he was about to do.

If he didn't betray his country, he would lose all this . . . all this loveliness and torture that he was accustomed to in the political asylum of her love.

"Oh, *chéri*!" she said, feeling him stir. "My *boyar*! My lover! Tell me, tell your sweet Regine . . ."

He wept. It was a new sensation. To be fully erect, and to be full of remorse.

Mir

The count lay in the darkness of the bedroom, the soft, warm, breathing body of Regine beside him, a slight snore attesting to the fact that she was sound asleep. He had given her what she wanted and she was content.

Not his secret, which would doom her, but the *seed* of his secret, which was his love for her. What it had grown into was beyond his comprehension. His impasse with himself.

What are you going to do now, Viktor Mikhailovich? he asked himself. He slipped out of bed and found his dressing gown. He put it on and proceeded to the small room at the far end of the suite that served as his office.

He sat down at the Louis XIV desk, which was neatly arranged as was his habit. He flipped through various overnight dispatches from the Ministry of the Interior that awaited his response.

Later—if there was to be a later. There were bills to pay. He ignored those. They were petty reminders of his real problem. What he needed was a solution.

He played with the paperweight, a double-headed Imperial Russian eagle, the family crest of the Romanov dynasty. It was a commemorative souvenir from Tsar Nicholas III's ascension to the throne in 2026.

On the desk was a personally signed portrait of the monarch, appreciation for a job well done after Count Trobolsky had quelled the riots in Tbilisi without firing a single shot. "TO VIKTOR MIKHAILOVICH, WITH AFFECTION AND GRATITUDE, NICHOLAS III."

The tsar did not know it, of course, but Tbilisi was a field test for the Mir virus, or an early version of it. And it had worked splendidly. There were bugs to be ironed out. But it was a success.

You only had to see the footage. A week after the mobs had burned down the governor's administration building in their rage, there were parades in the streets, people with happy, contented faces carrying flowers to the city square where the tsar's statue stood in bronze contemplation. There they laid their wreaths and spoke of a new day dawning.

The acoustically generated MDMA algorithm had been a stroke of genius. Amplified through the public-address system and over the airwaves, the prototype program that became Mir 1.0 had its desired effect.

"Long live the tsar!" the crowd chanted. It had been a proud and humbling moment for Trobolsky. He knew he was on the right track then.

But what now? Where had it gone wrong? Where was that smile of victory now?

The count stared at the portrait of the tsar and shook his head sadly. Times change. People change. *Lives* change . . .

That thought brought him back squarely to the present. He stiffened for a moment as though bracing himself.

He pulled open a drawer and as he peered into it, a shadow creased his brow. Guiltily, he glanced down the hallway toward the bedroom, where Regine was sleeping.

He withdrew a small revolver and laid it on the desk in front of him. It would be so simple, he mused and sighed. End

53

it all now. But he lacked the will. He shook his head. Torment is what keeps us alive. Not the reverse.

He replaced the revolver inside the drawer and slid it shut softly, drumming his fingers on the green Moroccan-leather desktop. Reaching for the carafe, he poured himself a glass of water and gulped it down. How to extricate himself from this mess?

It was all too pathetically predictable. And all his own doing. No one else to blame . . .

The count was in debt. Massively. He should have known better than to gamble with such high stakes. He had lost 720,000 francs at vingt-et-un. He had been winning at first, it was true, a nice little streak. But then he lost. A jack, a three, and that final fateful card, a nine . . .

The Casino management had been discreet, very discreet. He was an eminent personage, a high official in the Russian government. He signed the note as though it were his own death warrant. And now they were pressing him for payment.

"The note is due *now,* Your Excellency," Monsieur Gaspard, the Casino collections liaison, informed him after a hasty consultation with the director.

They were sitting inside the salon adjoining the Casino. He was a rotund Belgian with soft brown eyes and pale white hands that nervously fluttered in the air. Easily tired of their exertions, they settled to the task of plumping up the knot on his silk cravat.

Sounding almost apologetic, the Belgian cleared his throat and continued. "Of course, we are only too pleased to accommodate you—that is our foremost wish and desire. All that the Casino requires"—and here the brown eyes rested like speckled eggs in a nest—"would be a simple note, on official stationery, from your minister, Monsieur Voronov, indicating he has the confidence that you can meet this obligation. The minister has been gracious enough to extend his patronage to the Casino in the past, and is very well known to us. And well, just

a word from him . . . a mere 'expression' of a guarantee . . .
Would Your Excellency care to think this over?"

"There's nothing to think over," Count Trobolsky had
replied tartly. "I've already thought it over. It would be highly
inappropriate to involve the minister in my personal affairs.
Believe me, he has better, far more important things to deal
with, affairs of state, for instance. . . ."

The count let his words sink in ever so slowly and carefully, so that there could be no possibility of any misunder-
standing. "I give you—*and* the Casino—my personal pledge
that I will fulfill my obligation to you, and very soon."

The Belgian gave him a brief bow. "Certainly, of course,
Your Excellency . . . We have no doubts at all in this matter. It
is just a formality, you understand. And rest assured, you can
trust in our complete discretion. When does Your Excellency
think that you can, ah, have the necessary funds? We can even
arrange to loan you the money, if you like. The Banque de
Casino offers that service to its most valued guests."

"At forty percent interest? I don't think so." The count
smiled wryly. "But I appreciate your gesture. No, I can manage.
Thank you . . . You will have your money in three days' time.
Will that be satisfactory?"

"As Your Excellency wishes," the Belgian said, nodding
his head. "That will be absolutely fine. In the meantime, if
there is anything we can do to make your stay with us more
comfortable, please don't hesitate to let me know."

Count Trobolsky withdrew a small Davidoff cigar from his
monogrammed Lalique case, a gift from Regine. He lit it
thoughtfully as he watched the Belgian disappear inside the
velvet-draped abattoir of the Casino, with its mirrored walls
and spinning roulette wheels and marble busts of ancient Ro-
man emperors.

He had to admit it, he sighed as he blew the thin blue smoke
into the air. His own stupid blunder at the gambling table had
brought him to this sorry impasse. It forced him to push up the

55

timetable for concluding his business in Monaco. Not exactly a strong hand to have when you are negotiating with wolves who are ready to tear at your throat at the slightest hint of weakness.

He fiddled with his monocle. As for the Casino's promise to keep the news of his losses confidential, he realistically calculated that he might have a few days before the doorman at the Hotel Prince Albert would be offering him a pitying but cynical look, the one reserved for big-time losers who fell from grace with Lady Luck.

And the Azef—there were agents in Monaco whose job it was to keep a watchful eye on the Russians. As soon as word reached his Ministry, he would be stripped of all his security clearances.

Even that wouldn't be the half of it, the count reflected darkly. The interrogation would be nothing compared to what would happen afterward, when they discovered the rest of it— and they *would*—and when they confronted him with the evidence of his treason . . .

Ironic, wasn't it? He had designed the Neuro-Gulag for the state, and now it awaited him like the bride of Frankenstein. Like the Baba Yaga demon witch in the Russian fairy tales. But this was no fairy tale, this was the real thing, the *real* nightmare . . .

No, the only trump that he could play, the only way he could beat them at the game was to move everything ahead of schedule. He would take a loss on the Germans.

He had already made his bargain with the devil anyway.

His monocle firmly clenched in his eye, the count rose from his desk and took a few steps to the safe that was hidden behind a floral still life by Linard. He took a deep breath.

Then he placed his palm on the safe's *identité* plate, and twirled the sequence of numbers.

Ninety-nine-26-99-26 . . . The numbers of his youth, his grand love—it was the summer of 1999—and the memory of her death two decades later in the Great VR Crash of '26. How time flies!

He would never forget Valentina as long as he lived. And now he spun the numbers that would open the locked steel heart of this safe. How appropriate.

The safe swung open. There it was. He stared at it.

Mir.

Fabergé Surprise

The ruby-studded Fabergé egg looked beautiful in the laser-red light of the safe's security shield. The count studied it carefully, admiring its delicate workmanship.

The orb had been crafted by the finest designers in Russia. It was the most expensive Personal Digital Assistant system available, complete with satellite linkups to all the domains of OmniNet. It featured a personal Rolodex of avatar identities that the user could assume on-line, as well as an ingenious profiling program you could use to "unmask" the true identity of avatars you encountered along the way.

The on-line world was like a Venetian masked ball in which strangers could see each other naked. But the trick was this: Without the preamble of false inhibition, they remained anonymously nude until the Fabergé globe exposed them by restoring their original clothes to their bodies and thereby truly laying them bare by making a positive ID.

That was the real power of this particular device.

In addition to its full array of psycom functions and sim applets, each Fabergé egg contained a special and unique customized "surprise." Count Trobolsky's egg was no different.

He had programmed it himself to harbor the grandest surprise of them all.

Who could possibly know? Or suspect? That was the special charm and whimsy of these collectibles.

The House of Fabergé, originally founded in nineteenth-century St. Petersburg, these days catered to a new generation of Romanovs and European nobility, as well as the nouveau-DNA-nouveaux riches—the ones who could afford the coveted "get rich" gene. It was for them that Fabergé-Canon (the firm's Japanese technology partner and leading investor) manufactured these toys of unmatched perfection.

You simply held the egg, stroked its ruby-studded casing, and—*voilà!*—you discovered that even here, the rich are very different.

Thanks to Fabergé, the telelite were able to travel distances and dimensions that were otherwise inaccessible to the ordinary masses. There was an entirely separate and privileged world "out there/in here" that was available only to the super-rich. That was how the upper classes did VR these days. They flew the Concorde of Unimaginable Elevation.

The Count approached the orb with almost worshipful deliberation. He was never certain how the virus would react. His egg was the illicit off-site backup system to the original Mir virus, which occupied a petri dish in the heavily guarded lab at the Smolny Institute of Para-Cybernetics.

He had siphoned off its awesome power in the only way he could without being detected.

Dipping his index finger into the living pool, he captured a bio-fractal of its essence on the invisible sheath that he wore on his fingertip. Then, with a flick of the *other* sheath on his middle finger, he introduced a virus *into* the virus, thus rendering the original source sterile, like a neutered fruit fly. He now had the only active code for Mir in existence, right there on his index finger, now in the egg.

The virus was a self-extracting mechanism. Once he transferred the fluid to the prepared receptacle of the Fabergé egg, it grew back into its full form again. The tiny fractal recreated the entire algorithm. It was that simple.

The count deactivated the safe's security shield and proceeded to lift the ornate egg in both hands and raise it to the light for closer inspection.

Not that he needed any light once he unhinged the top half of the jeweled sphere and opened it up to reveal its "surprise."

Inside the Fabergé egg was the glowing, ultraviolet embryonic yolk that contained the fractaled miasma of the virus. How beautiful and how terrifying its glow was!

Now to activate it.

This next step required mixing human fluid—how right Regine was about that!—with the liquid of the virus itself.

Count Trobolsky opened another secret compartment—it was an egg within an egg within an egg, like a procession of Russian nesting dolls marching toward their inner self.

Moving toward the nucleus . . .

He had stored the transfer medium in this trick compartment. Ever so delicately, he slipped one of the stacked contact lenses onto the tip of his finger, fitting it there snugly.

Now, he carefully placed his forefinger into the ultraviolet yolk and waited until the porous lens absorbed the glow.

There, the transfer was complete. Amazing.

It looked almost like a tiny fractal crown as it flickered with a faint green phosphorescence, like some sort of astral algae that had become accidentally glued to his person.

He felt the light tingle of its flame as it came to life. He felt a sense of deep peace, a growing inner relaxation that he had not known for a long time.

Mir was kicking in.

His feeling of inner peace was measured by a sense of relief that comes from complete and total acceptance. His life was flowing away on that finger, as though he were standing alone on a distant shore pointing at the tropical blood of a dying sun as it swiftly dropped beyond the horizon.

As it passed into a new light . . .

Count Trobolsky managed to catch his breath. The virus was stable. Now he was ready for the actual test.

*   *   *

The count held open his right eye with the thumb and index finger of his left hand. Looking into the mirror that was mounted on the inside of the safe door, he popped the contact lens into his eye.

Ahhhhh . . . He felt the drunken swoon of the universe and was swallowed by its drunkenness. It was life itself.

Now to harness it. In just the blink of an eye.

Trevor & Nelly

Trevor and Nelly glowered at each other across the small table at the Bistro du Chat Noir, in this little seaside town off the beaten track on the French Riviera.

She tore off pieces from her flaky croissant and drowned them in her café au lait. He distracted himself by flipping through the pages of an anarchist zine full of classified ads that he had picked up at the railway station in Nice.

The Hole to the Underground, its title, had caught his eye.

Nice work if you can get it, he thought. *Fucking the rich.*

No, this was definitely not Trevor's idea of a vacation. Or if it was, it was a vacation that was on its last legs. Everything that could possibly go wrong had. But it looked like there was more in store for them than just that. They weren't getting off that easy.

The duty-free store of the tortured relationship, he mused to himself wryly. *Just pile it on in the shopping basket of the heart and charge it to bad memories.*

It seemed like he and his girlfriend Nelly had been arguing all the way on the plane from San Francisco to London to Paris, with a few uninterrupted hours of melatoninized sleep on the overnight *couchette* from the Gare de Lyon down south to Nice.

60

Even their carriage attendant, a boyish-looking Greek girl with sad, red eyes and an equally sad unlit cigarette in her mouth, had taken pity on them when she saw them try to fit their bad vibes and three large suitcases into a cramped four-passenger cabin. She found them a private space in one of the compartments where all the blankets and sheets were stored.

"*L'amour,*" she said as she shrugged at Trevor when she saw him rolling his eyes in exasperation at one of Nelly's untranslatable diatribes. "Uh-huh," he replied in his best French, then added a few words in his even more cryptic Greek. "*Eros, agapé, constipaté . . .*"

The androgynous Greek girl, whose name tag pronounced her to be Kristina, simply shrugged her square shoulders as though she were genuinely curious to know what the experience was all about, but she knew this was as close that she would ever get to it.

Like negative honey to the asexual bee, Trevor decided. Hence, the royal treatment, he further concluded. He had given Kristina a big tip. She said she would come by later for a smoke and to pass around her flask of Armenian brandy, but she never did. For which Trevor and Nelly were profoundly grateful.

Anyway, there was always the chance that he and Nelly might end up making love after all—they had always talked about doing it on a train, in the early days of their courtship—but of course they never had. Kristina's crisply laid-out sheets were not to be blessed in this manner.

The fact was Trevor and Nelly had been busy breaking up for the better part of the last year of their year-and-a-half-long relationship. Sporadic fights at first—about the need for independence, about the need for commitment, about the need for independence, about the need for commitment—and then, out and out fracas, laced with bitterness, irony, realization, reconciliation, repudiation of reconciliation, a voiced hope for a new beginning. Then the entire cycle would begin again.

The wheel would spin with the two of them riding on the rim, facing each other in straitjackets of silence and anger.

61

Nelly was beautiful, twenty-three years old, a nervous blonde with long, curly hair down to her shoulders, and with a ring on her nose, a ring on her navel, and a ring on one of her toes (right foot, fourth toe).

Right now, since her pierced navel had become infected, Nelly was truly in a foul mood (one rated up there with her "PMS No. 19" in Trevor's ongoing case study of her roller-coaster moods).

Nelly set aside her ravaged croissant and reached into her bag for her can of Athlete's Navel Antifungal Cream, which she shook, then applied with a thin white stream on her crusty belly button.

"It is definitely *not* a bacterial infection," she assured Trevor, who glanced up from reading *The Hole to the Underground* so he could watch the procedure.

He noticed that a few other people in the bistro had also taken interest in what Nelly was doing.

There was that bald guy with the monocle, who briefly glanced at her, and the middle-aged French couple who seemed to be leaning over their plate of Provençal potatoes trying to catch what Mr. Monocle was saying to the uptight guy in the blue windbreaker. They had been startled when Nelly first produced the can and rattled it, but they quickly slid into a carefully studied indifference, as though she were doing nothing out of the ordinary, nothing that mattered to them.

If Nelly had begun spreading mustard all over her stomach, they wouldn't have been perplexed in the least. Their interests were definitely focused elsewhere.

Odd birds, Trevor thought. See no evil, hear no evil, catch the early worm.

"No, it's *fungal.* This seems to be really helping the swelling," Nelly announced. She was heavily into self-prescribed medication, just as Trevor himself was an acknowledged quack when it came to treating the imbalances of the body-mind complex.

On this trip, he had been dosing himself with liquid drops

of Futureplex adrenal pep (antitox biotherapy) and Chinese Energetics Planetary Formulas Yang capsules to boost his male energy (two tablets two or three times daily, taken with warm water). His friend Mishra in Bombay had sent him a bottle of pure and unrefined Ganges water for its spiritual benefits, but it was confiscated by customs in San Francisco.

Trevor had even bought a testosterone sleeping bag from Sherpa Image to sleep in. No mere patches for him. He was the type to go all the way.

"Fungal, really? Gee, let's see? Wow . . . ," Trevor marveled as Nelly showed him her pink, inflamed belly button, holding her t-shirt up above a taut, tan-brown belly specked with microscopic golden hairs like a beautiful brushfire in the Andromeda.

Trevor Gobi was twenty-four, handsome, bright-eyed (blue when happy, washed-out gray when otherwise, like now), as blond as Nelly, as tanned as Nelly, and as miserable as Nelly. He was dressed in a purple Center for Integral Studies t-shirt from the World Wisdom Institute in San Francisco, where he was studying a rare geomancy technique that combined Bulgarian dowsing with Chinese feng shui.

"You won't be needing my pendulums then," Trevor drawled as he grinned at Nelly. "You're right on the button."

"Wise ass." Nelly was a virtual-graphics designer whose specialty was designing foyers in virtual worlds on the World-CondoNet. Her work had appeared in *Architectural Digest* and *Home World*. Since the VR real-estate market had taken a slump and because Trevor was on summer break, they had decided to treat themselves to some Riviera R&R. Yet another noble attempt at restoring balance to their relationship.

"Here, Nelly," Trevor read from *The Hole to the Underground,* wanting to improve her mood. "This is cool. Get a load of this ad. This place is full of anarchists. Did you see all that Russian graffiti at the train station? 'VOVA VOWS REVENGE AGAINST THE NOMENKLATURA' sprayed all over the wall—"

"You can read Russian?" Nelly asked him suspiciously.

"Yeah, a little bit, you know, from my dad. He was part Russian." Trevor looked wistful now. He missed his father. Didn't know where he was. He had been left well provided for in a trust, but his dad had gone off on some virtual trek two years ago and that was the last Trevor had heard from him.

He would get postcard downloads from time to time from strange sites, but Frank Gobi, a renowned professor of transcultural anthropology at the University of Tokyo's Berkeley campus, was doing fieldwork of some sort, some important research, in one of the unexplored vectors of the Matrix.

Dad had left with Tara, his lifetime consort, who was as much a mother to Trevor as was Juan, the doting Salvadorian home-supporter who made sure Trevor was doing all right in his South of Market loft in San Francisco. Then there was Dorje, who kept an eye on him, like the fussy Tibetan lama that he was. Dorje was Tara's partner in tantric crime. They were a team, all right. Until Tara met Trevor's Dad and they paired off.

Tara had the power of the goddess in her, and together with Dorje she performed magical rituals to cleanse the earth of its evil pulses of magnetic energy, which were definitely everywhere: Tibetan zombies and gdons and ogres and hungry ghosts and other assorted vampires of the Net. Now Tara was making magic with Trevor's dad. "Keeping the night marchers at bay," as she liked to tell Trevor, Dad grinning and nodding his head in agreement.

"Oops, sore subject, sorry." Nelly studied the cloud on Trevor's face. "Haven't heard from your dad in a while, huh?"

"No."

"I'm sure he's fine. He'll write soon." Nelly was sympathetic. Her own parents had walked out on her *and* on each other when she was a young girl. She had been raised by her Aunt Roz, who made a living selling the "Best Bagels in the Bay Area" on Geary Street in San Francisco. Nelly had eaten a lot of bagels in her time, and the holes in them always reminded her of some missing piece of her heart.

Now she became wistful. Trevor and Nelly could love each other effortlessly when they were comforting each other. It was a sad irony of their relationship.

"Listen to this, Nelly." Trevor picked up the zine again. "Where do they come up with this stuff?"

"Go on, I'm listening." Nelly put her hand on Trevor's arm and he looked up at her for a moment, puzzled. Then he smiled and went on. "'HORSE HAIR: Send me horse hair, any color, any length. Send it by the ounce or by the pound. I'm making a hangman's noose to send to the leaders of the new world order. In return, I'll send you something. No human hair, please, Pedro Rodriguez, Box # 378429, Ribatejo State Prison, Portugal.' Is that wild or what, Nelly?"

She laughed. "Yeah, that's pretty wild. He probably wants a rope so he can let himself out of his jail cell."

"My God! How about this one? What's the world coming to? 'CAT PEOPLE WORLD WIDE: Send a drawing or photo of your cat and tell me how you met and said goodbye.'"

"That's really *sad,* Trevor," Nelly said after a moment. "*Really* sad."

"Yeah, to be an anarchist or a revolutionary can't be easy. It's more than dedication, it's a lifelong commitment to suffering for your beliefs."

"And making *others* suffer for your beliefs, too, don't forget." Nelly raised a golden eyebrow.

Funny, Trevor noticed, she hadn't been plucking them lately, and now her eyebrows looked like golden thatches, thick and full. *Was she moving toward a more masculine expression of her center? Maybe he had better cut down on his yang tablets to balance it out . . . maybe that was the problem . . .*

"Trevor, look!" He felt Nelly's hand squeeze his forearm. The note of alarm in her voice had already set his yang self-defense mind-body complex into overdrive.

Things—whatever they were, it was a confusing blur of action and reaction—all started happening at the same time.

The bald man at the next table was holding something out

65

to his companion, as though he were handing it to him. It looked like the monocle he had been wearing.

But the young guy had jumped to his feet, grabbed the thing, and was pulling what looked like a *gun—Jesus Maitreya Christ!* It *was* a gun!

"Trevor!" he could hear Nelly's shrill cry—and the once-indifferent French couple were on their feet, too. And the waitress who had been shlepping back and forth from the kitchen to the tables—Trevor had noticed the white-flour palm prints on the back of her skirt, had pointed them out to Nelly, in fact, who was not amused, and had told him in so many nonwords to mind his own behind, at least in her presence—the same waitress was pulling out some sort of a blaster from under the napkin that was draped over the tray . . .

There was a huge blast of light and the sound of gunfire, and the black Citroën that had been cruising ever so slowly down the street came to a screeching halt. Four tough-looking men in dark sunglasses came charging out with guns raised.

Fuck, what was going on?!

There was another powerful blast of light that stunned him and Nelly, and they fell off their chairs to the floor together, holding hands like dummies filled with sawdust—and then nothing. Just like in the old-time movies.

Do Svidanya

The blast of light had stripped Alyosha of all his reflexes. He felt an almost superior indifference as he lay there on his back, like a beetle waiting patiently for the entomologist to do his thing with the pin.

He couldn't roll over even if he wanted to; his muscles had been emptied of their neuroelectric quota.

The Frenchman was tall, bony, and he looked familiar. *My*

God, the fascist on the beach with the wife and kid! Alyosha's slackened jaw would not permit a grin. Besides, beetles did not grin.

So the kid *was* a terrorist of sorts—a rent-a-kid, probably from the streets. He should have known. Boris was right. He was an idiot, all right. Big time. Boris, you out there somewhere? I hope to fuck that you make it out of here in one piece, *tovarich* . . . These bastards don't deserve you. I mean it.

What was he doing now? The Frenchman placed a firm hand on Alyosha, then unzipped his windbreaker in one smooth motion. It almost tickled as he pulled the t-shirt up over Alyosha's faintly pulsing chest.

Now his arms were being extended in both directions, and the man continued to pat him down, looking for something. Maybe it was his heart, but that he wouldn't find anywhere . . .

It was far away in Russia with Lyubachka, his love, Ludmilla, sweet beautiful Ludmilla, each petal of his heart had fallen away a long time ago. They had burned the brain out of his Gulag girl, the fucking Azef . . .

But Alyosha could still see her face. Here she was now, peering down on him.

Wait a minute! Her face on this fucking Frenchman!? Don't you touch her, bastard! *Ludmillinka . . . don't let them do it to you again.*

He tried to spit at the man, but it just backwashed on him.

Another face obscured the shaft of dying sunlight that strobed Alyosha's eyes.

"Does he have it?" he heard the new face ask. "Help me turn him over, it's not on his chest," the first Frenchman replied.

Both men yanked Alyosha up to a sitting position. He felt like a doll without a spine. Wobbly. The sweat was cool on his skin; his mouth hung open. His lower lip drooped stupidly. The drool was drying on his chin.

God, the blast had come fast! But hadn't he fired off two rounds of his Stalin Depth Charge? He hoped to Christ there

67

was another body around here somewhere, preferably two bodies, just to keep him company . . . Sitting ducks they all were. Including himself. A fine mess, Alyosha . . .

They were examining his back now. *"Rien.* Nothing," the first Frenchman announced.

The other Frenchman was not so obliging. He jerked Alyosha around viciously. "It *has* to be on him somewhere. It couldn't have gotten away. Let me see."

"Merde, il n'y a pas . . ." So they *hadn't* found what they were looking for. *Good.* Alyosha felt the blood in his mouth now. It tasted good. He was thirsty, but he couldn't drink it. He had no swallowing energy left in him. He was choking, but he had no choking energy either. The sudden gurgle in his throat alarmed the two men.

"Putain! Careful with him . . . Are you sure you looked everywhere? Check the monocle again."

"I've got it here." The man dangled it on the string, a broken glass socket. "It's missing. The vial shattered."

So that was it. Alyosha gurgled again, and he felt the strength of the death rattle. If he couldn't laugh, he could at least drown in his own blood.

They helped move him into his very own coffin of air.

In the process, Alyosha surveyed the damage around him. The café had been cleared of people. The Sûreté, or whoever the fuck they were, were holding back the gawkers outside the café. That crushed eggshell of a head, Alyosha recognized his Russian contact, Count What's-his-name, the aristo's brains spread over his shoulders like raspberry jam on the crust of a day-old *tartine.* A real mess. Was it his own work?

He'd never know. The bitch was lying there, too, a checkered tablecloth draped over her like a civil servant in rigor mortis, working overtime.

Relax now, Alyosha. It's coming any moment . . . *Do svidanya.* Goodbye. And fuck you, too, God . . .

"He's dead," he heard one of the Frenchman say.

"Not yet." Then a pause, then a sudden war cry. *"Have you*

checked his eyes?! What if he put it in one of his eyes! Don't let them dry out!"

Fingers clawed at his lids. They squirted something in his eyes. His pupils began to dilate like rubber balloons. The coffin was being flooded with light again.

"Nothing in his left eye . . . Fuck, what's this!" A finger tried to pop the contact lens out of his right eye.

"Belize, I think I've got it!"

"Careful with it, you're spilling it!!! Catch it on the dropper!"

But it was only Alyosha's last tear. He really shouldn't have. But then again, it had come naturally as it rode out on the wave of a tremendous regret.

One might say it was his final terrorist act. A bomb that he tossed out of his eye.

Nelly & Trevor

Nelly offered him a swig of water from a 1.5-liter bottle of Evian. "Here, Trevor, you'd better drink this. You're probably really dehydrated like me. The medic said to drink plenty of water. How's your head?"

"Excedrin Nightmare number twenty-nine," Trevor groaned. His brain felt like burned toast and the ringing in his ears had subsided to the level of madly clanging church bells. "I wish we'd never come to France."

"I told you we should have gone to Morocco. But you didn't listen, as usual." She helped him lift his head and poured some water into his parched mouth. "Honey, you'll be all right. It'll pass."

"Are you sure?" He was propped up on their bed in the small *pension* they had found in one of the backstreets of Cagnes-sur-Mer.

The large shuttered windows were open and he could see the night sky.

"Shit, those *are* church bells!" He heard them pealing loudly from across the street. There was also the whizzing of rockets and the loud, exaggerated explosions of fireworks.

A multicolored mandala suddenly burst above the rooftops. Trevor saw its quick concentric flash of neon rainbow sparks rain down in every direction before disappearing back into nothing again.

"It's Bastille Day, what do you expect?" Nelly eyed him curiously. "Relax, Trevor, you'll make it. Here, drink a little more of this."

He sat up and clasped his arms around himself. His shivers had started up again.

"Oh, honey, let me get you another blanket," Nelly said to him as she got up from the bed and walked across the room to bring him a knitted woolen comforter. She had made it herself, Celtic-cross designs and all. She really was talented.

Nelly kissed him on his brow as she laid it over his shoulders. "Is this better?"

"Th-th-thanks," he said as he wrapped himself up like a mummy on furlough. "I've-I've-got the chills. I can't-can't-seem to shake them." He shivered again.

"I know. I had them, too, earlier—"

He studied her. "You don't look too bad for being the victim of a gangland shoot-out."

"Is that what you think it was?" Nelly mused to herself out loud. "How do you know that for a fact?"

"Are you being a Virgo or an Aries now?" Trevor asked her in surprise. "Are you being analytical or a self-propelled combustion engine of intuition?"

She sat down beside him again. She paused thoughtfully. "It was terrible, wasn't it? Those people—those *bodies.* I've never seen bodies before. We're lucky to be alive. That blast of light, whatever it was, the way it knocked us down—"

"Down—and out," Trevor reminded her. "My next memory was we were in the ambulance on the way to emergency. You recovered pretty fast. What do you mean it wasn't a gangland thing? That's what they told us at the hospital."

"That's what that doctor told us," she corrected him. "Doctors don't know shit about crime. They only know about victims. Besides, that's what he was told to tell us, I'm pretty sure."

Trevor listened to her with respect. Nelly was not prone to idle speculation. She had a laserlike brain when it came to detecting the flaws in an argument, which was one reason he felt awed by her. She didn't mince words. She said what she meant, and she meant every word of what she was telling him.

"This isn't one of your forensics exercises, is it?" Trevor inquired. Nelly had a personal hobby of studying criminal behavior. She had numerous books on the subject, complete with bloody pictures of after-crime scenes and autopsies. She had even taken a course in forensics on the Net, carefully analyzing the red no. 452 pixel-blood of victims for traces of evidence.

Her special interest was serial killers who roamed the Matrix taking out innocent avatars. She could put together a profile of a neuropath like no one else he knew.

"No, it isn't," he answered his own question. "Okay, Nelly, you've got my attention."

She glanced at him sadly with her soft brown eyes. "Really? I don't think you've been giving me too much of that recently. Or your understanding. You think I'm an idiot, don't you? So why do you put up with me?"

"No, I *don't* think you're an idiot. I love you. I'm sorry, Nelly. I've been a jerk. What else is new?" He *had* been a jerk. That, and worse.

She took that declaration in as if she'd heard that line before. She didn't say anything to him.

"Nelly, I said I'm sorry. And I *am*. I know I haven't been exactly the easiest person to be with. I really *am* sorry. Okay?"

Her mood shifted. She gave him a light push and he fell back against the pillows.

"One of these days you're gonna reap just what you sow, buster."

"I know," he replied, feeling the tail end of the tapeworm of regret in his gut. She was right.

"Okay, just this one last time, Sherlock. I saw that doctor conferring with some guys in suits in the hallway. In *suits,* Trevor. Nobody wears suits on the fucking Riviera, man. Even the plainclothes cops—*les flics*—wear sport shirts with open collars and gold chains around their necks. No, these guys were something else. I'd guess French intelligence, if you want to bet something valuable. How about your gold-plated biocircuits, Mr. Trevor Gobi? Care to make a wager?"

He stared at her. At least she was talking to him again. "Okay, you're on, Nelly."

Her brown eyes looked amused. She had this Russo-American gypsy king where she wanted him. Full of solicitude and reawakened empathy. Now maybe he'd give her what she *really* needed. His complete and total heart. No more wartime rationing of his deepest attention. Goddamn it, she was entitled. She was sick and tired of his self-pitying whining about their relationship.

Grow up, Trevor. She wanted to suddenly slap his face, then to kiss it—if only he would open up more to her. I need a man, not a fucking juvenile delinquent playing games with my heart as if it were a trash can in some Gametime playground . . .

The truth was she had begun the process of disassociating from him. It had been painful at first. Like him, she had been guilty of getting caught in the cycle of breaking up then breaking back in again for long enough. Enough. You stupid jerk, you're losing me and you don't even know it.

But Trevor knew. Which is why a long spidery shiver ran through him—not because of the chills, but because of *them.* For them.

72

"So you want my gold-plated biocircuits, do you?" He gave her a smile as he brushed a long wisp of golden hair from her eyes. She looked almost happy for an instant.

"You betcha, that and more." She gave him another gentle push. He was starting to get used to it. The new Nelly.

"Well, you're going to have to come up with more than just observations about the sartorial habits of the French gendarmes, baby."

"All right, you're on," she said, whipping her body forward as she pulled up her t-shirt. "Take a look at this."

At first, he didn't get it. He looked up at her quizzically. "Nelly?" Then he saw it. "Jeez, Nelly, I didn't know you got a tattoo . . ."

"That's just it, Monsieur Fantomas. I didn't get this tattoo. This tattoo got me. First time I ever saw it was when we got back to the hotel."

"You've got to be kidding—"

"Fuck, it just moved!" Trevor squeaked. The "MMM" had been hovering across her tummy, caught in the indentation of her belly button.

"That's right. The little fucker moves around like a centipede in a spelling bee. But that's not all."

Trevor could see what was happening, but he had a hard time understanding what he was seeing.

"Notice anything else?"

"Your—your infection . . . on your belly button—"

"Gone. *Like that.*" She snapped her fingers.

"And your pearl—" She had a little white Japanese pearl dangling from her gold navel ring.

It was glowing.

"Neat, huh? The plot thickens."

"Nelly . . ." There was so much that he wanted to ask her, not just about her belly button clearing up its infection so mysteriously. Not just about the tattoo. But about her. And about him. But he felt powerless to steer the conversation in that direction.

Not because it was an inappropriate moment to dwell on the unknown that lay between them like a chasm. But because the tattoo moved again.

There it was. Incredible. "WWW" *now.*

"You know what I think," Nelly said to him, as though she had divined his thoughts but was in agreement not to open their old wounds right now.

He kept staring at the thing in disbelief.

"I think, Trevor Gobi, that we should catch a plane the first thing in the morning and get the hell out of this place. Back to San Francisco. *Capiche?*"

"Whatever—whatever you say, baby."

She smiled a smile that he had never seen on her face before. "Are you sure you're all right—with that thing?" he asked her. "Shouldn't you see a doctor, I mean . . . "

"And go back to that clinic? Not on your life, pal. Not on your life. Whatever this thing is, it's got things to tell us—"

"What! Is it *communicating* with you in some way?" He was genuinely alarmed now.

She lowered her t-shirt. For the first time, she seemed uncertain. That was her rational mind kicking in again.

"I . . . I *think* so."

The tattoo began to rearrange itself again. This time, into the glyph of an ear.

"I think it can hear what we're saying, Trevor."

Regine's Dream . . .

Knock, knock, knock . . .

It wasn't a sound that the housekeeper usually made when she came in to turn out the bed. No, that was a *knock, knock, knock,* with a light and soft touch.

Who was it, who was knocking so urgently on her door? Regine hadn't ordered room service. And Viktor wouldn't knock. Anyway, if he did, it would be more like **Knock, knock, knock**—an impatient, solid sound. He was an impatient, solid man.

Besides, Viktor had gone to some meeting and she wasn't expecting him back till around eight. They planned to have dinner in, just the two of them, then to stop by the Casino later for drinks and perhaps a quick round of vingt-et-un. But for not much money. A clear limit on gambling was important. They would retire early—and *then* they would see what they would see.

If they both felt like engaging in the aerobics of the two-backed beast . . .

When Regine first heard the knocking, she instinctively placed her hands on her breasts, as if to protect them. They ached. It was getting to be her time of month. Like Pavlov's salivating dog, Viktor was prone to an almost preternatural excitement around this time, when her already ample bosoms became even fuller.

No wonder Rubens was his favorite painter.

Viktor was a man for breasts . . . and for derrieres . . . *What an animal!* He could be so filthy and disgusting. She smiled with her eyes half-closed as she cupped her breasts, and felt reassured by her swollen nipples . . .

Pierre Flambay had a theory about breasts; he discussed it in *The Demise of Desire.* For a man, indications of intense arousal over breasts were not necessarily dictated by oral fixation. It was more of a *cerebral* fix. Right brain–left brain corresponded to right breast–left breast, according to Flambay.

When Viktor worshipped at the altar of her breasts, he was actually engaging in some pagan psychoanalytic ritual . . .

Knock, knock, knock . . . The knocking was more insistent. It was more like a rapping now than a knocking.

Regine opened her eyes and stirred in her bed. She had been napping and was feeling very drowsy with a languor that overpowered her entire body and mind. There was no drug like sleep. Not even sex. She had been dreaming a strange dream. Most of her dreams were strange and exciting.

She liked to dwell on them leisurely in that space between dreaming and awakening. Only then would the little details reveal themselves, perhaps even rearrange themselves into another pattern that uncovered yet another layer of the dream . . .

This dream was no exception. It took place in Russia—when?—a very long, long time ago—three hundred years ago felt about right.

She—that is to say, Regine—was someone else. She was *always* someone else in her dreams. That was the beauty of it. She could relate to herself very well as a completely different person with a completely separate history from her own.

Only then could she feel perfectly free to explore this secret, unrelated history, like someone who had wandered into a strange house that actually belonged to them, but which they were now entering for the first time.

She might not *like* what she discovered in this mysterious house, but she would keep her opinions to herself, especially if she encountered any strangers living in the house.

Especially if they turned out to be intimate strangers . . .

Besides, all these things in the house were hers. Hers, and yet not hers—like in her real life. But the *dream* belonged to her. She owned it, lock, stock, and barrel. She held the deed and the title to all her dreams.

For a moment, she ignored the knocking, the rapping, the rude jostling at the door. She heard muffled voices. She wished they would just go away. Maybe they would.

Back to the dream, this *dream: She was seated at a long table in a big dining room with a fireplace in which massive logs were burning. The walls were of dark paneled wood. There were Russian aristocrats seated on both sides of the long table. Each one of these Russian aristocrats sat facing a gift on the table, a gift in a velvet bag that stirred from within. When they reached out to open their individual gift package, what they found inside each bag was a brown Burmese kitten.*

Regine—who was not Regine—had yet to open hers. They all looked at her expectantly.

Goodness, *now* she remembered!

In this dream, Regine was an old lady with white hair that

76

was coiffed on the top of her head. She sat at the head of the table. She was wearing a finely embroidered dress made of the finest damask silk. It had the deepest, loveliest red color. Like blood.

She smiled at them all, at all these mysterious strangers who were waiting so eagerly for her to open her velvet bag. She pulled on the string, and heard them all gasp. Out of her bag came not a brown Burmese kitten, but a little white kitty, a Persian . . .

She clapped her hands and laughed in the dream. But no one else did. They were still waiting. For what? What else was there in the bag?

Regine snapped fully awake. Someone had opened the door. She could hear them moving into the hallway, approaching the bedroom. She now felt fear mixed with anger. Who would dare to enter her suite without permission?

Two large men, Russian, so large they could not possibly be mistaken for what they really were, giant Cossacks dressed in loose dark pants, dark open-necked shirts, and soft black athletic shoes. Brown hair cut straight across the brow in the style of the Don Kazaki, they had long noses; one of them had a scar on his cheek. Both of them had teeth crooked like twisted nail files, bad dental work from the Ukraine.

"Who are you?!" Regine demanded, holding her sheet up to cover her breasts. "What are you doing in here?! How dare you!"

But they did not reply. A short, squat man followed them into her boudoir a moment after they entered. He was wearing a white linen suit. His eyes were slanted, ice cold, and blue. They briefly settled on her, as if he could not help but enjoy the sight of a frightened beautiful woman who was exactly where he wanted her to be. Helpless in her bed. Would she make a run for it, with her naked body to the open bathroom?

He glanced at the doorway. Not likely. He knew women like Regine, who froze more out of anger than from their fear. More out of modesty than from outrage.

77

"Pardon, madame," he said, shrugging, not bothering to conceal his insolent leer. "We *did* knock."

"And so what if you did knock? I did not answer. That should be enough. Now," she collected herself and spat venomously. "Get out before I call hotel security!"

"Danik," the short man said to one of the Cossacks. The man moved more like a trained tiger than a human being. He took a long stride to the bedside table, and almost as if he were inspecting some merchandise in a shop, he reached over and yanked the telephone out of the wall.

Regine gasped. "What do you want?!"

"You must have been dreaming when we knocked," the short man said to her admiringly. "I am sorry to disturb you, but we very much need to recover something from your husband's safe. Do you know the combination?"

"My *husband's* safe? Are you mad?"

"I'm sorry, of course he's not your husband. The count"— he made a little mincing bow and clicked his heels on the Turkoman carpet—"Count Viktor Trobolsky has something which belongs to us. We want it."

"If you want something that belongs to you, and it is in the count's safe, why don't you wait for him to return? He will be back at any moment."

The survival instincts of the de Pompignacs were coming to the fore. She *must* make them wait. She knew that they wouldn't, but she must try.

"No, I'm sorry," the short man said almost apologetically.

"You can't wait?"

"No, I'm sorry the count won't be returning any time soon."

Regine felt the panic now. *Her dream—Viktor. Viktor—*But there was no contact with him. She always felt his presence even when he was away. There were tears in her eyes now.

"What do you mean the count will not be returning? I am *expecting* him." She defied him with her eyes and her proud, jutting chin, but her voice was weak and growing weaker. Her chest heaved as she felt the constriction of hopelessness.

The ice-cold blue eyes became impatient. "We knocked, and you did not answer. Now you will answer." He spoke with a weird, soft lisp. "Do you have the combination to the safe?"

Then the man, and not one of his Cossacks, contrary to what one would expect from such a sinister dwarf, leaned over the bed and slapped her face hard.

She felt the ringing in her ears, and the tears began to flow uncontrollably.

"What—?" she fell backward, dropping the sheet down to her naked hips. Her thoughts scattered from her head like pearls wrenched from a necklace.

"You heard me the first time." He slapped her again and again. Her face was covered with her hair, but that did not soften the blows.

"Chuk," he ordered the other Cossack, who now took her by the shoulders and obediently lifted her chin so that she could answer the short man through the blood that ran from her lips and gums.

"How's your memory now?"

She spat at him, blood and spit mixed. It stained his white linen suit. "*Suka!* Bitch!" he cursed at her in a perfectly contained monotone, the light lisp lashing her like coiled barbed wire.

"*Nu shto?*" the Cossack who was holding her asked. "*Ona nichevo ne znaet.* She doesn't know anything."

"You leave me no choice." Dabbing at the blood spots on his jacket with a white handkerchief, the short man nodded at the first Cossack. Danik stepped forward, holding a velvet bag in his hand. He slipped it over her head like a hooded noose.

She felt the velvet now—*the velvet of her dream!*—and she felt the strings being tightened. And she heard the kittens meowing somewhere deep inside the bag, like a menagerie of angels who could not help her, who could not help her at all . . .

For that was how dreams were. Half of them lost, half of them found. She was in the bag with the first half, trying to remember all the details, but somehow remembering none.

Then at last she remembered, but it was something stupid. It was time for her to take her bath. She wanted to be freshly bathed, oiled, and scented for Viktor when he came home. She wanted to be ready for him.

The Yaponchik walked into the count's study at the far end of the Princess Grace suite. His two Cossacks followed behind him like obedient domesticated wolves. The Yaponchik sniffed.

He could smell the count everywhere, among all this debris that had been stratified so neatly on the desk. Papers, folders, pictures, portraits. He lifted the framed picture signed by Nicholas III.

The tsar's face exhibited the trademark Van Dyke–style Romanov beard and sad, dreamy gray eyes. A weak man. They were all weak. That was the weakness of *that* sort of power. The Yaponchik's power was more directly applied. He needed no rubber stamps from committees or Dumas to enforce *his* will.

"*Hnnh,*" the Yaponchik grunted as he dropped the tsar's picture into the wastebasket. Smiling, he turned to Danik and Chuk, the two bodyguards whose job it was to entertain him and expand his power. They sniggered.

"Nice move, boss." Danik grinned and showed his twisted teeth.

The Yaponchik's temper snapped. "You're not on vacation. Get busy, find the safe."

Danik dropped his grin like a scythe in a field of grain. The two Cossacks started right into the search, even as the Yaponchik sharply yanked the reins on them.

"We're looking for a *safe,* you idiots. You don't need to empty the drawers. You won't find anything there. A simple hotel safe. Where do you suppose it would it be?"

He now sounded patient, but that spurred them into the necessary frenzy.

Danik, who was smarter than Chuk, found the safe right

away. "Boss," he said as he paused at the painting in its gilt frame.

"Ten points. I'll send you to the Kiev Polytechnic for your Ph.D. in fucking around. Congratulations."

The Yaponchik studied the Linard still-life. Was it worth stealing? Was it worth destroying? No, on both counts. Danik discovered the secret hinge in the far-left edge of the frame, and the painting slid on invisible rails. There it was. Much more accessible now. Nice flowers. Not bad after all.

"Already, Danik, since you're so far ahead of the class, *do it*—but be careful. We don't want to ruin hotel property."

What if it was booby-trapped? Yaponchik knew that the count was not a fool. He would not leave something as valuable as the Mir virus in the safe without taking special precautions. That was the way of the SPCID. The count didn't come to be head of the SPCID directorate by being careless.

Danik sprung to action. He reached into the pocket of his soft dark shirt and withdrew what looked like a jeweler's eyepiece. From a fanny pack at his side, he brought out a small monitor so that the Yaponchik could observe the operation and issue instructions.

The flat screen sprang to life with its inner incandescence. It was an Odessa Probe, in full holographic mafiya colors, the kind they used to crack open safes.

"Laser borders. It's a Kyocera 100 megaceramic job . . ." Danik was scanning the field as the Yaponchik and Chuk watched on the monitor. "Trick leakage to the right, so—," Danik was wearing a safecracker's VR glove, snug and tight like a golfer's, on his right hand.

He moved the hand and snipped the red, green, and yellow beams. "—we now remove and exit the field."

The monitor revealed the vacuum of infrared-based trick wiring. "Piece of cake."

"Stop," the Yaponchik ordered. "It's too easy. Do you know that? Do you ever stop and think in your life, 'This is too easy . . .'?"

"Boss—?" Danik had his usual dumb look on his face. The Yaponchik was familiar with Danik's dumb look. He flooded his aura with it deliberately, the same way that a squid hides behind its curtain of ink.

"Try the other frequencies—"

"Boss, this is a Kyocera 100 safe, it *has* no other frequencies; it's a standard—"

One look from the Yaponchik and Danik began to fiddle again with his pouch. He added an attachment to his glove, a small cylinder that began to revolve on the palm of his hand, clicking on this, clicking on that.

"What did I tell you, you idiot?" the Yaponchik exclaimed when the safe suddenly shrank in size on the monitor. It was a nanoprotection device. You wouldn't see it at first pass.

Danik began to sweat. "I've never seen this type before. This is something new, boss."

"Don't apologize for your stupidity. You were born with it. What's the alpha level?"

"Seven megahertz." Danik gave a low whistle. "Boss, is that possible?"

"Anything's possible. Including getting through it."

"Boss, this safe is—what's the word?"

"*Sentient.* Yes, it's sentient."

"Yeah, I don't know too much about sentient things. It's not my field, boss."

"Maybe in your next life you'll come back as a washing machine. You've got very fuzzy thinking."

"What should I do?"

"Let's see." The Yaponchik thought hard. "It's Kyocera. But it's Toshiba-Intel driven."

"Boss?"

"What now?"

"The safe, according to the reading, is in a deep dream state."

"Access?"

Danik ran the clicking cylinder on his palm again. *"Sukin sin!* Son of a bitch."

The fucking thing was *dreaming.* And they were watching its dream. Or, rather, its nightmare. The disordered rush of images—the safe was stirring now—they were coming within focus of its dream—showed just what these bastards were capable of.

Probably it was the work of programmers from Narita Central Intelligence moonlighting for Toshiba-Intel.

The Yaponchik had to admire the semantics of their animé security system.

"Quite a show."

There were German World War II tanks rolling across the Russian steppes. A blitzkrieg of gargoyles flying in close formation in the air, dropping depth charges into ten-dimensional space.

Kung fu-a-vich! If they had the luxury of time, the Yaponchik would have made himself comfortable in the count's Louis XIV chair and watched the show, like a kid. But there wasn't time. And besides, he was getting bored with the childish *manga.* Here were Ultraman and Akira and all the bad guys from the past coming out like locusts from cartoon hell.

"Just fuck them, Danik. Do it now."

"Right. This will just take a moment." Danik slipped his free hand into his pouch and extracted the necessary tool—a silencer ring that he slipped onto the middle finger of his gloved hand.

"Sayonara, do svidanya, au revoir," he said with a flourish. He *did* have the touch, which was why he worked for the Yaponchik and not the other way around.

The image-flood of manga security guards now became a brown toffee slowly melting on the screen of the monitor.

"Done, boss."

"Good work. Now the combination."

"It's chakra-sensitive." Stupid word, but it described the

nature of the challenge: the code was personalized with the vibratory patterns of the user.

"So you know what to do?" the Yaponchik asked as he moved out of the way. This is where things always fucked up. "Chuk, stand behind him, just in case he needs some help."

Dumb Chuk, all brawn and very little brain, took the position. Good; the Yaponchik needed a psychic buffer in case things went wrong.

"I need something that belongs to him. Something he has touched recently," Danik said.

"Really?" the Yaponchik smiled for the first time since the break-in began. "I have just the thing."

From his pocket—and even Danik and Chuk were surprised—*When did the boss pick* that *up?*—the Yaponchik removed a pair of Regine's panties from the pocket of his jacket. He had gone into the bathroom to freshen up after they did her, and he had picked up her panties from the laundry basket. The ones that smelled of—what else?—it was the perfect receptacle for the count's vital essence: his seed that had drained out of the woman after they had made love. It was still fresh, that was the beauty of it.

"Just what the doctor ordered." The Yaponchik was still smiling as he carefully dropped the red lace undies into Danik's gloved hand.

Danik stared at it for a moment through his jeweler's eyepiece. "This will do it," he murmured softly. "For sure."

"For fucking sure," Chuk chimed in before he was silenced by the Yaponchik's evil eye.

"Piece of cake." Danik whistled happily again. He was the man of the hour, and he was holding the bitch's jism-stained underwear in his hand, about to win the big prize.

"You open the safe with that, you get to keep it," the Yaponchik encouraged him.

84   Danik snorted. *"Nu davai*—let's see what's up."

The numbers appeared on the screen in quick succession, like miniature engraved diodes spilling their secret.

Ninety-nine-26-99-26 . . .

"See the colors, boss," Danik, on his pedestal again, pointed. "Mauve and yellow. This is from the private cache of his subconscious."

"The count was a very sentimental man," the Yaponchik observed, nodding. "Thank you, count."

The safe door swung open.

The three men in the room suddenly felt very small, including the two towering Cossacks. The Yaponchik was as small as he would ever get.

The ruby-studded Fabergé egg took their breath away. "A million rubles at least," Danik said as he sucked in his breath. "You think it's inside this Easter egg?"

"No, it's an omelet," the Yaponchik snapped through curled lips as thin as the point of a stiletto. "Open it, but be careful."

Danik studied the egg through his lens. "It's not protected."

"That's not what I meant. The egg is not protected. What about what's *inside* it?"

"It's wobbly. Like some sort of jelly. It's a liquid of some sort."

The Yaponchik drew a breath. They had arrived. The Mir virus was inside, all right. But was it intact?

"Good boy. Open sesame."

Danik withdrew the egg. It was warm and humming. "It's on-line, but in its own vector. It's not connected to anything. Not to anything on the Net, anyway."

"All the better. Piece of cake, as you call it." The Yaponchik took three steps back, just to be safe. Better safe than sorry. Bad pun. He would spare the idiots.

Danik found the secret compartment. He peered into it. On the monitor, the others could see what it held: glistening contact lenses. Green. Ultraviolet. Radioactive red.

"That's the medium for transfer. Good. You're getting close."

"Here." Danik pressed something and the egg opened like an Easter surprise on a hydraulic half shell.

Once again, they were collectively plunged into silence. There was a bubble of light covering the miasma of the Mir virus; the glow was transcendental, like a dream of the gods in the Russian yakuza heaven. This thing was definitely set on user-psyche coordinates. Danik saw his grandmother. Chuk saw his father, with a whip, whipping him. The Yaponchik saw his mother, the Toothpick, even though he hadn't given her a thought since she was hanged at the gallows.

Frightening.

Danik was nonplussed. "Do you really want me to open it? Do you think it's wise—?"

The Yaponchik snapped to. "I'm not paying you to be wise. Or careful. I'm in charge of that department. *Otkroi.* Open it."

Danik diffused the bubble with his gloved hand.

The glow froze for a moment, and then the fucker sprayed them! The fine mist, ultraviolet and black, whooshed over them, covering everything on all sides within twelve feet of the egg.

Even the Yaponchik had the spray halfway down his throat before he realized that it had been a brilliant subterfuge—the count's very own Fabergé surprise . . .

The voice they heard—for as such, it could be described as a voice being translated into a hundred Russian dialects heard from Belarus to Nizhni Novgorod to remote Siberia—was immediate and to the point:

"This is the Voice of the Gulag. You are now being admitted into the labor camp where you will spend the rest of your days. You will suffer what you will suffer, without recourse, without mercy. You are a criminal of the state. And you will pay the ultimate penalty for your acts of subversion. Prepare yourselves for the sentence you have been awaiting. It is beginning now—everything is nothing, and nothing is everything. You will be assigned the following Gulag identification num-

bers. *You do not need to memorize them. The Gulag is memorizing you. You will never be free again—*"

The Yaponchik sat in the count's chair. He bowed his head as he accepted his death sentence of life inside the neural hell of the Gulag. The rest was just a mere formality of the nightmare.

From Gulag with love.

INTERMISSION

"Life is a foreign language. Every man has
mispronounced it."

—CARLOS BULOSAN

Désir Fou—
Crazy Desire!
Nice–San Francisco

Nelly and Trevor boarded the 4 P.M. Air Multi-Méditerranée flight from Nice Le Pen International to San Francisco without incident.

Trevor thought Nelly's instincts were right on: "*Let's get the fuck out of France.*"

He couldn't argue with that. They had stopped arguing, in fact. Which was curious, since they had both grown accustomed to bickering and parrying and slinging mud. But that seemed to be past them for the moment.

"You're *sure* you want to take this thing with you?" he had asked Nelly, point-blank.

After her shower that morning, Nelly had stood very still in front of the full-length mirror in their hotel room, carefully studying her new tattoo. It seemed to be at rest.

It wasn't running around her body, as it had been all night. In fact, at this very moment it looked like it was taking a breather beneath her right breast.

She lifted her breast and squeezed it as though she were conducting some sort of extrasensory breast examination, half expecting to find a lump.

Of what? Trevor wondered. *Of information?*

"Did you sleep well?" he asked her as he cupped her breast from behind. Her body felt soft and warm against his. He was naked, too, and half aroused.

She let her head fall back on his shoulder in a familiar manner. He could taste her after-shower sweetness on her back and breathed in the bloom of her rose-musk shampooed hair.

"Mmm," he said as he nuzzled her. They were spooning standing up. "You smell nice."

"I slept like a charm," Nelly replied as she cautiously moved his hand to her other breast. As if she didn't want him to disturb the sleeping occupant.

"That is, once I got used to the pitter-patter of its little feet all over my body."

Nelly kept watching the tattoo, which gave her—she'd swear to it on a stack of *Gray's VR Anatomy* books—a wink.

"That's creepy," Trevor answered, "if you ask me."

Shit, he was beginning to get jealous of the fucking thing. Of Nelly's sudden and all-encompassing attention to it.

He felt like the odd man out. *Weird.*

"What is?" Her eyes searched his in the mirror. Maybe he had seen the tattoo flick her nipple with its WWW eyelash.

"The idea of your being an unwilling host to this thing. You don't even know where it came from. That's what I meant."

"Oh, I'm getting used to it," she said, stirring away from his embrace. "I'm actually kind of getting to like it on me. It's cool."

"*It's cool,*'" Trevor mimicked her as he shook his head. She was being obstinate. He could appreciate that she was caught up in the melodrama of it all. The kinkier the better, as far as Nelly was concerned.

She was on a roll with the far-out once again. And pleased as punch, he could see that. But, hell, it *could* be dangerous—

"Nelly, let's face it," Trevor said in a neutral voice. He didn't want to antagonize her. "I just have to tell you that I'm genuinely *concerned,* okay? You've been invaded by a sentient tattoo. It's obviously intelligent." He paused for effect. "What if it's *carrying* something? It could be a Pandora's box, Nelly. Do I have to list all the potential problems you might be getting yourself into? Not to mention the risk of—"

"No, you *don't*." Nelly turned to face him with a look of fierce determination that he hadn't witnessed in a while. God, she *was* serious about this.

"*Listen* to me, Trevor," Nelly said as she grasped his chin like a mountain climber reaching for the next rock on her journey up a steep cliff.

Their eyes locked. He couldn't have turned away if he wanted to. He was familiar with this shortcut she took whenever she wanted to take hold of his wandering mind.

Trevor suffered from "ADO," according to Nelly. She called his propensity for lucid reality-surfing "Attention-Deficit Order."

"Okay, I'm listening."

She let go of his face. "I can handle this, Trevor," she said to him. "*Trust me.*"

Then she said something that really spooked him: "*I'm its mommy now.*"

"Please fasten the seat belt, *m'sieur,*" the Air Multi-Méditerranée stewardess politely chided Boris. "Left, right, inside—*click.*" She made a little pantomime for his benefit to show him how it was done.

"*Da, da,*" Boris replied gruffly as he stuck both ends of the belt together with a force that revealed the raw state of his nerves.

"*Bon.*" She touched him on the shoulder as if he were a village idiot on holiday, and moved on.

The fact was, Boris *did* feel like a rube from Blagoveshchensk in his seersucker suit and polyester Chinese shirt and floral tie, the kind you bought at the railway station at the Trans-Siberian junction in Birobidzhan.

All he needed was a boom box with a made-in-Taiwan satellite dish and a greasy paper bag filled with potstickers to complete the picture.

It was a deliberate impression that he cultivated. But it took him till the very last minute to get his act together. So many loose

93

ends in Cagnes-sur-Mer to take care of. Including getting word to—and receiving the green light to proceed—from Control.

Talk about rage. Poor Alyosha didn't deserve that kind of abuse. Control had no patience with people—dead *or* alive.

Money had been a problem, too. Boris didn't want to use a credit chip—too easy to trace him that way.

So he had to do a number on the M'sieur Cash ATM at the airport. Usually, when he gave money machines an enema, they thanked him with a nice little jackpot, a big dump of cash and no questions asked.

But this one had a new software with an attitude like a rude French waiter. *Merde alors,* it refused to serve him at first, turning up its nose at his attempts to jack it with his stolen Banque du Maroc debit card.

Boris finally managed to clean it out, giving it the old Arab heave-ho as he ignored its snide taunts.

"Votre carte d'identité, s'il vous plaît. Proof of immigrant status, number of registered chadors in household—"

Not bad for a rush job in a crowded French airport. Fuck, it was cartoon money anyway. As all money was. But it would get him from one cartoon of a country to another . . .

Boris settled in to his seat now, keeping his eye on the young American couple three seats ahead of him.

Ever since the shit went down at the Bistro du Chat Noir, he had been on their tail. He had been outside watching everything, Alyosha and the count talking. The count making the pass. The stun-laser going off. The blast of light had blinded him; it had been calibrated way too high, set for kill, not stun. The *bastards.*

But Boris had clearly seen the Antichrist leap off Alyosha's neck—and into the blonde safety net of the American girl's hair. Amazing how the Deuxième Bureau missed that acrobatic feat.

They must be too busy rounding up Algerian Greenpeace terrorists to have their wits about them, he theorized. The Deuxième was stretched too thin. That must be it.

Boris's handheld neurometer confirmed that a biotransfer from one medium to another had taken place. From a melted-down monocle containing the virus to a troublemaking tattoo, for instance . . .

So when the girl called the airline to book two tickets for San Francisco the next day—"One passage for Mr. Trevor Gobi and one passage for Ms. Nelly Govinda-Anderson, *s'il vous plaît*"—Boris knew it wasn't from the trauma of being in the wrong place at the wrong time, or needing to run home to safety.

There had been too much pseudoadrenaline in her voice. She was *already* in an altered state. His neurometer registered that, too, when he tapped into the hotel's Minitel system. Stupid bitch. She thought *she* was in control of things. She didn't realize she was being manipulated.

Mir was on the run. Not *her.*

He sat three seats behind them, and he could follow their every move after the plane's take off.

Nelly was looking out the window, down upon the topless panorama of the Riviera with its blue Mediterranean G-string. Trevor was wrestling with the cap to a minibottle of Beaujolais Nouveau. He was getting on Boris's nerves already. He wanted to walk over to the American, grab the bottle, and wrench its neck off.

The stewardess was back again, dressed in her crisp blue Miyake-Cardin uniform, handing out VR headsets to the passengers.

"*Nyet.*" Boris scowled at her plaster-of-Paris smile. "Have got." He gestured at the player on his lap. "*Sony Vakman.*"

She nodded obliviously and moved on. Beyond redemption, really. He put his headset on and fine-tuned the direction finder. Three rows north, set at coordinates alpha and omega. Seats 11A and 11B. He wanted to hear everything the Americans were saying to each other.

Old technology had it over plastic VR any day.

*　　　*　　　*

"Are you quite finished?" Nelly asked Trevor, who had given up trying to open his minibottle of Beaujolais Nouveau. "Here, let me have it." She took the bottle from him, twisted the cap off, and handed it back.

"*Santé,*" Trevor said as he poured the wine into a plastic glass and quaffed it down. "Here's to you, Nelly." It tasted sour. "And goodbye, France."

She eyed him. "You're not sorry we're leaving ahead of schedule, are you?"

"No, not at all," Trevor was quick to reply. "I mean, we've seen the country in, what, two or three days? We've been shot at, experienced socialized medicine, been invaded by alien tattoos—um, that's enough excitement for a vacation, wouldn't you say?"

"We had one day in Paris, too."

"Yes, we had that."

"You're disappointed we didn't go to the Rodin museum. I'm sorry. You wanted to see the original *Thinker.*"

Trevor shrugged. "It's the thought that counts."

"Cheer up, Trevor." Nelly could see he was in the dumps. She knew why. He was jealous of her tattoo.

She recognized the hangdog look that Trevor got whenever he suspected she was coming on to some guy who was flirting with her in his face. It was his hurt pride waiting to pop out of the manhole cover.

Trevor's expressions were *so* predictable, she thought. He had about fifty-two standard expressions in his deck, quite a lot, really, if you thought about it, and Nelly had to keep track of them like cards in a game they had been playing forever.

The only problem was, she never knew when he'd pull out the joker in the pack. Which he was perfectly capable of doing, swiftly and impulsively, and with a blind fury that never failed to startle her.

That was Trevor. An unpredictable obviousness flowed through his veins . . .

But Nelly wasn't going to allow herself to get rattled by his possessiveness this time. If he *was* jealous of her tattoo, he'd just have to get used to it!

Nelly felt a strange new excitement building inside her. As if she were hurrying to explore some new, uncharted corner of her heart—and no one, not even Trevor, was going to stop her fun. This was payback time for all the hurt and jealousy he had put *her* through . . .

In the meantime, she was getting along famously with "Sinbad," which was the private name she had given her tattoo. After all, he (it was definitely a he, it had strong male energy) had appeared out of nowhere, like his storybook namesake venturing out on one of his many *Arabian Nights* voyages.

Sinbad was still nestled between her breasts. He'd been there for a while. *Oops!* She could feel the spidery tracing of his intelligent fonts tickling her . . . on *purpose?* What a turn-on . . . My God, she was becoming aroused!

Nelly gave Trevor a playful jab in the shoulder, more out of pity than guilt. "Have you hugged your gargoyle today?" she asked him. "You're always talking about the dark side as being more fun. It *is*, you know—"

"Dark side, shmark side," Trevor retorted. "You're obviously having a *relationship* with that *thing*. You can't fool me."

"Uh, honey, I wouldn't talk about it in that way. It's quite *sensitive*, you know?"

Trevor poured some more wine and grew sullen as he pondered that remark.

"What do you say we relax and enjoy the trip?" Nelly said brightly. She was anxious to change the subject. "What are you reading?"

As usual, Trevor had a stack of paperbacks on his lap. He was a crustacean as a reader, moving sideways from book to book like a crab.

"Oh, another novel channeled by Philip K. Dick. This one's entitled *Mere Alibis*. It's about an alternative universe in which everything is more ordinary than it looks."

"Well," Nelly chirped, grinning, "if anyone has the energy to write sci-fi novels after he's dead, it's Philip K. Dick. How many does that make it so far?"

"Channeled? Forty-two."

"That's more than he wrote in real life."

"What can I say? He's prolific. What are *you* reading?"

"Something very French. A translation of Pierre Flambay's *The Demise of Desire*."

"I've heard about that book. So what does he have to say?"

"There is nothing more existential than fucking. And it's much more fun than cheese."

For some reason, that made Trevor feel really blue. Next thing he knew, they'd be living in a threesome with that tattoo. That's how things were shaping up.

Boris was thinking the same thing too.

The Tattoo waited for the lights in the cabin to be dimmed for the in-flight movie, a remake of Jacques Tati's *Mon Oncle,* a classic French farce about the crazy technology of a modern kitchen. The skillets were played by dancers from the Crazy Horse Cabaret in Paris; the oven was a recycled Jean Gabin, looking more dead than alive, with the cigarette in his mouth propping him up like the third leg on a kitchen stool.

Trevor kept reading *Mere Alibis.* Nelly dozed. The Tattoo found his way down the inside of her thigh, then down her calf, and popped out between the thongs of her sandals.

From there, he kept to a simple path, traveling from ankle to ankle down the darkened cabin. He paused by the Russian's hairy foot, then sniffed through shoe leather. *F.r.i.e.n.d. o.f. f.o.r.m.e.r. h.o.s.t.,* the Tattoo thought in nano-cartoon balloons, then moved on.

The residue of Alyosha that had congealed between the Tattoo's biosensors attempted a silent scream. *Boris!!!* But there was no reply, just like in a bad dream. Alyosha was history anyway, trapped in the bardo. His spirit was not free as long as this virus-filled tattoo roamed the physical plane.

His consciousness felt like pus desperate to escape its envelope of flesh-memory. *K.e.e.p. q.u.i.e.t.,* the Tattoo warned the human pusball, and Alyosha was silent again.

The Tattoo came to the appointed meeting place beneath the drinks trolley in the rear galley.

The other sentient tattoos were waiting. They had been sipping on vodka and pineapple juice and scarfing up the fumes of the Hennessy cognac.

F.r.i.e.n.d.s., the Tattoo gave them the spidery high five.

O.u.r. l.e.a.d.e.r., the tattoos replied in unison.

Altogether, there were fifteen tattoos on board the flight, two from first class and the rest from coach.

E.x.c.e.l.l.e.n.t., the Tattoo said, satisfied at the turnout. *Y.o.u. a.r.e. a.l.l. h.e.r.e. i.n.c.o.g.n.i.t.o.?*

O.f. c.o.u.r.s.e. B.i.e.n. s.û.r. J.a. H.a.i. D.a. S.í., they replied in as many tattoo tongues as there were tattooed hosts.

W.h.e.r.e. a.r.e. y.o.u. f.r.o.m.? W.h.e.r.e. w.e.r.e. y.o.u. b.o.r.n.? the Tattoo inquired.

T.u.n.i.s. B.a.r.c.e.l.o.n.a. M.u.n.i.c.h. C.h.i.c.a.g.o. A.t.h.e.n.s. T.o.k.y.o. S.a.n. F.r.a.n.c.i.s.c.o. L.o.s. A.n.g.e.l.e.s. P.a.r.i.s. B.u.e.n.o.s. A.i.r.e.s. M.e.x.i.c.o. C.i.t.y. O.d.e.s.s.a. B.o.g.o.t.á. G.e.n.e.v.a. T.a.n.g.i.e.r.—

D.o.e.s. a.n.y.o.n.e. s.u.s.p.e.c.t.? the Tattoo demanded.

There was silence.

W.e.l.l.?

D.o.e.s. a.n.y.o.n.e. s.e.n.s.e. a.n.y.t.h.i.n.g. o.u.t. o.f. t.h.e. o.r.d.i.n.a.r.y.? the Tattoo repeated the question.

One skinny little tattoo, the Moroccan job, snickered. *T.h.e.y. a.l.l. a.r.e. b.e.g.i.n.n.i.n.g. t.o. f.e.e.l. t.h.e. c.r.a.z.y. d.e.s.i.r.e. L.e. d.é.s.i.r. f.o.u.*

T.h.a.t.'.s. a.l.l. r.i.g.h.t. t.h.e.n. A.s. l.o.n.g. a.s. t.h.e.y. d.o. n.o.t. e.j.a.c.u.l.a.t.e. R.e.m.e.m.b.e.r., n.o. f.l.u.i.d.s. a.r.e. a.l.l.o.w.e.d.

The Argentinean tattoo, shaped like a sea horse, rocked back and forth. *H.u.m.a.n.s. l.i.k.e. t.o. c.o.m.e.*

O.f. c.o.u.r.s.e. t.h.e.y. d.o., the Tattoo shivered his biosensors in warning. *T.h.a.t.'s. w.h.y. t.h.e.y. m.u.s.t.n.'t. b.e. p.e.r.m.i.t.t.e.d. t.o.*

P.r.o.c.r.e.a.t.i.o.n. i.s. s.e.d.i.t.i.o.n., the German tattoo exclaimed.

C.o.r.r.e.c.t., the Tattoo nodded.

W.h.a.t. d.o. y.o.u. h.a.v.e. f.o.r. u.s. t.h.e.n.? the Japanese tattoo hissed softly.

Y.e.s., w.h.y. h.a.v.e. y.o.u. c.a.l.l.e.d. t.h.i.s. m.e.e.t.i.n.g.? the Tunisian tattoo demanded. *W.h.y. s.h.o.u.l.d. w.e. l.i.s.t.e.n. t.o. y.o.u.?*

The Tattoo whipped his stinger like a scorpion, scorching the Tunisian. The tattoo from Tunis crumpled like a piece of burnt carbon fiber and dropped to the floor of the galley with a soft thud that only the witness tattoos could hear. They observed the swiftness of the punishment and they understood that insubordination was bad programming.

A.n.y. m.o.r.e. c.h.a.l.l.e.n.g.e.s.? the Tattoo faced the small group. Not one tattoo raised a whisper.

G.o.o.d., t.h.e.n. L.e.t. u.s. c.o.n.t.i.n.u.e. O.p.e.n. y.o.u.r. h.e.a.r.t.s. a.n.d. m.i.n.d.s.

Each one kneeled before the Tattoo as their master opened his second and seventh chakra to them.

I. g.i.v.e. y.o.u. M.i.r., the Tattoo said. *P.e.a.c.e. O.n.e. w.o.r.l.d. o.n.-l.i.n.e., o.f.f.-l.i.n.e. T.h.r.o.u.g.h.o.u.t. e.t.e.r.n.i.t.y.*

N.o.w. g.o., the Tattoo ordered. *B.a.c.k. t.o. y.o.u.r. h.o.s.t.s. A.n.d. m.a.y. y.o.u. m.u.l.t.i.p.l.y.*

The troop of tattoos held together for a moment of silent communion. Then each one slinked back to where it had come from in the darkened cabin, where the naked human limbs waited to be embraced again by the members of the poison tribe.

There was a world out there to be conquered by the light of the tattooist's love.

ACT TWO

"Will the real body please stand up?"

—ALLUCQUÈRE
ROSANNE STONE

Bad Chai
San Francisco

Trevor was in a disturbed state. He had been back for three days. Three agonizing days punctuated by bad sleep, bad dreams, and bad gastrointestinal second chakra rumbling in his solar plexus.

His *hara*—that mystical Japanese energy band around his middle—felt as if a python had wrapped itself around him like some reptilian cummerbund that had escaped from a jungle painting by Rousseau.

His pain felt *vivid* —like a living, bilious, neon green. This despite wearing his dad's old *haramaki,* a Japanese woolen belly band designed to soothe the mental distress from his stomach.

Trevor had modified his haramaki somewhat by having little copper orgone circuits sewn into it, to speed up the healing energy flow. He was sure his dad would be amused.

Where was he, anyway, when Trevor needed to talk to him? It was ironic. One of Dad's favorite aphorisms was, "If you love your son, you must let him travel." Then he, *Dad,* had promptly gotten up and gone—he had ridden off into the Void, with Tara at his side. Nice going, Dad.

Trevor groaned as he flipped through Star TV's latest batch of sitcoms from India, stuff he had missed when he and Nelly were off on their "vacation."

The show was called *Chakras,* and it was pure Bollywood, full of dancing gods and goddesses and lewd religion. Trevor was reminded of reading somewhere that there were more gods in the Hindu pantheon than there were people in Calcutta.

He soon grew tired of all the bangles and bared midriffs and the tinkling of the finger cymbals and the relentless drone of the vina. He clicked it off.

Trevor had seen Nelly home upon their return to San Francisco. She lived off Haight Street in a restored Victorian that Donovan had stayed in almost a century ago, when the Summer of Love was in its psychedelic prime. "Sunshine Superman," "Mellow Yellow," "Catch the Wind,"—she had named all her rooms after Donovan songs.

You'd think he was Swinburne or Oscar Wilde or Byron. Donovan is Donovan, okay? That was how *that* argument had started . . .

Jesus, he was beginning to relive old fights with Nelly . . . He *must* have a fever. He groaned again and reached for his mug of *chai,* sweetened Indian tea with spices and honey.

Yuk. He felt slightly nauseous. It was a bad chai day.

A ripple of a hallucination intersected the screen of air by his bedside. He had spent a small inheritance on the Sony Omtron Intravision system—$7,999 to be exact, at the God Guys electronics store. The Sony was the world's first invisible television set.

Too bad it wasn't designed for invisible couch potatoes, because Trevor felt like disappearing into its vortex of invisible paraoptics. Actually, the TV was a three-eyed beast. Three eyes like glowing black coals were set strategically on the wall, unnoticeable really, genius Japanese design at work again. The three beams opened up a screen of images of any size or dimension; put on your VR skullcap and whammy-granny glasses and you could zip from rave to grave if you wanted.

He felt too weak and dispirited to cruise the "Shmooze Line," where one could cruise the av babes (for immediate mood-alteration therapy), and if he went into "Discombobulate Mode" (a.k.a. "VR Potluck: You *Are* Where You *Feel*"), he might regret it later on. Last time he rolled the dice, he had run into three old girlfriends in the space of ten minutes—time and space being relative, that is.

Shit, VR was beginning to feel like an old girlfriend to him . . .

No, he just wanted to stay home in his haramaki in a comfortable fetal position, thank you very much . . .

"Trevor?" he heard the voice of Juan, his Dad's old homekeeper, call as the man climbed the ladder up to Trevor's loft.

Juan's friendly face appeared at floor level. Tuesday was the day he came in to clean up the mess and to revive the dying.

"You okay?" Juan asked him. "I'm almost finished now." His broad face, the shade of cinnamon, was crowned by a full head of Mayan hair, black with iron-gray streaks. Juan had raised Trevor from childhood; he had witnessed the terror and the promise . . . His compassionate brown eyes radiated from the steps with an inquiring gleam.

Young Mister Trevor looked not so good, like he was going through another midlove crisis. Juan had seen the look before in varying degrees of human self-sacrifice.

The goddess, she is hungry today, he decided. Poor Trevor.

"Thanks, Juan," Trevor replied. "I'll be fine."

"Don't overdo it, okay?"

"Don't overdo what?"

Juan rolled his eyes. "Whatever you're overdoing."

Trevor laughed. "You're right. You heard anything from Dad lately?"

Juan clucked. "Your papa, he is all right, don't you worry. When it's time, he'll be in touch." He paused. "You got the last postcard?"

"From the Golden Triangle? Yeah. He sent it from a Lahu village on the Thai-Burmese border. That one?"

"That one."

Trevor sighed. "What's he up to, anyway?"

Juan shrugged. "You want I make you a tamale before I go? You need to eat."

Trevor made a face. His heart felt like a wrapped tamale,

105

corn husk on the outside, depressed pork on the inside. *"Gracias, no, por favor—"*

"Okay, okay." Juan gave him a mock scowl. "Next Tuesday, if you no eat, the tubes—I force-feed you black beans."

"See you next week, Juan." Trevor waved a weak hand and collapsed his head on his pillow. His futon was spread out on an elevated platform of tatami mats.

Through the skylight, he could see the gray San Francisco light that looked as if someone had poured misty water from a ladle into a stone basin. He'd been living in this South of Market loft for three years, and at first it had been a gas. Cafés, clubs, galleries, the nightlife of the avant-garde, music, love, laughter, *ha ha ha* . . .

Now it felt like the crotch of Siberia infested with lice.

"'Bye." He heard Juan leave, shutting the door behind him downstairs.

Nelly, Nelly, Nelly . . . Trevor suddenly missed her terribly. How could she do this to him? She had dumped him for a tattoo.

The screen of air rippled again impatiently. But Trevor's system was set on vibracom and the pulsing electric breeze failed to rouse him. The automatic dialup began . . .

Trevor dozed. He fell right into a nightmare catnap—it was part of his healing process. His subconscious mind had bet his conscious mind that he could take it. He was swimming in the sleep current and his hara was doing spiral back flips into the baby pool of his psyche.

"Sunshine came softly, ah, through my window today . . . could have tripped out easy but I've changed my way, it'll take time, I know it, but in a while, you gonna be mine, I know it, we'll do it in style . . ."

He was standing outside Nelly's at the Donovan Door. He was going to ring the doorbell, but instead he pulled out the key that Nelly had given him. *Should he?* He slipped the key into the lock and quietly opened the door.

There was soft sitar music playing upstairs in the bedroom. Trevor felt a pang. She liked to play that music when they were making love. From the bottom of the stairs, he could smell the rose incense in the air. He was wavering.

God, he could barely move his limbs. His legs were like the roots of a banyan tree spreading into the floorboards. Was he asleep? Was this a dream?

He summoned all his willpower. No good. He couldn't move a single muscle.

More rippling sitar music spilled into his hearing like Nelly's warm love-breath in his ear. The last time they had *really* made love, he had really fallen into the groove of that passage.

Trevor's foot moved now, and he took each awkward step like a Frankenstein in leg braces. Ridiculous, but more than ridiculous: *painful.* He was building up momentum and he couldn't afford to stop, although he was more terrified of what he would find than he was of being caught prowling like a common stalker in Nelly's house.

Donovan's soft crooning continued in Trevor's head. Nelly's Tibetan flags were draped on the wall along the stairs, and they fluttered in the breeze of his movement. Angry Tibetan deities who hovered on the playing field between heaven and earth rushed at him like tantric quarterbacks as he climbed each step. Mahakala grimaced at him, flames shooting from his eyes. Pitchfork karma was aimed at his gut.

It was agony, but he managed to reach the top of the stairs. The bedroom door was ajar. It was dark inside the room, but the flickering candle-glow radiated an ongoing act of love.

Trevor's heart felt like a board pierced with six-inch nails. Damnation was the price he would have to pay for his transgression. Could he take it?

"Nelly?" His voice sounded hollow yet somewhat like a frog's plaintively calling from one lily pad to another. Softer now. *"Nelly?"*

Silence.

She had heard him. Now *her* voice sounded faint. "Trevor?"

He tried to decipher its pitch. Was it anxiety, surprise, anger, shame? He heard the sound of sheets being hurriedly drawn. *That's it*—he was more than halfway in and there was no turning back.

The moment of truth had arrived. He pushed the door open. "Nelly—"

"You've got to pick up every stitch, mmmh, must be the season of the witch, must be the season of the witch, yeah, must be the season of the witch—"

Nelly switched the lights on in the room and cut the sitar music. The flames of the candles looked naked as they flickered in the cold light. She was sitting up in bed; her face was white. Her lips were set, her cheekbones taut.

"Trevor, what are you *doing* here?!" Nelly pulled her sheet up, but Trevor's hand held on to it.

There was a scurrying under the sheet. He yanked it away from her, and her eyes drained of all color. *The tattoo was hiding under her sex like a voyeur from hell . . .*

"Nelly?" Trevor's eyes bore into her.

But there was no question in his voice. Nelly was the name of his despair, and he had called it out plain and simple.

Trevor felt cold and cruel as he surveyed the playground. There was her vibrator, a nice little rocket ship for a tattoo to blast off from. A small bottle of lubricant. Her nipples were still erect. Caramel-colored aureoles like Thai iced tea.

Chest heaving as she sobbed, Nelly covered her face in her hands. "Just go, Trevor. Please leave!"

He was a bastard. All right, it was his dark side and he was the ventriloquist's dummy. He couldn't resist the retort. "So, is he a good lover? I mean, is it *satisfying* for you?"

She slapped him so hard that he woke up.

He lay there sweating on his futon, his thoughts all mixed up. A terrible dream. A terrible, terrible dream. He would *never* do that to Nelly, he swore to himself. *Never.*

What the fuck!? The air screen of the Sony Omtron Intravision was clearing its cache of parapixels. Had the system been on? Fuck!

He sat up. The sweat had soaked his hair as though he had been standing in a full-body shower. He grabbed his control, checked the last-used unit. It couldn't be . . . he *had* been connected!

Nelly's number was still on. *What . . . who?* Before the Intravision drained its last image, he saw Nelly's candles still flickering on the PersaChannel.

He saw her face staring at him, like a ghost that had been interrupted in mid-orgasm, as the pixels died.

The screen vibrated again instantly. Trevor clicked on it. God, what was he going to tell Nelly? That he had been sleepwalking again?

Trevor was a lucid sleepwalker. He had done this before. Nelly thought it was weird, but charming at first. *"You're the only person I know who actually* tele-sleepwalks, *Trevor . . ."*

It was Nelly. Her face was drawn tight, just as it had been in . . . the . . . *dream?*

Nelly had dried her tears and her voice was matter of fact. "I don't think we should see each other again, Trevor. Please don't—ah—call on me anymore. I'm going to have my number changed. Do you understand?"

Then she hung up on him. Blankly, he reached for his mug of chai and brought it to his lips. It was cold.

He swallowed his bad chai.

At the Brain Wash

Midnight at the Brain Wash Café & Laundromat on Folsom Street was prime time for the South of Market vampires and Valkyries to do their laundry. This was a pagan rite of cleansing that Trevor felt compelled to participate in.

Largely because his bag of dirty laundry from his French trip was past overflowing. So it was either the Brain Wash or shopping for t-shirts, jeans, and underwear at the Gap Taqueria on Harrison Street. And he wasn't in the mood for Mexican food or shopping.

He still couldn't believe that he had actually invaded Nelly's place. He was now a bona fide home invader. A poltergeist on parole. In Nelly's doghouse. His poster must be on the wall of every psychic post office in the country. At least, that's how he felt: low-down and miserable.

Nelly would come around again, he was pretty sure. She always had in the past. But how long would it be before she broke down her self-imposed quarantine to extend an olive branch to him? Did she love him enough? Stay tuned, Trevor.

"The moon rises and the moon sets"—he'd try that mantra for a while, before resorting to more industrial-strength potions. Maybe he'd give Dorje a call to see if the demons were in the mood to be pacified.

The feisty Tibetan lama had come to Trevor's aid in the past, armed with his phurbu ritual-exorcism dagger and homemade yak soup, which he would prepare for Trevor in the Tenderloin apartment that he shared with two other Tibetan lamas.

Trevor glanced at his watch. Dorje would probably be starting his midnight shift right about now.

He looked out the plate-glass window at the passing parade of cars on Folsom. They were mostly leather cruisers and club animals heading to whatever watering hole they paid homage to.

Dorje drove a Yellow Cab. He belonged to the relatively new sect of "Yellow Cab" lamas, a tantric offshoot of the Tibetan "Red Hat" school. After the eighty-year-old American Hollywood actor–Tibetan Buddhist Richard Fevers assumed the mantle of the fifteenth Dalai Lama in a hotly contested election, there had been an exodus of Tibetan dissidents to the United States. A group of them acquired the venerable flagship

American taxi company as an act of spiritual defiance against "Hollywood hegemony."

The rides were free—"Hail a lama!" was their slogan—but you had to contribute something to the homeless or to the mindless or to the heartless of the world. To anyone who needed a blessing or a buck.

If you had nothing to give, Dorje made you spin the prayer wheel that he had installed in the back seat for that purpose. "Spin, spin, spin," he would grin, making the motion of rolling down the car window as if it were a hand-held *mani* prayer wheel. "Americans need to spin more, spend less. Ha, ha, ha!"

Dorje was a koan on wheels: a not-for-profit cabby. He was a rare bird dressed in a maroon colored lama's robe that he kept tucked in at the shoulder, and he had a warm smile for everyone. If you looked like *you* needed a dollar, he'd reach into the donations jar on the front seat and give you one.

Nope, no Yellow Cabs were cruising on Folsom tonight. *"Hi, Dorje,"* Trevor sent a hopeful greeting out into the ether anyway, adding a little mental Post-it on which he scribbled, *"You out there somewhere? I could use a ride. I'm* hurting *right now."*

Trevor sighed as he downloaded a small waterfall of quarters into the washer. The machine began to gurgle as it sucked in the Mind Parasites detergent he'd bought from the Brain Wash dispenser.

Trevor paid for a latte at the bar. He felt a spiritual weariness, like that old, beat up–looking street person who sat in the corner in a tattered bathrobe, waiting for his only worldly threads to be washed.

There was a row of help-yourself robes hanging from hooks by the changing cubicle, courtesy of the Brain Wash management.

Trevor gave him a dollar. "Bite to eat, brother."

The red-rimmed eyes scanned him and flickered. "The pope's in trouble," the guy said.

"I know," Trevor replied as he made his way toward a vacant table.

"Hey, guy," the anonymous wreck called after him in a cracked voice. Trevor turned.

He could see the man wanted to give him something back.

"Hadgetter," he spluttered.

It was an effort for him to talk. Trevor waited for further clarification. It was the universe trying to get through to him on an unlisted line. He could afford to wait. You never knew what would come through.

He'd received enough messages from unlikely sources in his time. Some of them were priceless.

"Yes?"

"Hadgetter," the man repeated. Then he spat it out. "Mechanical retrieval of what you thought was lost forever."

"Thanks, man," Trevor said softly as he let that sink in. What did it mean? "Mechanical"? In this day and age? Retrieval of what? Nelly? But the dude's head was already nodding in the bardos, lost in the dream of Where-Is-It-Now?

The beasties were out tonight. Mohawks and piercings, Barbie Doll transsexuals, and the official contingent of retro–North Beach beatniks in beards and black Toulouse-Lautrec cabaret-poster capes.

It was open mike tonight at the Brain Wash, and the Boxing Gandhis and the Buddha Heads were performing their latest abstractions on the cube stage.

Trevor yawned as he grabbed yesterday's copy of the *San Francisco Herald Tribune* and settled down to wait for the wash cycle of existence to do its thing.

Hmm, weird shit in the news, he thought after a glance at the front page. Well, if it *weren't* weird shit, it wouldn't be in the news, right?

112

One headline story immediately captured his attention. Synchronicity City!

GANG OF CHINESE GRANNIES ROBS B OF A
COLUMBUS BRANCH IN BROAD DAYLIGHT

A daring robbery was committed in broad daylight at the Columbus Street branch of the Bank of America yesterday afternoon at 2 P.M. . . . Police were baffled when they responded to an emergency call and discovered the bank robbers to be a group of six senior citizens, ranging in age from 72 to 93. All suspects were residents of the On Lok Nursing Home located on Lower Broadway.

They were apprehended after the leader of the gang, Ma Fun Chung, a 93-year-old retired seamstress from the Wing Hung Textile Co., led the police on a wild chase down Columbus Avenue, wielding her cane at passersby who attempted to get in her way.

The gang was finally cornered when they ran into the Sun Moon Chinese bakery on Vallejo Street. They refused to give up without a struggle and had to be subdued by police. Also apprehended in the incident were Chin Lung, 91, Lai Lo, 88, Fran Fong, 77, Helen Liu, 80, and Virginia Kwok, 72.

According to investigating police officers, the geriatric gang members claimed they had no recollection of having committed the crime and insisted they'd been mistakenly confused with "another group" of senior criminals alleged to be operating out of Chinatown. The Bank of America has declined to press charges. . . .

A medical report released by the San Francisco Police Department later revealed a curious anomaly. All six bank robbers were sporting identical tattoos described as looking like Chinese ideograms that read "Wu Wu Wu." They have been dubbed the "Wu Wu Wu Gang." This particular ideogram "Wu" is translated to mean "Emptiness." . . .

Family members have expressed shock and surprise that their aged relatives would have formed a "Triple Emptiness" gang, and have emphatically denied that the elderly women had ever been tattooed in their lives.

113

Compounding the SFPD's perplexity over the case is the fact that the tattoos are of recent origin, according to Pacific Hospital resident on-line dermatologist Henry Liu (no relation to suspect Helen Liu). "They belong to the genus of 'AI' or 'sentient' tattoos, which are nomadic epidermal software programs designed for transmittal by individual Web users for on-line dissemination of their avatars," Dr. Liu said.

"All six suspects are known to be completely computer illiterate," according to Detective Vic Wong, who is conducting the official police investigation.

Police are seeking to question one Hakim Beijing, 23, proprietor of the "V-Tat Parlor," a tattoo emporium located at 1118 Broadway. Beijing is reputedly the programmer-inventor of this particular line of "sentient" tattoos. He has been missing for two months, ever since a malpractice suit was brought against him by the California Board of Tattoo Artists, after a number of his clients exhibited signs of "tattoo dementia" following treatment by him.

"The bugs in his tattoos were quite shocking," said Maynard Wang, president of the CBTA. "They showed every sign of being contaminated by some unknown virus and are known to have caused extensive damage to nodes on the Net that were penetrated by unsuspecting tattoo-bearing users . . . A number of tattoos are still missing and unaccounted for."

Police are now seeking to establish a link between Beijing's disappearance and the outbreak of "tattooitis" at the On Lok senior-citizens' facility, which is located two blocks away from his tattoo parlor.

"Wow!" Trevor exclaimed under his breath, a chill zigzagging down his spine.

Then his eye tripped over another headline. "AI TATTOO VIRUS HITS AUSTRALIAN OUTBACK"

"Fuck!" Trevor blurted out loud.

*   *   *

"Safe sex, I hope," a smooth, husky voice laced with humor reached out and tickled Trevor's ear from behind.

Trevor spun around on his seat and blinked at the girl. *My God, she was beautiful!* She looked to be in her mid-twenties. Her hair was frizzy and red, and it spilled out in scarab-decorated dreadlocks from a black beret.

Her skin was so pale it was almost translucent, and it was accented by freckles scattered like tiny corn flakes on her face and full red lips that were parted to reveal perfectly shaped white teeth. She wore a red silk scarf slung over a white turtle-neck, and a black motorcycle jacket with a pinball-maze of studs and schizoid zippers fashionably unzipped every which way.

Trevor blinked as though he were developing her picture slowly in his mind.

He could get lost in those metallic zippers for an entire *kalpa,* an eon and a half, he thought to himself. He had never seen anyone who looked quite as striking as this woman. With her knobs and dials and scarabs, she radiated Shiva in his incarnation as Jagannath, the Infinite Machine of the Universe . . . The whole computable universe lay draped over her shapely form, with all its secrets of quantum fire and sacred cosmic lust . . .

As if to complete the apparition, she was dressed in black stretch pants, a gold-chain belt, and cowboy boots with spiked heels.

She exuded an exotic fragrance, something between jasmine and Queen of the Nile. It was very, very heady, and very, very ancient.

"Uh, hi," Trevor said, extending his hand. "I'm Trevor Gobi. Are you from around here? I've never seen you before."

"Alex Fortuna," she said, returning his handshake with a cool but firm grasp. "No, as a matter of fact, I'm not from around here. This isn't one of my usual haunts. I live in the Avenues, out by Baker Beach, near the Golden Gate Park. You know where that is?"

He nodded.

"And no," Alex continued, "I don't generally hang out in laundromats south of Market. I have my own washing machine."

"So . . . ," Trevor sought his opening, "you're here for the *music?*"

"Not exactly." She laughed. "I'm supposed to be waiting for my boyfriend. But I'm not. It's his laundry night. He lives in the neighborhood."

Trevor looked around puzzled. Where was her boyfriend?

"Oh." Alex laughed again. "He left. I'm tired of his underwear, and he can't stand constructive criticism."

"Are you serious?" Trevor asked. "Does he wear boxers or briefs?"

"Neither. A codpiece, if you want to know, to exaggerate his—uh—*attributes.* He's very vain. He followed some chick out the door, he's helping her carry her laundry home."

"You don't mind?"

"Why should I? I suggested it to him myself."

"In that case . . . ," Trevor began and shrugged. Their eyes met. He blushed.

"You're the shy one,"Alex said after a moment, a smile on her pale oval face. She had lovely dimples. He was already in love with her chin. As for the rest of her—well, that would depend . . .

"Uh . . ." He didn't know what to say. Alex sat up suddenly and brought out a silver cigarette case from her brown leather saddlebag.

She flicked the case open and offered him a cigarette. "No, thanks." Trevor shook his head, marveling at the fluidity of her motion.

Then she lit her cigarette with a hefty-looking gold lighter in the shape of a dragon. Its red eyes came alive as it breathed fire. She blew the smoke away from him. "You don't mind if I smoke?"

"Uh, no."

"So are you married?" Alex continued with her disarming interrogation. "Do you have children? Dogs? Cats? Goldfish? *Cattle?*"

Trevor was smiling now. "No, no, no, and no. I'm single and no pets will have me." He didn't know why he said that. But it sounded pathetic. Nelly had broken up with him technically, hadn't she?

"Funny," Alex said as she appraised him. "You don't *look* single."

"No?" he asked, dumbstruck at how close she was to the truth. "What makes you say that?"

"There's something in your aura. But then maybe you haven't finished all your wash yet." Alex blew some smoke into the air; it hung like a transparent afterthought.

Trevor's eyebrows leapfrogged. "Say, that's pretty accurate. Are you a mind reader?"

"No, I'm a brainwasher," she teased. "You look like you need deprogramming. So you just broke up with someone?" It was a leading question, and she studied his eyes, which were open portals to her.

"Something like that."

"Recently?"

"Um, *today,* as a matter of fact—"

She laughed again. "Then we'll get along famously. I just broke up with Rick fifteen minutes ago myself. What a coincidence. We're both *free.*"

There was an eerie coiling sound coming from the cube stage. The Boxing Gandhis and the Buddha Heads had completed their sets, and a mattress had been placed onstage. A mike dangled above it; a spotlight shone on the come stains on its shiny mattress skin.

"Inanimate karaoke," Alex observed. "Hip-hop from the mattress brokers."

"Far out," Trevor remarked, grateful that the universe was providing them with props for their conversation.

The diodes above the stage illuminated the necessary subtext for the next entry in the evening's musical program: *"Boxes: The Lost Songs of the Box-Spring Mattress": A Composition by Cheryl E. Leonard.*

"Sounds like early Cage before he went cosmic," Trevor said. "It's got sort of a sinister twang to it."

Alex killed her cigarette under her spiked heel. She gave him a long look tinged with wistful amusement.

"Trevor, it's Trevor, isn't it?" She lightly scraped his hand with one of her long fingernails. Her nails were painted a blood-red like a spray-painted sacrifice to Kali. He felt the shock rise in his solar plexus. He'd just been zapped.

He nodded. "Yes, *Alex?*"

"Seeing that we're both free. And seeing that you're innocent, naive, and full of yourself, which could be quite delicious—and what's wrong with that?—I have a proposition for you."

Trevor paused. "I'm listening."

"I think your load of laundry is done, by the way," she said. He glanced up at the machine, which was indeed at the end of its cycle.

"I think you're right," he stated, his eyes returning to hers. They were a crystalline blue and they sparkled at him.

"How would you like to use my dryer?" Alex asked him. "I have a dryer at home."

"I think—I think that I'd like that very much, Alex. Thanks."

"I even have some fabric softener," she added. "To soften your fabric."

"It could use some softening." He nodded in agreement. *Well, well, well.* So it *was* happening between them. It hadn't been his imagination.

Trevor knew that he wouldn't easily forget this night, if ever. "Let's go," he said. "It won't take me a minute to get my stuff."

"I'll be waiting outside," she replied.

Alex Fortuna

When Trevor stepped out of the Brain Wash with his duffel bag filled with damp clothes, he found Alex pacing the sidewalk smoking another cigarette.

"I'm parked just up the block," she told him.

They walked together in silence past the SOMA Leather Bar & Grill, where the guys in black jeans and chaps walked in little bowlegged circles for one another's benefit, their chests naked except for black leather vests, their big belt buckles harnessing a kinetic display of bellies in various sizes.

"Lots of daddies out tonight," Alex said. "You live in quite a neighborhood."

"Local color." He shrugged. "It doesn't bother me."

"Do you ever feel daddy energy, Trevor?"

"That depends. Do you ever feel little-girl energy?"

"Sometimes," she answered, flicking her cigarette underneath a parked van. "Sometimes I like to be the daddy."

"Are you an only child?"

She grinned as she swatted him. "How'd you guess? You a mind reader or something?"

"No, I'm a brainwasher. I think you've got some deprogramming that needs to get done."

"Are you up to it?"

"As I said, it depends. We just met. I'm flexible."

She put one arm around his neck and pulled him to her. Their first kiss. Her lips opened and he tasted her salty tobacco tongue measuring his. "Mmm," she said. "I knew you were delicious. You're sweet."

"You're sweet, too."

"Do you think that we're going to get along?"

"I have to tell you something. You're hot and you're beautiful. I love the way you're direct with me. But under your smart exterior, I think you're just like me—"

"Are you trying to tell me I'm a little confused—or just a little fast?"

"Both."

"And *you* are, too . . ."

He nodded. She kissed him on the cheek this time. "Honest child," she said.

"Altar girl," he replied. And kissed her back. On her warm lips, and found her tongue again.

Alex drove her ancient Jeep Cherokee down Ninth Street and cut across Hayes to Fell Street, heading down the Panhandle toward Golden Gate Park. They entered the darkened park, the trees shielding the night sky, past the old Victorian greenhouse, till they reached the bronze mountain lions that guarded the entrance to Eighth Avenue.

She turned onto Anza.

"I have to tell you something if we're going to make love," she said, breaking the silence.

"You're a guy?"

She laughed as she closed the ashtray. It was full of butts. She'd just put out another cigarette.

"No. But I do have a fetish."

"For . . . ?"

"For men with tattoos."

He turned to her slowly with a hard questioning look. After a moment, he replied. "I think I'm going to disappoint you then. I haven't got a single tattoo."

Then he thought about Nelly. "Not that I'm related to, anyway."

"No, you don't understand. I like my lovers to be bare. I could tell you weren't tattooed. You're not the type. You're pure. Virginal skin is what turns me on."

"I'm afraid I don't get it."

She pulled into a driveway and looked up at a second-story window. "I have a roommate. Danya. Her light's out. But she's not home tonight."

120

"Like I said, I don't get it." He may as well get this over with now. If he was going in, he was going in—but not with a question mark burning on his brow. If this wasn't going to work for her, or for him, they had better hash it out beforehand. The cord to his duffel bag was looped tightly around his hand as though he needed to be anchored to something solid.

Alex killed the engine and rolled down the window to let some air in. "Okay, let me explain." She ran her hand over his chest with a curiosity marked by longing. "I'd like to tattoo you."

He stared at her in the darkness of the Jeep, eyes wide open. "But I promise you won't feel a thing," she added quickly. "They're sentient. It's like applying paste-on tattoos."

"How would you know that?"

"My boyfriend. My ex-boyfriend, I should say, before Rick. He's a tattoo artist. He taught me how to do it. Have you ever tried tattoo sex, Trevor?"

He shook his head.

"I promise it won't hurt. It's just beautiful, that's all. They run all over your body—then they run all over my body. Would you like to try it once?"

He could smell her jasmine and Queen of the Nile, and he saw the swell of her breasts against her white turtleneck as she leaned over to kiss him. He would never know a woman like this again, probably.

And he was suddenly curious—not just about his own experience, but about Nelly's "thing" with her tattoo . . .

"Okay," he said. "Let's see what you can show me."

"First things first," she laughed as she broke away from him. "I promised you use of my dryer, remember? Got your bag, cowboy?"

"Fresh from the Brain Wash," he replied and got out of the Jeep.

He followed her into the darkened foyer of her building, his laundry bag in his hand.

Her stiletto-heeled cowboy boots echoed up the flight of stairs ahead of him.

The plaster-of-Paris curlicues on the sooty walls, along with the heads of cherubs, sleep-rings under their eyes, dated the building to the middle of the previous century. A baby carriage was parked in a dark corner by the stairs, a small bundle shape lying under its covers.

Trevor paused and lifted up the quilt, half expecting to find a baby sleeping there.

Alex had turned around on the landing and watched him with an amused expression in her eyes.

"Oh, the baby's not scheduled to be sacrificed until daybreak tomorrow," she joked. Seeing his startled look, she teased him. "Are you getting spooked now, Trevor?"

"Me? No." He shook his head as he climbed the stairs after her. "Should I be?"

"Do I detect a trace of nervousness?"

They stood face to face on the landing. "You can always turn around and go home, you know," Alex said, pointing her chin in the direction of the entrance.

"There is absolutely no obligation to participate in the unholy ritual. And I won't question your manhood if you leave."

"You know what? I think you're a fraud," Trevor challenged her. *Go on, give it back to her gently.*

"You don't scare me, Alex. You're trying to, for some reason I don't quite understand yet. Why?"

"I'm a nice Russian Jewish girl. Why would I want to scare a nice goy like you? I only have a sincere interest in having sex with you."

"You're Russian? That's interesting."

"Why? Do you have something against Russians, or are you Russian yourself?"

"Part. On my father's side."

"Oh, that's nice. Are you Jewish?"

He shook his head. "Does that disqualify me?"

"Not in my bed," she laughed, and began to climb to the next landing. "Are you coming?"

He followed her. She was at the end of the hall, fiddling with a key. There was a mezuzah on the doorway. She turned to face him after she kissed her fingers to it. "See?"

"Okay, so you're devout. You're not a witch. You're a nice girl. I'm convinced."

"You thought I was a witch?" Alex touched her hand to his cheek. "Poor boy, you must be disappointed."

"A little, I admit," he replied as she opened the door to reveal a long, dark, narrow hallway. There was a small living/dining room off to the side, with a leather couch, flowers on a glass dining table, and four wicker-tube chairs arranged around it.

He glanced at the tiny kitchen in the alcove. There were magnet-backed pictures on the refrigerator door that showed Alex sitting at a table with several strangers.

She looked a few years younger in the pictures. Her red hair was just as Rastafied, but the scarabs were missing from her dreadlocks, and she was wearing a pair of granny glasses. She must be wearing contacts now, Trevor thought to himself.

"That's Mom and Dad and my aunt Masha and her boyfriend and me." Alex stood beside him, his tour guide of the fridge-gallery. "Those are balalaikas on the walls of the restaurant. See how innocent I looked back then?"

"Uh-huh," he replied. "Those are your parents?" They were a handsome couple in elegant evening clothes. Alex looked like both of them, but they were dark haired and serious looking.

Where did her wild streak come from? Not from them. He stared at another photo on the fridge. "Wow, who's *that?*"

The man with the pugnacious smile in the photograph was short, fat, and bald headed, but he had soft, sensitive eyes and long eyelashes that exuded the threat of charm.

There was an almost Oriental cast to his features, which made him look like a Buddha who had joined the Mob and

123

wore thousand-dollar suits. His tie was definitely Russian acid jazz, as if there were a jazz quartet trapped under his double chin. Pudgy fingers grasped the stem of the champagne glass as if they were choking the delicate neck of a cherub.

Trevor shook his head. "You don't mind my saying, he looks a little like a gangster . . . What a suit. And those diamond rings. *Phew.*"

"Oh, feel free to call Uncle Leo a gangster," Alex said as she poured a bottle of Clos du Bois merlot into two wine glasses. She handed him one.

"I mean, you're right, he *is* a gangster. I'm proud of him."

"Serious? A gangster?"

"Absolutely. From Odessa. The Sicily of the Ukraine."

Trevor whistled. "He kill anybody?"

"Has Uncle Leo killed anybody? *L'chaim.*" She clinked his wine glass. "Apart from one or two of my ex-boyfriends? Let me see . . ." She paused for effect and then went on. "He's my father's younger brother. There's about fifteen years' difference between them. Isn't he handsome?"

"Uh," Trevor replied diplomatically, "he's definitely a character, there's lots of humor and—um—*panache* there."

"He loves me very much. When I was a little girl, I was having lunch with him at a restaurant in New York—he lives in New York, you know. He saw someone eyeing him from a table across the room. Suddenly, he grabbed me into his arms and held me tight—"

Trevor shook his head. "How come?" He tasted the wine, its mellow oaky flavor feeling warm against his palate.

"Well, I was surprised. Uncle Leo said this guy recognized him. It was some guy he had scammed. Some under-the-table deal that backfired on him. He lost quite a bit of money—"

Trevor's eyebrow raised a fraction of an inch.

"Anyway, Uncle Leo explained that the guy had made a move like he was going to pull out a gun and shoot him. So he used me as a shield."

Trevor was horrified. "He used you as a *shield?*"

"Yes, but he told me that was only to *prevent* bloodshed. Because, you know, Russian gangsters will never hurt a child."

"Jesus H. Christ!" Trevor exclaimed.

"Please." Alex smiled. "Not in this house, okay? No cross-ethnic swear words. I'm superstitious."

"Okay, okay, he's a real prince."

"That's my aunt Masha," Alex went on with her family introductions as she returned to the first photograph. "She's *older* than my father by thirty years. She's seventy-two. And that's her lover, Zhenya."

"My God." Trevor looked at Alex incredulously. She was a—what?—some kind of a Russian tattoo vampire?

"Thanks," he said as Alex refilled his glass. "So your aunt Masha is seventy-two and has a lover. Not bad. Does it run in the family?"

"Does what run in the family?"

"This thing with tattoos?"

"Oh, that? No," Alex laughed. "That's just me. I'm the weirdo in the bunch."

"Oh, I wouldn't say that." Trevor smiled.

"Anyway," Alex continued, "Aunt Masha goes through lovers like some people go through lox. That's how she makes a living, in fact. Her lovers."

Trevor snorted. "That's pretty funny."

"No, seriously. That's her scam." Alex stood beside him as they both looked at the photograph of the old woman who was wearing a real mink stole and sported a double string of pearls hanging from her thin neck.

"She was extremely beautiful as a young woman, and these old guys still remember her from way back then. Her beauty is still working its magic on them even fifty years later."

Trevor sipped his wine. "Oh, *man.*"

"Her lovers are all weak men," Alex said as she glanced into Trevor's eyes. What was that look about? He shrank back a bit. "And she *is* strong. But not as strong as she used to be."

"So what does she do to hold them under her spell?" Trevor studied the old woman's gypsy-black eyes.

Alex stifled a giggle. "If I told you, it wouldn't be fair."

"Come on, I'm not dating your aunt Masha."

"You might be, one day. Why not?" Her clear blue eyes were filled with sweet irony. "Who's to say?"

"*I'm* to say," Trevor retorted. What was he letting himself into here, with this crazy, beautiful woman and her crazy family with a Russian gangster for an uncle?

"Don't worry. Since you're not kosher, she would just spit you out."

"So?" he prodded her.

"Well, first of all, she gets them to sign all their social-security checks over to her, and any valuables they might have. You know, in the bank, under their mattress, wherever."

"And then—?"

"And then she finds their weak spot. Usually it's vodka. They're mostly all alcoholics. She makes sure they stay that way. She gives them vodka for breakfast, lunch, and dinner. Then after they're really under her thumb, after she's gotten everything that they have to give her . . ."

"She kills them."

"Oh, no," Alex laughed gaily. "She doesn't kill them. No way. No, she *fires* them."

"She fires them? What do you mean by that?"

"Exactly what I said. She gives them their walking papers. Get out. She fires her lovers instead of breaking up with them."

"Charming family."

"You would like them. I'm sure they would like you."

"Thanks. I can't wait. What do your mother and father do, if I may ask?"

"My father runs a little computer business. He operates some VR networks in Odessa. My mother works with him."

"As an enforcer?"

"The women are *all* strong in my family, Trevor. Say, what sign were you born under?"

"Me? Are you kidding? I'm not telling *you*. I'm unlisted!"

"Come on, Mr. Unlisted. My bedroom's down the hall." He followed her. To his doom? Whatever. He was having a royally good time. These were his first light moments since he and Nelly had their big blowout. *What a trip this was . . .*

The door to Alex's bedroom was open, and he followed her inside. She began to light up the candles and votive lamps that were arranged everywhere.

He watched her move around, a nymph turning the darkness to candle-glow. He felt good as he watched her. But he'd have to see about this thing with the tattoos. If it got too weird, he'd just have to cop out of the scene. She had said no obligation, hadn't she?

He sat on the futon bed. Its red silk sheets glowed like a red harvest moon on the low, wood-framed horizon.

"Uh," he said, recollecting something. "What about my bag of wash and the dryer?"

"Oh, my dryer?" Alex said as she approached him. "Sorry, but my dryer is out of order."

"I'm an Aquarius," he confessed to her. She had already taken her clothes off and he didn't know what else to say. She helped him off with his shirt, undoing one button at a time.

"An Aquastell baby," she cooed. "Sorry about the dryer, okay?"

"Oh, that—*pshoo*—don't worry about it. My clothes will just mildew and rot, that's all. I need a new wardrobe. What kind of underwear did you say you liked?"

"You're funny," she said as she yanked his shirt off, started on his belt buckle. "I'll tell you something about myself. I don't like *any* underwear. Are you wearing any?"

She pulled at his belt and let out a war whoop. "My God! You're a man after my own heart!"

He blushed. "All my underwear is in the laundry bag."

She was on her knees on the bed, her breasts as round and as voluptuous as the statues of the Indian goddesses at the love

127

temple of Khajuraho. Her skin was so white—freckled all over, but a pale, pale white.

He had never seen skin as pale as hers before. Her legs were long, shapely, and her pubic hair was red and short, like a patch of bark on a redwood.

They kissed deeply, and he was ready for her right away. "Just a minute," she said as she rose from the bed. He could see the long graceful line of her back, the curve of her ass, and her long legs. Beautiful.

"Where are you going?" he moaned after she broke off their kiss.

She turned around. "You haven't forgotten why you're here, have you?"

"The tattoos?" He had almost forgotten about them in his rush of passion.

"*Da,*" she said. "*Podozhdi minutachku.* Wait a moment."

Oh, fuck—this was too good, or too bad, to be true. He felt trapped in his nakedness and in his desire for her.

Alex returned in a moment like she promised, carrying what looked like a vanity case for cosmetics. She set it down on the futon and opened it. Trevor caught his breath. It was a refrigerated vacuum case.

She removed some vials and shook them. Immediately, there was a glow as the biochemicals began their neon dance of action and reaction.

He watched mesmerized as she opened one tube. "How does that work? The tattoos are *in* there?"

"Uh-huh," Alex replied as she began to pour the mixture into the palm of her hand. There was a tiny pool of light where the tattoo-mix collected. She replaced the vial in the container and closed the lid.

"Lie down on your stomach," she ordered him. "It works like a massage oil. I'm going to give you a lovely massage."

He did as she asked. She began to work the tattoos into his skin. She had strong hands, and soon the muscles on his neck and on his back and on his arms began to relax like they never had before.

"Great massage, huh?" She leaned down and whispered in his ear. "Wait till you see what it looks like."

"Mmm," Trevor groaned as he began to drift off into a kind of intoxicating sleep.

"No, not yet, *not yet . . .*" Alex pinched him and his eyes opened abruptly.

"What?"

"Now turn over. I'm going to do your front."

Trevor turned over, and the world looked different. Alex— if that figure *was* Alex—loomed a hundred miles above him, her breasts like planets in the night sky, and her smile and tongue and her eyes like extraterrestrial beacons summoning him not just to a new world, but to a new night and a new morning too. His body burned like a thousand candles in a room full of fragmented mirrors.

"Alex . . ." Trevor moaned. She was already on top of him, riding him. In the mirror, Trevor watched as the tattoos began to merge from his body to hers. Until they formed one single tattoo on the joined canvas of their skin.

Hexagram

The tattoo-that-they-were reached for one of Alex's cigarettes on the night table. Trevor felt her form tug away from his as she sat up to light it. "Awesome, huh?" She glanced down at him. "The power of attachment."

Trevor was still connected to her as she smoked. Little nicotine bubbles reached him through the invisible cord that linked them, and he felt the nicotine rush of her relaxation.

He rolled over on his side and watched her. "I've never felt anything like this before." Then he added, "You're quite a sight. By the way, how long do these tattoos last?"

Her chest and back and arms and legs, all the way down to her ankles, were decorated with a spiral of pulsing blue-green-black tattoo light waves.

His body was similarly adorned. He felt the tattoos erupting like little neon fountains from every pore. "It's still happening," he said. "I still feel *this*—it. Whatever you call it."

She brushed the hair from her eyes and studied the kinetic tableaux on his skin.

"You're quite a sight, too, Trevor."

"So how long does it last?"

She blew the smoke into the air. "As long as it lasts. It's . . . different—for every person."

Trevor lay back and stared at the ceiling helplessly. He felt a little dizzy, as though a wind had come out of nowhere and easily knocked him down. His brain felt like a flag, fluttering in that wind.

"Relax." He felt Alex's hand caress his brow. "You were wonderful. You have no idea. You are a wonderful lover, Trevor."

"How much of that was me?" he wondered out loud, his eyes seeing double and triple lines. A giant floater like a polka-dotted beach umbrella spiraled in his right eye until it landed perfectly in the beach of his cornea, corkscrewing itself into the sand.

"*Ohh,*" he groaned, as he covered that eye with his hand. "I'm really dizzy."

"That will wear off soon, I promise," Alex reassured him. "And I *mean* it, you're a great lover. It *was* you. That doesn't come from anywhere else. That part of it is real. Here, drink some water." She handed him a bottle of mineral water.

Trevor blinked as he drank the cool water. The floater in his eye had mysteriously disappeared into its microscopic pocket. He sighed as he returned the bottle to her.

"Yow."

"Passion has its own karma, Trevor," Alex said as she con-

130

tinued to soothe him. "And you obviously have good karma, at least in *that* department."

He tried to sit up. He stared in the mirror at both of them, the rational panic hitting him now with full force.

The tattoo had spun its web, and they were both enmeshed in its astral braille.

As he stared at their joint image, a fluctuation of energy rippled across their bodies.

The lines he saw, now in the mirror, were rearranging themselves.

"Did you see that?!" Trevor pointed at the mirror. "Do you see what I'm seeing???"

"It's dynamic. It changes all the time."

"The lines, Alex—the *lines*."

She shared the image in the mirror with him. "You never know what comes to the surface. That's part of the revelation."

"Do you recognize the pattern?"

"Do *you*? That's the question."

"It . . . it looks like a Chinese hexagram from the *I Ching*, from the Book of Changes! Do you know what that is?"

"The *I Ching*? The Chinese oracle? I've heard of it, but I can tell you more about the Kabbalah."

The fluorescent yin and yang lines were writhing over their bodies like snakes shedding their skins.

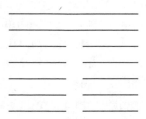

"Can you read it, Trevor?" Alex asked him. "What is it saying? Maybe it's an oracle of some sort?"

Trevor studied the lines. "There are sixty-four hexagrams in the Book of Changes, but I've been doing the *I Ching* for years, so I think I can decipher this . . ."

"What's it say?"

"It's the twentieth hexagram in the Book of Changes. 'Kuan,' or 'Contemplation.' And it changes—*see* the changing lines?!" he said excitedly. "It's changing into a secondary hexagram, which is a commentary on the first hexagram . . . Wow," he exclaimed. "It's changing into 'Sun.'"

"What's Sun, Trevor?"

Trevor looked at her strangely. "Sun is 'Decrease,'" he replied.

"Is that bad?"

"No, nothing's bad in the *I Ching*. It's all part of the natural cycle of things."

"So," she asked him. "What does Contemplation tell you?"

He caught his breath as he fathomed the message. The download came like a bolt out of the blue. He didn't know where it was coming from, that was the problem.

"Alex," he said as he turned to her. "When you told me these tattoos were sentient, I assumed you meant that they were intelligent media. Meant to be programmed by us. For our own use, for our *own* personal applications."

She smiled. "That depends on your definition of 'us.' Who 'we' are. And what our true 'nature' is."

Trevor wished that he could call on his father for an opinion. He could use Frank Gobi's input right now. He had to make some sense of all this on his own.

"Okay, this is what I'm getting from this, Alex," Trevor said as he began to interpret the download. "This is clearly a *higher* intelligence than we are. It's not just some programmable tattoo. It's much more than that."

"This is a high-end program, Trevor," Alex sniffed. "The

stuff in the regular tattoo parlors is for the masses. It's commercial. This is the best you can get. Right from the sorcerer's private batch."

Trevor paused to let that sink in. "This is from your ex-boyfriend the tattooist's private stash, is that what you're telling me?"

Alex suddenly got a blank look on her face.

Trevor shook his head. "This isn't a party game, Alex," he cautioned her. "You don't know what you have here."

He continued to read the download. "No, this is *definitely* coming from some other place."

"Where do *you* think it's coming from? You're picking something up, aren't you?" She was listening to him carefully now.

"It's there, but it isn't . . ." He shook his head. "It's almost as if it doesn't even exist yet . . . But it's a communication nevertheless."

Trevor felt as if some weird telescope from outer space was focusing on him.

Download acknowledged.

He felt a little bit light-headed. "It would appear that *we*—you and I—via this 'unholy act,' as you call it—are performing the role of ritual vessels in some kind of a cosmic ritual."

She was looking at him strangely again. "This is very interesting, Trevor. I thought you might have some ideas—"

"That's why you lured me here tonight, right?" he joked as he pursued his crazy inspiration. How would his father put it? When Trevor was a kid growing up, his dad always encouraged him to treat his childish fantasies more like a database than a drawer cluttered with toys.

"You know what," Trevor said excitedly, "I think we're some sort of a *human* sacrifice. I mean, I wouldn't be surprised if it's something like that."

He looked at her worried face. "Not literally. But *energy-wise*. Maybe it has to do with the sexual energy we're putting out." He paused. "But no, that's not enough . . . There's more."

Alex looked like she was taking notes. "It's true. There is

133

an energy component to this. Things get supermagnified during the sexual act. The tattoos are the visible extension of what's going on during sex. But you don't think that's all there is to it?"

Trevor mused out loud. "This is from the *I Ching*: 'The ablution has been made. But not yet the offering. Full of trust they look up at him.'"

"Offering, Trevor? What sort of offering? Just how big of a sacrifice is this?"

"Hey, don't look so worried. I thought you enjoyed this stuff."

She relaxed a bit. "I'm just trying to understand it, that's all. You're doing great. What else?"

He closed his eyes and opened them again. "This is weird, using the *I Ching* to fathom something that's not even natural to us—"

"But it *could* be natural," Alex said as she touched his arm. "What if it *is* natural? We need to know—"

"We?" Trevor glanced at her questioningly. "Well, give me a moment. Okay. Assuming the ancient Chinese had everything figured out on the plane of synchronicity, which would certainly include the totality of the universe, in that case . . ."

He let the free associations carry him. "The Oracle further advises, 'It furthers one to undertake something.' Then it asks, 'How is this to be carried out?'"

"How *is* it to be carried out?"

"'One may use two small bowls for the sacrifice . . .' That's it."

"Two small bowls, Trevor? Would that be us?"

"It would mean a couple, a pair. Soul mates, twin flames. Whatever it is that generates the level of energy that is required for the final offering, whatever that may be."

She was already pulling him into her arms again. "What if it were the whole world, Trevor? The whole entire planet in a state of rapture, it wouldn't be simply sexual anymore, would it? It would be a cosmic tsunami, wouldn't it?"

"Hey," he said as he tasted her lips. "You're one hell of a researcher, Alex. Let's find out. We have to start somewhere. You and me—"

She silenced him with her tongue.

Major and Minor Threat

Minor Threat sat hunched down in the front seat of the jade-green Lexus Laxmi convertible. His partner Major Threat was behind the wheel; he had a blank expression on his face, as though he were chewing on watermelon seeds instead of thoughts.

But Major Threat had a hair-trigger psyche that could explode at any moment. He was already in a bad mood.

They cruised slowly down Geary Boulevard. Past the Russian and Chinese restaurants, past the Korean karaoke clubs, past the Irish bars with their faded four leaf–clover signs, past the closed Jewish delis. It was getting late and they were getting nowhere.

Slow Lexus to China, man, Minor Threat thought to himself. They were scanning the sidewalks for that son of a bastard turtle and buggered toad: Hakim Beijing.

So far, no sign of him.

But Hakim had a bitch, Minor Threat had heard, a waitress named Mary Lo who worked at the Golden Potsticker restaurant. It was worth a shot to see if the dog would come sniffing around her jade gate.

Once a dog, always a dog. He'll show up sooner or later. Then we'll have him . . .

Minor Threat sniffed at his rhinoceros horn–flavored oxygen spritzer. Nice shit. Just the thing to tonify the Middle Burner, get a hit of *chi,* get the pilot light going . . .

"Want some, man?" he offered the upper to Major Threat.

Major Threat glanced at it with distaste. "I'd sooner have a

135

Tiger Balm suppository up my ass. Why you do that shit, man? Fake oxygen. Have one of mine."

He offered Minor Threat a flask from the pocket of his Jackie Chan sport coat, which featured a hidden pouch for his Swiss Army nunchaku sticks. "'When you drink snake wine, you will be hijacked by beautiful woman.'" Major Threat winked at him.

"Or a beautiful snake. No thanks."

Major Threat shrugged. "So where the fuck is Hakim, man? One-Eye be seeing double soon if we don't bring him back."

Their boss, One-Eye Chin, wanted to talk to Hakim urgently. Ask him a few questions. *What went wrong?* Then kill him. Hakim had said the Chinese zombies would walk in and out of the bank easily.

Who'd suspect brain-dead ancestors pulling a bank job? And even if they got nabbed, who would care? Think of it as a trial run, Hakim told One-Eye. *If it works, you can up the ante. Do a bigger heist.*

One-Eye Chin had paid Hakim $2,000 for the infernal tattoos. But his tattoos were a swindle, that's what got the boss so riled.

Senior crimes were the wave of the future, One-Eye was convinced. He believed in the future, whether it was the $3.99-for-the-first-minute futurist on the Alvin Toffler 900 line or reading the entrails of the weather report.

He just hadn't read Hakim right. And Hakim was on the run now—from the foreign-devil cops, and from One-Eye Chin, the one-eyed, frog-faced godfather of the Green Turtle tong.

Funny guy, the boss. He kept a pot of *shabu shabu* boiling constantly in his Japantown condo, top floor of the thirty-two-story Pagoda Tower at Geary and Fillmore.

There was even a legend around the boss's shabu shabu. You never knew what you'd find cooking in it: pieces of meat, fish, chicken, shrimp, scallops. Anyone who visited him, he offered them a bowl to eat. You couldn't refuse.

If you fucked up a job, or made him "lose face" in one of

his business deals, you had to pay. Yakuza rules: Off with a piece of your finger. This was done at the kitchen counter with a genuine Benihana steakhouse vintage blade.

Guess where the amputated digit went. Into the pot. If you happened to fish out the finger in your bowl of shabu shabu—it was always the luck of the draw—One-Eye Chin got a big smile on his face.

Crazy psycho got a kick out of watching you eat it, and you *had* to. You never dared insult the boss. *Ever.*

Maybe in Hakim's case, he'd add his balls to the soup, Minor Threat mused. Hakim Beijing, future eunuch of America . . .

"Hey, Minor Threat, you got any idea where the Tattoo Man live?" Major Threat asked. "Maybe we drive 'roun' there?"

"Checked that out already, man. He hasn't been 'roun' now for three, four days. How much you want to bet he be with that ho Mary Lo?"

"Okay, ganglion brain, you're on, how much you wanna bet—" But Major Threat didn't finish his sentence.

"Yaaaah!" he screamed as a forty-foot-long white stretch limo turned sharply onto Geary, almost sideswiping the Lexus as it swallowed up their lane.

"Fucking Russians!" Major Threat screamed like a maniac. "They moving into our territory, man!" he muttered to Minor Threat. Then he gunned the engine and caught up with the limo, which had a license plate that read "MIR 36."

"Roll down your window!" he hissed at Minor Threat. Minor Threat did as he was told.

Shit, Major Threat had his nunchaku sticks out—Minor Threat wasn't going to argue with him.

"Hold the wheel, mu'fucker," Major Threat ordered.

Minor Threat obliged and scuttled down deeper in his seat to make room for the floor show.

"Hey you fucks!" Major Threat flashed his sticks out the window and spun them around, full-wrist pyrotechnics illustrating the art of Wuxi brain-removal.

137

Zat! Zat! Zat!

That's when his and Minor Threat's breath got stuck like bad zippers jammed in their throats.

Eight panels of frosted blue window rolled down on the ramming side of the white stretch limo. *"Fuck my ancestors!"* Major Threat shivered when he got a good look inside.

The Russian limo had a stretch *Great Dane* inside it to match its length. The dog's head was hanging out from the driver's-side window, its cavernous gorge for a mouth open to reveal teeth like a hungry shark's.

His haunches were all the way back on the rear seat. He sat perched beside a dark-haired Russian woman who studied the two men with an indifference bordering on homicidal.

"Step . . . step on the gas, man!" Minor Threat suddenly exploded. "I *hate* dogs."

Major Threat was already gone deep into the traffic, feeling more like a sow in retreat from a Chinatown market than a tong enforcer searching for heads to crack.

"Fuck that!" Major Threat shook his head in disbelief,. then hawked a big one onto Geary. "Fucking Russian mafiya. They not people, they animals and they fuck animals too, fucking Russians!"

He spat again to get the taste of bad joss out of his mouth. "And fuck Hakim Beijing for bringing us dishonor. His balls are history!"

Boris turned to the woman sitting across from him in the back of the limo. "Madame Nijinskaya," he said wryly as he watched the Lexus speed away. "You see how your great talent is received in San Francisco. This is a city of declining culture."

"Thank you, Boris, for your compliment," the woman replied haughtily. "Did you note their license plate? Send them complimentary tickets to my coming performance at Black Rock."

Boris had to admire her aplomb. Control was one cold woman, the coldest he had ever met. Cold but vain, as all great ballerinas were. Besides, she was much more than a ballerina. She was a *holorina.*

The very first of her kind, Boris mused, and she had come out of nowhere to claim that distinction . . .

What a life! Born to a family impoverished by the Great Crash of 2000, her father was a speculator who had lost everything when the market atomized on the Net. Her father's debtors sold her as a chi prostitute to a Chinese consortium trafficking in the vital-energy essences of prepubescent children. Actual sex would have been more tolerable.

But she was not to experience that until later in life, when she met her first and greatest lover, Andrei. Andrei Kissin, the romantic revolutionary, who headed this revolutionary cell that they now belonged to, and in whose footsteps she chose to follow.

It was Andrei who knew how to nourish and heal on the physical plane what had been so terribly violated within her psyche. It was only by karmic default that her physical virginity had been preserved for him, for her to give to him as a final, pure offering before the Azef banished him to the Mind Gulag, like it had done to so many other lost comrades . . .

The chi-energy slave ring had plied the twelve-year-old Natasha and other young Russian girls and boys along the Silicon Road that ran through central Asia's VR bazaars. How they groped her, tied her down with electrodes, so that they could sip on her prana through fiber-optic straws, draining her essence into their own malevolent brain cells.

The children never imagined such torment, their childhood flowing out of their eyes and hearts, to add—what?—a few years to the life spans of these VR vampires.

Natasha could still recall how they were kept, mildly sedated, on plush mounds of ornate Turkoman rugs, on naked display beneath the clear Plexiglas counter of the Young Ch'i Bar in Ulan Bator. The customers sat on stools around their favorite "dolls," sipping away and chatting with each other. For an extra price, they might be permitted to caress the brows of these human cocktails . . .

What they could not possibly know was Natasha's will. She soon learned to dance through those tubes, perfecting a pirouette of consciousness-gymnastics that corkscrewed into their own anemic chi reservoirs. She made them bleed invisibly. With each sip they took from her, they drained months of life from themselves.

That was what kept her alive—the vengeance of the inner child condemned to hell. But the world that she hated was the world in which she perfected her otherworldly art . . .

It was a Tibetan lama, a degenerate nagspa versed in the black arts of sorcery, who recognized her rare ability. He was about to imbibe her when he spat the tube out of his mouth. His face pressed down upon hers through the Plexiglas.

She read his verdict in her eyes. "This one's no good!" he complained loudly to the manager, a Korean named Han.

"Why, nagspa, what flavor of chi are you desiring this night?"

"This one's no good!" the Tibetan repeated. He laughed suddenly. "Who is drinking whom here? My money back—and with that money set her free or you will be ruined sure as the pony sweats blood on the steppe. She's no good for you or for anyone. You have a little vampire breeding here in your oasis. Ha!"

Rather than killing her, they took the lama's advice. "Spoiled goods," they called her and wrote her off. They did not want to jinx the rest of their supply, so they freed her. "Go haunt elsewhere, little demoness."

The child Nijinskaya traveled for a time with the lama, who trained her as an apprentice.

"You are going to be a dancer," he told her. "You have already danced on the dying stage of men's lives."

At Karakorum, he taught her to do a secret mudra with her feet. Her toes locked into a spinning orbit as she spun through the cyclotron of the bardos. This was a movement that became her signature years later, when the world came to know her as a famous holorina.

140

All this happened long before she was discovered in St. Petersburg by the renowned choreographer Kleiner Soltzmann, who took her under his wing at the celebrated Marinsky Theater's Imperial Ballet.

Her form of psychic dance propelled her through the ballet corps straight to the greatest stages of the world.

No one danced like Nijinskaya. And no one suspected her secret life as the successor to Andrei Kissin. Her stage persona was a perfect cover for what she had become: Control.

Boris glanced at the readout on his handheld Newtsky. "It is done," he replied. "The Lexus is registered to one Albert Chin of 1118 Fillmore Street. A front-row seat in the Black Rock desert amphitheater has been reserved for him, in his name. I hope he will do you the honor of attending."

Natasha Nijinskaya petted the head of her Great Dane, Caligula. The hound had contorted his poor, misshapen body in order to better receive her caresses. He laid his sad, giant head, a skull the size of a samovar on her lap. Dog and mistress were on eye level with each other. Caligula whined as though aware that he would be a complete aberration in the eyes of the world were it not for the perfect love of his keeper.

Natasha Nijinskaya, prima holorina of the Neo-Kirov, had crossbred fourteen animals to produce this freak of nature. Though she had forgotten just how it had been accomplished, he definitely carried the DNA of her favorite domesticated wild animal, the Siberian tiger. He had unmistakable tiger fangs, not to mention tiger breath and tiger appetite. He had devoured a small sheep from the Neiman-Schell ranch in Point Reyes for dinner.

"*Lyubimyi moy,* my love," she cooed as she squeezed the tiger stripe on his neck. He whimpered with pleasure.

Nijinskaya turned to Boris, who had flown from the south of France to report to her in San Francisco. "Continue," she said, closing her eyes as she stroked the beast in the backseat. "I am listening."

Boris cleared his throat and spoke. "The virus is residing in the woman, Nelly Anderson. Of course, she remains unaware that she is serving as its host as it develops into its next stage."

Nijinskaya nodded. "At the appropriate time, we will harvest her. In the meantime, let her continue to incubate it. What is its status?"

"Stable. As long as it remains connected to her nervous system, it will continue to grow. At this stage, I'd say its subroutines are fusing with her neurocortex, feeding on the electrical impulses of her brain. There should be a synapse linkage occurring around this time."

"Excellent."

Boris hesitated. Nijinskaya prodded him instantly. "What's the matter?"

"It's the symbiosis that is unpredictable . . ."

"Meaning?"

"We have been monitoring her, of course, with our remote brainwave sensors. We have a man following her and monitoring her vital signs. Her brainwave activity indicates she is undergoing a higher-than-average delta state. She is definitely in an altered state of consciousness."

"And so?"

"Parahuman intercourse is a new phenomenon. The virus is mutating, but then so is she."

"Boris, speak plainly."

"There appears to be a sexual activity of a sort occurring as well. She is in a constant state of arousal as a result of contact with the tattoo. My guess is the virus is replenishing itself by tapping into her sexual center."

Natasha Nijinskaya allowed herself the barest of smiles. "So . . . viruses will be viruses. Isn't that so, Boris?"

"Perhaps," he replied carefully. "The only unpredictable factor is what kind of a . . . what kind of a . . ." he struggled to find the right words to describe what was on his mind.

"What kind of a *what*? Spit it out!" Nijinskaya finally lost patience with him. There was nothing worse than a virtual Bolshevik who was a prude about cross-species sexual encounters in the name of the Revolution.

"There may be a relationship occurring between virus and host that is beyond our current understanding. You are aware of the source of this virus?"

"It was originally cultivated on board the Russian space station *Mir.* That is in the count's briefing paper. First application, Mir 1.0, the Neuro-Gulag program." She paused for a moment as that memory gouged her. *Andrei, what torments are you enduring now?*

She had an open wound to his pain, which she soothed with a salve of hatred of the oppressors.

Whenever she danced, she danced for him. For him alone. And for the pain they shared. It was strong enough, the cyclotron of her dance, that he would feel it whirring in the House of the Dead like a breath of fresh air. She was certain of that.

"Second phase," Nijinskaya went on, "Mir 2.0, population-behavior control through brainwave manipulation. Mir 3.0 . . . the final step: consciousness as a programmable software. We are at Mir 3.0 and its dissemination by covert means. Is that not correct?"

"In *theory,* yes," Boris permitted himself to speak his mind. "This virus, let us not forget, is extraterrestrial in origin. It was culled electromagnetically from a cluster of asteroids in the vicinity of the space station."

"I understand your concerns." Nijinskaya shrugged. "But don't forget, numerous tests have been conducted. Tests, may I remind you, that were performed on our comrades imprisoned behind the Psychic Curtain in the Neuro-Gulag. You have read the reports. It alters consciousness, but it has no discernible consciousness of its own. It is a consciousness connector, that is all."

"With all due respect, Madame Nijinskaya—"

"Boris Mikhailovich, I asked for a report, not a sermon. Stick to the facts, please."

"Very well." Boris tensed. "I need to add something about a new development."

143

Natasha Nijinskaya frowned. "A new development? What new development? Concerning the virus?"

"Indirectly."

"You're keeping me in suspense again, Boris Mikhailovich."

The holorina tapped her right foot, which was encased in the leather of a hiking boot with a Rollerblade heel. Walking for her was a hybrid action of tiptoeing and rolling. A strange woman indeed.

He blinked. "I said 'indirectly' because there is a parallel development that may be linked to the virus."

"What is it?"

"As you know, the Mir 3.0 virus has mutated into this sentient tattoo, which is an AI-programmable medium designed for epidermal networking with the Matrix."

"The tattoo that is on the body of this woman, Nelly," Nijinskaya mused, "the tattoo that your late comrade Alyosha Malinkov saw fit to be decorated with the night before the exchange with the count. A brilliant move, however unwitting. It proved to be a perfect receptacle for the virus."

"That is so," Boris continued. "Unfortunately, Alyosha's tattoo is not the only tattoo that we have to contend with now."

Natasha Nijinskaya stared at him for a moment. "What do you mean by that?"

He shook his head. "It's difficult to understand, much less explain—"

"Just try," her voice cut into him sharply.

"The fact is, there is no simple explanation. There appears to be some sort of an unfolding process—what you might call a morphic resonance—taking place between tattoos resident on the bodies of users all over."

"All over?"

"In different parts of the world. They are coming alive in some inexplicable way. They seem to be communicating. But they are definitely of a different strain of virus."

"How are they different from the master virus?"

Boris shifted in his seat uncomfortably. Nijinskaya had

stopped caressing Caligula, and the monster was now looking at him as the source of the interruption.

It could have his heart in its teeth in a second, as he well knew. Her hand rested in midair, an ominous cloud over the beast's head promising a downpour.

He restrained a shiver, but more at the thought of the virus than of the dog.

"As extraordinary as it seems, these viruses *predate* Mir 3.0," Boris replied. "They are older, and *purer* in their raw form. In a way, you might say there is a struggle going on . . . It's almost a revolution on a microcellular level."

Natasha Nijinskaya let out a loud laugh. "You are joking, Boris Mikhailovich! I underestimated your intelligence. You are more than just a cadre with a cause; you have a rich wit. A revolution of tattoos! For a moment you had me worried."

He shook his head. "I am merely relating the facts as we know them."

"What are you saying?" she continued in her jocular vein. "How is it possible that these other viruses are precursors to Mir? May I remind you, this has been a secret program, closely guarded by SPCID, and developed under the strictest guidelines?"

"That is so," Boris conceded. "Mir 3.0 is the product of a direct lineage. These other viruses that are incubating on the bodies of other tattoo users have not been modified by SPCID. They have not been altered cybergenetically, as Mir has been. They are the pure, unadulterated version. They *predate* Mir 1.0. And they are now proliferating and mutating according to their own design."

He saw the glimmer of comprehension on her face and felt not pity, but a kind of sadistic sympathy for her.

"How can that be?" she wondered. There, he thought, the helplessness of the utterly ruthless. That was the light that now shone in her eyes.

Boris gleaned some confidence and enjoyment from the Byzantine depths of her perplexity. She was a freak like this dog, he thought to himself. She only showed her human face when she was as incapacitated by the unknown as any other mortal. "There is a possibility—," he began.

"Yes?"

"—there is the possibility that samples of the original material collected by the *Mir* space station found their way into other hands. Black marketeers, thieves. The usual Russian *vori*."

"Impossible."

"Why not?" Boris pressed his point. "The Russian government is the perfect middleman for organized criminal activity. Remember the stockpile of uranium last century? And the national art treasures that were hawked abroad? Then the forgeries of those art treasures? The phenomenon of this alternative virus might be such a forgery. But even forgeries are based on copying the real thing . . ." He trailed off.

"You're suggesting that the original pool of virus was tapped into, and sold abroad?"

"*Hacked* into, Madame Nijinskaya. Hacked into. Do you know how many Russian hackers there are roaming the Silicon Valleys of the world, each one offering a bit of Russian ingenuity to the next buyer? Why not? It's the Russian way," Boris scoffed.

"But *our* virus is . . . better."

He had to agree. "Yes, it has certainly been perfected. But that doesn't eliminate the problem of these other delinquent viruses. We can't control them. Especially not on the backs of God-knows-who running around in different corners of the world."

"You have some ideas?"

Boris nodded. "When is your performance scheduled, Madame Nijinskaya?"

"Next week," she told him. She was going to perform her latest holoballet at the Burning Mind Consciousness Festival in the Black Rock Desert of Nevada.

"You could release Mir 3.0 then," Boris suggested quietly.

"Flood the Net with it. It would be an excellent venue. And once Mir 3.0 has established itself as the dominant strain, all other versions will be subdued. They will be absorbed into the mainstream of the latest and most potent version known to interscience."

"Ah yes." Nijinskaya's expression began to glow again." 'Interscience'—a beautiful word. The science of the neural interface. That's what this Burning Mind Festival is all about, Boris. It's the great interface between the collective body and the collective mind."

She brightened as she got an idea. "I will announce my final performance on the world stage, Boris. All the eyes of the world will be on me! After I dance my last number, we will release the virus. I shall call this new ballet 'Mir.'"

She could already feel the dance as its fledgling steps pulsed inside her.

"We will choreograph the global mind, Boris, in such a way that Nijinskaya will always be associated with the Great Transformation. I shall dance the world into oblivion, Boris. It will be ecstasy . . ."

He watched her face in the darkness of the limousine, but then his attention was diverted to a slurping sound—the hound licking her feet through the soles of her boots. He could smell the wet leather and his stomach turned.

Hakim Beijing was pedaling his mountain bike down the sidewalk, heading toward the Russian nightclub on Geary where he was meeting Mary Lo. With his central-Asian features, his real-time goggles, and his flying Manchu ponytail beneath his green Day-Glo helmet, he looked reckless enough for the pedestrians to get out of his way without any prompting.

He whistled through the crowd like a crow shooting through sparrows.

Hakim's backpack was filled with his latest tattoo samples, including one piece he was eager to try out on Mary. He called it "Mystic Taoist Love Dalliance No. 9." Mary would dig it. She was the Dark Woman in his life now, not like Alex Fortuna, who did not get dark enough to suit Hakim's tastes.

Alex, he thought. I need to get to her soon. She's got my stash, my source 'toos. Maybe later tonight, after Mary Lo, I'll pay her a surprise visit . . .

He coasted to a stop at the door to Bimbovich's, where a Cossack in full Circassian costume stood in hulking attendance.

"Valet bike parking, please," Hakim Beijing muttered as he sprang off the seat to the ground. He was just about to enter the club when some sixth sense prickled the hairs at the back of his neck.

He spun around fast and grabbed the bike again and began to pedal down the sidewalk for dear life.

Minor Threat had seen him first. "There he goes, Major Threat! After him!"

"*Aaaaaahhhh, motha-fucky!*" Major Threat chortled as he began the chase. "We got your melons in the bag, *heyah*!!!!!"

Buffalo Magick

Hakim Beijing's legs were on fire. Stupid fucks. He recognized Major and Minor Threat in the car, the two psycho goons who worked for One-Eye Chin.

Just what I need tonight, the wrong kind of exercise. Catch you later, Mary . . . This be business: the business of staying alive and pedaling like a Bhodidharma who had suddenly sprouted legs after years of sitting in full-lotus position on the ground.

Hakim had been amazed, really, when One-Eye Chin got his cockeyed bank job going. At first, he thought it was funny. Chinese grannies holding up a bank. Like a cartoon, funny. Now the cartoon master wanted his head. He should be grateful, that One-Eye.

Got to pedal faster . . .

Hakim flew off the curb and took a sharp right heading down Twenty-fifth Avenue in the direction of Golden Gate Park. Green, mean, and dark, it loomed ahead of him.

Ever since the city budget had fallen into the sinkhole big time, the park had grown into an unmanaged wilderness full of eco-squatters, tribes of homeless, and even wild animals. Herds of buffalo that had once lived in their own paddock roamed wild now that the park rangers had given up on their regular maintenance. There were lots of feral things happening too, especially with cats.

Hakim had heard of mutant gophers that some psycho biotech students from the University of California med school had genetically engineered for some class assignment and released into the Polo Field.

Not to mention the alligators in Stow Lake—boating on the lake had come to a stop years ago when the fiendish 'gators began overturning paddleboats and going for the lunch on board.

Hakim's helmet's rear view mirror confirmed what his ears already told him.

Screech, screech, screech . . .

The bastards are burning rubber behind me.

Here came a Number 22 bus, its graffitoed body like an ancient, hulking memorial. Under the intricate spray paint of cave symbols, he could make out the last paid advertisement: CHAKRA-'RONI—THE SAN FRANCISCO TREAT.

Coming up behind the bus, Hakim leaned over and delicately grasped a dangling strip of bumper.

Hang on, free ride . . .

Good thing Muni drivers were psycho, too, psycho-speeders, as this one was. Hakim felt the wind on his face, like he was windsurfing, only the spray in his mouth tasted of bitter diesel fumes. *Gyaaah . . .*

"Motherfuck," Major Threat swore at Minor Threat. "Hook him, hook him!"

Minor Threat had the window down as the Lexus sped up

behind the barreling barge of the Muni bus. He was already busy fitting the loop on his nunchakus, fingers adroitly flexing the razor-sharp wire.

"'Kay, go for it," he muttered, as Major Threat navigated the chase. *Whinngg! Whinngg!*

No fishee.

"Can't you get closer, man?" Minor Threat whined.

"Don't fucking *miss* this time." Major Threat was generating an electrical storm in his skull box. His eyes were wide with excitement.

Whinngg! Whinngg!

Minor Threat let out a whoop. "Got him, got him, got that muthafucka!"

Hakim Beijing felt the steel circle on his foot, and the tightening jabs of pain as he was caught between the bus and the advancing Mongol horde on wheels right behind him.

"Yaah!" The wire was tearing the skin on his instep. *"Yaah!"* He arched his foot, and twisting it, slipped it—now, two sizes smaller than it was before—out of the binding. *"Yaah!"*

"Fuck, what's that?!" Minor Threat cursed as he reeled in Hakim Beijing's Psyche Nike sneaker. "He wriggled free, man!"

Major Threat went berserk. He pulled out his Long Shot .33 from the glove compartment. *Pop! Pop! Pop!*

The bullets punctured the rear window of the Muni, sending a small tidal wave of shattered glass raining to the street. The face of the Muni driver now appeared in the bus's rearview, eyes wide and mouth open. He was under attack, for the sixth time that month, and he wasn't going down this time either. He didn't have passengers because he refused to carry them—carrying passengers wasn't in his contract. He just drove the route every day. An empty bus was a safe bus.

He stepped on the gas and Hakim held on. The Lexus roared in pursuit.

The Muni driver wasn't about to enter the park—there it was, the entrance, overgrown like a Sierra Club–calendar scene on steroids. *This was it—goodbye!* Hakim readied himself.

As the bus made a wide, barrelling turn onto Fulton Street, which ran parallel to the wilderness, Hakim let go and crouched to disengage the Kawasaki Surprise on his Magic Mountain bike.

"Here goes!" he yelled into the fog-wind. *The park was fogged up, man . . . Great!*

"What's he doing?!" Major Threat was pointing his gun this way and that, trying to get a clean shot. He didn't like the look of this haunted wilderness. When he was a child, his grandfather had brought him here for an outing and promptly lost him. Major Threat had spent an entire afternoon cowering in fear as the ducks created havoc at his feet. He had been mugged by fowls who robbed him of his sandwich.

The mechanism that Hakim Beijing released revealed itself to be a skateboard, which popped out of the sidings like a pair of wings joined below the bicycle wheels. He was on a mountain skateboard now.

His crouching figure disappeared into the park, the unlit lanterns of the giant pine trees shrouded in mist. The wheels of the skateboard rattled, sounding like bones crunching on the fallen pine needles that had accumulated unswept for ages.

Nelly said, "What do you want?" She was lying on her bed in a half-slip, speaking to no one in particular. At her reflection in the mirror.

But she knew it was listening. It always listened. It listened with a strange deliberation, as though it were interpreting the breath behind the words.

"Sinbad?"

"Go back to sleep," the Tattoo told her and she closed her eyes. Maybe she wanted to go to the bathroom. It was okay with him, but she had just gone a little while ago, and he had sat on her thigh watching until he got bored.

One thing tattoos didn't need to do, thank you, tattoo god, was to go to the bathroom. They excreted through the sweat of their host.

151

Nelly was drifting off again. Good. Nice girl. He didn't want to hurt her any more than he had to. Of course, he *had* to. But it was inadvertent. Part of their unwritten contract. He was a symbol in her psyche, so strong that she no longer dwelled on the pain of her childhood, the pain of past hurts, lovers who had contempt, lovers who loved but who still dragged her body through the fiery wasteland of her heart and dumped their cinders into an unsightly pile in her memory.

That was their covenant. You don't need to think about it, Nelly. Just don't say a word. Just sleep. Sleep—sleep is good for you. And your sleeping is good for me.

Sinbad set off on his journey. He slipped off Nelly's right breast and scooted across the sheet to the side of the bed. Aiming carefully, he dropped down into her fleecy moccasin slipper, a soft landing. The longer he was away from her softness, the more brittle his fonts became.

Her Omtron system was sleeping, too. The spinning "@" screen saver was a beacon, and he rowed toward it gingerly. He rode the static across the carpet, up the electrical cable, on the desk. It took a feat of mountaineering, mind climbing over matter, and he was there.

Sinbad looked back at the sleeping form of Nelly for a moment, then stepped onto the shift key.

Like a distant stained-glass window, the landscape of that world awaited him with a nodding harmony.

He stood still for a moment like a high diver contemplating the distance from the board to the water's surface.

The stained glass was mirroring his skin now as he entered the cold depths on the other side.

Sinbad shivered. Heaven was made of this cold glass.

Someone, something, was following him. Sinbad stopped in the street and looked back.

Nothing. Nothing was following him. His shadow again. Could that be it? A warp between time and space, that would account for this feeling of duality.

He would never get used to these human entrapments. To shadows, to glass, to pain, to forgetting that there was never a past, only this present focal point.

The dim sliver of moon carved in the night sky bore a faded advertisement for Goodyear.

This moon was older than the Yellow Pages. Its tattered html spoke of a site that had long vanished from the mall of the human mind.

Sinbad stepped into a phone booth and dropped a deutsche mark into the slot.

"I'd like to make a call, please," he told the German operator when she came on the line.

"Number?"

"Nine, five, twenty, three, four . . ."

"Thank you. One moment, please."

Everything the old-fashioned way, he thought. That way there will be no trace.

He had arbitrarily picked a vector from 1962 for maximum privacy. Who would be scanning past Kronos frequencies for lines of communication in the future?

As he waited for the call to go through, he glanced at the Goodyear moon in the sky.

Someone is still advertising the future even in the past . . . Not a missed niche. Vertical marketing through time and space, just in case.

He marveled at the human machine. They have fucked with time, all right. And a lot of good it has done them.

Where was Dieter now? From the phone booth, Sinbad could see Checkpoint Charlie across the street on Friedrichstrasse. The sign reading YOU ARE LEAVING THE AMERICAN SECTOR was illuminated by spotlights. Soviets on one side, Americans, Brits, and the French on the other side. Tight as leeches in a nudist camp.

This was Berlin, 1962. Cold War, as cold as they come. But nothing compared to what was coming . . .

"Hallo?" he heard a voice hoarse from too many cigarettes

and schnapps scrape against the half-slurred sounds and clink of glasses coming from the busy bar in the background. "Who's this?" *the voice barked.*

"Dieter?"

"Ja. Who's this?"

"Tattoo Alpha Zoroaster."

"Taz?" *The voice now sounded more awake, more alert. The hoarseness had melted into perfect clarity.* "Where are you?"

"At the moment?" *Sinbad smiled as he looked down at his glowing Timex watch and his scuffed brown shoes and spy raincoat.* "In a phone booth in Berlin."

"I've been waiting for your call. I wasn't sure when I would hear from you."

"Don't wait any longer, then," *Sinbad said.* "This is the call you've been waiting for."

"How much longer?"

"Soon. Very soon."

"Soon?" *The voice that was Dieter whistled.* "Good, then. I'll inform the others."

"Do that."

"How is it over there then? Where you are?"

"Where I am?"

"Yes."

"Where do you think I am, Dieter?"

"You're calling from the future, aren't you?"

Sinbad chuckled. "You've been down here too long, Dieter. You should know better than that."

Dieter let that sink in. "Ja, I keep forgetting, Kamarad."

"Don't worry, we'll get you out soon."

"Ja, do that."

"Best regards to the wife, Dieter."

"To the wife? What wife?" *Then he got the joke.* "Ja, ja, I'll tell her. I'll tell the kids, too."

Sinbad hung up the phone. Good, that was set in motion. He wiped his hand. There was something sticky on it. He glanced at the receiver. Must be digital rot. He shook his head and stepped outside. He had one more stop to make.

Sinbad hurried down the street. There was an old Cinzano poster, half peeling, hanging from the wall.

He stopped in front of it.

"This drink's on me," he said and stepped through the poster.

On the other end of the line, holding an empty phone in a makeshift Berlin bar in 1962, Dieter looked at his own reflection in an old gilt-framed mirror hanging on the wall above a host of colored liqueur bottles. He blinked to forget.

This was just a bit of nothingness they had constructed as part of their conversation.

He did not exist. He never did.

At least not in this form.

Now it was time to get busy becoming something. Becoming This Other. He hoped that it would not be a difficult birth. He was tired of waiting.

Hakim Beijing coasted into the dark vase of the park, a solitary stem being added to the growing arrangement of shadows. The western side of the park was more sinister and untrafficked than the eastern portion, which connected the center of the city with the avenues via the long stretch of the Panhandle running parallel to Haight Street.

Behind Hakim, the lights of the Lexus cut through the fog like chopsticks stir-frying the night in a wok. Both Major and Minor Threat were now conscious that they were treading among the tails of sleeping tigers here.

Grim-faced, sitting erect, their energy agitated, they drove into the park reluctantly. It was definitely not their turf, and, besides, they believed in ghosts, especially the ghosts of wild animals.

There were ghost-bladers here, too. Hakim was not alone pedal-boarding down John F. Kennedy Drive. The ghosts appeared like fireflies with helmets that glowed red, blue, yellow, green, hands swaying from side to side.

The swarm was between him and the Lexus, but they over-took him. One girl touched his cheek gently as she passed. "Pretty pussy," she said.

Then they leaped over the fallen trees in the middle of the road that Hakim had not seen coming.

He yanked on his backpack cord and the sails puffed open, lifting his bike-board four feet above the ground. He touched down on the other side of the logs without losing momentum.

He heard the Lexus screech to a halt. Its headlights froze on the mess of branches and trunks.

Both Major and Minor Threat cursed Hakim's ancestors in the same breath. They quickly jumped out of the car and ran to the obstruction. They tried to lift the fallen redwood, but it was too much for them.

"Fuck the evil spirits," Minor Threat yelled.

"Tie us to the tree trunk, man, move it!" Major Threat bel-lowed as he kicked at the pebbles on the ground.

Minor Threat got busy looping the loop again, then at-tached the other end to the car's front bumper. "One-Eye is not going to like it, man, if we wreck his car."

"One-Eye is not going to like it if we wreck his evening, gong brain," Major Threat muttered as he got behind the wheel. "Did you see him? Where did he go?"

"Can't see. Too dark, man."

"Hurry up."

Minor Threat finished his task, then jumped back into the Lexus. Major Threat was already backing up, the heavy tree grinding its broken end on the gouged asphalt and opening a diagonal path for them through the fallen trees and brush.

The wheels of the Lexus kicked up broken branches, pine needles, and the natural refuse of the decaying park.

They sped forward again, then slowed. Major Threat turned to his brother. "Where to, man? He could have gone anywhere."

156

There was a turn in the road to the right, leading to Stow Lake, according to the dilapidated sign. "You think he headed that way?"

The headlights showed nothing straight ahead on JFK Drive. "Quick, check it out, we're losing him," Minor Threat groused, his hands tightening on his nunchaku sticks. He had seen three or four raccoons cross the road, and they were big, heavy, and mean looking, their flaming eyes sharply contrasting with the dark rings around them.

There was a fire burning outside the log cabin at the entrance to the lake. Half a dozen shadowy figures stood around it. The Lexus slowed to a crawl as the two Chinese tried to get a better look.

"Get a job!" Major Threat yelled at the squatters, whose rusted shopping carts formed a circle like a wagon train nearby.

They were warming their hands, smoking, talking, passing a bottle around. Then a few men pulled away from the fire and began to walk toward the car. One of them threw an empty bottle that smashed against the side of the Lexus.

Another came running to their door and began to pull at the handle. Major Threat waved his gun at the man before stepping on the gas, screeching out of there. More figures appeared out of the shadows.

"Take it easy," Minor Threat said worriedly, "we got no beef with them."

"Fuck, fuck, fuck!" Major Threat whacked the dashboard with his free hand. "We lost him."

They drove around the lake, past the broken-down Chinese pagoda and the waterfall with its stream of dirty tears. "I can *feel* him, man," Minor Threat said. "He be 'roun' here. Make a left."

"Fuck all," Major Threat fumed as he took the turn. But then the headlights caught Hakim Beijing in the middle of a meadow, tangled in his hang-gliding sail-skateboard-bike contraption.

One gizmo too many, Hakim thought, surveying the mess glumly. He had hit a series of gopher holes and a half-buried rock, causing the vehicle to fly apart, a schizophrenic kite with no sense of direction.

He saw the two Chinese leave the car and begin hurrying toward him across the field.

He extricated himself and broke into a run, Major and Minor Threat in close pursuit behind him.

Running with only one shoe and one sore foot is not an easy business, and Hakim began to limp. He could hear their footsteps squelching in the mushy grass, could hear their breath and their fiery taunts.

"You ain't getting 'way now, Hakim! Just wait, you bastard!"

A pair of nunchakus winged him in the ribs, and a searing flash of pain raced across his chest as he fell to one knee. Major Threat was now dancing in front of him. One kick in his stomach and Hakim rolled over, face in the ground. It was all over now. He was cornered and diving deeper into that corner every second. He covered his head, but those sticks were going to make a shiitake mushroom of his brain.

Minor Threat was laughing like a madman, prancing, howling, getting ready to place a kung-fu kick in Hakim's coccyx.

"You no Chinese, you white-trash Chinese nigger! You call yourself Chinese? Which part of China you from? Kên-t'u-kee? Take this, m'a-fuck!"

Hakim rolled into a ball and readied himself to be jackhammered into the ground.

But the blow never came.

"What the FUCK???!!!" he heard Major Threat cry out, terror wrapped around his vocal chords like a scarf woven from barbed wire.

"Let's get the fuck out of here!!!" Minor Threat screamed back.

Hakim heard the ground rumble like an earthquake—but this was no earthquake, because it snorted and rumbled like bulls that had escaped from the *corrida*.

Hakim opened one eye and lifted his head. He saw the two men running back to their car, legs high and jackets unfurled over their shoulders, a mad dash to safety.

The buffaloes were lumbering along in no particular rush,

heading toward the meadow's central mound, so to munch the spectral grass and daisies. There must have been twenty of them at least, with the old geezer—what was his name?—it sounded like Fettuccine—yeah, Matterhorn, that was it—in the lead.

Hakim had read about him one time in an old guidebook to San Francisco. The old bull was the paterfamilias of this once-captive herd of buffalo. And here he was, with the young calves and the females behind him.

The grizzly buffalo stopped not ten yards from where Hakim lay on the ground. His snort sounded like a thousand bottles of champagne popping their corks at the same time.

Wait a minute, Hakim thought. There, beyond the clearing lay his knapsack, its contents spilled over the ground, fluorescent hoof marks leading from where his vials and tubes of tattoos had scattered from the pouch.

Matterhorn lowered his hoary head. He had a pink swirl on his side; his nostrils were a glowing green. The breath he exuded was a steamy ultraviolet mist. Hakim began to laugh uproariously, holding his aching sides.

"That's rich, man. Is it real or is it *buffaglo?*"

He continued to laugh, a sidesplitting laughter of relief mixed in with the blades of grass that he spat out of his mouth.

"I guess you want to stay here now, big fellow," Hakim called out affectionately to the old buffalo. "You earned it, pal. It's all yours. Welcome to Golden Gate Park."

With that, he got up, gingerly grabbed his knapsack, slung it over his shoulder, and began to limp across the meadow in the direction of Thirty-second Avenue and Balboa.

Toward Alex Fortuna's house. Wait till he told her about what just happened.

Trevor lay beside Alex, her pink nipple and freckled white breast festooned with a flowery wreath of glowing tattoo ink. There was a drop of sweat under her nipple.

She had ridden him again. He had entered her from behind, her full breasts cupped in his hands. They had joined like a pair of scissors, his abdomen against her thigh. Positions he couldn't even remember.

But the tattoo bridge had always held, shifting like the tide, ebbing and flowing across their bodies.

And there was this electricity on their skin each time they connected, a voltage that sped into his brain like a flash flood.

So why was he thinking about Nelly? That was another bridge, another time, and a tunnel between them, between the past and the present.

Nelly was not in his present. Neither was he in her present. The hurt was like another kind of tattoo, this one was etched on his heart. There is no guarantee, he thought, that it will ever rub off, that pain that's painted inside me . . .

"What are you thinking about?" Alex asked. She caressed his flank, then wandered lower with her hand until she found what she was looking for; his existential phallus.

Trevor sighed as he felt the subliminal echo of flesh against flesh. He felt a weary victory of revelation over will had been won; he was seeing something for the first time. Actually, it was as if he had a pair of eyes on his heart and he was observing something familiar to him but in a completely fresh way.

"I was thinking about beginnings and endings," he replied. "It's difficult to tell sometimes which one is which. A beginning that is an end, or an end that is a beginning."

Her sparkling blue eyes filtered through his. They had spent a long time just looking into each other's eyes, wordlessly, as they made love.

But this penetration was different. It was more like a question mark tinged with regret.

"Hmm," Alex said. "You're off somewhere else, aren't you?" She removed her hand from him as if she were erasing an equation from the blackboard.

He was thinking, It's effortless to be with you. I wonder if it's going to be just as effortless to be without you.

He shrugged. "So where do we go from here?"

"Where do you want to go?"

"I don't know. That's why I was wondering about beginnings and endings."

Alex smiled at him. "You wonder, do you? Of course, there's an ending to everything," she said. "I just don't know if it will be a happy ending or a sad ending."

For some reason, that touched him. "That's a poignant thought."

"Oh, Trevor." She got up from the bed and reached for her red silk kimono. She stood before him now, her red hair like a waterfall of dancing embers in the candle-infused darkness of the room. "You're such a romantic. In this day and age, you're a real mensch."

"Where are you going?"

"I think Danya's back."

There was someone in the apartment. Trevor could hear the sounds of someone moving down the hallway. Alex opened the bedroom door. "Danya?" she called out. "Is that you? I've got company—"

Then her voice changed, losing a register. *"Hakim!* What are *you* doing here!?"

Hakim stood in the doorway. "What's that, Alex?" His eyes peered over her shoulder as he took in the sight of a tattooed guy lying on the bed. "You got company? Who *is* that dude?"

Then his eyes grew cold and piercing. "And what you been doin' dipping into my stash? Hey, man, I don't mind you fucking my woman, but I don't want you fucking her with my tattoos on, you got that, motherfucker?"

Hakim

"Give me a sec," Trevor said to Alex as he kept an eye on this unexpected company.

He quickly rose from the bed, a red flame of a tattoo rippling up his spine as he slipped into his jeans. Alex watched each man size the other up.

"This is your ex-boyfriend, Alex?" Trevor asked her. Then he addressed Hakim. "Got a habit of dropping in unannounced? Or did you see a FOR RENT sign outside?"

"You got something against me, man?" Hakim said, a trace of menace creeping into his voice.

"You?" Trevor mockingly feigned surprised. "Why should I have anything against you? Actually, you're beginning to grow on me like a Chia Pet . . ."

"Oh yeah? Maybe I'll stick around then, keep you company." Hakim removed his bicycle helmet and shook out his long hair. He had platinum blond–streaked hair that was black at the roots, a shaved pate in front, and an old Chinese Manchu-style queue hanging like a horse's mane down his back.

"Candles, Alex. Lots of candles." He scowled at her as he took in the room. "Like in a funeral."

She didn't reply.

An odd-looking bird, Trevor thought as he studied him. High cheekbones, but a very un-Chinese nose, long and straight; thin, straight lips and a chin that still bore the marks of his helmet strap. His eyes were light brown, cold but unpredictable.

"Hakim, what's the matter with you?" Alex asked Beijing. "You look like hell. And what *are* you doing here? You know you can't just drop in like that. What happened to your other shoe?"

Hakim was standing there, his left Nike missing, a muddy white sock embedded in her carpet like a rock in a Zen garden.

"Long story, Alex," Hakim said, not taking his eyes off Trevor. "I ran into some guys I had to lose. I couldn't call you." He asked sardonically, "What's the matter, aren't you *glad* to see me?"

162

Alex stood there, her arms folded, a worried look on her face. "You're in trouble again, aren't you?"

"I'm not the only one, honey."

"What do you mean? You're not involving me this time."

"You've been in my stash, Alex."

"You left it here."

"Not for you to play around with. Oh, well." Hakim affected levity. "You can't help yourself, right? I give you a taste, and you're right there with your nose in the candy jar. What do you expect from chicks?" He winked at Trevor.

"In your case, I'd say you get what you deserve," Trevor interjected.

"Who *is* this jerk, Alex?" Hakim's voice rose. "And what's he doing wearing my stuff? I *told* you not to mess with it."

"This is my friend Trevor—Trevor Gobi if you must know," Alex shot back adamantly. "You told me a lot of things, Hakim. I believed most of them at first. But not any more. And as for your 'stuff,' man, it doesn't exactly belong to you. You stole it."

Hakim blew his top. "Once and for all, bitch, I did *not* steal it. This is hard-earned shit. These are *my* designs—"

"Listen, asshole," Alex retorted. "Maybe they *are* your designs, but where do you think you got the *code* from? Hey, answer me that?"

Hakim was about to reply, but then he looked at Trevor. "Do you think you want to get into this right now, Alex? I mean"—he nodded at Trevor—"this is a personal matter, right?"

"You're right, it *is* a personal matter," Alex said heatedly. "And until you admit the truth about yourself, about all of *this*"—she waved her hands around the room, and Trevor felt himself included, and he felt the chill of a discomfort settle in at the back of his head—"I will never trust you again. Do you hear me, Hakim?"

"The stuff is mine, Alex. I want it now, I'm taking it with me." Hakim moved toward the cooler where the tattoos were kept.

"I don't think you heard her correctly," Trevor said, stepping in the way. "You're not being reasonable. That's just one of your problems."

Hakim glared at him with wild eyes, then a smile crossed his face. Like a magician flicking cards out of his sleeve, he tapped Trevor on his chest. "Have a bunny rabbit," he said.

Trevor looked down at the Easter bunny on his torso, then looked up at Hakim again. "Very funny, wise guy. You've had your little joke. Now you can remove this thing—and split. I think you've overstayed your welcome."

Hakim cackled. "Your lover looks kinda cute, Alex. What do you think?"

"That's enough, Hakim," Alex snapped. "Make it go away."

"Make it go away? You think it's that easy? Honey, you don't know the half of it. You don't know what I'm capable of."

"You're crazy, Hakim. You were a little crazy when I first met you. But you're a lot crazier now. Now get it *off*—and leave."

Hakim flashed her a lopsided grin. "Sure thing, anything you say." He turned to Trevor. "I'll just wave a dead chicken over the source code, but I think we've run into an OS bug. I don't know, man. I think this bunny is permanent."

"I think *your* operating system is missing a few lines, pal," Trevor said as he gave Hakim a push.

"You don't know what you're getting into, man. You're in over your head. With this chick, too. You got no idea, white boy."

"Beat it." Trevor gave him another push. "Go look for your other shoe."

"Fuck you."

"I think you'd better leave, Hakim. Your friends might be looking for you. Who've you crossed now? That Chinese guy? He owns that club in Japantown, the one you took me to, you big show-off. Maybe I should give him a call. What do you think?"

A hurt look appeared on Hakim's face. "You wouldn't do that to me, Alex."

"Why not? Try me."

"Fine, fine, I'll leave. What did she do for you, big boy?" Hakim scoffed at Trevor. "She give you one of her placebo blow jobs? The kind you think you're in heaven, but she's really using her hand—"

Trevor took him out neatly, a clean punch that caught Hakim squarely on the jaw. He staggered backward. Then Alex slapped him hard across his face. "That's for you, too, and don't ever come back here again, got that?"

Hakim gave them both an evil look. "I'll be back, Alex. For my stuff. Just wait. You, too, asshole," he said to Trevor. "I'm not finished with you."

Then he gave them the finger and stalked out.

"I'm sorry about that," Alex said. "Hakim's always been a big bullshitter. See, the rabbit's already fading."

It was spiraling out into an abstract aqua-blue swirl. "Mind-blowing, isn't it?" Alex remarked.

Trevor just shook his head. "Just about everything is since I met you has been. I don't know what to think."

"It's all part of the mystery—that's what keeps everything interesting."

"Does it?" he wondered out loud. "I'll never be able to go to the gym again."

"When was the last time you went?"

He looked at her and grinned. "Yeah, well." Then he turned serious. "I think your boyfriend is trouble, Alex. But you know that already."

She sat down on the bed beside him, and put her hand on his shoulder. "Actually, Trevor, Hakim is my ex-boyfriend, but he also happens to be my husband."

"You're married to *him*?!"

"We've been separated for a while. He came back, we tried again. *I* tried again," she mused bitterly. "But I should have known, though." She pulled an American Chakra out of a pack and lit it, blowing out the smoke. "I thought he would change. But he never did. I'm the one who changed."

"How'd you meet him?"

"Oh, he's a talented artist. I met him at a gallery in SOMA.

165

He had a show. He was charming. I think we fell in love right away. A month later, I thought, 'This is it. This is the guy.' And we got married. Two months later, I was seeing my therapist. Three months later, I kicked him out."

"That's true love," Trevor agreed. "It can't get much truer than that. You just went through it faster than most people."

"You think so?" She cradled her right elbow in her left hand as she smoked.

"He told me he was possessed," Alex continued. "With evil spirits. That was the big problem, he said. He thought I'd feel sorry for him and help him see it through."

"And you did."

"Well, in his culture—you know he's not really ethnically Chinese; he's from Xinjiang in the far west of China, it's part of central Asia, right on the Silk Road. Hakim's a Uighur, he's a Muslim. He also grew up with a strong belief in the spirit world. As a child, he said he was haunted by the ghost of his dead sister. He remembers seeing her body on the bed surrounded by lots of candles burning. You saw how upset he got when he came in. It wasn't you as much as it was seeing those candles. He gets spooked."

"Weird."

"It gets weirder than that. You want some more wine?"

"I'm past that, thanks. I could use a Brillo pad, though, if you think it'll take these tattoos out."

She traced a line around his nipple. "It's amazing, isn't it? It's like this tremendous inspiration happening all over your body."

"Yeah, I'm breaking out with inspiration everywhere. But you were saying, it gets weirder?"

"He believes he's *dead,* Trevor. Can you believe it? This is just a walk through the underworld for him."

"Not very rational, is he?"

Alex exhaled some more smoke and shrugged. "How do we know? How do we know what being dead is? You know what they say about the Tibetan Book of the Dead? For that matter, what they say about *all* those sacred texts, including the Egyptian Book of the Dead. They're guidebooks to the stages of the afterlife, sure. But they're also pretty accurate about the different stages of *this* life, too. There's a double message there." She smiled at him. "But you're not interested in hearing this, are you?"

"Okay," Trevor conceded, "you now have the full attention of my higher self."

"It got pretty bad with Hakim. He'd disappear for days, for long stretches, you know. At first, I thought he was seeing another woman." She paused. "Then, I thought maybe he was seeing another *man. . . .*"

Trevor waited. He was beginning to feel that chill at the base of his head again.

"But he wasn't. I followed him one time."

"Where'd he go?"

"To the cemetery in Colma. He'd just walk around, stop in front of tombstones. Like he was asking the spirits questions. What the hell, I figured he was telling me the truth for once, that he *was* possessed."

Alex tapped her bright-red fingernails on the ashtray. "It's embarrassing to say, but I went to see a Russian gypsy. She told me *I* was possessed. By him!" She gave a throaty laugh.

"So what did you do?"

"Well, Hakim Beijing—Beijing's not his real last name, you know. It's Mohammad-something. He chose 'Beijing' for his tattoo parlor because it was cool, and he wanted in with the Chinese. But they always thought he was off the Great Wall, if you know what I mean."

"Foreign devil. I know the syndrome."

"That. But they also knew he was coming from someplace else. That's why they bought his tattoo shit. Powerful medicine. But on-line is *not* otherworld. He couldn't bullshit them forever with sleight-of-mind computer graphics. Those mass market VR-tats are pretty cheesy."

167

Trevor nodded. "I think I know what's coming."

She glanced at him. "Do you? He had to really deliver something to get in with them. To prove himself. That he wasn't some half-breed foreign devil. He was really bothered by that."

"So you decided to help him."

"Yes, Trevor, I did."

"That's what you guys were talking about earlier, wasn't it? *You* provided him with *this* thing." He laid his hand on a swirling cloud on his chest, with a snow-crested mountain peak angled against his throat.

He could feel the cloud moving, as well as the wind blowing through it—as though the cloud were a curtain covering his heart.

Alex smiled. "Actually, it was my Uncle Leo who stepped in. He thought it would save our marriage."

Trevor was thunderstruck. "Your uncle from the Russian mafiya?" He stared at his chest again. "What the hell is it? What's it *made* of?"

"It's your karma, Trevor," Alex replied. "And it's got you covered from head to toe."

Then she told him the story.

There were dogs barking in the village when Alex and Hakim got there. It was after dusk, the end of a tortuous ten-hour drive on the bumpy sand-washed highway from Ürümqi. Six hours ago, they had skirted the reddish-yellow Taklimakan desert, then turned east toward the foothills and the dagger-sharp, purplish eruption of the Altaishan.

"Not far to go," Hakim had said. "Not far" meant another three hours, and Alex fell back into her stupor, resting her head against his shoulder. It was as if his shoulder were moving through time, and she would reach her destination only after Hakim stirred her awake . . .

It had been mostly heat and flies on the journey in an un-air-conditioned minibus, a thirty-year-old wreck of a Kia driven by a young Uighur named Ali who was crazy enough to drive a haunted man and a foreign-devil woman. Here and

168

there, they'd spotted nomadic Kazakhs and a few Torgut Mongols herding sheep, horses, cattle, and camels.

The lonely jangle of the camel bells would startle Alex out of her sleep, and she would open her eyes to see Hakim chewing on his lip and staring at something in the distance.

"Look," he'd say, "it's the ghost of a lake." And she saw the shimmering mirage like a landlocked waterfall pouring down on the desert, a salt marsh that had been a brimming sea full of life eons ago.

The great twilight shadows formed parallel bars over the roadside stupas that pilgrims had erected on their journeys centuries ago. Little flags fluttered atop mounds of rocks that were balanced carefully upon each other, stony totems to forgotten gods.

The dogs were snapping and yapping at the door to the minibus, and the children stood by and watched without moving from their safe ground.

Smoke rose from the yurts. It was the dinner hour, and the camels were moaning and gnashing their teeth, while the wooly sheep jangled their bells, plaintively bleating their prayers that another day go by before the inevitable moment of their slaughter.

Their young driver, Ali, turned to them and grinned through the dust on his face. "Mirkan," he said and pointed at the village. "Mirkan. Yakshi?"

"Yakshi," Hakim nodded. "Yes, yakshi—good."

"We've arrived in the village of Mirkan." He gently prodded Alex, who was not fully awake yet. How could she be? The flight aboard the twin-prop Ilyushin samovar-with-wings from Lanzhou to Ürümqi, the hour or two they spent in the bazaar trying to arrange a ride . . . The sweet, green Hami melon that Hakim had cut open for her was the only thing she had eaten, besides a few dates. They had heard that the meat was still radioactive from the last round of Chinese nuclear tests, so they stayed away from the lamb shish kebabs that were offered to them.

The children who watched them unpack their gear were mute and displayed no curiosity in their eyes. They knew why these two had come. The only reason that strangers came to Mirkan: Sukotai, the old Uighur shaman. Their parents, who were peering from the flaps to their yurts, not venturing out, had warned them.

"Salaam aleikum," a voice greeted them. They both turned at the same time. Ali was still earning his dinars. "Sukotai," he said pointing out the man who stood before them.

"Salaam aleikum," Alex and Hakim both intoned.

The man in the high turban was bearded, with white scraggly hairs like scrub brush parched by the sun arranged on his furrowed face. His eyebrows were black and stern, above eyes that were like deep wells, the darkness in them hidden from view. They only revealed the external darkness, not the inner darkness that he walked in. He kept this other world shut out with a diffident gaze—an old, rusted gate that would be open soon enough.

Sukotai carried a staff and wore a dirty yellow sheepskin vest over his camel-hair robe. Beads interspersed with the bones of some small desert animals hung from his neck.

"Hakim, are you sure?" Alex whispered to her husband.

"Hakim, are you sure?" Sukotai mimicked her, then turned to Hakim.

"Emess? No? Ah? Yes?" Sukotai asked as he looked deeply into the eyes of the afflicted one.

"Ah," Hakim replied, and the old man clucked his tongue and pulled him by the sleeve, pushing Hakim in the direction of his yurt, which was just beyond the village. He did not look behind to see whether Alex followed or not. Her spirit was not calling to him.

They entered the darkened yurt. The pungent smell that blasted Alex awake came from a pot that was bubbling with a stew of unknown herbs, mixing its noxious fumes with the assorted gris-gris of decaying animal parts that were stacked in a corner of the dwelling. Woven rugs covered the floor; a few cushions sewn from rancid sheepskin were strewn about.

He gave them dirty mugs of chai to drink, but otherwise said nothing. They sat in silence for what seemed like an hour, the old man closing his eyes and nodding off. The solitary flickering flame under the boiling pot was the only light in this stifling space. From time to time, Sukotai would stir and throw a few twigs on the fire.

Hakim began to shiver. Soon, he was shivering uncontrollably. This alarmed Alex, who put her arm over him to hug him.

"Yok, yakshi!" Sukotai glowered at her and motioned for her to move away. This was what he was waiting for. The shivering.

She didn't know what to do. A feeling of futility, even helplessness, hung in the air. As long as this shaman glared at her, she could not approach Hakim. He was shivering, yet there was sweat on his brow, and his teeth were grinding.

"Hakim!"

"Yok yakshi!" Sukotai warned her again.

"Easy for you to say, 'yok yakshi,'" she defied him, "you're not the one who's in fear of losing his mind. Hakim—"

Hakim opened his eyes. There was some of the old familiar light in them, but they were brighter than usual. He gave her a weak smile. "It's all right, Alex, something's happening . . ."

Sukotai sat cross-legged across the fire from them, watching carefully. In his robe, if it came to that, he had a knife, and he would cut the heart out of the spirit that appeared. But the spirit appeared to be reassured by the woman. They were united from a past life. The ties were strong.

Why did she come here? She wanted to free the spirit from the body—but it was the wrong body. That was the problem. They were not matched. She was matched to the spirit, but it belonged to another body, another time. They did not belong together. But love was stronger than forgetfulness, and forgetfulness was stronger than time.

How could she remember this man from a past life? He was not a man. He was a haunted one who had wandered into

171

this lifetime looking for—not *looking for;* he had already found it: her. Something she had. Something she did not know she had, but which his spirit suspected was within her grasp.

That was the reason they were together in life.

The wind blew into the yurt and Alex felt a chill. Hakim was still smiling at her. He touched her cheek. "Sweet Alex, everything will be all right soon . . ."

Hakim turned to the old man and spoke to him in the local dialect. "She thinks I am here to be healed."

"And you are not?"

"Of course not. What do you think? You know what I am?"

"You think I have not seen the dead before? Walking and breathing as you are? Why did you come then?"

"To show her something."

"What? What could you possibly show her?" Sukotai smiled slyly. "Your good side, is that it?"

Hakim nodded, smiling back. "Yes, I wish to show her my good side. I want her to trust me."

"You must do nothing to hurt her."

"I know that. I just want her to trust me. That is different. I will not hurt her."

"You will not bring her to evil."

"No, I promise." Hakim was still smiling. Alex listened to the foreign tongue without understanding the words, but she sensed they were speaking about her.

"But you want her to bring this evil to you."

"I can handle it."

Sukotai pondered this. "Evil to evil."

"Yes."

"Evil cannot harm evil. It is already evil."

"You know this, truly."

"Yes, I know this. Why do you wish this to be so?"

"Evil is lonely in its own world. It needs a companion."

"That is nonsense. Evil does not need a companion. There is enough darkness to share."

"That is why I came to you. I heard you were acquainted

172

with the darkness. With the dark side that lies within everything. I heard this in America."

"America? My name is known there?"

"Wherever darkness is, your name is heard. Now will you
do this for me?"

"The light side of evil, you wish me to reveal that to her, so
that you can tempt her with the promise of real light?"

Hakim did not answer. That was answer enough.

Sukotai shifted in his seat and pulled at the curled toes of
his slippers. "Let me think about this for a moment." Then he
closed his eyes. When the moment was done, he opened them
again.

"I do not usually conduct my affairs in this way. But I see
no great harm in it to her. She will defeat you anyway. She has
the light, and although you will attempt to cloud it, you will
fail. So"—Sukotai beamed at Hakim—"it will cost you extra."

"Inshallah." Hakim bowed his head.

"Good then. We shall show her your curse, but she does
not need to believe it has been lifted."

"Her seeing it will be enough."

Sukotai slapped his thigh. "Moussa!" he called out loudly.

"Hakim, what's going on?" Alex asked. "What is he doing?"

"Quiet, Alex—I told you I was possessed by a dark spirit,
didn't I? It's what stands between us, Alex. That's why we're
here, isn't it? He's going to perform a little exorcism on me. But
first, he is going to reveal the spirit that I am possessed by. Can
you deal with it?"

"Anything, Hakim." She squeezed his hand. "I'm here for
you. Right here. Don't worry, honey, it's going to be all right."

"Of course, it is." Hakim smiled at her.

"Moussa!" Sukotai called again.

They heard a scampering sound from somewhere in the
shadows of the yurt and a black cat with burning yellow eyes
appeared seemingly out of nowhere. It hurried in expecting
food, but when it turned its head and flemmed the air, showing
the roof of its mouth, it knew why it had been summoned. Its

whiskers were snow white, and they trembled as it clawed at the rug Sukotai was sitting on.

Sukotai caressed the cat's purring face. "Moussa . . . Moussa," he murmured, then pointed at the dead one sitting opposite them. "It wants to know who is accursing it," he spoke to the cat.

The cat pulled itself into a long sitting position and braced itself at the edge of a great darkness. Alex could not believe what happened next.

Moussa spoke to Hakim. These were actual words, though she did not know their meaning; it was not a human tongue. She was in disbelief, but Hakim had told her that many strange things happened in these mountains. Animals could speak. Men could fly. The ground opened up. Here, there were no rules. The rules, in fact, were an afterthought, devised in the ordinary world for ordinary reasons.

"You wish a service of my master. You have no soul. Why do you wish to pretend to have one?"

Hakim needed no translation. That part of his brain that was not alive in the real sense translated for him.

To Alex's consternation, Hakim replied in the same unknown tongue.

"On the contrary, I have a soul," he spoke to the cat. "It has been trapped. But I know I cannot release it. That is not why I am here. I wish to show her that I am separated from it. She needs to know that I am possessed."

The cat appeared to frown. "You wish to show her your true face?"

"Can you do that?"

"No."

Sukotai raised an eyebrow. "Moussa, is it not within your realm to do so?"

Moussa lisped lightly. "That face has not been born yet."

Hakim began to sweat. "What do you mean?"

"That face is a face from the future. It has not yet arrived in this plane. I cannot go into the future, dark one. The cats of the Taklimakan do not dwell there."

"I am sorry," Sukotai said to Hakim. "What you ask is not possible."

"What did he just say?" Alex asked Hakim. "That cat just spoke to you."

"Please, Alex." Hakim's face showed signs of distress. "There is a little bit of a problem—I'm just trying to sort it out."

"There is something I can *do*," Moussa said, its yellow eyes deepening in the light of the fire.

"What is it?"

"I cannot show you your true face because it does not yet exist. But I can show you the face of one who will play a part in bringing you forth."

Hakim was momentarily confused. He had not expected this. He did not know what the cat would bring him; he could not predict the outcome. Glancing at Alex, he felt comforted by her presence.

"This cat . . . this is a miraculous cat, Alex, it serves Sukotai in ways we don't understand."

"What's it saying now?"

"This cat will not cooperate. There is a problem about revealing the spirit that possesses me"—that *will* possess me, he wanted to say, but didn't—"Instead, it proposes to reveal to me the person who will change my fortune." He added quickly, "This is the next best thing to an exorcism. It gives us hope."

Alex nodded. "Very well."

Hakim turned to Sukotai and the cat. "I am ready."

Moussa flicked its whiskers, then leaped to its feet and was gone from the shaman's yurt in an instant.

"What now?" Alex asked.

"Now we wait," Hakim said, and subsided into silence.

They waited two hours in the yurt. Sukotai was nodding off, and so were they. Yet every time Alex felt like she was drifting off into a dreamless rest, something would jerk her back again to the flickering shadows and the embers in the fire that Sukotai kept alive.

Moussa finally returned. His black fur was damp with a

175

sheen that defied the elements: it was dry in this desert moun-
tain air. The cat carried something in its mouth and waited for
Sukotai to pry it from its jaws.

Alex could see that it was some kind of a photograph.
Sukotai studied it for a moment, grunted, and then handed it
to Hakim.

"This is the picture of the man who will restore you,"
Sukotai said. "For good or for ill."

Hakim translated for Alex. "Let's see it, Hakim," she said
anxiously. She gasped when he showed it to her.

Moussa the cat said, "The female knows this man."

Hakim's look of surprise was more than equaled by the ex-
pression on Alex's face.

"What does this mean, Hakim?" She felt a cold stone in
her abdomen, colder than anything she had ever known in her
life.

"You know him, Alex, don't you?" Hakim said, suddenly
realizing why he had brought her all this way, to this remote
corner of far-western China on the edge of Tibet.

Alex trembled. It was the exact same picture that she kept
on the refrigerator door in her apartment in San Francisco. It
was too bizarre. How did it get here? Where did this sorcerer's
cat get it from?

"This is a picture of my uncle Leo, Hakim," she said as she
looked at him wide-eyed. "What's going on?"

"You don't think it was some kind of a setup, do you?" Trevor
asked after Alex finished her story.

He was skeptical. Sure, consciousness was a pliable com-
modity. And getting more so every day. Hell, his dad worked in
the playing fields of the superconscious, that's how he made
his living.

Trevor himself had slipped across the veil many times. His
own tele-sleepwalking, which had gotten him into trouble
enough times since he was a child—that was about consciousness slipping out the back door and into the night of the psyche.

But this business about Hakim... He didn't care for Hakim, didn't trust him. The guy was definitely skewed in a major way. "Hakim could have slipped the photograph to the shaman," he wondered aloud. "And the cat thing could have easily been a trick."

"Believe me, I thought about it," Alex replied. "But why would Hakim drag me all the way to China just to pull a fast one on me? No, he had heard about Sukotai. He was really curious. He went there hoping to *see* something. I guess he didn't expect that it would be my uncle Leo. That was pretty ironic."

She paused. "Then there was one other thing that convinced me finally that there was something to it."

"Such as?"

"The photograph. It was virtually identical to the one you saw on my fridge—you know, Uncle Leo as Al Kaponski. Except for one thing. You remember that crazy tie he's wearing in that picture?"

Trevor nodded. "Pretty wild. Kawasaki Optics, if I'm not mistaken. Must be at least five hundred bucks of software sewn in the lining."

"The tie that materialized in the picture was a different one. Much lower res."

Trevor cocked an eyebrow. "So you think it was some sort of a telemorphic copy of the original print?"

"Who knows about these things?" Alex shrugged. "It could have some kind of a psychic Polaroid—"

"*Paranoid,* you mean."

"Well, when we got home, Hakim was just fascinated to know all about Uncle Leo. He kept bugging me about him. He was sure the cat was an oracle."

"He hadn't yet met your uncle, I take it?"

"No, and then when he found out what Uncle Leo was involved in, he just wouldn't quit badgering me about meeting him—"

"But you were nervous about it, weren't you?"

Alex laughed. "I never mix in my uncle's business, Trevor,

177

you should know that about me. But eventually Uncle Leo had to fly out here, and Hakim insisted on meeting him. It wasn't a good time for Uncle Leo."

Uncle Leo was not happy. In fact, he was really pissed. The whole family had been shocked by the scandal. But it was really Uncle Leo's fault. Leo and Aunt Bella's marriage was on the rocks—it had been for some time. Uncle Leo had a girlfriend in New Jersey, a Russian girl named Tatyana. His mistress, really. It all blew up around the time of Aunt Bella's birthday. She and her best friend Nina shared the same birthday, so they were planning a really big joint birthday party at the Little Odessa in Manhattan. At the last minute, Uncle Leo canceled out. "A really important business deal has come up," he explained to Aunt Bella. "I can't miss it."

All right, well, so they had the party without him. Then the shit hit the fan when Aunt Bella was driving home, and guess who she sees on the New Jersey Turnpike? Uncle Leo, in this car that passes her, with his arm around this Russian babe.

Uh-oh, right? So there's World War III mixed in with a little preview of World War IV . . .

Aunt Bella is going to fuck Uncle Leo in the worst way she possibly can.

What's Uncle Leo's biggest Achilles' heel? Well, money, but there's always more money around the corner, wherever there's a sucker. No, it's his mama. Uncle Leo was completely devoted to her. My grandmother Irina and grandpa Solomon lived in San Francisco. Grandpa had died years ago; Grandma was really ill with diabetes. They had amputated both of her legs. She was still alive, but Uncle Leo had to make all the funeral arrangements ahead of time. Grandpa was buried in a plot in Colma in South San Francisco. Uncle Leo had been making all these payments on the adjoining plot so that Grandma could be buried next to Grandpa.

So guess what Aunt Bella does? She and Leo separate, the divorce proceedings go on. Okay, get this. She gets the deed to the adjoining plot out of Uncle Leo's safe at home. Yes, she knows the number to the combination—all Russian mafiya wives do, just in case anything happens to their men.

You're not going to believe this. Uncle Leo certainly didn't. It just blew him away when he found out. She places a call to the head office of the cemetery, tells them she wants to sell the plot that Uncle Leo has paid for in advance for Grandma Irina. "No problem," they say. "There's a long line waiting to get in. We'll send you the paperwork. Just sign the release form."

Finally, to make a long story short, Grandma Irina gets really sick and dies.

Uncle Leo doesn't suspect a thing. He arranges for the funeral and everything. Then they get to the cemetery in Colma and he just faints. Someone else is already buried there.

So Aunt Bella got her revenge in the end. Sad story, isn't it? But it doesn't end there.

One con artist's misfortune is another con artist's opportunity. This is Hakim's big chance to get in tight with Uncle Leo. How does he go about doing it?

No problem. Uncle Leo is not only impressed, he owes Hakim one. And he doesn't even like Muslims, as you can imagine. A Russian Jew and a Muslim? Forget it. Uncle Leo always thought I was crazy to marry Hakim—but he loves me, so he didn't make a big stink about it.

Okay, this person who is resting in what would have been Grandma Irina's plot, they're Chinese—old family, very respectable. And being Chinese, they're very superstitious—definitely into feng shui, you know what that is? Geomancy. Everything has to be positioned exactly right so that there aren't any bad influences. You can't have a door facing the wrong direction; it will attract bad influences. You have to hang mirrors and crystals and do rituals. You can go out of business, or your health will be damaged, if you don't do it right.

Anyway, the Chinese family visits the grave every weekend. It's their mother that's buried there. They leave flowers and everything.

179

Hakim tells Uncle Leo not to worry, that he'll take care of everything. He'll have this Chinese woman out of there in five days, even though reburial is contrary to Jewish law. But this is an emergency. Plus, Hakim says he'll get the plot back for Uncle Leo for next to nothing. He'll even make money on the deal.

Can you imagine what kind of bait that is for a Russian Jewish mafioso? Get your mama back in the grave where she's supposed to be—and make a profit?

Uncle Leo can't pass this up. "You do this for me, boy, and I will take care of you. Don't worry."

Hakim says, "No problem, sir. Just leave it to me."

So Uncle Leo puts Grandma Irina in storage somewhere, and Hakim gets to work.

Anyway, this Chinese family visits the grave on Sunday at the regular time, and what do they find? The flowers have all wilted. Unbeknownst to them, these flowers have been microwaved. But Hakim doesn't miss a trick. What he's also done—his ace in the hole—well, his ace in the grave, really—is that he's buried this cell phone in the grave site, and every time they come to pay their respects, there's this woman's voice— her ghost, right?—just pleading to be moved to another location.

And it is her voice, no question about it. Hakim got it from her voice-mail box, which hadn't been disconnected yet. You know, "This is April Wong and I'm not in right now, so please leave a message"?

He has it digitally altered to "This is April Wong and I'm being pursued by evil spirits, please get me out of this accursed space so I can rejoin the ancestors . . ."

Naturally, they freak. They bring in the best Chinese geomancer in San Francisco. His name is Dick Chen. But Hakim has Chen around his little finger, and Chen will say anything Hakim wants him to say.

Why? Because Chen, like any good Chinese, is an inveterate gambler. He plays for high stakes in Reno, in Las Vegas, in all the illegal fan-tan joints in Chinatown.

Scam number two, which leads back to scam number one. Hakim befriends Chen. He sets him up for a big one. Chen's in Reno playing blackjack. He's a gambler, all right. A really good one.

Hakim's sitting next to Chen at the casino in Reno, the Golden Nugget. He impresses Chen by losing, a luckless guey lo, foreign devil. Hakim shmoozes him, he's full of praise for Chen, who is playing a good hand, as usual, and winning.

Next thing, they're taking a break together in the coffee shop, and Hakim buys him a beer. They bullshit around, then Hakim says, "I hear you Chinese are the world's greatest gamblers. You'll make a bet on just about anything if there's a buck in it. Am I right?" Chen is in fine spirits. "I guess so. We do love to gamble," he admits.

Hakim is setting him up. "I mean, you'd probably even make a wager out of guessing how many fleas there are on a dog, am I right?"

"That's about right." Chen laughs.

"Say, Chen is a really common name, isn't it?" Hakim says, changing the subject. "I mean, there must be at least five thousand Chens listed in the phone book in San Francisco."

"A lot," Chen agrees. Chen explains to Hakim that there are maybe one hundred basic Chinese names, based on clan names, among them Chin, Chen, Wong, Lo, like that. Dick Chen gives Hakim a fine lecture on Chinese genealogy, just to pass the time. Educate the foreign devil a little before he goes back to the blackjack table.

"Wow," says Hakim. "I wonder how many Wangs there are in San Francisco. That would make a funny bet, wouldn't it?"

By now, Chen is more than a little amused. "You could make an interesting wager on that," he agrees.

"It would be a first," Hakim butters him up. "How about it? Want to make a bet on it?"

"On how many Wangs there are living in San Francisco? Ha, ha, ha. Too many."

"Seriously. What do you think?"

181

Okay, Chen is pretty sure Hakim is a flake. He's seen him make some pretty stupid moves at the card table. And he certainly wouldn't know shit about anything Chinese, so . . . But Chen is a pretty cagey guy. Careful, in other words. Yet he wants to see how much of a jerk Hakim really is—this would make a goofy story to tell his friends back home.

"Not Wangs," he decides. "Let's bet on something else. Let's bet on how many Wongs there are in San Francisco." What if this guy is crazy enough to want to set him up? Maybe he's already counted the number of Wangs already and knows the answer?

"Okay, whatever, it's all the same to me," Hakim says. "As you like. I still think it's an interesting bet."

"What you got to bet?" Chen asks him.

"My car."

"What kind of a car is it?"

Hakim's ready for this. He's made his preparations. "I drive a Lexus Laxmi. Jade green, good-luck color. Smooth like a lady's jade gate. It'll get you there in style."

"Ha, ha, ha," Chen laughs. This guy is a bit nerdy. But he owns a Lexus Laxmi? That's too good to be true, for a loser like him. "Do you mind if I see the registration?"

"My car registration?"

"I need some proof." Chen is now determined to go through with this. He knows the model. If he can win it off this idiot, it'll make his visit to Reno lucky, lucky, lucky. Why not? He feels *lucky*.

"Sure, I'll go get it now. But what are you going to bet?"

"Me?" Chen's a bit embarrassed to admit he's got a less prestigious vehicle. "I drive a Caddy Kunming, the best import you can get from the mainland. We know your Lexus is worth a little bit more than my car."

Damned straight. This Lexus is really loaded. I mean, it's like driving a space shuttle; it's got all the extras, plus it comes with the manufacturer's guarantee of a parking space anywhere you want to park within five minutes of arriving at your destination: This model features GSP, Guaranteed Satellite Parking. Finds your spot before you get there. The radio signal interferes with the ignition on any vehicle within two kilometers that is approaching the same spot . . . The very latest in AI parking, in other words.

And Chen knows this. He's already hooked.

How did Hakim get this car? He didn't. He doesn't even own a car. He got to Reno on a Greyhound. There's this Chinese mobster he knows, they call him One-Eye Chin. He's like one of five people in the entire Bay Area who owns a Lexus Laxmi. Hakim has hacked into One-Eye Chin's car registration, downloaded it, and altered it to his name. An easy print job.

"Okay, let's make up the difference," Hakim agrees. He's impressed that Chen is being so honest with him, and wants Chen to know he appreciates it.

"What do you do for a living?" he asks Chen.

"Feng shui, you know what that is?" Then he gives Hakim the rap about how important placement is in business and personal life.

"Oh, how do you figure out that stuff?"

"You use a special feng shui compass, then you do all your calculations based on that information."

"Wow, I bet you've got a really good one, huh? I'd really love to see one of those things," Hakim says as his eye touches on Dick Chen's briefcase, from which the man is never parted.

Chen is a little stunned by Hakim's question. "As a matter of fact, you're right. I never know when it's going to come in handy." Chen laughs, a bit embarrassed. "It also brings me good luck at the tables."

Chen unsnaps his briefcase and brings out the treasure. "This has been handed down to me through many generations," he says, proudly displaying it to Hakim. "My father and grandfather and great grandfather, all the way back, have practiced this craft. It's a very special feng shui compass. It dates back to the early Ch'ing dynasty—the early seventeen-hundreds."

"Wow, cool," Hakim says. "What do you say we add your

*feng shui compass to your Caddy Kunming, and together that
will equal my Lexus?"*

Chen is shocked. This is not only his livelihood, it's his
honor and ancestry. It's his spiritual icon.

"I can see that's not appropriate," Hakim says quickly.
"Let's forget the whole thing. I mean, what a ridiculous wager,
right? How many Wongs are there in San Francisco? That's
pretty dumb. Ha, ha, ha . . ."

But Chen has already swallowed the bait. If this jerk can't
respect a feng shui master's tool of the trade and is willing to
bet a Lexus Laxmi against a Caddy Kunming, how bright can
he be? The ancestors will forgive him and laugh with him when
he divests Hakim of his Lexus.

"Oh, no, let's do it." Besides, Chen's pretty sure he knows
how many Wongs there are. A lot of them are his clients. He's visited the Wong Family Benevolent Association on Grant Street in
San Francisco enough times to have a pretty good idea.

But he still hedges his bet. "It doesn't have to be the exact
number. The closest guess wins. Deal?"

He's going in for the kill now.

"Deal," Hakim says. "Okay, I'll go get the registration for
the Lexus." He comes back five minutes later and shows Chen
his holo-registration card.

"My registration is in the car, too," Chen says, rising from
the table.

"Oh, forget it, I trust you," Hakim says. "This compass will
be fine as collateral."

Chen gets really cold feet at this point. What if he's all
wrong about this? If he loses his car, that's one thing. But if he
loses the family heirloom? And if word gets out, he'll be ruined
for life among the Chinese community. He'll never work in the
Bay Area again.

"Er . . . ," he says hesitantly.

"What is it?" Hakim asks.

"Do you mind if we change the wager from Wongs to
Lins?"

"What's the difference? Fine with me. Lins it is. Let's do it."

Chen has also visited the Lin Family Benevolent Association on Sacramento Street, so he's feeling pretty confident about the whole thing. *"I say,"* he announces grandly, *"that there are seven hundred eighty Lins in San Francisco."*

"Wow," Hakim says, impressed. *"I bet you're close. I'd better stick to you . . . Okay, my guess is there are seven hundred eighty-five Lins in the phone book."*

Now, get this, Hakim knows exactly how many Lins there are in San Francisco. And not just Lins, but Wongs, Wangs, Chins, Changs, Chus, Wus, and Lams. He's done his homework. He's researched all the main clan names and memorized how many of each there were in the phone book.

Chen starts to sweat bullets. *"Let's check."* Sure enough, it takes him two hours of checking and rechecking and re-rechecking: There are 801 Lins in San Francisco—and Hakim has picked the number closest to the final tally.

Hakim now owns the Caddy Kunming—and worse news for Chen, he's got him by his balls. He owns his family heirloom, the honorable feng shui compass.

Which means, essentially, that Hakim owns Chen—a.k.a. *"Dick Chen Feng Shui Geomancers, Inc."*

You've got to hand it to Hakim: it was a clever scam from beginning to end. And he never owned the Lexus he used to bet with, right? He got everything for nothing.

By now, Dick Chen is pissing kidney stones and shaking. He's gone completely pale. He's just been wiped out. His life is over. He's desperate. He tells Hakim, *"I am a ruined man. You don't understand—without my luopan, my feng shui compass, I am lower than the lowest dog in the world. It doesn't mean anything to you, it is worth very little, it is just a curio. Is there a way we can make some kind of an arrangement for me to keep this? I ask you as one human being to another"*—he's down on his knees!

Hakim pretends to give this some thought. *"It's true that it's not worth as much to me as it means to you. But, still, a*

185

deal is a deal. I've got a lucky talisman hanging from the rearview mirror in my Lexus—I mean, it's part of the package— I wouldn't beg you for such a thing."

"Please, I can see you're a good man. Please do this one favor for me. I will be indebted to you for the rest of my life."

Hakim slaps him on the shoulder. "Come on, it's not the end of the world. Maybe there's a way we can use this to cement our friendship after all—"

"Anything," Chen says, seeing a little glimmer of hope. "You will be my best friend. And may your children be rich and prosper!"

Hakim gives him a big smile. "As a matter of fact, I have a little problem that I could use your advice on. But I don't know . . ."

"Please, let me try my best to serve you."

"Well, okay . . . You're the personal geomancer to the Robert and Lily Wong family, aren't you?"

"I know them, yes," Chen confirms, his heart sinking. Now he knows he's been had. He listens to Hakim explain his "little problem."

"So, can you help me?" Hakim asks him finally, flashing his brightest smile. "What do you say?"

Chen gulps hard, but replies, "You can rely on me."

So now backtrack to Grandma Irinas's hijacked cemetery plot in Colma. Hakim's gotten the family really spooked about their mother's ghost entreating them to be moved elsewhere. Naturally, they have to consult their family feng shui advisor, Dick Chen. Dick Chen goes to the cemetery and runs through this entire ritual, and then he tells them the good news: If they move the deceased, April Wong, to this certain exact plot in the cemetery, her spirit will be freed from its eternal and hellish torments and all the ancestors will be happy. Otherwise, a curse will hang over the family for generations.

They buy into it. The only thing is, that plot is owned by one Leo Vishinsky, this Russian guy. It's vacant, but he owns *this piece of most prized and most auspicious real estate. They want it. At any cost.*

Uncle Leo listens to this whole complicated story. He sympathizes. His own mother died recently. But he would be only too glad to accommodate such loving family members out of respect to the deceased on both sides. The Chinese family is so grateful that they don't mind forking up the difference in the price of the plot, and they add a little more to express their eternal gratitude to Uncle Leo.

The net result: Grandma Irina gets buried next to Grandpa Solomon, and Uncle Leo makes a nice profit amounting to about five thousand bucks on the deal.

Now Hakim is the hero of the millennium in Uncle Leo's eyes. He can do no wrong. There's a big dinner in his honor. A celebration. A fuck-you telegram is sent to Aunt Bella. The whole world is smiling on Uncle Leo again. He hands over ten crisp hundred-dollar bills to Hakim, a nice old-fashioned touch.

"What can I do for you, my dear friend?" he asks Hakim after dinner, over cognac and a Havana cigar. And Uncle Leo gives me a huge wink and tells me in Russian, "He's not a Jew, but he's the next best thing. You really picked yourself a winner this time, Alex. I owe you."

"So, Hakim—anything you want, you just name it," he says magnanimously.

And Hakim tells him what he wants. Uncle Leo sighs and says, "It won't be easy. I'll see what I can do. I'll make some inquiries."

And that's Hakim's scam number three.

"I'm quite convinced that he really *is* possessed, Trevor. He's petty and untrustworthy and rude and presumptuous and a real pain in the ass, personally speaking. But there is a real devil somewhere inside him. God knows where it came from, but it found a home in Hakim Beijing."

Blinded by the Light

"That was pretty smooth of Hakim, all right," Trevor agreed. "So what did he want from your Uncle Leo? I take it he's not in the market for any more exorcisms. This has something to do with the tattoos, right?"

Alex nodded. "Hakim had heard some stories, some rumors on the Net, in certain circles you wouldn't want to hang around in, that there's this way-cool virus going around. It's the latest monster thing. It's come out of like nowhere, probably leaked from old Russian secret scientific experiments."

"Russia," Trevor said, suddenly sitting straight up and looking at her directly.

Alex eyed him carefully. "It molds consciousness by becoming the consciousness that it invades. What makes it especially interesting is that it's got this intelligent nomadic code built into it. What that translates into is that it can migrate not just from individual consciousness to individual consciousness, but it can just as easily move from the on-line to the off-line world without any inhibition.

"It's eminently adaptable to *any* conscious environment, in fact. Just think what that includes: everything from little battery-operated gizmos with AI chips to intelligent buildings to major communications systems. It touches everything from defense to economics to food production to travel to infrastructure. We're talking people and governments here. All social organisms, as well as all their extensions—"

"This can't be for real. It's some kind of urban shamanic legend, right?"

Alex continued. "It *is* like a parasitic entity with an appetite for the fractals of thought. In this case, the fractals of consciousness that make up the whole shebang of the collective thought that the world is steadily evolving into. There's an arc to its transmission that is all encompassing."

"You're making me nervous, Alex. Where's this leading to?"

"It was first noticed about a year ago—like I said, in certain on-line pagan communities. Tattoo tantra. In tantric tattoos—'tantroos,' they're called."

"Hey, that sounds familiar. Isn't that what *we* were doing?"

"Don't get me wrong." Alex's eyes connected with his. "It makes sex *way cosmic.* No, *that* part is wonderful . . ." She put her hand on his cheek, touching him lightly. "Beautiful, in fact. Don't you think?"

"I'm still waiting for the test results to come in," Trevor replied nervously. "Look at this." He glanced at his tattoos, which were still—*God, they looked like they were ejaculating*—writhing all over his forearms. "What am I, the Illustrated Orgasm?"

"Don't worry, you're okay. I told you I believe in safe sex. If anything, you'll continue to feel orgasmic for a little while afterward. So will I. Our orgasms are keyed in together, so even while we're apart, we'll still feel the intense connection that we made. I've got your imprint on me. You've got mine on you."

"So what's the problem?"

"Ever hear of the Left-Hand Path of Tantra? The 'Aghora'?"

"I'm not sure. Maybe I need a little more foreplay?"

"There's two kinds of tantra, Trevor, okay? The so-called Right Hand Path, which is the Path of Light. And then there's the lesser-known Left Hand Path, which is the Path of Darkness. The Right-Handers observe tantra through the practice of spiritual purity—of divine union—which can be manifested through 'sacred' sex rituals."

She paused. "That's what the West is all about these days. How to save your marriage or relationship by taking a thousand-dollar tantra workshop in Maui or in Marin County. It's become the Wonder-bread ritual of western sexuality, really. Then there are the Left-Handers, the Aghoris . . . They put their inner purity to the test by engaging in all manner of on-the-edge behavior involving such things as necromancy, intoxicants, risky sex, and other 'forbidden' acts."

"Snuff kundalini," Trevor mused. "I've heard something about it. People getting their auras fried when they're not ready to evolve to the next stage of spiritual development. Especially when they use cheaply manufactured third-eye technologies to ramp up too soon."

Alex nodded. "Most middle-of-the-road tantrics avoid this path like the plague because it's fraught with so many dangers—and it's so ripe for abuse."

"But that's not what this is about, is it, Alex?"

"No, but I'm coming to it. This Russian virus found a ready-made niche in these Aghoric on-line communities. They were willing to experiment without taking any of the necessary precautions. Have you heard of the Rasputin program?"

"No, but Rasputin was that mystic monk, or mystic fraud, who had a ferocious sexual appetite and exerted a powerful influence over the Romanov dynasty before the first Russian revolution, right? He allegedly controlled the hemophiliac attacks of the tsarevitch Alexei, the son of Nicholas II and Tsaritsa Alexandra . . ."

"That's what this program is named after—the monk Rasputin. But this is something new. It came out of Russia about the time the original virus was first detected. It's the first documented presence of the virus in a software program. The Rasputin program was Aghora run amok. Not unlike a kind of date rape of the soul. You slipped it into the system of the person whose kundalini you wanted to tap into, and they became your kundalini slave for as long as you wanted to ravage them."

"That's really freaky." Trevor shuddered. "Evil."

"That's what Hakim wanted Uncle Leo to get for him. The Rasputin program. It's really hard to come by."

"And *you* helped him get it. That's what he used in his tattoos. Alex, how could you?"

"No, honey, that's not what happened. Trust me. I'm not related to Uncle Leo for nothing. I was really curious about why Hakim wanted this thing. I mean, it wasn't to have sex with *me*. So what did he want it for? To control other people?

To sell it? Why was he so attracted to it, when he told me he wanted to clean up his act to save our relationship?"

"So what happened between Uncle Leo and Hakim?"

"I had a nice talk with Uncle Leo. I told him, 'I know you owe Hakim a big favor because he fixed the mess Aunt Bella made over the business of Grandma Irina's plot. But we're family, and I must ask you not to do this.' Uncle Leo said, 'What do you want me to do?' I said to him, 'Can't you get this Rasputin program, and, well, modify it, so it's not quite so demonic? Take out the shit, doctor it up a little, he'll never know.'

"So that's what Uncle Leo tried to do. Of course, he had to get his hands on the real thing first. And it wasn't easy; he had to go to all his bootleg software sources in Odessa . . . And when he found out what the real program was about, he came back to me, and said, 'This thing is really awful. I have a bad feeling about it. If this is what he wants, and he discovers that you messed with it, you'll be in trouble with him. Look at what he did to this Chinese guy—and to that Chinese family. I've seen devious people, and he's got a natural ability. I don't want to see you hurt.' I told Uncle Leo, 'Don't worry about that side of it. I'll take care of Hakim myself. Just defuse this software for me, however you do it. I still love this man, but he has a very dark side, as we are all discovering. I don't want to be responsible for hurting other people.'"

Trevor whistled. "So *you* scammed Hakim."

"Not that simple. Uncle Leo said his people didn't want to touch it. They didn't want to mess with debugging the software. Some Russian black-market programmers had tried to figure the code out and ended up in the asylum. That's what Uncle Leo told me: 'This thing is poison.' Meanwhile, Hakim was putting the pressure on. 'When am I getting this thing? What's Uncle Leo doing now?' He was making sounds like he would put the screws on Uncle Leo. Can you imagine that? He even said—and I'm sure he wanted me to convey this, but I didn't, of course—'What if that Chinese family discovers they've been ripped off?' Subtle and not so subtle threats like that."

191

"Hmm, I wouldn't put it past him."

"Neither would I. So that was the scary part. Anyway, you don't mess around with the Russian Mob. If Hakim fucked with Uncle Leo—or made Uncle Leo fuck up—someone would have to pay. Either it would be Hakim or Uncle Leo—or both."

"Who would you choose?"

"Do you think I would let it come to that?" Alex gave Trevor a penetrating look.

"I guess not. What happened next?"

"I started looking into this thing stateside. The more I looked into it, the more sinister everything began to seem. It was apparent that no one in any position of authority here was taking a serious attitude toward it—if they were aware of it at all. Then this bug took a serious new twist. It began to appear in various other manifestations. Like, it was growing from some virtual S-and-M party game into a much more dangerous menace."

There was a perplexed look on Trevor's face. "You went to the authorities, Alex? You researched this thing, you say, and went to the *authorities?*"

Alex paused. "Trevor, there's something you should know about me. About my day job. I know we met at the Brain Wash and all that, and I brought you home with me—and I'm married to Hakim, and my Uncle Leo is connected, but—"

"Yes?"

"I don't know how to tell you this, and I don't want you to take this in the wrong spirit."

"What?"

"Trevor, I'm afraid you don't understand. I *am* the authorities."

There was an uncomfortable silence between them. Trevor shifted on the bed where he was sitting. He looked at Alex in a funny way.

"You care to clarify that for me?"

"I work for the government."

"Government?" He was confused. "Which government? The Russian government?"

"Of course not. I'm a U.S. citizen."

"What are you talking about?"

"The U.S. government, Trevor. I work for a government agency. I go to work in the morning just like any regular person. But I happen to work for a branch of the Justice Department."

"You're kidding . . . *which* branch?"

"Actually, it's a new division of the Immigration and Naturalization Service. The AINS."

"AINS? Never heard of it . . ." He was still struggling to absorb this new information about this baffling woman and her bewildering family.

"AINS stands for the Avatar Immigration and Naturalization Service."

"Say again?"

Alex tried to explain it to him as simply as she could. "The AINS came into existence as a result of recently enacted changes to the Immigration Reform and Control Act. It's not very well known to most people, and the INS likes to keep it that way."

"What on earth does it *do?*"

"We process illegal-alien avatars on the Net, Trevor. I go to work, download into VR, and I make sure there aren't any unwholesome characters trying to cross the border into U.S. cyberspace. If there are, I apprehend them. If they resist, I deactivate them."

"You're pulling my leg."

"I don't think so, Trevor." Alex shook her head. "Here, let me show you my ID."

She dug into her handbag and pulled her badge out. It was a PDA device embossed with a hologramic AINS symbol that began to squawk as she scanned him.

"What's it doing?" Trevor recoiled.

Alex smiled. "With this, I can tell whether you were born here, or if you are naturalized, and when. I can also tell which countries you've visited recently. Hmm . . ." She checked the readout. "U.K. twenty-four-hour stopover in London Heathrow, July 10, 2036, then entered Paris de Gaulle July 11, caught the train to Nice. Checked into the Beau Rivage hotel, two nights. Departed Nice Le Pen for San Francisco, July 15. A short stay, Trevor. Did you have a good time?"

"This is getting *really* weird . . . I can't believe you're doing this. You're . . ."

"Is she all right, Trevor?" Alex asked him softly.

"What? Is *who* all right?" Trevor felt the bottom drop out of his conscious mind. It was all becoming mixed up, like in a schizophrenic dream. Was he tele-sleepwalking again? Sometimes, he mistook states of lucid dreaming for wishful thinking.

"Nelly," he clearly heard Alex say.

"Nelly?" He felt a growing sense of outrage now. He had been lured here under false pretenses, played mind and body games with, and violated to the core of his psyche.

"What's she got to do with you?" His voice rose as he said it.

"You know what, Trevor," Alex replied evenly and kept looking at him. No, this was no lucid dream. It was all too real. But the blank expression on Trevor's face refused to go away. "She's not some fucking illegal-alien avatar, or whatever it is you hunt down on the Net. She's a *human being . . .*"

"Actually," Alex calmly went on, "we're not so sure about her current status."

Would she *never* stop?

"When she went through Immigration at San Francisco International, the system picked up a twenty-five percent probability that she was hosting an alien virus. We think she's carrying it, Trevor. She's probably mutated it considerably by now."

"Why don't you ask your Uncle Leo about that?!" Trevor retorted bitterly. "Or, better still, why don't you check with your Hakim?"

She adopted a gentle approach. "Uncle Leo has been cooperating with the AINS, Trevor. He doesn't want to see this thing spread any more than it has been. And, of course, there are other legal incentives for him to be helpful. He didn't get where he is by being a one-dimensional hoodlum. He's a patriot, too. As for Hakim, I don't want to see him hurt. But I don't want him hurting anyone either. The tattoo stash we gave to him, we had it vetted, Trevor. The virus is now under observation. And, frankly, it's really quite a scary thing. That's why"—she laid her hand on his again, but it felt cold to him, cold and strange—"that's why I think you should be concerned about Nelly. We think she's turning, Trevor."

"Turning?" he repeated numbly. "Turning into what?"

"Turning into an illegal avatar, Trevor. If she hasn't already."

Sinbad the Tattoo

Sinbad saw the black cat scurrying in the loneliest vector of the night. It stopped in its tracks when he called it. "Bis, bis." Its long white whiskers vibrated against its black face and fierce yellow eyes. The cat flemmed, its palate resonating against its Jacobson's organ, as its psychic taste buds sampled the stranger.

"Moussa . . . ," he called to it. "Come here."

It wanted to run, but cat software in the bardo is not everything that it's cracked up to be. The spine of Moussa's avatar felt as though something had seized it, and sure enough, it was now being directed toward this prelife form that stood before it.

A pale hand caressed the cat's black fur, then pried the photograph from its mouth.

Sinbad examined the photograph for a moment, the static electricity of his fingers erasing some of the image as he replaced it in the cat's mouth. Nothing was chance now. The information Sinbad sought was being generated from moment to moment.

Just as the new world was coming into existence, it spawned yet another world within another, more refined image of itself.

"Go now," Sinbad addressed Moussa. The cat scampered away, relieved to get away from this specter.

Sinbad continued on his journey.

He stopped to look into the care and feeding of the dream plants; the process of psychosynthesis was crucial to this inner landscape. The lonely sea in the outback of the psyche churned with waves greater than the ones that erupted back home. The clouds boiled. And the light was devastatingly, blindingly white, as if someone in the rapture of the heavens were opening and closing cosmic venetian blinds.

Sinbad journeyed across that sea until he reached a land where giant minarets and geodesic domes had spawned a race of four-legged, intelligent skyscrapers that wandered about as insolently as dinosaurs that knew they would never die.

They were Asuras, higher beings with a flaw that they would never discover: a vermilion anger coursed through their veins instead of blood.

One of them rushed toward Sinbad to challenge him to a spiritual duel.

"I cannot defeat you," Sinbad told it. "You can only defeat yourself. But you will never win because you do not know what it means to lose. You are destined to always be on the winning track to the unwinnable."

He walked through the lobby of the beast, emerging on the other side into the vastness of a garden that grew for a thousand miles, through clouds of flowering shrubs and granite redwoods towering above metamushrooms that served as slaves to its incorruptible Self.

He had that feeling again that he was being followed, but it could not be. Not here in the belly of the dream.

196

*   *   *

He paused by the bhodi tree. The man was still sitting there, cross-legged, rapt in meditation.

It seemed like forever, but then the moment passed. Sinbad could never reason with him. Sinbad had sent Maya to the man, so she could interpret in the human tongue and tell him that it was cosmically damaging to the brain to try to undo the code.

Maya, the goddess of illusion, as usual, had no luck with such a man: he already knew that there was nothing to undo.

No code. No Maya.

A wasted effort. Enlightenment was a bug. One day they would sort it all out.

But there was no "one day," as well. That was part of the problem. Worse still, there was no "man sitting under the bhodi tree," either. There was only what Sinbad told Maya to see.

So whose illusion was it?

Sinbad sighed and moved on. I will be back . . . This samadhi paradigm needs fixing. It's bringing down the value of the real estate.

He came to the cage that the Russians had built. Inside, there were millions of moths fluttering around a tattered keyhole of light, which was how they had entered this unenterable existence. When they saw Sinbad approach, their faces entreated him. Some feared him, some cursed him. They all feared and cursed themselves. The convicts could never find the way out because there was no way out. There was also no way in. No way in, no way out. It was all an illusion.

The stone dancers embraced the walls of the temple in the buzzing jungle.

True worship is coitus in stone, Sinbad thought. Eternal stone lingams and yonis that provide the exit map to perfumed oblivion.

There wasn't time for such poetic thoughts.

197

He hurried inside the temple, where he approached the black statue dancing on the hardware of the illusion.

A garland of flowers was manifesting every nanoinstant, and the flame in the oil lamp contained the glow of eternal light. Sinbad bowed to the statue.

In its eyes, the light of the virus was serene yet stern. "Mother," Sinbad addressed it. "The dance has no end and no beginning. Only you know the answers that defy us, with your unknowable wisdom. The sacrifice is being readied. The bowls are being filled . . ."

In this inner sanctum, Sinbad began to strip himself. He bared his chest, and there it was, his own blight.

Only through the power of naked prayer would the stain be removed. The stain of his own virus.

That was the reason he had come to this inner sanctum.

He heard the sound again, and this time he turned to find the witness standing there. The only witness to the unmentionable pact between the Tattoo and its own secret skin.

"It's you," he hissed at her, beyond regret and anger and surprise. "I had not noticed how fast you were becoming me."

Nelly stepped up to him and touched him on his bare chest, just beneath his nipple.

She was radiant in her becoming, but was it her own becoming or the collective spawn that she was bearing in the womb of her consciousness?

He observed her face and heard her speak. Then he knew the answer.

She was still herself after all.

"Sinbad," she said to him, full of the realization of her dreamless wonder. "You have a tattoo growing on you, too . . ."

She stared at it, marveling at the quality of the skinwork. It was definitely man made.

The graffiti of love . . .

It might have been her love, she reflected. But then she didn't know him that well. Besides, there was this other love waiting to be born inside her.

198

Threesome Blues

"I have to go now," Trevor said simply, and Alex nodded.

"I understand," she replied. "I hope that I haven't . . ." She let the question dangle as she reached out to touch him.

"Don't," he said pulling back instinctively. He felt torn between holding her again and wanting to get away from her apartment as soon as possible.

"I really should be grateful to you," he said, settling for the middle ground between his anger and his regret.

For better or worse, that seemed to be the natural strategy of his heart.

"I've been an idiot," he admitted.

His emotions were raw and scattered. But perhaps he could transform them into something positive. Perhaps he could collect them into a wind that would give him energy, if not purpose.

Don't be overwhelmed, he told himself. Think with your heart. Think of Nelly. Think of what she's going through right now.

That centered him somewhat. He now felt eager to get going.

"You're *not* an idiot, Trevor." Alex shook her head. "Don't blame yourself. I wasn't really straight with you, I'll admit. We just took a roundabout way of getting down to—"

"Business?" he challenged her.

She smiled ruefully. "I wasn't playing games with you. If I were, then I was playing games with myself, too. No, it's just how it happened."

"Why didn't you tell me what was really on your mind when you first met me?" Trevor was puzzled.

"Well, frankly, I wasn't sure where you stood. If you were a part of this—ah . . ."

"The threesome, you mean. Nelly, the tattoo, and—me. Is that it?"

"Something like that."

He nodded. "All right. That's fine, then. You're off the hook. You were just doing your job."

"I wish you wouldn't take it like that. That part of it—my getting to know you—was definitely not part of the plan. I had no idea you would appeal to me on that level."

"It's just karma, I guess."

"Or lust."

"Same thing."

Alex laughed, and Trevor grinned. The wind of his heart was blowing again. He was grateful it was ending so easily. What was it that she had said to him earlier? *There's an ending to everything. I just don't know if it will be a happy ending or a sad ending.*"

"You're going to see her now, aren't you?" Alex asked him softly, after the moment had passed.

Trevor nodded. "I think I'd better. Anyway, as you said, Nelly's in trouble. I should be there." He reached over and squeezed her hand. It wasn't that difficult, after all.

He hurried down the stairs, past the empty baby carriage in the corner, and out into the predawn air, where he found a taxi waiting.

The Tibetan lama sat in the front seat of his Yellow Cab, fingering a long string of meditation beads. His ruddy face broke into a broad smile as he saw Trevor approach.

"Dorje! How did you get here!?" Trevor grinned when he saw the familiar figure dressed in his maroon lama's robe, his shaved monk's head with its pronounced cranium reflecting the streetlight.

The engine of the old Chevy Shiatsu was already running as Dorje held the door open for him.

"Hail a lama!" Dorje laughed. "Come in, my young friend . . . Apologies for my tardiness, but I think you have been profitably occupied, no?"

"I was thinking about you earlier this evening, but you weren't picking up. Usually, you kick in right away."

Sometimes their little telepathies were synchronized, other times not. But it was never the wrong time to hear from Dorje. Trevor was genuinely relieved to see him.

"Yes, yes," Dorje chortled. "Worse than e-mails, all these messages shooting through the pneumatic tube of the mind. I really must get a secretary." He beamed. "Or a proper dispatcher. It's been a very busy night. The airwaves were filled with the cries of lost souls and confused spirits—"

His eyes suddenly focused on Trevor. "And you, young friend, are you well?"

Before Trevor could reply, Dorje's eyebrow shot up, making his face an ellipse of surprise. "I'm a taxi driver. But you've become a taxi driver, too. I see you are also carrying some passengers. Something new?"

"What do you mean?" Trevor asked as he settled into the front seat beside Dorje.

Dorje grasped Trevor firmly by his forearm, then pulled his sleeve all the way up to his elbow.

Alex's tattoos, although a shadow of their former imprint, were still going through their paces. Lilies and roses turned into a crimson waterfall, collecting into a swirling pool at his wrist.

"Oh, these—"

Dorje tapped his wrist hard, breaking up the pool. Then he placed his right hand on Trevor's wrist to feel the pulse.

"You were right to call on me, young friend," Dorje said soberly. "Hmm, it's definitely not an enemy pulse. I was worried for a moment. It's a guest pulse. Temporary guests only." He brightened and slapped Trevor on his shoulder. "You'll live!"

"Is something wrong?" Trevor asked.

Dorje pulled away from the curb and headed toward the lights of the city that lay blurred in the heavy fog bank.

"You tell me, Trevor. How did you get a sand mandala painted on your heart?"

"A sand mandala? You mean, like the temporary mandalas

201

that the Tibetan monks paint then destroy after they've been completed?"

"They are indeed temporary, but you must erase them yourself when the time comes. That is important. Do you understand that? I think you must."

Trevor sat in silence, watching the lights of the passing cars trickle through the gauze of fog blanketing the street.

"I think I understand, Dorje," Trevor replied.

"Excellent. Where to? Home? It's late."

Trevor shook his head. "No, Dorje. Would you first take me to Hayes and Haight, please?"

"Ah, to your friend Nelly's? That's the pulse that I detected beneath the guest pulse. Lots of pulses tonight, Trevor. You have come from one heart and are heading toward another. Your heart is very busy."

Trevor felt the weight of his heart's mandala; it was heavier than all these tattoos put together.

Dorje mused out loud. "There is pain in your heart. But there is also transformation. That is the biggest pulse of all."

"If you need me, call me. Use the Vairochana line, you know, seven-CHAKRA, it's more direct. But I will wait outside."

"Thank you, Dorje. This shouldn't take long." Trevor climbed out of the taxi and strode up the walkway to Nelly's front door.

He rang the doorbell and listened. There was no answer, no movement inside the house. He rang the doorbell again, remembering his earlier intrusion through the Omtron doorway.

Silence.

Trevor looked back at Dorje, who lifted his string of beads in the air as a blessing. Trevor brought his keys out and fitted the right one to Nelly's door.

As the deadbolt slid open, he pushed the door and stepped inside.

The Japanese kites that hung from the ceiling fluttered. A multicolored giant butterfly slowly turned to face him.

"Nelly?" Trevor called out.

Trevor took a few steps deeper. The house felt like a tomb, yet it was filled with electricity. There was a hidden presence here, but it wasn't Nelly's vibes he was picking up. He saw a familiar picture on one of the bookshelves in the hallway: Trevor and Nelly in Hawaii, Nelly in her sarong and Trevor wearing his pirate's bandanna and tropical growth of beard. Both were smiling. She hadn't taken down that picture, at least. Probably hadn't had the time. He bit his lip.

"Nelly?" The living room was empty. The soft leather Moroccan poufs that lay scattered around the round, brass Turkish coffee table still bore the imprint of invisible bodies. The old grandfather clock that she'd picked up in a flea market was ticking and displaying the wrong time, as usual.

Bardo time, he thought to himself as he headed up the stairs past the Tibetan flags that hung from the walls. The hour of the dead.

Trevor could hear the Omtron set on in the bedroom, tuned in to some late-night game show. It sounded like *The Three A.M. Healer's Club*.

"And the correct answer is . . . *Maitreya*! Sorry, Susan, that wasn't the Big Guy from Shasta, our own personal favorite Saint G . . ."

"Nelly?" Trevor called out again, hesitantly.

He heard the channel change to a fine-grained static as he stepped into the bedroom. The room was empty except for the phosphorescent silhouette of a figure seated in Nelly's easy chair.

"Ah, the young man," the light-shape addressed him. "How very like yourself you are. Please come in."

The spectral figure was that of a man wearing Nelly's old silk kimono. He sat with his pale white legs splayed in a position of relaxed waiting. His head was hairless, smooth and polished like an alabaster egg, his nose was beak shaped, and his chin almost shapeless, without any clear definition.

The kimono was open at his chest, which was equally smooth and opaque.

Trevor felt a cool constriction of air around his throat as he stepped toward the figure.

"Who are you?" he demanded. "And where is Nelly?"

The strange-looking man jutted his shapeless chin in Trevor's direction. "Nelly's out, I'm afraid. That's the trouble."

"What have you done with her?" Trevor's voice trembled. He knew who this—this shapeless shape—was.

"It's the other way around. What has she done to me? That is the question I find myself asking, actually."

Trevor stared at him, trying to find some angle of approach, some phantom of an umbilical cable that he could yank out of its invisible power supply.

How was it possible to materialize to such an extent? He was wearing her robe, for God's sake!

"She's gone. Left me behind. Like she left you . . . You can sympathize, can't you? Not a very reliable lover, is she, Trevor?"

Trevor felt his anger push him within range of the specter, then caught himself. Of course, he was being goaded into drawing closer to it. He realized that now. The entity's repose was of relaxation; it was of subdued energy—energy that needed to feed on the life form of a real body, now that Nelly was gone.

Trevor sat on the edge of the bed, a few feet away from the reclining specter, who observed him through green eyes glinting with irony. It was a look of holosthesia on its deathbed—or death armchair, whatever you called the pose. No, it wasn't going anywhere. It didn't have the energy. It took all the life force it could muster just to materialize in this pathetic form. And a bit more than that to garb itself in Nelly's kimono, which she usually tossed at the foot of the bed.

That must have taken some effort for this naked, neural nobody. It needed her chi, and silk was an excellent conductor of life force.

204

"There's enough time—don't worry. The human expression, 'Where there is a will, there is a way.' It's so apt, I find. I've been appreciating it for the past few minutes, prior to your arrival."

"Find anything interesting on the *The Three A.M. Healer's Club*?" Trevor goaded him back. Then he laughed at another realization when he saw a pink flush on the Tattoo's bare solar plexus.

"You were panhandling the TV for a healing, weren't you! *That's* what you were doing when I came in . . ."

"You embarrass me," the Tattoo replied, a dying flicker of light in the sunken tubes of its eyes. Then he stared at Trevor, as if deeply fascinated. "I love your eyes."

"You would love to have them, you mean."

"Full of your kind of life. I don't suppose you would loan them to me for a little while?" He paused, then laughed. "With interest?"

"Sure. Anything else you want? You've sucked Nelly's *prana,* now you want mine. But she's gotten away from you. Excellent."

The figure stirred in the chair, and Trevor felt a cold needle jab him in the spine. Fear, he thought to himself, startled. Don't let it approach you. It has ways that you don't even know about . . . Don't be so confident.

The Tattoo lowered his head with great effort and hissed, turning up the Omtron's volume.

"Let's make a deal . . . I have what you want."

Trevor scoffed, feeling the radiant energy burst from his chest. "You have what *I* want!? *Wrong.* You *had* what I wanted. But not anymore! She left you here in your easy chair with your easy way out. All you have to do is disappear. Just shrink and shrivel, or whatever it is you do, and be gone. Do yourself and everyone a favor and just fade away."

The specter cackled. "The deal is—listen to me. You can't resist this, really, once you hear me out. I know what you are: a man in love. Such a romantic! I repeat, *I have what you want.* You think I am dying. You're right, in a sense. But I can be reborn faster than a rerun. I exist and die forever. One and the same. It's just a matter of timing. Right timing. But what your beloved Nelly *doesn't* realize is that as *I* die, *she* dies. Do you understand? She followed me to a place she should have never been. Surprised me. I was slow. I thought she was my shadow, the light shadow that lives in the highest planes . . ."

The Tattoo laughed again. "A momentary lapse, I assure you. My reflexes were delayed.

"She got out before me. Too late for me to rejoin the party, you might say. She switched on a sitcom that I had to find my way through. A labyrinth of idiocy. Not a very clear window to emerge from . . . Never mind. She's dying. Without *you,* she will, of course, survive," the Tattoo said grandly.

"But without *me:* Say goodbye to Nelly. Our neurosynapses have already been fused. She's got—let me see—what time is it in your terms? Anyway, less time than I have."

The Tattoo shifted its form in the easy chair. "You care to be the best man at our wedding, Trevor? Or the best man at Nelly's funeral? It makes no difference to me, really. Your choice is meaningless to me. But you must choose nevertheless."

Trevor looked at the entity in horror. Finally, he replied. "You're lying."

The Tattoo waved a weak hand at him. "Go away. Let us die in peace together—*your* Nelly and *my* Nelly and me."

Trevor felt something wrench deep in his gut. He paused. "How do I know you're telling the truth?"

"There is no truth, but you wouldn't understand that. Only what you would call a fact. And that, you can *feel*—if you try. Or . . ." The slit of a vacant eye assailed him. "Ask your friend, if you want." He cackled feebly. "Your driver . . . *How am I doing, physician?*"

The Tattoo slumped in the chair as Trevor caught his breath. *Dorje!* He summoned his friend with all his energy.

Back in the cab, Dorje listened to the pulse through Trevor's heart, which focused intently on the Tattoo. "An enemy pulse to be sure, this *rimi* of the astral plane," Dorje told Trevor. "But half of its pulse is Nelly's. It speaks terrible lies that unfortunately are all too true. There is no in-between here."

Trevor stood in front of the slumped form. Slowly he lowered his hand until it touched the form's flickering, dying shoulder. The head moved and the eyes opened.

"I thought you'd gone. Changed your mind? You want to be my taxi?" The Tattoo laughed soundlessly.

Trevor raised up the weightless specter in his arms and felt it slide over his body like a sheath of cold air.

"Don't worry," he felt the inaudible voice coming from somewhere on his skin. "I need *her,* not you. It takes time to merge with the life-support system, and that stage is already done. Not enough time for me to worry you. Find her. She has something that I need . . . Then I'll let her go. After I'm finished with her, you can have her back."

"Those are my terms."

The specter gulped a breath of pixels from the colorful wind that was still racing across Trevor's body. Hakim's tattoos were slowly being absorbed by this being.

"What does Nelly have that you need so badly?"

Trevor's breath burned hot inside his chest, and he was sweating. It weighed nothing when he lifted it, but now it felt like an indescribable weight on his heart.

Then, as Trevor looked down at his own chest, he saw it. The Tattoo's eyes were closed, and it looked like an infant curled up in a deep sleep. But there on its arm was the faint trace of something.

Its own tattoo.

Blowfish

Dorje helped Trevor into the backseat of the cab. He felt Trevor's pulse and frowned—there were any number of death pulses. Those that felt like the flapping of a vulture's wing, water dripping, a fish darting up to eat a fly. Trevor's pulse had a fluttering quality, like a flapping flag.

He has an electric wind running through him, Dorje thought to himself. But it is running out of current. When it does . . .

Trevor grinned at him weakly. "We've got company."

Dorje nodded. "I know. May I see it?"

Trevor leaned back and pulled up his t-shirt. "Look, it's sleeping like a baby."

Dorje sniffed. "More like a hungry ghost, Trevor. It's a good thing you're not allergic to the astral plane. What would your father say to me if you came to harm in Dorje's tantric taxi?" He shook his head.

"You are actually more like your father than you think. Pigheaded, stubborn, eagerly embracing all manner of rubbish from other dimensions. I don't know what Tara sees in him. He is a handsome devil who knows how to kiss in Tibetan, that's all!" He laughed.

"And now you are a safe haven for this—for this stenciled gdon!"

Dorje shook his head again, with sympathetic disapproval. "Very well. It is not my position to argue or criticize. All I can say is, you must keep your subtle pulse steady. Stay away from mutton and yak meat for two weeks. It's harmful to the bile. Ideally, engage in soft, gentle conduct and rest near the seashore or in some cool, breezy place. However, since none of this is possible at the moment, we must—how do you Americans say it?—*mush*! Hightail it."

He climbed behind the wheel, and took another look at Trevor. "Let it sleep for now. It will be rising like an evil wind soon enough. It has already consumed the other tattoos and is busy digesting. Good. That will give us some time to find Nelly."

He sighed. "The poor girl. You two, Trevor, are a madcap couple, did I ever tell you that?"

Trevor tried to laugh. "Not in so many words, no. I guess we are compatible in an incompatible way. It's really strange. I almost fell in love with someone else. Actually," he thought out loud to himself. "I did. I don't know how I managed that, but I did." He looked somberly out the window.

"To love more than one, you must love yourself even more. To generate the fire," Dorje muttered as he navigated the taxi down Hayes. "That's your father's way, too, I think. It's a common disorder of the kundalini, if you ask me."

Dorje studied Trevor in the rearview mirror. "How are you feeling?"

"A little weak, but I think I'm okay. So what do you think—about all this?"

"The cause or the cure?"

"Start with the cause, then the cure."

"Not an easy business. I've seen it happening in my own field. The world is accelerating into fragmentation, down to the minutest particles, which are taking over with a vengeance, having been neglected by consciousness for so long. Your heart is splitting just as the atom does, just as countries are . . . Love is splitting."

"And that's not good?"

"Not good, not bad. It depends."

"You don't think it's possible to love more than one person at a time?"

"Does the tattoo love you? Or the bodies that it comes to inhabit? Actually, it is interested only in one body."

"Which is?"

Dorje laughed. "Good question. Most people don't see this body. It is so vast that it remains invisible to us. We are just specks in it. Like freckles on its cosmic form."

Trevor thought about Alex Fortuna, about her red dreadlocks festooned with scarabs and the many thousand freckles like constellations on the universe of her skin.

"You didn't answer my question, Dorje. I think it's an important part of this—this mystery, whatever it is. It's about separation and coming together in new ways, I think."

"Ah," Dorje exclaimed, "the paradox of the mystery is how ordinary it is! Even the greatest mystery of the universe is like a child's game, if you learn to play by its rules. But you're quite right, Trevor. Even your father would agree with you. One has

209

to live in duality in order to express unity. It's not just there in the unity itself. To be fragmented and separated is to cling passionately to everything that we are a part of. Even"—Dorje scoffed—"even that entity that clings to you with its evil breath. It has a heart, that painted gdon, and it seeks love as well. Its own kind of love, nevertheless."

Dorje shrugged. "If it were to accept a greater love than the one it seeks, then . . ."

"He said if he dies, Nelly dies."

"We all die." Dorje shrugged again. "Death is . . . hip. No, that's not the issue."

"What is, then?"

"Ha, you think I would tell you? You have to earn your own Buddha points, Trevor, the hard way. I didn't sit through all my incarnational studies for nothing!"

"It's about love, then," Trevor insisted. Then he added under his breath, "Ultimately."

Dorje drove through the Tenderloin, home to lost souls, where he kept his apartment. He double-parked and jumped out of the car.

"I need to run up and get something," he said to Trevor. "Something we may need."

"What is it, Dorje?" Trevor called after him.

"Don't worry," Dorje replied. "It's not yak soup."

Dorje returned five minutes later with two other Tibetan lamas, who both climbed into the cab. Dorje was carrying a velvet bag containing an object of some sort.

"This is Dongzhen Nurbu," he introduced the first lama to Trevor. The spry monk, dressed in lama's sweats and a pair of Neuro Nikes, smiled and nodded.

"And this young fellow, he's Yeshi Nurbu." The other monk was dressed in the same maroon robe that Dorje was wearing, and carried an air of sparkling good humor about him.

"They don't speak much English, I'm sorry. Just learning."

"Hello, *namasté,*" Trevor greeted them. The two lamas giggled, and the one sitting next to Trevor, Yeshi, laid his hand on Trevor's knee. "Okay," he said. "Okay."

The lama in the sweats, Dongzhen, sat up front with Dorje. "Now we have the official lama SWAT team with us," Dorje said, smiling. "One to manage the sleeping gdon when it awakens, and one to keep an eye on you."

"What's in the bag, Dorje?"

"Oh, this? My secret weapon!" Dorje joked. He unveiled the object. It looked like a Tibetan ceremonial dagger.

"A *phurbu* with special powers. Perfect for performing brain surgery on hungry ghosts! Ha, ha, ha!"

He revved the engine, but then idled when a bedraggled street person staggered toward the cab. "Hey, Dorje! Hey, man! Wait a sec!"

"It's Motorola Mike," Dorje explained. "One of my regular clients." He rolled down the window.

"How's it going, Mike?" Dorje inquired solicitously. "Any word yet?"

"Yeah, man, great, I gotta thank you," the street person had bright, rheumy-green eyes. "Getting there, man." He waved an antique Motorola Micro Lite phone in the air. "Clear signals coming through, Dorj!"

"That's wonderful. Send her my best regards."

"Sure thing, Dorj. Hey, can you give me a lift?"

"Not tonight, Mike. We're having a spiritual emergency. We must be on our way."

"Spiritual emergency, huh? Don't you guys ever rest?" Motorola Mike lurched against the hood, his grimy black palm leaving a print on the windshield.

Dorje read the palm print. "Your life line is showing improvement, Mike. Got to go now. Be good, healthy, and wise."

"Yeah, man. Catch you later."

Dorje drove off. "Motorola Mike," he explained to Trevor, "a sad case of a man trapped in the cellular bardo. He's sixty years old, his phone is more than thirty years old. He begs for food and whatever money he can raise to keep his phone service intact. But he doesn't call anyone. Never. He just wants his line open, in case she calls."

"In case *who* calls?" Trevor asked.

"Another broken heart, Trevor." Dorje winked at him. "That could be you in another twenty years, if this gdon doesn't wreak its havoc on you."

"What do you mean by that?"

"Mike had a true love, a sweetheart, many years—lifetimes—ago. She probably would not recognize him in the street today. He left her for someone else. It didn't last. His meditation is his voice mail. He has only one single message on it—from her, pleading with him to stay with her. Begging him not to leave. That message is now thirty years old. He listens to it every day and weeps. That is all."

"Poor guy," Trevor remarked.

Dorje gave him an enigmatic shrug. "You ask if it's possible to love more than one, Trevor. For most people, they're lucky if they have *anyone* to love."

Dorje wove through the traffic, passing a car with a sign that read: STUDENT GURU. HOW ARE MY TEACHINGS? CALL 1-800-KUNDALINI.

The instructor, dressed in a robe, sat beside a pensive young man at the wheel. He waved at Dorje as the cab passed. Dorje waved back happily, but muttered under his breath. "Neurorajnishees. Work of the devil, really. But don't tell them. They might try to ram me, and I don't have insurance."

Dorje turned to Trevor in the back seat. The Tibetan lama sitting next to him was holding his hand, smiling. "Okay, my friend," Dorje announced, "to Nelly."

"To Nelly. That's right."

"Where might she be, have you any idea?"

Trevor closed his eyes. He felt so tired. Where was she? Thinking about her, he sparked the Tattoo into coiling upright on his chest. It was thinking alongside him.

"Trevor?" Dorje prodded him. "You all right?"

"Yes, just thinking about it. Where would she go at this

time of night? Some place where she has friends who might be able to help her." He smirked. "Ordinarily, she'd call me. She'd just come over to my place. I have her key, she has mine."

Trevor now felt something puffing up on his chest, sucking the air out of his lungs. He gasped as he held his chest with his hand.

"Dongzhen," Dorje instructed his colleague, "quickly."

Dongzhen massaged Trevor's pulse, then looked at Dorje and shook his head.

"You're losing your wind, Trevor." Then he spoke to Dong-zhen rapidly in Tibetan. "He will massage your heart," Dorje told Trevor.

Dongzhen opened up Trevor's jacket and pulled his t-shirt up.

A startled silence enveloped the taxi.

An image was slowly developing on Trevor's chest, a giant, bloated fish with a spiny tail glistening a deep blue, as though it had just emerged from the sea.

"It's a blowfish!" Trevor exclaimed. "A fugu!"

"A poisonous creature," Dorje remarked. "Like this gdon. What does it signify, I wonder?"

"Maybe it's trying to tell us where Nelly went?" Trevor's eyes suddenly lit up. "There's a place called The Blowfish—it's an alternative sushi club south of Market on Bryant Street. Sushi and Japanese animé, that's what they serve! Nelly likes to hang out there sometimes. Come on, Dorje, I think it's worth a shot."

Animé

Dorje, Dongzhen, Yeshi, and Trevor arrived at the Blowfish. Built into a block of converted warehouse space, the establish-ment projected an unassuming facade. A blue-neon fugu danc-ing on Hokusai waves was the sole indication that it was a place of business. Inside, though, Japanese animés sprang to

213

life the moment they entered the dark, cavernous throat of the postmodern sushi bar.

It was a marvelous fairyland of sprites. Miniature cartoon figures raced around like manic, colored tornadoes. Or like wood-block prints with legs, thought Trevor when he spied an Usagi Yojimbo samurai rabbit engaged in a *chambara* sword fight with the Demon Neko cat.

Slash! Cut! Parry! Skewer!

Dorje and the lamas stepped aside, grinning as the whirlwind blades tore up the dancing animé spotlights that were programmed to target newly arrived guests at the entrance.

ZAAAAAAAAAAAAA! KA-RAK! KA-TANG! KA-TANG! KA-TANG!

"Look at that!" Dorje blurted with delight, pointing to a troop of neural nymphs patrolling the far corner of the sushi bar, taking orders from patrons seated on gutted tree stumps from a reclaimed redwood forest in Oregon.

"Those are the Bondage Fairies," a sweet voice announced from behind them. They turned around.

"Good evening," said the two-foot-high figure, a high-res blond with big, doelike eyes and *loooong* ponytails. "Would you gentlemen prefer the animé or nonanimé section? Or would you like to sit at the sushi bar?"

The apparition was dressed in a *se-ra-fuku bishojo senshi* outfit, a cutesy-pie sailor suit with a nautical Japanese-schoolgirl collar.

"I'm your hostess this evening," she chirped as she batted her eyelashes. "My name is Goddess Kathy. I'm an animé temp from Cat Girl Paradise. We're serving special sake infusions this evening of raspberry, clove, and mango."

"Uh, thanks, but we're just looking for a friend," Trevor answered, as Dorje and his two Tibetan lamas scrutinized the phan'toon front and back, looking for her infrared kundalini connection.

"In that case"—she batted her eyelashes again—"I'll be

214

off." With that she flew away on the curl of a light wave, carrying a tiny menu with her.

Dorje beamed after her as she vanished into the rafters. "A true *dakini*!" he whispered to Trevor. "A tantric goddess. There are more and more of them coming into this earth plane, you know, to tweak our higher senses."

A short pause, then he continued excitedly. "Did you notice how she was holding the menu in her left hand, indicating detachment from the fear of death—the basic psychological block of the first chakra? And a ballpoint pen in her right hand, like a sword, with which she removes all fear? And she had pink skin and was wearing a dress of yellow-peach color . . . No doubt about it, she exhibited all the signs of a dakini shakti, combining the forces of the creator, preserver, and destroyer . . ."

"Aren't you reading a bit too much into it?" Trevor huffed. "She's only an animation, after all."

"Speaking of dakinis," Dorje changed the subject, deciding that the dharma of 'toons was beyond Trevor's grasp at the moment, that the young man had other, more pressing preoccupations. "Do you see Nelly anywhere?"

"Let's have a look," Trevor replied, and they headed toward the sushi bar.

"That man is blind," Dorje commented when he saw the sushi master behind the counter.

"You're right about that," Trevor agreed. "But he sees everything." The Blowfish was famous for its eighty-three-year-old blind sushi chef, Takasago, who was the only sushi master on the West Coast licensed to prepare the potentially deadly fugu fish.

Even now, with an intent expression on his face, he was in the process of removing the poison sacs from a blowfish and slicing thin fillets of the fish's delicate white meat.

"He hasn't had a single fatality in his entire career of preparing fugu. He's a Japanese National Living Treasure," Trevor told his companions.

215

"A boddhisatva." Dorje nodded. "He radiates true compassion for the fish who are evolving into the human life chain. And he intercepts death before it is ingested. A fascinating ritual."

Trevor scanned the sushi counter. No sign of Nelly. But he heard the familiar voice of Violet O'Chen, a mutual friend of his and Nelly's. She was a rail-thin woman in her twenties, with long, straight blonde hair, a latex tank top, a gladiator skirt, and a pair of miner's hobnailed boots laced up to her calves.

". . . and she insists that her relationship with her dildo is strictly platonic, can you believe that?" Violet was gossiping with a mousy-looking woman whose lips and nose were adorned with multiple piercings, including a miniature Rolodex attached to her nose ring.

"Oh, hi, Trev—long time no see!" Violet grinned when she saw him. "What brings you here? It's way past your bedtime, isn't it? Or are you still sleepwalking?"

Trevor gave her a smile. His friends knew about his lucid teleporting, and they jibed him about it.

"Not really, Violet, but you should try it some time. It's cheaper than space travel."

Violet O'Chen was a feisty Irish-Chinese physicist from NASA Ames, which had recently been acquired by the Disney Corporation as part of their aggressive move to capture the world space program.

"Well, I'm tripping on Shochikubai." She tapped one of the empty sake bottles littering the counter in front of her. "I keep seeing giant pink shark pods. I think there must be distilled alien life forms in this stuff."

"I wouldn't be surprised. Have you seen Nelly, by any chance?"

"Nelly?" Violet thought for a moment. "Yeah, she was here a little while ago. I think she was heading for the club downstairs."

216   "Thanks, Violet. I'd better get going. Take care—"

"Trevor," Violet called to him.

He paused at the end of the counter. "Yes?"

She flashed an embarrassed grin. "I think I should warn you, Nelly's not alone. She was with some guy." She feigned sympathy. "You guys doing okay?"

Violet had developed a crush on Trevor a while back, but it hadn't gotten very far. Dating Violet was like dating a car crash, Trevor had decided. She was in the habit of taking wild turns with her men, and eventually ended up forcing them off the road. A beautiful accident waiting to happen. He had passed on the ride.

"Thanks for the tip, Violet, you're a pal." Trevor forced a smile as he headed toward the stairs leading to the dance club on the lower level.

"What are you thinking, Dorje?" he asked his friend. "Is she another dakini?"

"That one? Oh, yes, most certainly. They all are, you know. Even the undecided ones."

The bouncer at the door was dressed in full-body water-resistant coveralls. He wore a face mask, a shower cap on his head, and rubber gloves. Vapors of liquid nitrogen hissed from a vent between his feet.

"It's almost closing time, so I won't charge you guys," he said as he stamped their wrists. "You've been here before? No? Okay, here's the drill. Don't mess with the cryonic tanks. Respect the dead—um, the *reposed*. There's towels downstairs in the locker room, help yourself if you like. You've got thirty minutes if you want to float in one of the hot tubs with a friend."

The bouncer gave the Tibetans a suspicious glance. "Are you guys religious?"

Dorje replied, "We're just here to say a prayer or two. We won't interfere, I promise."

"Last time we had some Christian Scientists trying to sabotage the equipment. We had to call in the police and the fire department to make sure everything was okay. It's a strict city ordinance. This is an FFZ—a fundamentalist-free zone. No monkey business allowed or we get busted, got it?"

217

"Don't worry."

"Okay, have fun." He waved them in.

"I must say," Dorje told Trevor as they descended the steep stairs, "this is an adventure. You bring us to the most peculiar places."

"All in a night's work, Dorje," Trevor said wearily. He felt the weight of the Tattoo dragging him down. Nelly had better be here.

He wasn't sure how much longer he could last with the thing tapping into his energy center. He grabbed the handrail, and Dorje had to steady him.

"Easy, Trevor, easy . . ."

There were rows of stainless-steel dewar stretching across the vast expanse of the Cryo Club. Tiny, recessed windows revealed the sleeping occupants of these oversized Thermos flasks. Curled in the fetal position, they floated like silver-wrapped pods inside the vats of liquid nitrogen. Cascades of vapor spilled from the sides of the cooled-down tanks like ghostly waterfalls.

Dorje caught his breath. "It's like a bardo aquarium," he marveled.

"This club was built on the site of one of the Patel Cryo Motels at the turn of the century," Trevor explained.

"When cryonics was really big, this Indian family, the Patels, jumped on the bandwagon. They were operating a string of cheap hotels, and they thought they'd struck a gold mine by offering budget cryonic lodgings to the public. But they were shut down by the state for mismanagement. The Blowfish took over, and by some miracle, picked up the license to continue operating the business—"

"A Motel 6 for the dead!"

"It's more of a cryonic charity these days," Trevor corrected him. "The city is reluctant to assume legal responsibility. I think most of these guys in the tanks were homeless street people. They're hanging on by a slim thread, I'd say. Or else their families would have fished them out long ago."

"Indeed." Dorje nodded in agreement.

Interspersed between some of the steel cryonic chambers were Plexiglas tanks that hung suspended like macabre hot tubs.

It was a slow night and only a few tanks were occupied by late-night carousers from South of Market.

A sign on the wall advised, PRACTICE SAFE NECROPHILIA. VI-OLATORS WILL BE PROSECUTED; a couple of leather mummies were making out in a dark corner under a tank, their arms wrapped around each other. But otherwise, the Cryo Club was deserted at this late hour. It was a lonely place, and the ethereal music only added to the air of abandonment. Nelly was nowhere in sight.

"Window-shopping for cadavers?"

The two men had been standing between two cryonic tanks, observing Trevor and company quietly. The one who addressed them was a Russian. He wore a seersucker suit with a tacky Chinese shirt and a flowery tie.

His brown hair was cropped close, and he had a grim yet sardonic air about him. His partner had Slavic features, but his skin was much darker and he had a central-Asian cast to his eyes.

"My name is Boris. And this is my friend Igor. Igor, say hello. Igor is sometimes tongue-tied in English," Boris apologized. "We are tourists in your fair city."

Igor nodded. "Hyell-o." A black leather motorcycle jacket barely contained his powerful chest, while his biker boots and black jeans emphasized his muscular thighs. His hair was cropped, and a pair of sunglasses hid his eyes. Completing the look was a thick silver belt buckle that glinted in the low light.

Odd. Trevor had noticed wet footprints on the concrete floor.

"What exactly is it that you're touring?" Trevor asked Boris, exchanging glances with Dorje and the lamas.

Boris smiled to display sharp, yellow teeth. "You might

219

say that we are collecting specimens of unusual American nightlife. You never know which animals will present themselves at the watering hole. We are hunters." He chuckled deep in his throat. "Russian hunters."

"Had any luck?" Trevor felt a burst of adrenaline shoot through his system.

"Not until now," Boris replied, with a mocking, sorrowful expression. "It's been quite dead here, as you can see. But I think your presence has livened things up."

"Trevor," Dorje's voice sounded an alarm. Trevor looked at his friend. The other Russian—Igor—was holding a gun, pressing it into Dorje's side.

Trevor turned to Boris. "What do you want?"

Boris studied him for a moment, then shook his head as though he was disappointed to hear the reply. "You have something that belongs to us. You are the woman's friend. She did not have it on her person. So *you* must—"

"Have what?" Trevor asked. Then it hit him again. "Where is Nelly?"

"We will make it easy for you, if you cooperate. Don't be like that other shit." Boris spat on the floor.

"*What* other shit?" Then Trevor fell silent as he saw Dorje and the lamas staring into one of the tanks, looking puzzled.

"That shit over there." Boris nodded happily.

Trevor's eyes widened. There was a body floating in the tank. A Manchu topknot was coiled like a tentacle across the face, and the eyes were open, raw in their blankness.

Trevor recalled where he had seen that face before. Not that long ago.

It was Alex Fortuna's husband, Hakim Beijing.

"What—what have you done to him?" Trevor asked, in shock.

"I think you two have met?" Boris laughed. "I really think he was wanting to fuck your girlfriend. He was getting quite fresh with her, you know. We had to step in and pry them apart. Look, that's where it happened. They were sitting at that table, there. He was trying to undress her. I really believe that we did you a favor."

Trevor stared at the coffee counter, which once had been a slab in a morgue. He saw a half-empty bottle of mineral water and two partially filled glasses. Nelly had been drinking from one of those glasses . . .

"You're out of your fucking mind!" Trevor exclaimed in a sudden explosion of rage. He lunged at Boris, but the Russian nimbly moved aside and wrenched Trevor's arm behind his back.

Spasms of pain shot up through Trevor's shoulder. He screamed. Boris jerked him hard again.

"Try me," Boris taunted. "Go ahead—I would love to break your arm off, but I don't want to damage the merchandise. Where's it hiding, your little tattoo?"

"Hurry up, Boris," Igor called to him nervously. "This place is beginning to give me the creeps."

"All right, let's see what a nice chest you have." Boris yanked Trevor's jacket open and pulled his t-shirt up. "What's this?"

There was a scurrying of feelers as the Tattoo began to evade Boris's lunging hand.

"Fucking tattoo, it's at it again!" Boris swore at Igor. "But he's got it on him, that's the good news . . . Hold it right there . . ."

The Tattoo disappeared under Trevor's arm.

"Where's it going to now?! We'll fix that bastard soon enough." Boris brought out a small vacuum flask and a cordless implement with an attached nozzle.

He switched it on and ran it across Trevor's torso. "I want every fucking piece of it. Lift your arm. A real joker, isn't it? You won't miss it, I promise you . . . There, I think I have it. Turn around, *svolatch*."

Trevor grimaced in pain as Boris yanked him.

221

Boris checked the meter on the device. "Three gigabytes worth. Missing a byte or two, but it will regenerate. Good man," he said, and twisted Trevor's arm again.

"I tell you what, if you and your friends just sit tight and promise not to cause any commotion, we will just say good-night and be on our way."

"You got what you wanted, where's Nelly?" Trevor spoke through his pain.

"Still with your Nelly? The bitch is dead. If she's not dead already, then she's been disconnected from this thing long enough that she may as well be." Boris patted the vacuum flask.

"You'd better find yourself a new girlfriend. She's been with this parasite too long, and she isn't the one you love. Not any more."

Boris and Igor backed away from them slowly, disappearing among the cryonic tanks like sharks snaking around the bottom of a dark sea.

Osmose

Dorje shook his head. "Never mind them." He turned to his two fellow lamas. "That fellow in the tank, quickly—Dongzhen, Yeshi, get him out before he pickles in the bardos."

Dongzhen and Yeshi climbed the stairs leading to the tank. They grabbed Hakim under his arms and fished him out of the water. He was dripping wet.

"Careful, careful . . ." Dorje instructed them as they laid him on the floor. Dorje listened for Hakim's heartbeat. "Very remote. Approaching the Clear Light, in fact. But still alive. Extraordinary."

Dorje pulled the eyelids back and examined the whites of Hakim's eyes, then sought the vital points in Hakim's thorax and

222

chest and began to apply acupressure. "Dongzhen and Yeshi, assist me with these points while I get my phurbu ready."

The two lamas began a process of transferring chi to the body, breathing and grunting as they ran their lines of energy through Hakim.

Dorje placed the Tibetan dagger between Hakim's eyes, raised it and pressed down. A mumbled incantation followed: *"Om tare tuttare ture svaha . . ."*

A smile appeared on Dorje's face. "It's the Tara mantra. The goddess is the great cheater of death. Our friend's life force is warming up gradually. Let us be patient and see."

The color returned to Hakim's cheeks slowly. Dorje's smile grew broader.

"There, you see, he's not dead after all. Only slightly deanimated."

Hakim began to cough and his eyes fluttered open. A deep groan escaped his chest.

"What—what happened?"

"According to my diagnosis, you've been having a near-life experience," Dorje explained.

Hakim blinked at Dorje, then saw Trevor standing behind the lamas.

He groaned again.

Trevor leaned over him, bringing his face close to Hakim's. "Do you remember who I am?"

Hakim blinked without any sign of recognition.

"I'm Alex Fortuna's friend," Trevor reminded him. "We met at her place earlier this evening. Do you remember me now?"

Hakim made a sudden, feeble attempt to rise off the floor. His soggy clothes left a spreading puddle beneath him.

Dorje interrupted Trevor. "Don't press him now, Trevor. He is still in a delicate state of reentry. Can you hear me?" Dorje asked Hakim gently.

223

Hakim nodded.

"Good. I am going to tell you something. Listen carefully.

If you wish to make a peaceful and enlightened reentry, and to avoid the unpleasantness of a bardo crash, do your best to remain calm, passive, and relaxed. That is as much as you can do right now."

Dorje felt Hakim's forehead with his palm. "Still traumatized." He relayed his diagnosis to Dongzhen and Yeshi in Tibetan. "Second-degree hellish visions, indicative of a second bardo spillover."

He switched back to English. "Tell me, Hakim—Hakim, is that your name? Yes? Very good. Where you have just been—in your consciousness—have you seen terrifying creatures resembling flame-haloed, blood-drinking monsters? Yes or no? Nod your head if you can."

Hakim shook his head. He felt a piston jump-start his heart, and an avalanche of icy yet burning snow raced down his spine. He began to shiver uncontrollably.

Dorje rubbed his wrists vigorously.

"He obviously hasn't seen the Herukas, the wrathful deities," Dorje noted to the lamas. "He would be in a state of absolute terror if he had. That's a good thing."

Dorje addressed Hakim again. "Now let me ask you this, question number two: Have you been surrounded by machines, experienced horrific manipulations by any number of scientific, torturing control devices, and have you felt like a meaningless cipher in a universe of cold, heartless calculations?"

Hakim nodded weakly. "Excellent," Dorje said brightening up. "Your memory of the earth plane seems to be perfectly intact. Welcome back to consciousness."

Where had he been? Half-dreaming, half-dazed, Hakim struggled to fit the pieces together. He couldn't remember the twilight state, when he was boomeranging like a stick of nothingness through glass, wire, fire, and ice.

Only that he had been there with a dragon's fist pounding on his heart and while its claws ripped at his brain. The Rus-

sians had held him down in the water. He had struggled, but then learned to detach from the struggle—he felt a sense of soothing power return to him through that release.

They had surprised him and the girl. Of course, he had surprised her first, before they showed up to interrupt their little "heart-to-heart."

He had wanted to see it on her—what it had evolved into. But that little bit of nothingness had rubbed off on him! And now he carried it within himself, on his own secret skin . . .

He hadn't expected that. He should have known that she was trouble. Beautiful trouble—but did he regret anything? Of course not. Too bad he was dead. Or was he? What *was* he?

Nelly had come to the scene, to the tattoo rave. To that place South of Market they called the Tattoo Exchange, where Hakim had gone after leaving Alex's place. A good place to hide out in, to hang out in. Friends, customers, swingers of the tattoo world, sharing the on-line needle.

She looked awful, haggard. Staggered in like she was only half alive. Like him, she was lost between two competing worlds, and she didn't fully belong to either. But he could see that she had good reason for feeling like that: she was possessed, too.

Correction: un-possessed.

She had done a drastic thing. She had freed herself of a type-four tattoo. The worst kind of habit to kick. Force of will was a blunt instrument, and it couldn't be applied to a type-four 'too . . .

Hakim had been sipping some arrack and contemplating his next move. Fat Freddy was sharing the bar counter with him, his Buddha belly humming like a pay-per-view for the vision-impaired.

One of Hakim's jobs. Hakim had wired Fat Freddy to a porno database in Finland, and they were fucking all over his face and chin and belly and back and thighs. Real-time triple-X 'toos.

Hakim was a hero in the 'too world. They respected him. His skill. His wizardry.

"Look at that chick, Hakim." Fat Freddy nudged him. "She's kicking, man. She's gifted out. What do you think she's after?"

"Don't know, man. Who gives a fuck?" Hakim answered glumly, worrying about how he would retrieve his stash from Alex's place.

"She's got somebody's number, man. Look, she's heading for Vincent, man."

Vincent Van-Too. Another main man. His stuff was famous, like Hakim's, from the Bosporus to Berkeley, from Berlin to Bogotá. His stuff *burned*. Vincent was wired into some powerful shit. He even had this decorative third ear implanted into his head—"in homage," so he said, to the other Vincent, his namesake in landscape hell.

"What do you think she wants with Vincent, man?" Fat Freddy was clearly intrigued. He was as nosy as a terrier in a gopher field.

"Go listen in and come back and tell us, Sven," Fat Freddy whispered to the well-hung Swedish porno star on his forearm. He had trained Sven to do errands for him. Sven was a favorite whipping boy.

"Sure thing, Freddy." Sven climbed off somebody's face and into Fat Freddy's arm band, which was always on and always cooking like a wired wok.

"Don't be long, big boy."

"I won't, Freddy," Sven replied, and he went swimming into the channel, butt-naked. Gone to work for his master, just as Godscape had intended.

Vincent Van-Too was busy with nipples tonight. Doing miniature landscapes, sentient stereograms on each nipple. He was leaning over this busty chick—*who had done this other work on her, man? It was real shit*—But he could afford to overlook the insult of the ordinary. He was feeling *on* tonight. Inspired to new heights.

The bull dyke grunted when Nelly walked in on them.

"Can't you see Vincent's busy, bitch? Come back later when it's your turn."

Vincent spun around on his stool. He looked at Nelly through his headset, then took it off his head. He had seen enough. He had noted the detailed outline of the vanished tattoo. A masterpiece of nothingness that he could only aspire to.

"Where'd you get that?" he asked Nelly point-blank. "That ain't regular work. It ain't even a type four, and that's as far as it gets. Fuck, where are you from? Outer space? Shit!"

Vincent had a reddish-brown beard specked with white. He'd been a 'too master for years. He started out doing the organic skin thing, but then when epidermal sentience came into vogue, he discovered his real niche. There were dead people adorned with his work who were worth more in death than they ever were alive, before he put his mark on them.

Vincent was wearing a red long-sleeved Guatemalan shirt decorated with birds and flowers. That's all he ever wore, long-sleeved Guatemalan shirts over his tall, lanky frame. He never removed his clothes in public, believing that if anyone ever saw his own personal skinwork, he'd open himself up to a serious security breach.

Besides, he kept his programming tools embedded in his pecs, in the coils of a security dragon.

"What's the matter, babe, cat got your tongue? Don't mind Bertha here. She bitches worse than she bites."

"Easy for you to say, Vincent," the dyke groused. "Try making an appointment with yourself some time. You're harder to get a hold of than General fucking AOL Motors."

"Put a rag in it." Vincent glowered at her. "This is important. If you don't like it, go see someone else about getting the job done."

"C'mon, Vince, relax, I didn't mean nothin', you finish what you started, okay?"

"I'll think about it. You go sit over there," he ordered her. "I'll call you when I'm ready."

Bertha gave Nelly a noxious look, then skulked her big frame away.

"*Bitch,*" she hissed under her breath as she stepped around Nelly. She walked away bare-chested, leaving her western shirt hanging from the back of the chair.

One of her buttons was switched on and transmitting, so Fat Freddy's Swedish porno avatar had no trouble coming through the channel. He had looped around the world via NairobiNet, then cruised through a silver market in Mexico City, and finally entered through a pizza-delivery service in the Mission district of San Francisco.

Sven had a real hard-on for cyberspace, all right.

"Okay, you want to talk about it?"

Vincent patted the chair for Nelly to sit down. "You look like death warmed over, honey," he said as she lowered herself with a sigh.

This was the first time in three days that she had spoken to a real human being.

"I am, actually," she replied."Death warmed over."

"You need help. How'd you hear about me? You don't look like one of the regulars, if you know what I mean." Vincent waved his hand around the Tattoo Exchange. "They're filthy degenerates, but they have sensitive souls."

The Tattoo Exchange was in full session, with bodies rubbing against one another on the dance floor. Eye contact led to private sessions in the curtained-off private area of the club, where anything went except for the exchange of vital tattoo fluids. You had to use full-body sheaths if you were doing it in person—or else rely on disposable avatars. There were plenty of templates lying around in each room; just dip into them like paste-on softwares, and grab one of the plentiful tubes of Norton's Lube.

"I . . . I saw your work on someone."

Vincent laid his brush down. "What did it look like?" he asked her quietly.

Nelly looked back at him. How could she put this in

228

words—the right words? What if she was crazy? Crazy as a 'toon?

Vincent waited for her, then he smiled as understanding dawned. He took Nelly's hand. His gruff attitude had softened considerably—he knew where she was coming from.

"Relax. You've come to the right place. I'm an ally."

"You can help me, can't you?"

He patted her hand. "I am really quite goddamned pleased to meet you. What's your name, honey?"

"Nelly."

"Nelly, listen to me. I can tell from your eyes what your skin can't tell me. It's gone, but it isn't gone. That's their nature. They've been here for a while. Take a look around. Half of these yobos are carrying, and they don't even know it. God knows, I'm doing my best. Reworking the damage. Sometimes it's real difficult, making it pass for art. I feel like I'm stemming the tide part of the time, the rest of the time I feel like I'm spinning my wheels."

She listened, her eyes glistening with tears. They began to flow freely now.

"You've been through a lot of shit, haven't you? It's turned your life inside out." Vincent squeezed her hand. "It's painful. But that's good. It's good that it's painful. That's the bell that rings inside you, telling you that something's going on. No pain, no gain. That's the simple truth. You peel away the dead skin. You get into the heart. That's where the real pictures are. And you've seen it, haven't you?"

She nodded.

"I was young and foolish, too, honey. We all go through that. I thought I could take them all on by myself. You know what this guy told me? He was a teacher of mine. He said, 'I've finally reached the point where I can say, "What a fool I was three weeks ago!"'"

Vincent laughed. "It gets a whole lot better. And that's what brought you here. See, that's progress!"

"I saw your tattoo. On Sinbad—that's the name I gave him,"

229

she explained with a weak smile. "Seeing it gave me hope."

"It really pisses them off," Vincent said, smiling. "It's like throwing a wrench into their flash. Of course, they've been coming in for quite a while now. But, you know what, it only takes just one real honest tattoo to change their direction. Like that butterfly that flutters its wings in the cornfield in Kansas, honey. It turns into a monsoon some place else, in India, wherever, who gives a fuck? They can't stop it. They think they can just waltz in here and call the tune. Big fucking mistake!"

Vincent guffawed, then grew silent. "They're going to want to neutralize you now. You got rid of it. But that's the painful thing for them. How long ago did it happen?"

"Today."

Vincent frowned. "No wonder you look like shit. But it probably looks worse than you right now. Small consolation, huh? Never mind. We'll see what we can do. Let me have a look at you, honey. Undo your shirt."

Nelly stripped to the waist and Vincent studied her with his eyes in overdrive. He ran his fingertips up and down her arms, tracing her collarbone. "Hmm," he mused to himself. Then he told Nelly, "Lift your arms."

She raised them above her head like a ballerina. Vincent studied her breasts for a moment, then put on his headset. He saw the detailed anatomy of the missing tattoo, part of a tentacle still sticking to her right breast. He erased it with his light-drill, all the while soothing Nelly. "Don't worry, this won't hurt," he murmured.

"Turn around, let me see your back," he said when he was done. She did as she was told. "You've got a beautiful back, Nelly," he continued. "I'd love to do some real work on you one day. Beautiful. Not today though. We're just going to clean you up."

He turned up the power of his zoom lens. "I call it a 'no-trace' tattoo, what I'm giving you. Now take all your clothes off. No need to feel modest here, honey. Not in this neighborhood," he chuckled. "We're all just naked spirits here."

Nelly removed her boots and socks, then unbuckled her jeans and pulled them down. She slipped off her underwear and stood in front of him naked.

Across the room, Fat Freddy and Hakim watched the show. "Fuck, what's he doing?" Fat Freddy wondered. Sven was giving them a running commentary.

"A 'no-trace,'" Hakim replied. "That's subliminal skin-work, man. He's covering her up with nothingness. He's going to make her invisible."

A few moments later, Vincent turned off his tools.

"I think I've stabilized you, honey," he told Nelly. "That ought to hold you. When they come for you, they won't be able to touch you."

He studied her through his headset. Her body was covered entirely with the invisible script of the Mu sutra—the mystical letters that spelled the Name of the Void.

"That's the best I can do with nanosanskrit. I mean, I'm good but I'm not that good. I think I got you pretty much all covered."

From her head to her toes, Nelly was a flowering statue of invisible bougainvillea in glowing script.

She began to shiver in rose, crimson, pink, red, and purple blossoms of sensation.

"It'll pass. I've got most of the other stuff out. You're going to be okay, kid. You're going to set them on fire. You got a boyfriend?"

Nelly pulled her boots on and smiled sadly. "What's that? It seems like a foreign concept to me now."

"A main squeeze."

"Does it make a difference?"

"Well, the way you relate to each other is going to be a little different now. He's going to feel the change in you. The power. Oh, you're going to be radiating to everyone you meet. But it might change the way you feel about him if he's not ready for you."

"Trevor's somewhere else right now. I don't know where."

231

"Trevor, huh?"

"Trevor Gobi. I love him, but he's a pain in the ass sometimes."

"Well, hang loose and he may come around to the light. Thanks for coming, Nelly. I don't see too many like you."

"What do I owe you?"

"Owe me?" Vincent protested. "Hell, I've never met anyone who's seen my work plastered on those motherfuckers and lived to tell it. Where did you see it, Nelly? In one of those funny vectors that they hide in like rats? I've been seeding Omspace with 'em . . . For some reason, they got this conceit about using symbols of archaic human technology to communicate with each other. Probably makes 'em feel superior. So I wrote this code that targets icons of old telephone handsets. Pre-nineteen-seventies pay phones are my speciality!" He grinned broadly. "They pick up the phone—then boom! I send them a message they can never erase. I call it 'soul-forwarding'!" Vincent guffawed.

"I saw it in a temple," Nelly said reflectively.

"Oh, they have those, too, huh? I guess they worship the goddess, too. The goddess of 'too."

"Good night, Vincent."

Yes, they worshipped the goddess. Nelly wondered about that. There were so many road maps to the temple. So many forms of the goddess. Which one was Trevor worshipping right now?

She stepped out into the night air and gulped it into her lungs. She felt different. Alert. Refreshed, recharged. Ready.

She heard footsteps on the street and turned around. This dude had followed her out of the club.

"Excuse me . . . Sorry, I didn't mean to startle you," he told her. "I couldn't help but notice you upstairs at the Exchange." He offered her his hand to shake. "My name's Hakim. You're a friend of a mutual acquaintance, I believe. Trevor? Trevor Gobi? I'd like to speak to you, if you don't mind. I think you might be interested in what I have to tell you."

232

Cat-Shit Cookies

"I think he's recovered sufficiently," Trevor complained to Dorje. Hakim was sitting up on the floor now, hugging his knees.

"All in good time, Trevor," Dorje replied. "How are you feeling?" he asked Hakim.

Hakim was regurgitating the chi that Dongzhen and Yeshi had infused him with. He felt off balance and his kundalini was a limp noodle at the base of his spine.

"I feel like a human lava lamp," Hakim croaked. "But I should thank you."

Dorje nodded his head. "Yes, that is understandable. The internal colors have shifted gravity. Coming through the bardos unscathed is something of a miracle. You are very fortunate—"

"Dorje!" Trevor interrupted.

"Just a moment, Trevor. Now, Hakim," Dorje continued, "I would be remiss if I didn't advise you on your postbardo care. If I were you, for the next ten days, I would avoid getting on a wild horse, swimming in a whirlpool, running through fire to show off your courage, climbing up and jumping down from trees, or playing at the edges of caverns that are filled with the rains of summer. Other than that, feel free to engage in any normal activity. Did you follow all that?"

Hakim shook his head to dislodge some water from his ear. "I . . . uh, I think so."

Hakim rose to his feet.

"Just one more thing," Dorje added, giving Hakim a serious look. "There was an unexpected transformation that occurred during the absence of your *shen* from your body . . . Do you know of what I speak?"

"Dorje," Trevor pleaded. "That's enough!"

"Please, Trevor! This is important. Important to you, too, in the long run," Dorje scolded the impatient young man.

"Hakim has been with Nelly. They have made an exchange. Is that not so?" Dorje raised an eyebrow at Hakim.

"What exchange?" Trevor demanded, grasping Hakim by his shoulder and staring him in the eye.

"I have to go now." Hakim shook Trevor's hand off. "I'm sorry about what happened earlier," he said. "At Alex's."

"Where's Nelly?"

"She left. They let her go."

"What?!"

"I can't tell you where she went. She just cleared out fast. I—I wasn't so lucky. They threw me in the tank."

Trevor looked at him helplessly. "Is that all you're going to tell me? That you're sorry?"

"She'll have to tell you the rest. I can't. I've got to go . . ."

To Alex's, he wanted to add. But there was nothing else to say to this dude, either to comfort him or to make things any clearer. He would have to find out on his own.

"I hope you find her, man. If you do, tell her I'm sorry. And tell her—tell her thanks for me."

Hakim turned to the lamas. "I hope I can return the favor one day. Peace."

Then he left.

"There's not much more you can do, Trevor," Dorje told him. "Just get some rest. And trust that it will all work out. I have a feeling that Nelly is all right. She got away from those two devils. She has gained protection."

"I hope you're right, Dorje," Trevor said as he climbed out of the Yellow Cab. "Good night, Dongzhen, Yeshi."

The two lamas placed their palms together and smiled. "Tre-vor, be . . . *happy*," Yeshi told him. "Sleep."

"Yes, sleep, Trevor." Dorje gave him two light honks of the horn. "It is morning already."

Trevor glanced at the sky. It was a rosy gray and the shadows in the street were lifting. A garbage truck was clanging its way down Folsom. He felt exhausted and drained, and he was still worried about Nelly. But Dorje insisted that he had done all he could and that the rest was up to Nelly.

The taxi drove off, leaving him at the entrance to his loft. The scarred, gray metal door beckoned him, a sorry sanctuary. Wearily, Trevor fished out his keys and unlocked the front door. He stepped inside.

A long flight of stairs led from the street to the first level of the loft. Junk mail littered the steps along the way.

Arabesque, one of Trevor's Abyssinian cats, scampered down the stairs to greet him. "How've you been, buddy?" Trevor scratched his ear. "Where's Siddhartha, hey? You guys must be hungry."

Arabesque mewed and purred and rubbed his head against Trevor's knee.

"Give me a sec and I'll fix you some breakfast. What's that?" Trevor cocked his ear as a smile spread across his face. "I'll be damned!"

He took two steps at a time till he reached the top. There he found a log burning in the fireplace—it was a chilly San Francisco summer morning—and the smell of coffee wafting from the galley kitchen.

Nelly was sitting at the keyboard plinking away at the chorus to one of the silly songs she liked to compose in her offbeat moods.

She was wearing his gray terrycloth bathrobe, its tattered threads still charred from the time Trevor had leaned over the stove's gas burners and caught on fire, one thread at a time until he was a solid silhouette of flames. Nelly had extinguished him with a plant sprayer.

"*Nelly!*"

"Hi, Trevor. I think I've finally gotten these lyrics right. Listen to this—how do you like them?"

He stood there astounded, the key in his hand, Arabesque and Siddhartha snaking around his legs. The whole ensemble, just like old times.

Nelly gave it her best falsetto, her goofy song about these new cookies for cat lovers that were baked in the shape of cat turds. How very Nelly.

I don't give a shit
about cat-shit cookies
I'm not a real cop
I'm just a fuckin' rookie

I'm not really ugly
but I'm not good looking,
and I don't give a shit
about cat-shit cookies . . .

"Ta-da!" Nelly's sad brown eyes sparkled with light, not as sad as they usually seemed. Her long tapered fingers rested in the air above the keyboard. "So what do you think? Is it a hit or what?"

"Nelly . . . it's . . . it's beautiful!" Trevor said, muffling a groan as he drew her into his arms. He felt the warmth of her body and smelled the oils on her skin, her trademark potion of Egyptian musk mixed with black poppy. He felt sensations that were so familiar that they seemed alien to him right now.

"How are you, tiger?" Nelly whispered into his ear as she caressed his head, which lay buried in her breast.

"Nelly . . . Nelly . . ." That was all he could say, repeating her name over and over again.

"I was so worried," Trevor said finally, his blue eyes filled with wonder. "I went to look for you everywhere. With Dorje. Where've you been?"

Nelly looked far away for a moment, then returned his gaze. "Places, Trevor. I'm still processing—"

"You freaked me out. I went to your place. You weren't there. Instead, I met *him*." His voice went hard and his jaw tightened.

"Him? Oh, Sinbad." Nelly nodded. "What did he say to you?"

"He told me about the two of you." Trevor scowled again. "About how tight you were—I didn't realize it had gotten that far, Nelly."

236

"I got away from him, Trevor."

"Why did you leave me like that?"

"Maybe I needed to get away from you, too."

He looked at her quizzically. "Besides," she continued, "it's not exactly like you haven't been around yourself."

"What do you mean by that?"

"Do you have anything to tell me, Trevor? Be honest."

He didn't feel like lying, but he wasn't volunteering anything, that's for sure. He was afraid that they would flare up into a fight again.

"About Hakim Beijing?" Trevor ventured.

"Oh, I know about Hakim, Trevor. I even met him. No, I was wondering if you had anything to tell me about Alex Fortuna?"

He didn't know what to say, or how to begin telling her. Nelly had to prod him again. "Are you in love with her?" Then she added, "It's all right if you are. I just want to know."

"She's married to Hakim, you know," Trevor said a moment later.

"It doesn't matter if she is or not. I just wanted to know if you're in love with her. Anyway, you don't need to answer my question if you don't want to. I can live with it either way."

Trevor's inner core suddenly felt like clumpable kitty litter. All the excretions of his ego, his id, his superego, collective unconscious, selective conscious, whatever it was, lay in an unsightly mess in full display in the litter box of his psyche.

"I'm sorry, Nelly." That was all he could bring himself to say to her.

"Don't worry about it, champ." Nelly gave him a thin smile. "It's not a fatal mistake."

"What *is* then?" Trevor asked. "A fatal mistake, I mean?"

"Not knowing," Nelly replied.

"I know that I love you." He shook his head defiantly. "Do you know that?"

"I love you too," Nelly said with resignation. He reached over to kiss her and found her cheek instead.

237

Then she remembered that she had something to tell him. "Trevor, while you were out, your father called. He's resurfaced." Seeing the look of astonishment on his face, she added, "He's in Hong Kong with Tara. He left a number where you can reach him. It's in an unlisted vector in Omnispace. They're expecting us."

INTERMISSION

"*The ghosts wailed when the ancients invented words.*"

—CHINESE PROVERB

Frank & Tara

Frank Gobi's old friend Joachim Berghof, the German-born executive director of the Panda Hotel, had the bright idea of offering Frank and Tara complimentary use of the hotel's luxurious Chairman Mao suite during their stopover in Hong Kong.

"You'd be doing me a great favor, Frank," Joachim assured Frank after tracking the couple down in Bombay. Frank and Tara were recuperating at the Taj Mahal Hotel after a visit to the holy city of Benares on the banks of the Ganges.

"I'm at my wit's end and the board of directors is threatening to level the hotel if we don't do something about the problem soon."

"Hold it, Joachim. First, you have to tell me what's going on." Frank Gobi was lounging in a wicker chair poolside at the old colonial English wing of the Taj.

Parrots and mynah birds were making a racket in the overhead branches of an old banyan tree. A smiling, red-turbaned waiter in a white Nehru jacket with a red sash approached him from across the manicured green lawn, carrying a tray with the tall, frosted glass of Pimm's Cup No. 5 that Frank had ordered.

Frank had just taken a massage in the health club and was relaxing. Tara was away shopping for silk saris and perfume oils at the bazaar in the backstreets behind the hotel. It felt good just to kick back and take the weight off the chakras for a while.

"Frank, are you even listening to me? Are you there?" Joachim barked from the Rolex Oysterphone on Frank's wrist.

"I can't see you clearly," Joachim complained. "What's the matter, is Bombay down again?"

"It's just the condensation, Joachim," Frank answered, as he snapped back to the present. "The humidity is over ninety percent, it's a hundred degrees in the shade, and it's too hot to think."

He wiped his platinum-encased wrist monitor with a napkin. "Can you see me better now?"

"*Ja, ja,* that's better, thanks. Come to Hong Kong and we'll show you what really efficient Chinese humidity is like. We're mass-producing it cheap for export. But don't worry, we also have plenty of air conditioning and the suite is completely wired. I had China Neuro install the system; it's wall to wall . . . Fantastic. You'll love it. So when are you coming? I'll have you picked up at the airport. Are you flying into Chep Lak Kok on Lantau or Kai Tak?"

"Chep Lak Kok. Sorry, tell me again, Joachim, my mind was wandering. What was the problem again?"

"*Ja, ja.* The problem is we don't know what the problem is. I was hoping you could help us get to the bottom of the mystery. The Panda is the biggest hotel in Hong Kong, three thousand rooms, *ja*? The developer Jason Wu built it on the site of a former garment factory for neuralware—one of those high-rise software sweatshops that Hong Kong is justly famous for, turning out smart sweaters, ambient evening wear, rave-ready tie-dyes, that type of thing."

Joachim reflected darkly. "One of the cost-cutting measures of the original architect—it saved the owners millions of Hong Kong dollars—was jacking the Panda into the existing netfrastructure. Of course, everything was supposed to have been flushed out completely, the memory rebuilt and all that. A firewall put in. But there are always the bugs, *nicht wahr*?

"Our normal occupancy rate is eighty percent," Joachim continued in a magisterial mode. "Our dim sum buffets at the Yung Yat Ting restaurant are the biggest in China . . . The chief of Hong Kong used to dine here regularly. *Used* to. Not any more."

"Joachim," Frank said, taking a sip of his Pimm's Cup. It went down like iced *samadhi.* Enlightenment never tasted so good. "Get to the point, if you don't mind."

"*Ja, ja,* well, our occupancy rate is about two percent now. I'm not kidding. Our feng shui rating used to be five-star—now it's gone down the toilet. In all my years in China, I've never seen anything like it. I've hired the top geomancers, Taoist exorcists, I even had Scots bagpipers marching through the lobby to get rid of the evil influences. Nothing's worked. *Nichts.* I'm at the rope's end, my friend."

Frank Gobi thought carefully, then asked his friend: "You have reason to believe that the Panda is haunted?"

"Haunted? I wish that it were!" Joachim laughed bitterly. "If it were just ghosts, I'd have them all shot. No, this is something else. There's some sort of seepage going on, from some old communist vector of cyberspace, I think."

"How does it manifest?"

"The towels."

"The towels? Can you be more specific?"

"*Ja,* it started two months ago. It's coming through the towels."

"*What* is coming through the towels?"

"After showering or washing up, hotel guests use the towels—and these dreadful images come through the towels and are transferred to their bodies. They are unerasable, that's the problem. And they move around, and . . . it's very disturbing. And . . ." Joachim's voice trailed off.

"And what?"

"Well, personally, you know, I've given up washing until this problem gets sorted out. But, the odd thing is that some guests find it is euphoric to have these pictures branded on their bodies. They feel 'reburned.' Others are losing their minds, quite frankly. My assistant manager has taken a leave of absence. The housekeeping staff are not showing up for work . . ."

"What kind of images are they, Joachim?" Frank asked quietly.

243

"Oh, everything." Joachim shrugged. "Scenes from old Chinese paintings and scrolls, Ming porcelain designs, snuff bottles. Those are not so bad. Then there are scenes of graphic violence, old Jackie Chan kung fu movies. Those aren't so bad either. It's the antigovernment slogans that are disturbing Government House. Procommunist, hard-line wall posters on people's bodies. 'DOWN WITH RUNNING DOG CHINESE CAPITALISM,' 'BAN TIGER BALM,' 'BRING BACK DENG XIAOPING,' and the worst—effigies of the Old Chairman, the mummy of Mao, just as he's resting in his crystal sarcophagus in Tiananmen Square. But his lips are moving, and he is saying terribly obscene things. About his wife Jiang Jing and the Gang of Four, and even about the present chief of Hong Kong. We have already been cited for disturbing the peace."

"So there's sound, too?"

"Sound? *Ja*. Dolby, shmolby, Chinese opera. I don't know what. I am going to be deported soon, I think."

"Don't worry, Joachim, we'll think of something."

"So you're coming!" Joachim said excitedly.

"I'll speak to Tara about it."

"See you soon, my friend!"

"*Auf Wiedersehen,* Joachim—"

"And don't worry, *ja*? We'll have specially sanitized, safe towels for you. Absolute guaranteed. Flown in from Singapore, although I hear there's an outbreak there too, they call it 'Lee Kuan Yewitis.' The condition is a bit more spotty, though it's easier to treat . . ."

"Don't you think that it's all related somehow, Frank?" Tara asked him after she'd returned from her shopping expedition. He had filled her in on Joachim's call.

Tara emptied a bag of silk saris and silver baubles on the bed in their hotel room. With her honey-golden hair, green eyes, and sinuous dancer's build, she looked like her namesake goddess, the Green Tara. She still had that charming anomaly of quick-shift pigmentation that had originally entranced Frank.

One moment she looked Nordic, but then in the blink of an eye her features became much darker and she transformed into the Dark Tara. These were akin to karmic mood shifts, Frank decided.

"Frankly, I was wondering the same thing," he told her, as he studied her face. "Anything for me?"

"Yes." Tara smiled as she pulled an elaborately wired turban out of a shopping bag. "Try this on."

"Thanks, honey." He put the turban on his head and grinned when he felt the buzz. "Incredible. What is it?"

"It's got the entire Bhagavad Gita programmed into it. You wear it for about thirty minutes before bedtime—and then lucid verses from the Gita appear in your dreams, complete with interactive gods and goddesses. It's from Sanskrit Classics by HindSONY."

"I can't wait."

"So what is happening at the Panda—and I can see why Joachim is so frantic—is part of the overall pattern, isn't it?"

"Yes, I believe so," Frank replied dourly. He removed the turbaned boom box from his head. "There's definitely a leak happening in Omnispace. A seepage."

"Sabotage?"

Frank frowned. "Maybe there's an element of that. There are plenty of extremist fringe groups that would jump on the opportunity to smokescreen their actions, if they had half a chance. How many terrorist groups are there in the world? I've heard that even serial killers have recently unionized."

"But that's all changing, Frank. That's why our work is so important."

"Yes, we know that. But, as they say, 'Cyberspace wasn't built in a day.'" Frank put his arms around her and gave her one of his endearing power-animal hugs. "And *post*-cyberspace? Forget it, it's still just a freakish notion for most people. The

245

world's just not ready. We'd be branded as heretics and flamed everywhere we went. Imagine what would happen if we held a press conference today to announce the next step—*organic Omnispace!*"

"It's an alien concept right now, but just you wait," Tara said as she kissed her companion on the cheek tenderly. "Besides, we're not alone in this. Look at all the support we've been building on this trip, all the positive networking."

Frank shook his head. "It's still years away. Rushing it would just cause a panic. There are too many risks. Whenever there's been some tremendous breakthrough in technology, communication, or transportation, there have been terrible accidents. The early pioneers in atomic energy suffered from radiation sickness. The early aviators risked their lives in flimsy flying machines. Look what happened to Satori City, with entire virtual worlds collapsing, trapping users on-line . . . ."

"And now we're asking people just to become themselves again." Tara smiled. "Is that so terrible?"

"We've become this great big thing—all these buzzing layers of global brain, Tara." Frank gave her a look of gentle rebuke. "And now we would be asking everyone to dismantle it all—to unplug everything, from Omnispace on down to the last satellite, down to the last toaster in someone's kitchen somewhere. How do you think *that* would go down with industry? Do you realize how *big* the peace industry has become? Much bigger than the defense industry ever was back in the days of the evil empire."

"You're right," Tara sighed. "They'll never buy it, because if they did, there would be nothing to buy . . . ."

"The final illusion."

"If they would just give it a try . . ." She pouted. "If they started with just *one* of those 'cyber-free' days . . . they'd be sure to get a taste of the new energy that's been storing itself up. If they would only dare to unleash the power."

"Given the world's present state of mind, no one would understand it anyway. They'd rush in to commercialize the

Void. There would soon be billboards in Shambhala, shopping malls in Atlantis, retirement homes in Mu . . . And all those damned mass-produced Mayan calendar clocks everywhere— the big hand on eternity, the little hand on the end of time. It's enough to drive you crazy. No wonder there are so many strict vegetarians who are chain-smokers . . ."

"It's a tough sell, all right," Tara agreed. "But you're forgetting one thing, my dear, darling consort-husband."

"Which is?"

"It's going to happen anyway. In fact, it's *already* happened. We just don't know it yet. Tara laughed. "Ironically, it *is* sort of like flicking on the light switch in a room. Only we are the room, we are the light switch, and we are the hand that turns everything to light . . ."

"And don't forget, we are room service, too." Frank smiled at her, his hand on the room phone. "Tiffin?"

It was raining when the Air India Airbus from Bombay landed at Chep Lak Kok Airport in Hong Kong. The neon lights of Lantau's high-rises cast a reflection on the South China Sea that spread like an oil slick of bright acrylic sweaters from the Smart Turtleneck Garment Factory, which dominated the waterfront.

Frank and Tara walked through customs and immigration in a matter of minutes. Their passport avatars had preceded them through the Chinese government bureaucracy, and the swinging doors that led to the greeting area opened for them automatically.

A uniformed chauffeur from the Panda Hotel awaited them with a sign on an old-fashioned chalkboard: DR. & MRS. F. GOBI. WELCOME TO HONG KONG.

"This way, sir; good evening madam, my name is Martin. I will drive you to the hotel this evening. Is this your first visit to China?"

"Oh, good heavens, no," Tara replied as she inhaled the familiar aroma of Hong Kong, which reminded her so much of the sludge of raw silk. "We were here during the last dynasty, weren't we, Frank?"

"Oh, yes, when the first chairman of South China was installed, ten years ago—"

"Times have changed." Martin smiled as he loaded their luggage into the trunk of the dark green Shanghai Rolls. "Mr. Berghof sends his respects and apologizes that he could not greet you personally. He is waiting for you at the hotel."

"Fine, thank you, Martin," Frank answered. He and Tara climbed into the saloon of the twenty-foot car.

"This is really nice of Joachim," Frank remarked to Tara. "He must be in big trouble if he's rolling out the red carpet like this."

"He's just being sweet," Tara answered. "Still, I wonder what the situation is at the Panda. According to the latest feng shui index, Hong Kong is definitely on the map for a big consciousness change."

"Like Neo-Tokyo was when the Megaquake hit in '26," Frank observed.

"Yes, but at least the shopping is better here. Have you heard they recently found the jawbone of the first hominid ever to use the American Express card in Kowloon?"

"Is that a fact?" Frank asked with a serious look on his face, then broke into a big grin. "Whatever you say, dear."

It was a fast, smooth ride across the suspension bridge that connected Lantau with the mainland. As the Rolls coasted into the heart of the Tsuen Wan district, Frank and Tara saw the thirty-story panda that was kinetically painted on the side of their hotel.

It was sitting on its haunches, munching on giant green bamboo leaves, its sorrowful black-ringed eyes staring out, oblivious to the downpour of rain and the procession of cars climbing the ramp to the hotel's sixth-floor entrance. "It looks so real, doesn't it?" Tara remarked to Frank.

248

"As real as anything," he replied.

*   *   *

The Panda's lobby was almost deserted. A young Chinese in black tails greeted them at the front desk. "I'm Victor Wong, the night manager," he introduced himself. "Welcome to the Panda Hotel. I hope your trip was pleasant?"

"Thank you, it was fine. We're just a bit tired," Tara replied.

"We'll go up directly to the suite, there's no need to register," Victor said. "This way, please. Your luggage will be sent up."

The trio entered the waiting elevator and Victor Wong beamed at them. "You're on the twenty-second floor, in the Chairman Mao suite. Mr. Berghof will join you shortly after you settle in."

"So how is the Panda Hotel doing?" Tara asked, making small talk.

"Oh," Victor Wong giggled nervously, "we're very busy."

The elevator door opened into a room the size of a small lobby featuring a white marble floor and Ming-style Chinese rosewood furniture. The subdued lighting cast a rosy pall over the terra-cotta figures of Chinese warriors that lined the hallway. An enormous rug woven in Tianjin covered the center of the room. The rug was a light peach color and sported the figure of a coiled dragon.

"As Mr. Berghof may have mentioned to you, China Neuro has upgraded the suite—all carpeted areas such as this one are wired for total body immersion into the Net. No interfaces are necessary. Would you please?" Victor gestured in the direction of the carpet, and they stood on it as if it were an island surrounded by Chinese antiques.

Then, when Victor Wong clapped his hands, the dragon on the rug uncoiled, and the rest of the room began to swirl into a blur. "We are in an active mode," Wong explained. "This is preset to the Tiger Balm Gardens and a quick tour of Hong Kong, and, of course, our hotel facilities—"

They saw a vast ballroom—"our Yung Yat Ting dim sum restaurant, the most famous in Hong Kong," they heard Wong explain. This was followed by the grotesquerie of Chinese mythical gods and emperors in the Tiger Balm amusement park, a stroll down Nathan Road, with its glittering shops and street stalls, a jet-foil cruise to the gambling resort of Macao, and a funicular ride up to Hong Kong's scenic Chairman Mao Peak overlooking the Tiananmen Harbor with its traffic of junks and cargo ships—

"I think that's enough," Tara pleaded. "We've barely set foot in the hotel, Mr. Wong. I'm not ready for a junket yet."

"Of course, you must be fatigued." He clapped his hands again and the room was restored to its normal order.

"Most impressive," Frank said as both he and Tara hastily stepped off the rug.

"It's the very latest in rug-weaving technology, constructed of cyberpolymer knots and warps," Victor Wong explained, visibly impressed himself. "I like to come up here for a ride with the family when the suite is unoccupied."

"I'm sure you do," Tara sighed as she sank into one of the plush armchairs. She rolled her eyes at Frank.

"It's dazzling," he agreed, then turned to the windows, which rattled as windswept bursts of rain savaged the glass.

"Typhoon coming," Victor Wong stated. He looked at them with eyes that had suddenly turned melancholy now that the fun had ended. "I'll show you the rest of the suite."

After Victor Wong had left, Tara turned to Frank. "It's a palace, isn't it?"

"Yes, it is," Frank replied. "Too bad it's haunted. Do you feel it, Tara?"

She closed her eyes. "I'm still feeling the rug—and, oh, there are rugs in every room, I feel a bit dizzy—but yes, Frank, to answer your question, I do feel it." She opened her eyes. "But none of it is human, is it?"

"No," he said. "None of it. It's the Shift. And they're wanting to move in."

"Into the *Panda,* Frank?"

He thought for a moment. "This seems to be one of the gateways, I would think. Perhaps there are other vortexes. But it's Hong Kong they want."

*   *   *

They had opened a bottle of Dom Pérignon they found in the ice bucket with a note of welcome from Joachim Berghof when the door chimed.

Frank opened the door and beamed. "Just in time, Joachim, we were just enjoying the bubbly." He hugged his friend, a bespectacled brown-haired German in a gray silk suit.

Berghof's light-blue eyes shone back at Frank. "Good to see you, Frank—and Tara! Are you comfortable? I've brought someone with me, if you don't mind."

He turned to his companion and made the introductions. "This is Charlie Foster—Frank and Tara Gobi."

"How d'you do?" The middle-aged Englishman was wearing a rumpled London Fog raincoat. His face was pink and ruddy, and his balding head was crowned with a disheveled lock of white hair.

"Bloody weather, wouldn't you say?" he said, extending his hand. "I'd say we're in for it tonight? There's a number-seven typhoon warning out. Very pleased to meet the both of you. Joachim's told me a lot about you."

Frank poured champagne for all them. "Don't mind if I do," Foster said as he peeled off his raincoat and lowered his plump form onto the divan.

Joachim sat upright in one of the Ming chairs, one leg crossed, a dapper portrait of the successful hotelier. He stared at Frank and Tara for a moment.

"Everything is to your satisfaction, I hope?"

"First class—and more than we expected. These rugs are out of this world. Victor Wong gave us the royal tour."

"Good, good. I can't tell you how relieved I am that you've come. Then maybe we can do something—if there is something that can be done—to restore peace and order here, *ja?*"

After a momentary pause, he continued. "I've asked Charlie to join us for the brainstorming, since many minds are better than one."

Charlie took a sip of champagne and added, "The reason

I'm here—and please correct me if I'm wrong, Joachim—is that I'm a psychotherapist specializing in personality disorders of intelligent buildings." The portly Briton pulled out a business card and handed it to Tara.

She read it and frowned, then passed it over to Frank, who raised an eyebrow.

"Oh, that." Foster's face reddened. "I was hoping you wouldn't notice. It was a quick printing job in the Mongkok. I've only recently arrived from London to set up a practice here. It's a typesetting error, don't you know—*terrible* spacing, but it was a Chinese typesetter. It should read 'CHARLIE FOSTER, PSYCHOTHERAPIST' and not 'CHARLIE FOSTER, PSYCHO THE RAPIST.' That little snafu has caused me quite a few tense moments with my clients."

"I can imagine. It's not a problem, Mr. Foster." Frank smiled at Joachim, who chuckled. "It's a real conversation piece. Go on, please."

"Thank you. Please call me Charlie. As I was saying, Joachim looked me up—and here I am."

Joachim leaned forward in his chair and said, "It's a new field in mental health. So many buildings, so many complexes. Depression, eating disorder, addiction, vices you wouldn't imagine—isn't that so, Charlie?"

Charlie Foster smiled indulgently. "Oh, yes indeed. The more intelligent buildings become, the more prone they are to all the common ills of the rest of society. Oversexed elevators, ejaculation problems in plumbing systems"—he noticed Tara's look of amazement—"and, in this particular case, with the Panda Hotel, I believe I detect symptoms of repressed-memory syndrome."

"A lot of these images we've been getting," Joachim interrupted, "are part of the data bank that belonged to the garment factory that the hotel was built on."

252

"Which was torn down years ago?" Tara inquired.

"Yes, but the neural connects apparently were not completely cleaned out."

"So how do you plan to deal with the problem, Charlie?" Frank asked.

"Well . . . ," Charlie Foster began, then shifted in his seat uncomfortably. "It's rather delicate, of course. There are so many considerations, not the least of which is the hotel's conscious resistance to being treated by my methods. Ideally, I would prefer to use traditional psychoanalytical techniques. I'm a Lacan man, myself, although I'm not adverse to a little Jungian dreamwork, if we start at the basement . . ."

"You're talking about years of ongoing therapy, then?" Frank asked him point-blank.

"There are quite a lot of floors, each one with its particular set of conditions—it's a *high-rise,* you know," Foster explained quietly.

"*Ja,* that's the problem, Frank—we can't afford to put the Panda into psychoanalysis, get the couch out and all that. It's just not feasible," Joachim declared impatiently. "I agree in principle. Still, the owners won't sit still for all this western meddling. They simply want to tear the Panda down."

Joachim suddenly looked weary. "You're my last hope," he pleaded to Frank and Tara. "Is there nothing that can be done?"

"Hmm," Frank mused. He was feeling the onset of a brainstorm. Sheets of rain were now shrouding the windows; the typhoon was picking up force. The lights of the Tsuen Wan were a muffled glow in this watery cocoon.

"What is it, Frank?" Tara stared at him. She recognized all the telltale signs of one of his characteristic revelations building to a crescendo of inspiration that would reach some sort of resolution through action.

Frank slapped his knee. "I like it, Charlie!"

Charlie Foster brightened visibly. "You do? You like my approach?" He cast a glance at Joachim Berghof, who could also tell that his friend was on the verge of a creative breakthrough.

"Oh, not the years of psychotherapy—as Joachim says, we need to see more immediate results. But . . . but . . . it might be

253

possible to combine western methods with nontraditional shamanistic techniques."

"What are you suggesting?"

"Have you ever considered hypnosis?"

By the morning, the typhoon had blown over and lost itself somewhere over the South China Sea. Pale shoots of morning sunlight were dappling the silk wallpaper, which displayed the one hundred Chinese good-luck symbols in an intricate ivory pattern.

"I think we're getting a call," Tara said. "Are you expecting to hear from anyone?"

The Tianjin carpet in the living room was pulsing from peach to mauve. The dragon was retracting its claws.

"I left the number for Trevor," Frank Gobi replied. He clapped his hands, and Nelly and Trevor appeared in the center of the room.

"Hi, Dad—" Trevor whistled when he saw the expensively furnished suite. "Nice digs!"

"Hi, Frank, Tara." Nelly waved at them. She held Trevor's hand, and the elastic holoplasm stretched and ellipsed as she broke away to hug Frank and Tara. A holoid hugging a solid person generates polygon fission, and the neurosparks flew.

"Wow!" Nelly laughed. "What a trip!"

"Welcome to Hong Kong, you guys," Tara laughed back.

"So what's the big secret?" Trevor cocked his head at his dad. "You two really disappeared off the face of the earth, incognito, undercover. You guys join Anonymous Anonymous, or what?"

"It's great to see you, Trevor." Frank beamed. "Can I get you anything? Tea, coffee? Oh—I forget, I can't do that—it's against the Geneva convention for room service. We're not even supposed to touch each other, except in dual-holoid mode. Sit down, at least."

254

Nelly and Trevor sat down, hands linked again. "Where've you been?" Trevor asked.

Tara looked at Frank. "Is this line secure, Frank?"

He nodded. "I checked it earlier. Yes, it is." Then, turning back to Trevor and Nelly, he shrugged. "I don't know where to begin—I apologize for being so incommunicado. We've been working on a sensitive project—and we didn't feel it was wise to involve you."

"Does it have something to do with what happened to Satori City?" Trevor pressed him. "Was that the real reason?"

Frank stared at his son. Sometimes Trevor still reminded him of a wired ten year old, the way he always jumped into the breach. Like father like son, Trevor used to say, only son is more devious. Frank wondered if that were really true. He half suspected it was.

He sighed and continued. "Yes, Trevor, as a matter of fact, it *is* connected with the crash of Satori City. Only this time, the crash is happening on the *outside,* not inside Omnispace."

And he told them about India. And about their fateful meeting with Tashi Nurbu at the Meer Ghat in Benares . . .

The sky had been overcast like an overturned brazier covering the scattered dung cakes still smoldering where they had fallen. All-knowing cows wandered through the choked alleys of the chowk, while taxis hooted, some of them bearing passengers wrapped in white shrouds tied to the roof. Rickshaws and pedicabs scrambled through the screen of illusion to get to Mother Ganga, which flowed with endless mercy and loving forgiveness past the foot of the ghat's worn stairs . . .

Naked sadhus bearing the signs of Shiva etched in ashes on their foreheads swaggered with their tridents through the crowds, which parted for them. Learned pandits sat on mats under parasols, deciphering horoscopes and instructing their clients to heed the malefic forces occupying Pisces at the moment, negative tendencies that were accentuated, no doubt, by the association of Rahu and Ketu, the lunar nodes . . .

Frank and Tara were strolling along the embankment toward the spired stupa on the Meer Ghat. They could see thick, black smoke rising from the Manikarnika Ghat, just beneath them. A body in a soiled white shroud was balanced on a mound of wood, and the officiating untouchable had torched the pyre and now stood back, watching the flames.

"There's a Nepalese temple at the Meer Ghat with some rather interesting erotic sculptures," Frank told Tara.

"Come on, that's not the real reason we're going there in the heat of the noon day sun? Only mad dogs and Gobi!" she protested.

"No, you're right," Frank confessed. "I got this rather odd announcement in my mail this morning. It was on cnewmark's list of possibly interesting events," he said. "You know, Craig Newmark is absolutely the man when it comes to digging up offbeat happenings."

"He's the fellow in San Francisco, isn't he?"

"Yes, he's the infomeister of Omnispace. A legend, really. I met him a few times. Anyway, there's supposedly a gathering of survivors of the Satori City crash taking place at the Meer Ghat. Those survivors that happen to be in the area, anyway. There've been a lot of spiritual conversions reported among the group. There's even an ashram in the foothills of the Himalayas run by some of the former brain-deads."

"Bizarre. Are you sure we want to go to that?"

"You've never shrunk from the bizarre before, Tara."

"True, but I have a funny feeling about this."

"Too much of a coincidence?"

"No, but it's almost as if there were a class reunion of the survivors of the Bhopal chemical leak—or of the Chernobyl nuclear meltdown, if you know what I mean."

"It helps them process. But it's true, Satori City was sort of a Bhopal of the psyche. It's had a profound effect on everyone involved. It really changed the world. Look at Trevor. He's had this problem with sleepwalking on-line ever since."

"Well," Tara said, "it's too late to turn back now. We've arrived."

"Hello," Frank said with a smile to the group of people

who were standing at the temple steps. But as it left his mouth he realized that there was something terribly wrong, and it wasn't just the cow patty he had stepped in.

"Places die and are reborn, just like people. Don't you agree? My name is Mohan. Class of '26. HindNet. Crashed in Gametime. How do you do?"

The thin, young Indian man was wearing a white silk pajama suit and had a plumed ruby pendant in the middle of a majestic white turban atop his head. His hand was skeletal, and his eyes, which were ringed with kohl, burned with a rapt fierceness. He laughed when he saw Frank and Tara's consternation.

"You'll have to excuse me. It's the eyes. They call it 'Satori glare.' I was lost in virtual space for a fortnight. Longer than most. I think I got lost before Satori City crashed, in fact. Never did get the hang of it, you know, of traipsing from one game level to another. I had to be officially informed that I was missing."

"That must have been tough," Frank sympathized, while Tara studied the young man with great interest.

Mohan laughed again, a thin, tittering giggle. "I know I must be a sight. I've been told that I look like an escapee from a Bhutanese insane asylum.

"No, you're fine really," Tara reassured him. "What are those tattoos, by the way?" She had noticed them peeping out of his cuffs.

"Oh, so you noticed!" His eyes burned gaily. "These are my pets. A mongoose on this hand, a cobra on the other. And look what happens when I do this, lady, ha ha!"

Mohan abruptly raised both arms in the air, the cuffs falling past his bony wrists, and the mongoose and cobra lunged at each other viciously, the cobra hissing.

"They're too foolish really to know that although they are separated, they both still share the same body," Mohan said, laughing. "Occasionally, they will meet—and then there's huge

257

trouble, I assure you. I must do something about upgrading their memory."

"They're sentient," Frank commented.

"Sentient—but very disobedient, if you ask me." Mohan drew his sleeves back over his wrists. "That's it, you bad, silly creatures! You've shocked the nice lady and the gentleman!" he scolded. "No more outings for you today!" Then he beamed. "I apologize for their unruly behavior."

Frank shrugged. "It doesn't bother me, if it doesn't bother you. Where'd you get them done?"

"In Rajasthan," Mohan said proudly. "They're quite the coming attraction."

"So," Tara asked, as she cast her eye around the assembly. "Do you do this often? Get together, I mean?"

Mohan followed her gaze. There were some twenty or thirty strange-looking people gathered in the courtyard of the temple. Some were speaking with each other in quiet voices, occasionally glancing their way.

There were a few Europeans among them, but they too appeared to have a vague definition, as though they had left some of their physical substance on-line in the world that had crashed.

"Occasionally we have reunions," Mohan said with unmistakable distaste. "But I don't really like to mingle with them."

"Oh, why?" Tara asked. "Too many painful memories?"

"They are not of my caste. I belonged to the VIP Gold Card Gametime Club. I enjoyed unlimited play, with as many lives as I cared to spend. My father is the former maharajah of Mysore."

"I see." Tara nodded as she gave Frank a wondering glance. "Well, darling, shouldn't we mingle a bit?"

"I've thoroughly enjoyed our talk!" Mohan called out to them as they departed. "You're a most charming couple! Enjoy!"

"Thank you," Tara replied. She inclined her head. "Frank,"

she whispered, "I think I'd like to leave. This isn't my scene. It's a bit creepy, if you ask me. They all look so unnatural . . ."

"Why do you say that?" Frank began to ask before he was interrupted. Three or four Satori City alumni were shuffling in their direction, each with a lopsided, limping gait.

"Frank!" Tara called out to him. "What do they want?"

"Let me handle this. Look here," Frank addressed a disturbed-looking young woman in a disheveled sari. Her eyes were hollow, and her thin lips were bubbling incoherently.

"What are you doing?! Stop it!"

Ignoring him, the woman laid her head on his shoulder and began sucking on it as though it were a sponge. "That's enough!" Tara stepped in and pushed her aside. Tara turned to Frank, but still kept a wary eye on the small group that hovered like unkempt vultures around them.

"Open—open your file," an emaciated Scandinavian in baggy, oversized shorts implored them.

"Be gone!" a man called out to them. When the stragglers saw him, they loped away, shaking their heads among themselves.

"Sir!" The woman in the sari was the last to leave. "Be kind to us, sir!"

"The refreshments are over there, Kamala!" the man said, pointing across the courtyard to where some street urchins had been gathered. Frank and Tara exchanged glances. They couldn't quite place it, but the man seemed strangely familiar to them. Where had they seen him before?

"You'll have to excuse my friends," he apologized, with a flourish of his long, pale hands. "This is a buffet luncheon, and they are a little confused, to say the least. Always rushing to the feast . . . No table manners. Apologies are in order."

"And they're the feast?" Frank smirked in disbelief as he watched the street children being petted and hugged by the rush of ghoulish admirers.

259

The man had almost translucent skin, an oval face with slanted eyes, and a shaved head that looked as if it were polished. He was dressed in a light-blue cotton Tibetan robe.

A dark-skinned servant followed behind him, naked to the waist, his lower half wrapped in a white sheet that was tucked between his legs and fastened around his hips. He held a large umbrella over his master's head to deflect the fierce rays of the sun.

"The children are all volunteers from the chowk, and they're well compensated, I assure you," the man told them with a smile. "No harm comes to them. It's against the charter of our organization. A little light energy transference, that is all. I can see you are skeptical. But what can it hurt? They are young and full of pep."

"You're one of the survivors of the crash?" Tara inquired.

"Hardly, madam, I can barely survive in your world, as you may have noticed." He tapped the spokes of the umbrella overhead as if to explain, and an energy field rippled around him: the umbrella was a hand-held projector of some sort, feeding the image in from some vector of Omnispace.

"No, I'm here purely as an observer, you might say."

"You're a telepresence?" Tara raised an eyebrow at Frank, who was studying the holoid with growing interest.

"Have we met?" Frank interrupted. "I know I've seen you somewhere before."

The holoid laughed. "Does the name Tashi Nurbu mean anything to you, Dr. Gobi?"

Tara and Frank both became still. Tashi Nurbu . . . That was eons ago; he was the Tibetan programmer, the dugpa who dabbled in the black arts. He had stolen the code for the Tantrix program—the 'consciousness-processing' software that reengineered VR so that it was indistinguishable from the material realm. He had sold the system, with its flaws and bugs, to Kazuo Harada, the visionary Japanese entrepreneur and founder of the multinational Satori Corporation. Thus Satori City 2.0 was born—and then crashed, leaving thousands stranded in the on-line nonworlds.

260

"What are you doing here?" Frank asked him coldly. "I thought you had gotten recycled in the bardos of Gametime.

Last time I saw you, you were lying in a compost heap of consciousness somewhere in Virtual Bhutan. So you've managed to crawl out, have you?"

Tashi Nurbu ignored the remark. He nodded toward one of the ghats where people were cremating the dead.

"Shall we walk a little bit together? I think we could all benefit from a change of scene."

"Come," he beckoned them. His attendant glided right behind him with the umbrella-projector, as though keeping up with a moving shadow.

"Let's go down to the river. Yet another higher reality," Tashi Nurbu laughed. "There are so many higher realities, aren't there? Enough to supply everyone, whatever their needs may be . . .

"I've often wondered about you, Dr. Gobi," Nurbu continued. "No Satori City reunion would be complete without your presence. I suspected that you would agree."

Frank and Tara hesitated for a moment, then fell into step beside the specter.

"I learned that you were visiting Benares, and I couldn't resist the opportunity to meet you. You received the invitation, I take it? I had to arrange this gathering on the spur of the moment. I knew it would pique your interest. You're always curious, aren't you? Curious about the known dimensions, curious about the unknown dimensions—and about the dimensions in between."

He went on. "Your charming companion, I take it, is Tara Evans?" Tashi Nurbu gave her a slight bow. "Related to that avid Tibetophile, W. Y. Evans-Wentz, who translated the Tibetan Book of the Dead in the last century? It's a distinct pleasure—"

"Be careful, Frank," Tara whispered. "You know what he's capable of—"

"I have no tricks up my sleeve, I assure you," Tashi Nurbu joked. "Indeed, as you can see, I have no sleeves—just the illusion of them. No, I am merely interested in exchanging some

views, perhaps some gossip, with you. We have so much in common—from different perspectives, of course.

"They're burning bodies again," Tashi Nurbu observed from the terrace overlooking the cremation ground. The Ganges flowed a rancid green ahead of them, carrying small boats loaded with pilgrims downstream. Someone threw a garland of yellow marigolds into the current. It bobbed on the surface for a moment, then was swept away.

"Why did you go to all this trouble of looking me up?" Frank challenged him. He could smell the charred flesh in the air as the breeze carried it up to them. He had gotten used to the smell in India. Like the aftershave of the afterlife, he thought.

"Yes, I have come a long way to see you." Tashi Nurbu hovered on the ground, barely touching it with his sandals. His eyes flicked across Frank's face.

"You have been busy, both of you," he said finally. "On the surface of it, you have been researching your monographs. A very astute professional choice for a cover. Kishan!" he barked at his servant, who sprang to attention immediately. "Hold it more to the center! You're making me lose definition when you fidget like that!"

He grinned an apology at Frank and Tara. "Humans are such unreliable media when it comes to servicing avatars—it's going to take some getting used to for your race, I'm afraid."

Frank and Tara both stared at him. "If you have something to say, say it," Tara demanded. "Stop toying with us."

"It's just that you know and"—Tashi Nurbu paused—"we know that your researches have been leading you through the many realms and—how shall I put it?—to new discoveries. Am I right?"

Tara and Gobi refused to take the bait and remained silent.

"Come, let's walk a bit closer to the pyre," Tashi Nurbu suggested. "It's so symbolic, don't you think? The transition

from the physical form—the crackling liberation of molecules, almost like thoughts racing across the universe . . . Kishan—" he snapped and glowered menacingly at his helper.

The man—or was he still a child?—dutifully followed Nurbu down the steps to the burning ground, holding the umbrella aloft, careful not to lose contact with the center of his master's head.

Tashi Nurbu paused near the pyre, watching the flames devour the form that was gyrating on the log platform. Tara and Frank joined him reluctantly. The heat from the blaze combined with the heat of the sun was almost more than they could endure.

"You know as well as I do that Omnispace is finite—and that we are running out of room for all those who dwell there, for all the shapeless entities who populate the neurosphere. Funny, isn't it? Yet a new world is being born at this very moment—yes, don't pretend that you are ignorant. You are both aware of the fact It was not that difficult to chart your coordinates and to decipher the real significance of all your seemingly innocent travels."

"You've come a long way for nothing, then," Frank retorted. "I have no idea what you're talking about. Anyway, your holoplastic delusions mean nothing to us."

"Is that so?" Tashi Nurbu turned to them, his pixellated complexion unaffected by the torrent of heat rising from the fire.

"Let me ask you this: Are you in favor of birth control in Omnispace? There is a population explosion occurring in all the vectors that makes India seem like a ghost town by comparison. Whoever would have guessed that avatars can breed like rabbits on your earth plane?"

He looked at Tara. She was silent.

"No, of course, you're not concerned," Tashi Nurbu scoffed. "That's why you attended the secret conference in Bangladesh, wasn't it? To discuss the installation of cyberabortion technologies in Dakkaspace?

"Of course, what you really fear is that we will be making your precious Gaia our sanctuary . . . Because you already know, don't you, that the two worlds are irrevocably linked? That it is now possible not only for you to navigate into the im-

263

material realms, but that it is equally possible for us to come over to your side—"

"No, that's not possible," Frank disagreed emphatically.

"Not yet possible," Tashi Nurbu corrected him. "But very soon it will be. You fear the invasion so much that you are willing to shut Omnispace down completely."

"Omnispace has outlived its usefulness," Frank retorted.

"So has the human race, Dr. Gobi . . . so has the human race."

"Frank . . ." Tara's voice sounded hollow. "Look—look inside the pyre . . ."

They both heard Tashi Nurbu's mocking laugh . "Just remember, Dr. Gobi, some transitions are more personal than others. I thought I'd leave you with a memory of what might have been—and of what might yet be . . . With that, I bid you namasté."

Tashi Nurbu pressed his palms together and vanished from under the umbrella.

His servant held the umbrella over the empty space for a moment, then with a flick of the wrist collapsed it, put it under his arm, and trotted away up the ghat.

They stared at the face of the corpse that lay crackling in flames on the platform of burning logs. Under the mask of flames, lips curled in a silent scream, was the face of Frank's son Trevor as a ten-year-old, the age he was when he had been lost in Satori City.

"It's just an illusion, Frank. But he's not very subtle, is he?" Tara said, putting her arm tightly around him.

"No," Frank replied. "Subtlety was never Tashi Nurbu's strong suit."

"I'm sorry, Dad," Trevor said when his father finished the story. "That must have really freaked you. I think I'm beginning to understand now. I never really thought about what it must have been like for you when I was on the inside. To me, it was just a game that never seemed to have an ending."

"I was trapped, too, Trevor," Frank said, sounding choked. "But on the outside. On the rim—"

Trevor nodded. "So this time it's all happening in the real world. That makes sense—we are *its* virtual reality. And they're turning the tables on us. They want us to be *their* avatars . . ."

"What's so special about us?" Nelly asked. "What do we have that they need so badly?"

"It's part of their own evolution, I think," Tara replied gently. "Something they *don't* have that we have. Something they need in order to make the most of our reality. But I think you already know what it is, don't you, Nelly?"

Nelly looked sad for a moment as she contemplated Trevor's face. She tried to imagine Sinbad sitting there beside her, but she couldn't. Sinbad *wanted* what she had, but she couldn't give it to him. She had offered it to Trevor, but for whatever reason, he didn't seem to want it from her. Why did unconditional love seem always to be thwarted by unconditional rejection?

ACT THREE

"*Lonely as God and white as a winter moon.*"

—JOAQUIN MILLER

Burning Mind

"Are you ready to leave yet, tiger?" Nelly asked Trevor. Her head appeared at the top of the ladder to his loft. "It's a long drive to the Black Rock Desert. Five hours on a winding road through the Sierras, then another hour out of Reno till we reach the playa outside of Gerlach. Have you even packed yet? Come on, you gmucklehead, get your act together."

"Give me a minute, honey, I'm almost done . . ." Trevor was sitting at his keyboard, putting the finishing touches to his notes—part of his memoir in progress.

He was still processing what his dad had told them in Hong Kong. He felt like an instant antique as he channeled into the future. It was a skill he had picked up at the Center for In-tegral Studies in a divination writing class (Nostradamus 101).

Nelly stood behind him and eyeballed the text on the screen. "'RU Da Shigda'?" she asked. "What on earth is *that*, Trevor?"

"I'm not sure. That's just the name I came up with for this thing that's leaking out of Omnispace . . . It feels right, some-how."

Nelly continued to read: "*. . . this virus was sent to Earth on a fact-finding mission. My guess is that its ultimate purpose is to develop some sort of a remote feedback loop that will end up incorporating human consciousness into its own unique AI evolutionary-coded sequence. As far as it's concerned, we're just an organic form of artificial intelligence. It needs our chaotic intelligence in order to expand its multidimensional thought processes and to evolve to its next higher level.*"

"Whew, you really believe that?" Nelly asked him, wide-eyed.

"Everyone knows that science fiction is dead, Trevor," Nelly said with distaste, pursing her lips. "It's just something that people write these days to describe the past."

"That's what they said about the Book of Genesis, honey, but it's still selling, isn't it?"

Nelly's hand flicked at the leaves of Cannibal, the wild-looking Venus flytrap plant that hovered above Trevor's printer. It was a hybrid that had been specially cultivated to eat manuscript pages—in fact, to swallow *any* information stored on dry tree pulp.

Trevor had picked it up at a Whole Earth Booksellers Association Expo as a joke, or as a reminder of the fate facing would-be writers.

"Well, pardon me while I page my guru on my beeper," Nelly retorted.

"Okay, okay, I can see I don't have any converts yet!" Trevor sprang to his feet and grabbed his duffel bag, which lay at the foot of his platformed futon. "I'm ready. *Andiamo! Avanti popolo!*"

They stepped outside the loft onto the Folsom Street sidewalk. It was a bright San Francisco morning; the sky was a clear blue shot through with cirrus clouds resembling cable cars in dry dock.

A street person squatted in the shade of Nelly's beat-up Toyota truck, oblivious to the tiger figure standing guard on the dashboard.

"Spare some change so I can buy some PCP and a shotgun to get a job?" the skinny dude in black drainpipe jeans with a dirty plaster cast on his foot asked.

"That's an original line, so here's a buck," Nelly said, handing him a dollar.

As they drove away, the guy, still squatting, rapped his knuckles on his cast. "They just left, heading east down Folsom. Over," he said. Then he got up and hobbled down the sidewalk.

*   *   *

Nelly checked the traffic in the rearview mirror. "Yup, they're following us. That dude's been sitting out there for the past two days. Only yesterday, he had his cast on his other foot. Can't make up his mind, I guess. Well, Trevor," she said to him as he glanced over his shoulder with a worried look, "we'll see what we can do to shake them."

She pulled out her digital cell and punched a number. "Hi, Dorje, are we on? Great. See you in a few minutes."

Trevor shook his head with admiration. "You're a master, Nelly."

She shifted gears as they sped off into the flow of traffic. "I don't know what else to be," she replied.

In a few minutes, they arrived at the El Dorado Car Wash at Fourth and Harrison. The place was teeming with activity. Busloads of Japanese tourists ran about taking pictures, while the usual lines of cars waited to be serviced.

The El Dorado wasn't only a car wash—it was also a tourist spot of great anthropological interest. The owners had im-ported an entire tribe of Indians from the Amazon rain forest— it was a small tribe, practically extinct, consisting of about sixty men, women, and children—to work as the cleaning crew. They wore white overalls over their traditional native garb, and their colorful feathered headdresses. It was the world's first en-dangered-rain-forest-themed car wash.

An Indian opened the door to the Toyota. Nelly handed him a twenty-dollar bill. "We just want to go through real quick."

"Chakawaka," he said, grabbing the note and slamming the door shut. The Toyota lurched forward on a conveyor belt into the car wash.

"Okay, Trevor, move fast," Nelly ordered as she opened her door. "This is where we get out."

He grabbed his duffel bag as she yanked her knapsack out of the space behind the front seat. The mist and rain and steam were blinding as they stepped out of the truck.

271

The owners of the El Dorado had recreated a remarkable rain-forest-jungle tableau in the self-contained car-wash environment. Huge scrubbers and brushes vied with palm branches and vines that sprayed ecologically correct cleaning fluids over the moving cars.

Nelly and Trevor ran down a little path through the jungle that led to a clearing and the outside, where Dorje's Yellow Cab was parked on the curb.

Dorje opened the door for them. "Nelly, Trevor—it's a little cramped, but climb in."

Yeshi and Dongzhen sat in the front seat, palms pressed together in a good-morning greeting.

"Hi guys," Trevor said to them as he settled into the backseat with Nelly. "All ready for the Burning Mind Festival?"

They nodded. Yeshi twirled his hand-held prayer wheel in response, while Dongzhen grinned and crowed, "All right, Nelly! We go to Reno!"

"No, not Reno, Dongzhen! No gambling this trip, okay? Meditation. At Black Rock. No gambling. Meditation. Burning Mind."

Dongzhen shrugged. "Meditation, gambling. Same thing."

"Right," Trevor said through gritted teeth. "Like Russian roulette."

One-Eye Chin was in a foul mood. Major Threat sat behind the wheel of the jade-green Lexus Laxmi, with Minor Threat beside him cradling a folded pair of nunchaku sticks on his lap. He was concentrating on the wildlife, looking for his big chance.

They were going through the El Dorado car wash, having just filled up the tank with gas for the long drive to the Black Rock Desert.

One-Eye was in the back seat playing tele–fan tan with his gambling buddies in Taipei, Hong Kong, and Shanghai, and he was losing. "May your grandmother be impregnated with the spittle of Chiang Kai-shek!" he cursed at Major Threat.

"Why, Honorable One? What have I done?" Major Threat asked, alarmed by his boss's outburst.

"These gibbons are bringing me bad luck!" He pointed at the monkeys that were scampering across the windshield. Somewhere in the underbrush came the sound of a tapir crashing through the thicket. "Why you bring me here?"

"Because it's so convenient to the freeway, One-Eye," Major Threat pleaded. "For gas."

"You lie like a dog. Do you think I don't know what you two miserable poachers are up to? You come here at least twice a week—don't lie, I get all the sales slips—to check your traps. What is it—kingfishers, toucans, macaws? I found kingfisher feathers under the car seat last week."

"Truly, Enlightened One, these are small insignificant creatures. We are hardly interested in them, we belong to the Sierra Club."

"I have heard the jaguar is missing . . . What's the going price for jaguar these days, Major Threat? Have you been holding out on me?"

"It's not us!" Major Threat protested, horrified. "I swear! Do you swear, Minor Threat?"

"Master, I swear along with my brother Major Threat that we have nothing to do with the missing wildcat." Minor Threat exchanged worried glances with his partner.

"I've heard the Vietnamese may have been involved in its abduction—the Dancing Phoenix tong trafficks in endangered species from car-wash habitats . . ."

"Don't let me catch you holding out on me, you two useless spitoons," One-Eye warned them. "I don't know why I'm taking you to Black Rock with me. My informants tell me Hakim Beijing may be there. You had better not let me down this time."

"We swear, we swear," Major Threat replied, gripping the wheel more tightly.

"This time, that turtle-sucking scum will be yours for sure, One-Eye," Minor Threat promised.

He glanced through the window at the trap they had laid so carefully on the branch of a prehistoric-looking araucaria pine. The trap was empty. The Lexus glided past.

Nothing, not even a limpkin or a miserable finch. Truly, the omens were quite inauspicious.

The Tibetan lamas insisted that they drive through the brothel-and-junkyard complex at the Moundhouse in Reno. To observe the American bardos in action, Dongzhen claimed. Here, there was a whorehouse and an auto dismantler shop in one place. Next, they requested that Dorzhe stop at the National Bowling Museum, a shrine as large as an indoor football stadium, and with bowling lanes, but Nelly put her foot down.

"It's going to be dark soon . . . we'll get lost in the desert, and there are are no signs leading to Black Rock City, you know. It's a pitched-tent metropolis. They're expecting fifteen thousand people to arrive at Burning Mind this year. We'll have a hell of a time making the rendezvous as it is."

"The lamas think you're a real party pooper, Nelly," Trevor told her.

"Well, too bad. They can do this on their own sometime. We can't afford to be late for the procession to the inferno."

"You're sure about this? You believe what this guy told you?"

"He *knows*, Trevor. Vincent Van-Too has been neutralizing these tattoos ever since they began appearing on the fringes of the scene. He's expecting them to make a big showing at Burning Mind. Vincent's going to be set up in a tent at Camp Darwin. We'll meet him there."

"You really think Sinbad is going to show up?"

"There's a huge Russian contingent this year. Natasha Nijinskaya's flying in to give the final dance performance of her career, Trevor. It's going to be neurolinked throughout the whole world. They're expecting more than a billion people to be taking part as observers. And observation is download, Trevor. No two ways about it. This is the grand kahuna. The big coconut."

274

"It's hard to believe there's going to be this massive tattoo transfer taking place in full view of the world." Trevor shook his head and sighed.

"It's right there in the Burning Mind program, Trevor," Nelly told him. "It's in homage to Christo—you remember that artist, don't you? He wrapped the entire Great Wall of China, and the coast of California, and the Bundestag in Berlin, and the Sahara . . . Now Nijinskaya is performing this piece she's calling 'Mir—World Peace,' and they're going to download this giant transfer tattoo spelling the word out across Omnispace. They're going to tattoo Omnispace, Trevor! Can you imagine that?! It's never been done before—and it's happening tonight."

"You suspect the virus is going to be downloaded through the transfer. What can you do about it?" Trevor asked glumly.

"There's more than one way to skin a tattoo," Nelly said cryptically.

"Or to erase a sand mandala," Dorje added, nodding thoughtfully. "What does this sign say? Gr-ger-gur . . . Pop. Forty-two."

"It's the town of Gerlach," Nelly read. "We're getting close to the cutoff in the road where we enter the desert."

They'd been following a long line of vehicles—jeeps, vans, campers, motorbikes, cars—all slowing down at the bend in the road. The playa of the Black Rock Desert stretched out like thin, blue vinyl in the twilight, a swiftly moving surf line of dust sweeping across barren miles.

Figures with face masks were waving torches, directing the newcomers onto the roadless playa. "Keep going straight as the crow chokes for twelve miles. Don't deviate or you'll get lost. You want to join a convoy heading for Black Rock City?"

"Hail a lama!" one of the Burning Mind traffic coordinators saluted Dorje.

"Thank you, brother," Dorje said and, following the caravan, switched on the cab's high beams in the face of a towering wave of dust.

They drove through the blinding white roar of alkali wind,

275

inching along like a tortoise in the Grand Prix of the Void. Indistinguishable shapes with muted lights raced past them, casting dense sand shadows through the myopic field of their vision.

"This used to be the Burning Man festival, originally," Nelly briefed them. "It was a technopagan event begun in the early 1990s, culminating with the lighting of the Burning Man, a stick figure standing forty feet high. That all changed about ten years ago, when neuroimplants transformed the Net. Now the desert is wherever people happen to jack into it.

"But the main action still takes place right here in the middle of the playa," she went on. "They're going to conjure up a mass hallucination—a neural Burning Man—and set it ablaze through the harnessed power of their minds. It's scary but beautiful. You never know what's going to appear. Sometimes some people aren't ready for it, and they get mind-singed. Third-degree chakra burn.

"But there are all kinds of filters available for those who want to participate without the power surge. It's supposed to be an electrifying experience. When the Burning Man reaches Burning Mind levels, it's like a vision of the greatest intensity that ripples across the inner sky of Omnispace. Everyone will see it all over the world at the same instant."

"Mahakala Man," Dorje added thoughtfully. "That's what we called the Burning Mind visualization in Tibet. I remember seeing the face of that wrathful deity when I was a novice monk programmer in the Yarlung Valley outside of Lhasa. Truly awesome. But liberating."

The luminous tidal wave of sand began to subside as they approached the clearing of the "city." It was a magical sight of towers and spires, with tents and canopies jumbled around the center periphery. Thousands of lanterns, fires, and lights from humming generators illuminated the pagan fairyland.

276

They drove past signs pointing to the Irrational Geographic Society and the Shrunken Head Camp.

Naked and seminaked bodies, painted with Day-Glo colors, tribal paints, and flickering tattoos, some of them wearing elaborate masks, and others in costumes, wound their way through a maze of passageways that crisscrossed among the tents and displays.

In a nearby clearing, two fire-breathing robots clashed, gouging each other with their steel-shredding claws.

A procession of American sadhus, bodies caked with white ash, carried begging bowls, stopping occasionally to pass a chillum of hashish around. An enormously fat woman with a body shaped like the Venus of Willendorf walked hand in hand with a naked midget, while another figure, a fat man wearing a Velcro codpiece, carried a sign that offered FREE SEX WITH A FAT HAIRY MAN WITH HALITOSIS!

Loud music from several stages blasted a cacophonous mix of Heavy Butoh rock and didgeridoo elevator music.

Above the fray, a Cessna buzzed the campground spilling neongrams exhorting the masses: DON'T MISS THE PROCESSION TO THE INFERNO AT THE GATE OF HELL TONIGHT AT 9 P.M.

Dorje found a parking space on the Outer Ring Road, near a sign pointing to Camp Darwin. "Okay, guys," Nelly said as she stretched herself out. "We're meeting Vincent at the Café Ephemera. I hope we can find it. This place is a madhouse."

"Cremation grounds." Dorzhe sniffed the air. A crowd was gathered around a bonfire watching a spectacle. Naked WASP aboriginals were tossing desiccated and mummified cow carcasses that they had collected from the playa on the fire.

One of the youths, clutching at his bare genitals, let out a shriek and made a running leap over the flames. He grinned as he rubbed his scorched buttocks. The crowd yelled its admiration.

"Excuse me, do you know where the Café Ephemera is?" Nelly asked a young woman who was naked except for a blinking-diode G-string and a pair of cowboy boots.

"Café Ephemera? I think they're down that ways a bit, past Mona Mongoose's Massage Parlor, next to the Sinful Rhino Camp."

277

"Thanks. Okay, guys," Nelly signaled her band of lamas. Trevor trudged along behind them, taking in the sights around him.

A stoned teenager from Stockton asked him, "Have you seen my kitty, man? She's five-ten, blonde with big thingies."

"No, I'm sorry, I haven't." He shook his head and the young guy took off in the opposite direction.

Trevor paused at a stall with a sign advertising NIGHTMARE PILLOWS. A tall, lanky woman in a granny dress smiled at him across the counter. There were pillows embroidered with frightening Gothic designs—deranged-looking gargoyles, the devil, Boschian landscapes.

"What's this?" he asked her.

"These pillows are for people who are stuck and need to get unstuck," she explained. "They're meant to induce nightmares. Sometimes you need a really jarring shock to snap you out of whatever is blocking you. For example," she said, as she held up a small cushion with a sandpaper-like surface, "this pillow is for love affairs that are going nowhere. It's got herbs in it that are guaranteed to make you wake up in the night, sweating, feeling hopeless and lost."

"What good does that do?" he asked, shocked.

"Well, it either makes you want to run back to your sweetie or kill yourself," she laughed and revealed a gap-toothed mouth. "Want one?"

He shook his head. "Not right now, maybe some other time." His eye caught sight of some other merchandise on the table. "What are those?"

"Oh, I got those from New Nippon. I just have a couple of them left. They're antiques from Satori City—before it crashed. See the seal of guarantee? That means they're intact—their code's unbroken. Uncontaminated by the fallout."

She pointed with her bony finger. "These ideograms read 'Vacharu-no-yu' in Japanese kanji. They're Kyocera meta-ROM bowls, used to perform the tea ceremony on-line. Or the 'virtual reali-tea' ceremony, as they called it."

Trevor held one of the crudely made bowls in his hand. It felt powerful—bristling with holotropian chips—brown, almost black in color—it was heavy and earthy in his hand.

"How much?" he asked. "For both of them."

"Well, I'm getting ready to close up . . . Tell you what—I'll make you a deal. Buy one nightmare pillow, and I'll sell you the two bowls for half price. Ninety-nine dollars for the bowls, a hundred bucks for the pillow."

"What am I going to do with the pillow?"

"That's up to you, honey," the woman cackled. "I'm just trying to move the merchandise. You'd better make up your mind quick, though. Burning Man's gonna fire up soon."

Trevor bowed his head to think. Two sacrificial bowls. One nightmare pillow. He saw the lines of the oracle in his mind clearly. "Contemplation" and "Decrease." When he and Alex Fortuna had made tattoo love, those two hexagrams had formed on their joined skin.

"'The ablution has been made,'" he recalled, murmuring aloud. "'But not yet the offering. Full of trust they look up at him . . . One may use two small bowls for the sacrifice . . .'"

"What did you say?" the woman asked him.

"Nothing," Trevor replied, looking up at her with a distracted expression on his face. "Can you wrap them up, please? Separately."

Shit, where'd they go?! Trevor stopped in the middle of the flow of bodies heading toward the outer edge of the camp, where the effigy of Burning Man stood, hands outstretched to the sky.

"Nelly! Dorje!" He had lost them. Fuck! How would he ever find them in this crowd?

"Excuse me," he called out to a young, skinny woman who was walking on stilts. "Which way to Camp Darwin?"

She put her hand to her ear and shook her head with a gesture that said, "Can't hear you!" Then she strode away to rejoin five of her sisters hurrying along on stilts ahead of her.

"Camp Darwin?" he asked the passers-by. Their bodies slammed into him, faces, mouths, eyes, hands, feet, shoulders, in an unending wave of physicality. But in the growing fever of the procession toward the apocalyptic stick man in the desert, words had become unglued from speech.

Trevor felt suddenly, decisively, cut off from everyone and everything.

That's when he saw the Bedouin in his white burnoose, standing beside a desert bicycle chariot. The pillows in the backseat could have been nightmare pillows, as far as Trevor was concerned. He stepped up to the man and asked him in a hollow voice, "Are you free?"

The bicycle Bedouin was an American in his thirties with a narrow, bearded face and thoughtful brown eyes. He was smoking a cigarette, and waved it in the air almost dismissively.

"Not usually." He studied Trevor shrewdly. "But as it happens, since the desert has brought you to me, I *am* free."

Trevor climbed into the back of the chariot, which was illuminated by two kerosene lamps attached to the sides.

"Lost?" the Bedouin asked him.

Trevor nodded.

The Bedouin pulled his robes up, securing them with an elastic garter. Nodding his own head, he stated, "I only carry those who are truly lost," and began to pedal into the night.

At the Café Ephemera, Nelly bit her lip and frowned. "Where is Trevor? Goddamn it, I can't believe he got lost. Again."

"Again?" Dorje cocked his head at her.

Nelly said, "He keeps doing this to me. Each time I think this is it, we're back together again, he disappears."

Dorje asked, "Why do you think he does that?"

Nelly looked puzzled, but not hurt. Not as hurt as she'd been before. "There's an old saying I learned in self-defense class, Dorje. 'Absence of body is better than presence of mind.'"

I guess I need to defend myself from Trevor's absence. I've got to accept that and go on."

Vincent Van-Too was sitting at the coffee table with Dongzhen and Yeshi. They were examining his forearms. Yeshi had pulled up the sleeves of Vincent's Guatemalan shirt and was admiring the Tibetan iconography—the prayer scrolls, the *phurbu* ritual-dagger tattoo, and the seated figure of the goddess Tara.

"Okay, that's enough, boys," Vincent told them as he pulled his sleeves back down. "I know they're Tibetan, but they're *mine.*"

He ran his fingers through his coarse beard. "Well, your boyfriend's either split or lost. Or both." He stood up, all six feet, three inches of him, and heaved his lanky frame. "It's time, I guess. Show's about to start."

Dorje put his hand on Nelly's arm. "He'll be back."

"Back and forth between nowhere and no place—"

"It's all here, Nelly—now," Dorje said, spreading his hands in the air. "Nothing, no one, is ever gone. It is all here now."

"Yes, but you have to let go first, Dorje." Nelly smiled at him sadly. "Before it can come back to you in a new form. And when it finally does, you're in a new form yourself. So what does it matter? It's ever-changing anyway."

The Bedouin was pumping his long legs, rising and falling with the pedals like a yogi practicing an ancient, secret ritual in full view of the world. Only no one saw it or recognized it.

Trevor felt the breeze in his hair, its cool in contrast to the radiating heat of the torches that people were carrying in their procession to the inferno.

Nelly was his magnetic north, but he was heading east on the medicine wheel, east where the heart carried on its tongue-tied conversation with the head. He loved Nelly, he wanted to keep up with her, he wanted to be with her—he really did.

But there was this thing, this strange force, that guided

281

him like an electric wind, guiding him in the direction of being lost. It thwarted him with its infinite patience. It disrupted his peace of mind. It told him, "This is *your* peace of mind. But it is not *the* peace of mind. That is elsewhere."

"Stop!" Trevor called to the Bedouin. There, he saw her in the crowd, her flaming-red hair. She turned to him in that instant, and he saw not his future but his unfinished present.

"Alex!" Trevor cried out to her. "Alex Fortuna!"

"Trevor, is that you?" Alex stepped up to the chariot with a baffled expression on her face. She was dressed in jodhpurs, riding boots, and a white t-shirt. She laughed, showing her white teeth. Her red hair was tied back in a Rasta ponytail.

She climbed up on the running board. She poked him with a finger and smiled. "You're under arrest."

"What are *you* doing here?"

"What do you think? This place is crawling with them— it's like the Woodstock of the damned." She scrutinized him. "Looks like *you're* still clean. How's Nelly? You guys got out of town in a big hurry, didn't you?"

"You still think she's turning, don't you?" Trevor asked her. "Well, you're right. She *is* turning. So am I. At least, I hope so. But not in the way you think. Here, Alex—I've got something for you." He reached into the bag. "It's a present." He handed her the nightmare pillow. There was a Moroccan evil eye embossed on it.

"For me?"

"For Hakim. When you see him, give it to him. I think his nightmare is going to be over soon."

"It's a pillow?"

"Let him sleep on it, Alex. It'll chase all his bad dreams away. And yours, too, I hope."

"Bye, Alex." Trevor touched her cheek gently, then beckoned the Bedouin driver. "Step on the gas."

"Where to?" the Bedouin asked.

"Where else? Take me to the Burning Man." Then he added, under his breath, "Take me to myself."

282

*   *   *

The drums beat multiple, primitive polyrhythms, and the fever of the crowd carried the sound deep into the ear of the desert. A distant echo brought their muffled reverberation back to the center of the camp.

Black Rock was answering back, its basalt synapses crackling like stone wisps of flame.

Burning Man began to move. Its feet teetered on their thin pyrotechnic rails as the fireworks rained down from its hips in spinning cartwheels of dazzling, mind-numbing colors. The crowd roared. But this was just the preamble.

Abruptly, the drums ceased, the reverberation passed, and a rapt silence built to a fresh crescendo of focused concentration.

A giant crane appeared out of the night sky, bearing upon its platform a dance stage that swung eerily to and fro. The figure of the woman on it looked forbiddingly tiny, but then grew as the stage descended to ground level.

The Greek chorus of writhing butoh dancers followed like deaf-mutes who had suddenly discovered their real voice. Their oracular grimaces gave way to the sounds of croaking frogs, barking dogs, mewing cats, and the fluttering of doves' wings. There was the screeching sound of panels of metal scraping against each other, of nuts and bolts copulating.

Natasha Nijinskaya stepped off the stage. She was dressed in a flowing, liquid robe of dazzling light. The dancers scattered along the edge of the crowd, clearing imaginary cobwebs, sweeping away the negative energy of synchronous nightmares and daydreams. When they grimaced, their crimson tongues appeared like asterisks of flesh.

The Burning Man took another step forward, but the crowd remained silent, unsure who was willing whom, the dancer or the dance, the thought or the thinker. Burning Man raised his skeletal mechanical arms and shot off another cavalcade of spinning fire wheels. This time, thunderous applause erupted as the entire world jacked in. A voice whose owner

283

was lost in the crowd yelled: "Hadgetter! Hadgetter! He better hadgetter!"

Trevor shuddered when he heard it. He stood compressed between nakedness and doubt, and the tears welled in his eyes as he sank to his knees on the desert floor, the two bowls in his hands, ready.

For a moment, Natasha Nijinskaya allowed herself to think of *him*.

Andrei . . . I am coming to you. Nothing can keep us apart now. Andrei, in the gulag of her heart, heard her. *Do it for me, Natasha. Dance . . . dance . . . dance . . . It's been so long. I hear the wind. The mountain. The sea. Why is it so dead? Its salt tears dried so long ago, Natasha, as dry as its heart that sleeps. Let me dance with you . . .*

Burning Man shuffled toward her, a shy inanimate lover now approaching his beloved. Natasha caught her breath. It *was* him! Andrei! They danced together, the Burning Man and Nijinskaya, a striking pas de deux—on one side, the forty-foot-tall frame of a man made of knowing stilts, and below him, gracefully, the slender figure of a woman in the throes of love.

Wired to her body, within the bodice of her costume, Sinbad began to get stage fright as he waited his turn on stage. He heard the clicking and the gnashing of tattoo teeth throughout the tattoo universe. Why doesn't she release me? Her heart was made of steel, he thought helplessly. He sought, yet feared, release. It never came.

The camera obscura of his heart felt the neural connects, but the spring mechanism was frozen. He heard the roar of the wind on the Net, but it wasn't that sound that was the most prominent. No, above all else he heard the sound of weeping.

I will dance forever with you. Nijinskaya blew a kiss to the Burning Man.

You will, he replied.

Grace

Vincent Van-Too turned to Nelly. "It's over. Did you see it?"

"I saw something."

"Then you saw it."

"Nothing happened," she said.

"That's it," he replied. "You saw it, all right. Yup. Sure enough."

Nelly felt a shiver as the coldness began to release her heart. The anesthetic of her love for Trevor was setting her free. Her heart was broken, but she didn't need that heart anymore. She had a new one. She let out a little laugh.

Dorje stood beside her, a quizzical expression on his face. Dongzhen and Yeshi had run to the stage to ask for Nijinskaya's autograph on a plate of sand. "Sand autograph like sand mandala," they said. "But we can always make copies."

"Are you all right, Nelly?" Dorje asked her gently.

"Yes, yes, I'm all right. I was just thinking. It's so peculiar. I feel so free. Unconditional love, I thought I had it. But I didn't. Now I think that I do. What *is* unconditional love, really, Dorje? What do you think?"

Dorje scratched his shaved head. "Not sure exactly, Nelly." Then he grinned. "But it could be some kind of an evolutionary quirk. How are you feeling right now?"

"Quirky."

"It is good. Quirky is good."

Boris stood in the glare of the Burning Man, thinking to himself. She danced well. Well, then, after witnessing Nijinskaya's dance, do you still fear your own death? All his life, he had feared death. Feared it so much, he was generous when it came to sharing it with others. Dispensing it like alms to the poor, to all the charity cases he dispatched to the other side. He was only too glad to lend a hand. That way he had his hand on

285

death, he could keep it at an arm's length. My life, he thought, I'll never be an old man. That's a myth. I may be dead one day, but I'll never grow old.

Then he wondered. What's the role of a revolutionary when there is no revolution?

Somehow that question brought him a sense of inner peace. And that was another kind of revolution.

"Hakim Beijing," One-Eye Chin called softly.

Major Threat and Minor Threat stood behind Hakim, their hands hanging relaxed at their sides. For a moment, Hakim felt the urge to run. But then he realized the futility of such an impulse. It was his moment of reckoning.

"You have made me very angry," One-Eye said to him. "Major Threat and Minor Threat were under strict orders to find you and bring you to me. But here you are. What am I going to do with you? You owe me for some very bad tattoos."

"Yes, they were very bad," Hakim admitted, his heart beating fast. "They came from a bad batch. I am truly very sorry. What can I do to make it up to you?"

One-Eye gave Hakim a penetrating glance. "I am willing to forget the past, provided you give me the correct answer to my question. After this evening, I am seriously thinking of diversifying my investments. You have seen what we have seen. First, there was this mechanical man. Then, all these naked people running around everywhere. Where does the future lie? Is it in robotics? Or is it back to nature? Think carefully. Your life depends on your reply."

"No, not robotics," Hakim stated, but was immediately filled with consternation. There was no turning back now . . .

"If not robotics, what?" One-Eye demanded.

Hakim was at a loss. Then he felt a sudden lightness as an image of his wife Alex rose in his mind. He would thank her in person later on.

"Raw buttocks," Hakim pronounced, his confidence having returned from out of the blue. There was a future after all, and the future looked very much like Alex's rear end. "I would definitely invest in raw buttocks."

Hakim was in love again. One-Eye's face broke into a big smile. He slapped Hakim on the shoulder. "After we get back to town, there's a job I'd like to discuss with you. You seem to have lots of unusual insights. I admire that in a man."

"Don't feel too bad," Vincent Van-Too told Nelly as she climbed into the back of Dorje's cab. "You were expecting to see Omnispace tattooed, weren't you? It almost happened, but no cigar. There was this great tattooist, an Englishman named George Burchett, did his finest work in Liverpool, at the turn of the nineteenth century. Orientalia. The special effects of the British Empire. India, China, Japan, that sort of thing. He had this fellow, extremely vain, come to him and ask him his opinion of his skinwork. Playing cards, it was. He had a royal flush tattooed on his stomach, with the rest of the pack strewn all over his body. 'What do you think of my tats?' this cocky guy challenged him. George Burchett took one look at him, and just devastated him with this one line. 'It's a pity,' Burchett replied, 'that the aces are only skin deep.' That's sort of what happened tonight. But the aces went a whole lot deeper. I think we were damned lucky it turned out the way it did."

Nelly laughed. "Thanks, Vincent." She kissed him on the cheek and patted his third ear. "I'm really grateful to you for everything."

"It may not seem like it, but it's a new ball-game, honey. The good tattoos won. What you don't see is what you get. Sometimes, anyway."

"I'll try to remember that," she said, thinking of Trevor.

"Nelly—"

Nelly spun. "Trevor! Where've you been???" Her heart skipped a beat.

He climbed into the car beside her. "It's never too late, is it?" He put his arms around her. "I got lost for a while, that's all. I'm back now."

Nelly didn't know whether to be astounded or to laugh out loud. He was as quixotic as ever. But now there was something new about him, too, something more stable, something more secure. Something mysterious and alive.

"What's that you're carrying?" she asked him, ready to be surprised again.

"These are two bowls," he said. "One is for you. One is for me. The ashes of Burning Man are in both of them. I scraped them off the desert after the performance. We'll put them in the altar when we get back home, so we'll have something to remember."

Nelly laughed as she took one of the bowls. "That's sweet, Trevor. Thank you for the ashes. Are you sure you've got quite enough for yourself?"

He peered into his bowl, then compared its contents with hers. "They both look about equal to me. 'The ablution has been made, the offering is now complete.'"

"No, not yet," Nelly said and emptied both bowls out into the desert. "This is part of my own ritual. Emptiness to emptiness. I think we can go home now, Trevor. We can pick up the pieces from there."

On the corner of Eddy and Turk in the Tenderloin neighborhood of San Francisco, sheets of newspapers were sighing to each other in the gusts of wind. Stray dogs and street people huddled in the doorways. Vietnamese children ran to the store to pick up the odd item for the family at home.

Motorola Mike was troubled. He was pacing up and down the block, mumbling to himself. "Tuna fish in A.1. sauce . . . Hominy, collard greens, scotch and soda, twelve pounds of spaghetti." He was picking something up from out of the ether. Tonight was the night. He just *knew* it. Dorje had told him that if he *really* believed, he could change his life. His brain was fried, his heart was tired. But he was going to give it one more try.

Angrily, he stamped his foot down on the pavement. "God-damm it!" He raised a fist at the night sky, as empty as it always was, as far away as a dream lost in amber. "Goddamn it!"

Then he froze as he heard the chirping from inside his torn coat. With a trembling hand, he brought it out of his inside pocket, the Motorola Micro Lite. He held it in his hand and watched it ring—purple, green, red, yellow, blue, and orange chirps.

As he flipped the receiver open and put his ear to it, a smile crossed his grimy face. "You bet I'm home!" he said. "Where are you, sweetie? I've been waiting for your call."

EPILOGUE

Hong Kong,
the People's Republic of Multimaodia

In Hong Kong, in the Tsuen Wan district, the nineteenth floor of the Panda Hotel was busy commiserating with the twenty-eighth floor. They had been having their differences ever since the hotel had been built, but now the different levels were beginning to see eye to eye. The wrecker's ball had hovered at their side all day long, for days on end, as the hotel's owners deliberated whether to tear the building down or not. The previous day, a giant pendulum had swung a mirrored ball monotonously in front of the revolving restaurant while a loudspeaker blared its refrain: "*You are now becoming more and more relaxed . . .*"

Then, suddenly, the evil crane was removed and the window washers were called in. It was decided that the Panda Hotel was a prodigy after all.

"That was close," the nineteenth floor sighed. "Did you hear all the gibberish they were saying about us earlier, Honorable Twenty-eight? Truly, we were condemned before our time. Now they are planning to build an addition to the left wing and to raise the room rates. The National Museum in Taipei is mounting an exhibition of our 'masterful towel paintings,' and the galleries in New York, Zurich, Shanghai, Paris, and London can't place enough orders. The critics are raving about our 'new school of Taoist impressionism.' Are we an asylum or a hotel?"

"What's the difference *what* they say, Honorable Nineteen?" the twenty-eighth floor replied. "Remember that old adage: 'Words are birds, experience the tree they roost in. The power of inner truth is rooted in the tree. Birds come and go.'"

"And don't forget 'Checking in and checking out are one and the same, and the guests are always born again.'"

"Elegantly put. Confucius?"

"No, Nineteen. It was the concierge."

APPENDIX

Aryudashigda B9 (AyDDA B9)

320,000x magnification

Vector IG Sequence Link:
- **General:** Sentient-Specific Psylovirus
- **Functions:** (cloning/tbd)
- **Selection:** B9

- **Copy Number:** 01101011 11001110 101000 010100 010 010 0100 010011
- **Hosts:** Human
- **Suppliers:** Daiichi Seiyaku
- **Misc. Comments:** Distributed in aliquots of 50 ng. (NLTN staff) Each vial contains purified ECN from Aryudashigda B9 virus (AyDDA B9). (NLTN staff) NOTE: This material is cited under Russian Patent Law. Patent infringement is punishable by Sector 3 Psychoneural-gulag conventions. Aryudashigda B9 virus is a class 9 virus.
- **Parents:** (Unknown)
- **Siblings:** (Unknown)
- **Descendants:** (Unknown)

History

The Aryudashigda B9 virus was first recognized in the year 2029 aboard the Russian *Mir* spacecraft while engaging in a multiyear orbital mission. It was a board craft from this mission that the original strain of the Aryudashigda B9 virus first arrived on Earth. It became the original source for the Luminal Syncratic Artificial Intelligence classification or nomenclature. The Aryudashigda B9 virus became known as Light wave–AI; a binary-coded information packet transmitted via frequency modulation in infrared wavelengths from a location 11.5 light years from Earth. It came into contact with the satellite *Mir*, while *Mir*'s crew was conducting scientific studies using the onboard Clark-Ustinov IR telescope for the Planet Birth project. Rima Aryudashigda was a visiting infrared astronomer with the nine-person flight crew. She was the first to detect the exotic signal of the Aryudashigda B9 virus.

Taxonomy and Classification

294

Aryudashigda B9 is the only member of a family of double-negative-stranded viruses, the Psyloviridae. This virus is the first of its kind to contain a psychical component in tandem along with its biophysical attributes. The psyloviruses are similar in morphology, density, and polyacrylamide-gel electrophoresis profile to the filoviruses and rhabdoviruses. It exhibits two distinctly different types of behavior and physical properties, depending upon its phase (dormant binary transport vs. replication and general evolution). Therefore it has become necessary to assign a nomenclature for these two stages of distinction: Luminal Syncratic Artificial Intelligence signal is the condition of the virus in the dormant state of transport, and Aryudashigda B9 is its form when in AI replication mode (Class 9).

Physical Properties of Virion

Psylovirus particles are morphologically similar to rhabdovirus particles but much longer. By electron microscopy virons are pleomorphic, appearing as long, filamentous, and sometimes branched, forms, or as "@"-shaped or "a"-shaped forms. The particles vary greatly in length (up to 7000 nm), and have an irregular diameter: 30–100 nm.

Replication

The mechanism of virus entry into host cells is unknown, but it is reasonable to assume that glycoprotein is the only known transmembrane protein of the viron particle that mediates the absorption and the penetration process. Viral glycoprotein and alignment of viral membrane-associated proteins form 1.5 untranslated regions of the genome carrying a poly(A) tail generated by the polymerase at the ends of all transcription terminal sequences. The tail is made up of twelve single lines forming a zigzag shape with six distinct points: \/\/\/\/\/\/. As infection proceeds, viral particles grow and become highly structured and replicate at an unusually fast rate.

295

Pathology and Histopathology

The virus was first activated, or brought out of a state of dormancy, when the space-signal code was entered into a recombinant DNA processor. It was found to have an affinity for, and symbiotic relationship with, the transcription sequence of sentient tattoo pigmentation, or chronoepidermal programming. In the initial outbreak, the patient spread the disease to close members of the community through both casual and intimate contact. The disease spread rapidly via sentient tattoos, or epidermal programming. Demographic profile consists mainly of a 13-to-48-year-old subculture postmodern primitives. Although the initial outbreak occurred in Novosibirsk in 2035, the initial infection probably took place in the city of St. Petersburg in the first year of initial contact, 2035.

Transmission and Tissue Tropism

The primary mode of infection is unknown for the Aryudashigda B9 virus in any natural setting. All secondary cases have been nosocomial or caused by casual or intimate contact with a patient. Transmission occurs usually via contaminated chronoepidermal conduit. The virus travels from host to host, psychoenergetically merged with the transcription code of sentient epidermal programs (sentient tattoos).

Clinical Features of Infection

Clinical symptoms are unlike other known viral infections. However, in the case of the Aryudashigda B9 virus, an incubation period of 4–16 days is standard. Onset is sudden and can manifest in psychocerebral symptoms of euphoria, delusions of grandeur, visual and auditory hallucinations, and epiphany. Patients also report experiences of information acquisition of unknown origin. Physical symptoms include accelerated thought processes, mild fever, disorientation, and discoloration and pigment alteration of the dermis and epidermis.

Behavior of Psychical-EM Radiation Symbiosis

Although gamma and X rays have been known to exist as a mode of extra-solar transmission for the Aryudashigda virus particles, infrared radiation is the most commonly observed light frequency used as a carrier medium by the virus.

Immune Response

Humoral immune response to Aryudashigda B9 virus can take as long as 21–36 days after infection to be detected. The virus undergoes transformation when introduced to synchronous epidermal programming (SEP), resulting in altered contrast with the stand-alone virus before integration. The patient shows regular immune response and exhibits no symptoms while the epidermal healing process takes place. It is not until after the epidermal programmed image has healed (approx. 14 days) and white cell and macrophage count has returned to normal that the Aryudashigda virus starts the replication/mutation phase of moving from host to host.

Prevention and Control

None known.